Scoundrels AND HEROES

WHATEVER IT TAKES SERIES
BOOK 2

D1712994

ANNA SVOBODA

To Mom and Dad.
Thank you for being the best parents anyone could ever wish for.
I know I don't say it often enough, but I love you.

Chapter 1

Clara Redwood was standing in front of the mirror, brushing her long, fiery red mane of hair, all the while trying to stop her hands from shaking and tears from filling her eyes. Both unsuccessfully. In the past few weeks, her life had been nothing but a series of disasters and now another one was looming just around the corner.

There were two sets of clothes laid out on the bed for her to wear. One was a beautiful ornate gown, suitable for the royal palace halls and the other, leather breeches paired with a simple white shirt and a well worn jacket, something that a squire would wear. She hadn't chosen which outfit to put on yet, a decision that was going to shape her life from this day forward.

Up until recently, Clara had had a good life. She wasn't entirely happy, but she would have said she was content, at least. Then her father died in some stupid skirmish with pirates along the eastern seaboard. The man Clara had loved and cherished the most in her life; the only person in the entire world who'd understood her and respected her even; the one person she considered solid and certain, was gone.

"He was a soldier and soldiers die. Deal with it," her mother had said. She was never a heartfelt person but those words sounded cold, even for her.

However, Clara's father wasn't just a soldier. He was also an important lord, an admiral, and a loyal supporter and good friend of King Hayden himself. Which, under normal circumstances, was a good thing for Clara's family. However, since her father was now gone, suddenly she had become the king's responsibility.

Apparently, it was unthinkable for a woman to live alone without a man in the house to take care of her. Although Clara officially had two older brothers living at home, one was a soldier like her father, away on an assignment in the northern mountains, the other was a diplomat, traveling the world as a representative of the Kingdom of Orellia.

All of that meant that Clara had not only lost her beloved father but a few days later, she'd lost her home as well, being forced to move into the Royal Palace in Ebris. Her mother had gone with her, more than a little excited to discover the king had become Clara's guardian.

Sophia Redwood was a very ambitious woman who'd often remarked that it was entirely possible that instead of finding a suitable husband for Clara, the king might want to marry her himself, which had made the young girl lose her sleep for days.

Marry the Burning Fury? Even the thought of spending time with the morose, snappy, and perpetually angry king frightened Clara. Being his wife? Fulfilling her duties in his bed? Clara had sworn to herself that she would end her own life before that would happen.

Of course, she couldn't have said that to her mother, who'd adamantly pursued the idea, constantly bugging the king to have dinner with Clara or to take a walk with her through the palace gardens. Naturally, it hadn't improved the king's disposition so when he and Clara finally had dined together, it was in awkward silence. He was furious to be there and Clara was so frightened of him that she'd had to fight back tears the entire time, quite certain that if she'd let them fall, he'd have started yelling at her.

At least one of Clara's prayers had been answered. The king wasn't interested in her and soon, he'd been so fed up with Clara's mother he'd firmly but politely ordered her to stop with her actions. Sophia was disappointed, naturally. What mother wouldn't want her daughter to be queen? But it hadn't stopped her from trying to find other suitors for Clara, all very important, rich, and powerful.

Why couldn't they just leave Clara alone? Why could a man live just fine on his own but a woman needed someone in charge to decide everything for her? Clara was only seventeen. She should have had her whole life in front of her to do as she pleased. Not be married off to some wealthy idiot and forced to keep her legs spread, birthing one child after another, all while keeping her mouth shut.

The king had then left to wage war against a neighboring kingdom. Everyone in the palace had breathed more freely for a couple of weeks, without the constant fear of doing something that might set the king off. Clara had avoided people as much as possible, her mother especially, spending most of her time in the gardens. On a few rare occasions, she'd managed to sneak out of the palace and head to the training grounds, calming her turbulent mind by firing countless arrows into distant targets, a secret and unbecoming hobby that made her mother absolutely furious.

She would have loved to take a horse out for rides through the countryside but her mother insisted that she use a side saddle. Clara hated that stupid saddle so much she'd given up riding altogether.

Just as she'd gotten used to her new life, another disaster had struck. Clara hadn't cared for politics overmuch, but she knew that Orellia was the most powerful country on the continent. Therefore, it came as no surprise when news of King Hayden winning a large battle against their neighbor, the Kingdom of Levanta, reached the palace. But that was not the only news the messengers had brought. No more than a few days after the battle, Clara had received a letter from the king himself. It was more of a short note than an actual letter but the parchment had carried a life sentence.

Her mother was ecstatic. King Hayden's letter had clearly stated that Lord Huxley was an important figure at the Levantian court and his family was wealthy and influential. That's all Clara knew about the man she was now supposed to marry in a couple of weeks. No amount of crying, begging, or arguing could stop her mother from swiftly replying to King Hayden that Clara would be honored to marry Lord Huxley at his earliest possible convenience.

Ever since that day, Clara had barely eaten or slept. She'd spent her days hiding in dark corners where her mother wouldn't find her, crying her eyes out. Every night she went to bed praying she wouldn't wake up the following morning. It was so unfair. Wasn't it the Levantians who'd lost the war? Clara was fairly certain of that. Then why was she being thrown to the enemy as a conciliatory peace offering?

The Orellians had killed her future husband's king and took over his country. How could he not hate Clara for that? Would he take his anger out on her once they were married? Would he make her suffer in revenge?

This was all her mother's fault. If she hadn't annoyed King Hayden by trying to get him to marry Clara, then perhaps he would have forgotten about her. But no, Sophia had to go and make him angry, so when he needed a young girl to offer as a sacrifice to placate the Levantians, he'd immediately thought of Clara.

Now, he was returning to Ebris with his new queen by his side, bringing Clara's future husband along. The wedding was planned for the day after their arrival. Clara most likely wouldn't even see this mysterious Lord Huxley until she walked down the aisle, let alone have the chance to talk to him.

Last night, her mother's patience had finally run out. Sophia had started yelling at Clara for not eating and looking no better than a skeleton which now caused the girl to be too thin for her wedding dress.

"You will stop with this nonsense! You are not a child anymore, Clara. You are an adult woman and you have duties."

Clara had known better than to waste energy on arguing with her mother, preferring to simply turn away from Sophia and stare aimlessly out of the window. At least that way, Sophia hadn't seen the tears that had filled Clara's eyes.

"You should feel honored," her mother had added.

Honored? That stupid word had reignited a defiance hidden so deep within Clara's mind she hadn't thought it existed anymore. She'd turned to her mother. "Honored?!" Clara shrieked. "For being given to our enemy like a worthless breeding mare? For being forced to marry a man I've never even met? No, Mother," she'd spat out, her voice strong and full of venom, "I will not do that. I am not a slave and neither you, nor King Hayden can make such decisions about my life! I'd sooner put an arrow through that man than marry him."

Clara had seen her mother's hand raise and move swiftly but she hadn't realized what it meant until she'd heard the smacking sound and felt a sharp, stinging pain across her cheek. She'd blinked in confusion, her own hand flying up to touch her suddenly painful and swollen skin, stray tears rolling down her face. Her mother had never struck her before.

"That is enough, you stupid girl." Sophia was no longer yelling anymore, her voice dispassionate and so cold it sent chills down Clara's spine. "The time in your life where you get away with talking back to people is over. You will do as you are told. You will obey King Hayden's orders. You will marry Lord Huxley. You will be a proper and obedient wife and you will please your husband in any way he sees fit."

Incapable of response, Clara had watched her mother walk over to the large wardrobe and open it. Horror had filled the young girl when Sophia had pulled out a long piece of wood, carefully hidden between the gowns. "And this?" Sophia had hissed with so much contempt it had actually made Clara flinch.

"No, please," the girl had tried to whisper but no sound came out of her mouth.

Her mother's lips had curled into a cruel smirk as she'd raised Clara's bow. "I've told you to stop with this nonsense countless times. Do you have any idea the dishonor and shame you could bring upon our family if anyone found out?! I will not let you embarrass your husband in this way. From this day forth you will act like a proper lady. This rebellion ends now."

Clara had watched on helplessly as her mother had grabbed the bow with both hands and forcefully brought it down against her knee. She'd screamed and lunged forward out of instinct but she was never going to be fast enough. The sharp cracking sound the wood had made as it had splintered and broken into pieces had her freezing mid lunge in the middle of the room. With tears streaming down her face, she'd stood paralyzed, forced to watch on as her mother had tossed the broken weapon to the ground, giving Clara one final, contemptuous glare before striding out of the room.

That was the final straw. The bow itself was just a standard weapon, the same as any archer in the army would be issued. But Sophia knew what it meant to Clara. It had been a gift from her father, the one thing Clara had held dearest in her life.

After spending the night sobbing inconsolably, Clara had wiped her tears away unceremoniously, pulled two outfits out of her closet and was now standing in front of them, faced with a life altering choice. Would she put on the gown, stay in the palace and abide by both her mother's and the king's wishes? Or would she put on the simple squires' clothes and sneak out of the palace, stealing a horse and running away? Become a fugitive? How long could a lone girl survive on the run before someone robs, rapes, and eventually murders her? Clara scoffed. At least she would die free.

Who was she kidding, her decision was already made. Clara reached defiantly for the shirt and breeches.

Chapter 2

The horse she'd stolen wasn't the fastest animal alive but since Clara was still moving through the labyrinth of narrow back streets that made up the Lower City, speed wasn't really an issue. Merchant stalls lining the streets and alleyways offered various goods for sale. The mouthwatering smell of food was invariably mixed with the foulness of garbage and the rancid contents of chamber pots being tossed out onto the pavement.

As Clara passed by a small bakery, her stomach rumbled and she cursed herself for not getting breakfast from the kitchens before she'd left. But that would have been too risky.

Right now, her mother probably assumed that Clara was hiding somewhere in the palace, yet again, and it would be hours before Sophia realized that her daughter was missing. Clara needed that time to put as much distance between herself and the palace as possible.

She'd been tempted to rent a boat and sail down the river. It would have been much more comfortable than having to spend all day on horseback, but someone in the docks would have noticed a young boy traveling alone.

And when the guards eventually came after her, they would have an easy trail to follow.

The thought made her shudder. Opposing her mother was one thing, Clara had been doing that most of her life and there really wasn't much Sophia could do about it. But, by running away from the wedding, Clara was disobeying the king's orders. And disobeying King Hayden was something not many people dared to do because the consequences were always severe. The Burning Fury didn't forgive easily. But what could he do to her? Condemn her to a life in prison? Hadn't he already done that? Or he could have her executed? So be it. Clara didn't want to die, but life without freedom was no life at all.

Following the eastern road out of the city, she passed through the inner gates unnoticed, nervously pushing a lock of hair back under the cap she was wearing to cover her long red curls. It would probably have been smarter to cut her hair altogether, it made her easily distinguishable which was dangerous in her current situation, but Clara simply couldn't bring herself to do it.

She was headed east because Levanta was west and that's where King Hayden was returning from. Wouldn't it be ironic if she rode straight into the middle of his entourage while being on the run from him? Clara might be insane for trying to oppose him, but she certainly wasn't stupid.

Her eyes were inadvertently drawn to the other side of the valley, where Ebris was located. One of the large mansions dotting the mild slopes over there used to be her home. Now it was nothing more than an empty house filled with lots of memories that only brought Clara pain.

Her father. Teaching her to ride a horse. Giving Clara her first bow. She couldn't have been more than eight at the time. The pride in his eyes when she'd drawn the string back and the arrow had hit the dead center of the target. All of the good memories in her head were connected to that man and now he was gone. It felt like a part of Clara's heart had died with him.

Will King Hayden punish her family for this? He wasn't known to do that but maybe a girl disobeying him would make him lose control of his anger? Clara didn't particularly care what would happen to her mother but she hoped her actions wouldn't have a negative impact on her brothers' careers. There wasn't exactly love between them, the two boys having mocked and ridiculed her ever since she was a little girl, but they were her family.

Maybe, if at least one of them was actually living at home when their father had died, Clara wouldn't be in this situation. Having a man to 'take care of her', she wouldn't have ended up being the king's charge and he would have had no reason to marry her off to a foreigner. But Clara's oldest brother Sebastian was a diplomat, currently away somewhere, traveling beyond the eastern sea and even though he was supposed to return in the following weeks, it would be too late to stop what was happening now. Plus, Sebastian was loyal to King Hayden and would never go against his wishes, even if he were willing to help his little sister.

And Nicholas? He'd never really liked Clara. Being two years older, he considered himself stronger and smarter and thought he could order her around. Every time Clara had outsmarted him he'd been furious and when she'd dared to beat him in a small archery contest their father had held in the garden, he'd slapped her so hard she'd fallen onto a rock.

Clara was only twelve years old at the time and had needed several stitches to stop the bleeding. Their father had punished Nicolas but it hadn't helped to improve the relationship between them. Clara had been relieved when her brother had joined the military and even more so when he'd been stationed far away in the cold mountains, fighting primitive tribes.

Looking at the simple peasant houses lining the road, with flocks of children running around, dressed in rags but laughing heartily, Clara wondered what it would feel like to be part of a happy family where people actually loved each other.

A mutinous tear slid down her cheek and Clara wiped it away swiftly with the back of her hand. Why was she crying? She should be happy. For the first time in her entire life, Clara was free to do whatever she wanted, go wherever she wanted. Yet, despite the beautiful day, all she felt was fear and desperation. She was alone and her future was uncertain.

Could she stop by one of the houses, ask the people to take her in? Perhaps they would, she had money to pay for shelter and food for some time. But, then what? Would she become... What exactly were these people?

Clara's eyes scanned the signs along the road. Seamstress, weaver, bakery, pottery, inn, smithy. She was almost at the edge of the city now, the blacksmith's house was standing slightly back from the other buildings. Clara guessed it was because of the increased risk of fire. She had no idea how to perform any of those crafts. Maybe she'd manage to serve ales in the inn but it would hardly be a good hiding place.

Clara knew how to be a lady; how to dress properly, talk and smile politely and how to dance or recite poetry. Skills that nobody outside of her privileged world would appreciate. Plus, she was an excellent marksman. But who would want a female archer? She did her best to pass herself off as a boy, wearing men's clothes with a tightly wrapped bandage around her chest to conceal her breasts. Luckily, she wasn't very blessed in that area. But, upon closer inspection, a careful eye would recognize she was not a young boy with feminine features.

What was she doing? This was insane. Perhaps she should just accept her fate and return to the palace. She glanced back at the city she'd just left. Streets rose steadily behind her, the Royal Palace towering high above the city on a cliff overlooking the river, A sudden realization sent shivers down her spine. A dark-haired man on a gray horse was following her. There was no doubt about it.

Clara had noticed him before and remembered his ridiculous purple cloak which didn't fit with the rest of his outfit at all. He couldn't have been simply going in the same direction as she was since she'd made at least one full circle while wandering through the many alleyways of the Lower City. With all of the twists and turns Clara had intentionally made, along with those she'd made by mistake, there was no way anyone could still be behind her, not by coincidence.

Clara tried to act as if she hadn't noticed anything but was probably really bad at it since her whole body suddenly felt stiff from fear. Had the king expected her to disobey his orders and thus, told someone to follow her at all times? It couldn't have been Clara's mother. Sophia would never waste good money on providing Clara with a personal bodyguard. Or maybe the man following her was merely a thief who'd recognized Clara as being a person of wealth in disguise and thought her to be an easy target? It hardly mattered.

Before Clara could weigh out her options and decide what to do, the man was sidling up to her, guiding his horse so close to Clara's left flank that his knee brushed against hers. When he grabbed hold of the reins, Clara opened her mouth to cry out but then froze as she felt a sharp blade being pressed against the other side of her chest. Quickly turning her head to the right, she saw the blade was held by a second mounted stranger. His mouth twisted into an evil smirk and his gray, steely eyes were filled with contempt.

"Stay silent, little lady," he said quietly, his voice brimming with malice. Clara bit back her scream as she felt the blade press hard against her clothes. Being from a military family, Clara knew full well that the blade was lodged firmly between two ribs and that with one good thrust it would slide between them, right into her heart.

"There is someone who wants to talk to you," the man continued. "After that, you are free to go wherever your noble heart desires. Now, you can either come with us willingly, riding your own horse, or I can tie you up and toss you over my saddle like a sack of potatoes. Your choice." From the way he chuckled as his eyes slid over Clara's body, it was obvious which option he preferred.

Clara desperately looked around for an escape, but they were beyond the outer border of the city now. There was nothing but distant farmhouses and fields spreading around them for miles. A couple of wagons wobbled along the road ahead, but they were too far away for anyone to notice that Clara needed help. Besides, even if they were close enough, it was unlikely they would willingly risk their own lives to help Clara. These two thugs looked well-armed and extremely dangerous, any common merchant would probably just ignore her cries for help, not wanting to get in trouble as well. She had no choice but to nod in acquiescence, still unable to produce actual words.

The first man yanked on the reins, tearing them out of Clara's hands then leading her and her horse down one of the side roads. The gray-eyed bandit remained close behind her, ready to attack should she try something stupid like jumping down and running away.

They traveled like this for more than half an hour before reaching a disheveled farmhouse, one seemingly long abandoned. Clara shivered involuntarily when they stopped in front of it, the gray-eyed man waving at her to dismount her horse. As soon as Clara's feet touched the ground, he roughly grabbed her arm and led her inside, both of them stumbling over broken furniture and rubbish strewn across the floor until their eyes became accustomed to the darkness.

The room was lit by a single torch, the barred windows preventing sunlight from getting through. There was one man standing in the center of the room. Most of his face was covered by a scarf, leaving only his short brown hair and his eyes visible. His eyes scared Clara more than the stranger's knife had earlier. They were obsidian black, devoid of any inner light, illuminated only by the reflection of the flickering flame from the torch. Even King Hayden's eyes didn't seem anywhere near this dark.

As Clara's eyes adjusted further, she realized there was someone else in the room. A man was curled up in a corner, dressed in dirty, bloodied rags, with a black bag over his head. The ropes securing his ankles were tight, digging into his flesh, and his hands were tied behind his back. The prisoner was alive, Clara noticed him moving a little from time to time, an occasional muffled groan of pain coming from beneath the cloth covering his head. Clara didn't have time to ponder over who he was because the dark-eyed man turned his attention to her.

"Lady Redwood," he gesticulated with a bow. Clara was certain he was smirking at her under the cloth covering his mouth and nose. "I'm very honored to see you accepted my invitation."

As if she had a choice. "Who are you?" she asked, finally finding her words as she tried to sound calm and brave. Despite all of her effort, it came out as more of a little girl's sniffle.

"That's not really important."

He was right, it didn't matter who he was. There was one question Clara needed to ask that was much more important, "What do you want from me?" The man had said earlier that they wanted to talk, then she'd be set free. Clara seriously doubted it would be that easy.

"Well," amusement sparked through the darkness of his eyes. "Firstly, I want to congratulate you on your engagement."

Clara didn't know how to respond, a horrible thought suddenly crossing her mind. Were these her future husband's men? Did Lord Huxley send a bunch of thugs to make sure his pretty little Orellian bride didn't slip through his fingers?

"Since you are running out of time to return to the palace unnoticed, I'll get straight to the point, my lady." So they were here to force her to go back. "The man you are marrying is a very close friend to our new queen, which puts you in a unique position." The man fished a small glass vial with clear liquid out of his pocket and held it against the light. Clara's eyes widened in fear. There was no doubt what was in it. Poison of some kind. "You will use your husband's friendship with the queen to get close to the king, then pour this into his drink."

Clara's fists clenched at her sides. "No."

"Because you love our king so much? Has he always been so kind to you? Selling you to our enemy like a horse? A slave?" Sarcasm dripped from the man's voice.

Clara shook her head, trying to sound stronger than she felt. "I might not love him. But that doesn't mean I'm going to poison him." They couldn't make her do this.

"Such a brave and loyal little thing you are. Adorable." His chuckle sounded almost demonic. "You will do it. Want to know why?" Clara didn't want to know why but she didn't really have a say in the matter. The man who'd brought her inside stepped forward, heading to the body lying helpless in the corner before dragging the struggling person closer to the torch.

When he removed the bag from the prisoner's head, Clara screamed. She tried to lunge forward but the third man, the one in the ridiculous purple cloak, grabbed her from behind.

"Sebastian!" Clara cried out, tears streaming down her cheeks.

The man on the ground squinted in the light, his eyes widening in recognition and horror upon finding hers. "Clara?" He tried to say more but a swift kick into his stomach stopped him, pushing the air from his lungs and leaving him huddled on the dirty floor in the fetal position, dry heaving.

"Sebastian!" Clara kept struggling against the man holding her, even though it was pointless. But this was her brother, the one that was supposed to be overseas on a diplomatic mission. Somehow, he was here, tied up on the ground, half of his face caked in blood, one eye swollen shut, squirming in agony. The man above him lifted his foot to kick him once more. "No, please!" Clara screamed. The leader raised his hand, stopping the gray-eyed man from hurting Sebastian again.

Holding out the vial, the masked man walked closer to Clara, his obsidian eyes piercing her own. Clara stopped trying to free herself from the steely grip, her eyes jumping between the poison and her brother.

"It's really your choice, little lady," the man said. "Once you are married, you will have five days to get the job done. If you do, we let this piece of shit go. If not, well...he's been a very annoying hostage, so I'm going to enjoy killing him. Very slowly and very painfully."

"Please, you can't make me kill the king," she sniffled, long having lost control over the tears. "I'll do anything else. We have money, I can-"

"I'm afraid, we didn't bring you here to negotiate, that's not how this works," he interrupted her with a chuckle. "I've been told the effects of the mixture aren't immediate so if you do your job carefully, you might even get away with it. Then you can live happily ever after with that Levantian scum you are marrying." Knowing she'd murdered someone.

Clara saw her hand reach out for the vial as if she weren't the one in control of it, before glancing once more at her brother. He looked just as frightened as she was, shaking his head. When her fingers wrapped around the tiny piece of glass, he shouted, "Clara, don't!" A fist hit his chin, knocking him out.

"Don't worry, he's alive. For now." The man's tone wasn't very reassuring. "And, I almost forgot. I mean, it's only logical, but still. I feel like it should be said out loud, just for clarification. If you try to tell anyone, your brother dies. And we will know if you have. The palace is full of eyes and ears sympathetic to our cause."

Then why the fuck did they need her to do their dirty work? Clara thought but nodded anyway, carefully tucking the vial into her pocket.

"Go home now, little girl. You don't want to miss your own wedding. I bet it's going to be...magical." His ensuing cackle haunted Clara long after she'd left the farmhouse. Spurring her horse into a sharp gallop toward the palace, Clara's mind whirred. No, she couldn't miss her wedding now, even though she might not live long after her nuptials. Even with everything that had just happened, it didn't make her upcoming marriage any less scary.

Chapter 3

K arina stirred in bed, panting heavily as she found herself waking up from a hot dream. Even without opening her eyes, she knew it wasn't all just a dream and began spreading her legs to give the intruding fingers better access. She bit down hard, locking her jaw in a vain attempt to stop her loud moaning. There was no need to alert the whole camp as to what was going on inside their tent.

To be fair, they probably already knew. Karina rarely stayed quiet when reaching climax and these tent walls did nothing to muffle her sounds. One good thing about their arrival to Ebris would be having actual solid walls around their sleeping chamber. Sadly, in Karina's eyes, that was pretty much the only good thing about their pending arrival to the capital.

Being on the road with a regiment of Hayden's army was surprisingly fun. Karina enjoyed staying in a different place every night, spending her days in Seraphina's saddle, riding first through the countryside of Levanta which Karina knew well, and then through Orellian towns and villages she had never seen before. It was interesting, even adventurous.

The soldiers skillfully set up camp every evening and packed it back onto the wagons every morning. The caravan moved slowly but Karina wasn't in any rush to reach their new home.

She loved to watch Hayden around his men. Why did he ever think his people didn't love him? Yes, the soldiers were afraid of the infamous Burning Fury, but it wasn't all they felt. They looked at him with a mix of fear and respect, even admiration, especially when he joined in as they performed their duties, of which there were many with the camp constantly on the move. He wasn't a king who sits idly by, watching people toil their asses off while sipping wine out of a priceless glass. He was one of them and they knew it.

The fingers sliding in and out of Karina's vagina, pressing and rubbing her sensitive spots, were too distracting to continue with that thought. Something large moved under the blanket followed by a mouth attacking one of her nipples, making her gasp in pleasure. Teeth pulled gently, adding to the pressure she'd already felt building up.

Karina reached for Hayden's pillow and pressed it over her face in the hopes of at least muffling her scream of pleasure as the joint effort of Hayden's mouth and fingers pushed her over the blissful edge. She came hard, her back trying to arch itself up and away from the barrage of sensations before a strong pair of hands held her down, forcing her to stay still, which amplified the pleasure even more.

When Karina finally calmed down, she could feel Hayden slowly kissing his way up her neck before finally reaching her lips. "Good morning, my queen," he chuckled. "You are a heavy sleeper."

"I'm a normal sleeper," Karina grumbled when she finally caught her breath, "it's you who doesn't sleep enough."

Hayden was used to getting up before sunrise, a thing that seemed nearly impossible for Karina. His hair was wet which meant he had already exercised and bathed, probably in the freezing stream that ran below the camp.

"You know, bathing in blood and eating newborns aside, you truly are a madman," she teased him, brushing the wet hair from his face with her fingers. "Getting up so early to run around the forest with Lamar is insanity." But it did cause him to have the perfectly sculpted body of a god of war, so as long as he didn't force her to get up with him, Karina didn't really mind.

Hayden smirked and was about to answer when they were interrupted by a hesitant knock on one of the wooden poles holding up the roof in front of the tent entrance. "Gods! Seriously?" Hayden's smirk was replaced by a scowl that would be more fitting on a toddler than a king. Karina had to suppress a giggle as he glared angrily. Moody as always. But in this case, he was entitled to be. "What?!" he barked angrily.

"Uhh, sir, there is a messenger from the lord chancellor." The man standing guard sounded frightened and Karina could hardly blame him.

Hayden rolled his eyes. "We will arrive in Ebris tomorrow, that idiot couldn't wait one more day?" he grumbled, more to himself than to Karina. She knew he didn't really mean it. After all, Hayden trusted and respected Lord Egmont enough to let him run the entire country while he was away on a war campaign. "He can wait!"

"I... I'm incredibly sorry, my lord, but it sounded really urgent." The soldier was desperate now, torn between his duty and fear of angering the king.

Before Hayden could snap at the poor man, Karina whispered, "It's alright." She gave him a brief kiss and slipped out of bed, straightening her hair and putting on a long robe to cover her thin nightgown. "Send him in," she ordered, smirking at Hayden, who was now sitting on the bed looking incredibly annoyed.

"Thank you, my lady." The guard answered, sounding relieved. Another, slightly more nervous man entered the tent.

The messenger was covered in dust and mud. Clearly he'd ridden through the night without rest. While bowing deeply to Hayden, the poor man staggered. The king's anger evaporated as he jumped to guide the exhausted man to a chair. Karina brought over a glass of water, trying to hide her own worries. What could possibly be so important? Nothing good, that was for sure.

The man gladly accepted the water, only now noticing Karina's presence. "Thank you, my lord, my lady. I have an urgent message from Lord Egmont, sir."

"Well, what is it?" Hayden was asked impatiently.

The messenger nervously glanced at Karina, lowering his head to avoid Hayden's gaze. "It's, umm, it's for your ears only, sir."

Right. Karina was not supposed to be involved in matters of the state. Hayden had already broken several customs by allowing her to attend his council meetings so she didn't want to push this, especially not in front of his soldiers. "I'll go grab something to eat." Her smile was honest, she trusted Hayden to tell her what was happening later.

"No." His answer was quick and definite. "Stay. I already brought you breakfast." Hayden turned back to the messenger, "You, speak."

The man's eyebrows rose but he didn't dare argue with Hayden. "There's been an attack in the northern mountains. Several actually. The Ruthians have resumed their hostilities, attacking and destroying a number of trade caravans as well as several of our units and patrols."

"Why didn't the Blackwater outpost dispatch reinforcements to protect caravans after the first attack?" Hayden was frowning again. "There's like six hundred men stationed there."

The room was quiet for a few moments before the messenger drew in a deep breath. "Sir,...the Blackwater outpost was destroyed. Completely. There are a couple dozen survivors who made it through the woods to the nearest fortress but the outpost itself was ransacked and the remnants burned to the ground."

"What?!" Crouching in front of the man, Hayden stared into his face, trying to see if he was lying.

A sealed envelope appeared in the man's hands and he handed it over to the king. "I'm sorry, sir, that's all I know. This is the Chancellor's report."

Hayden quickly regained his composure but Karina could sense he was both confused and worried. He grabbed the envelope and while his fingers were breaking though the seal, he shouted to the guard outside. "Marley! Tell Warren and the other lords to meet me in the big tent in twenty minutes. And make sure this man gets some food and water and has a place to rest."

The guard saluted before helping the messenger outside, leaving Karina alone with a very tense Hayden. "Eat and get dressed if you want to come," he commanded her, his eyes flying over the parchment in his hands, frowning more and more as he continued to read.

Karina quietly did as she was told, quickly washing herself, brushing her hair and putting on a simple dress all while eating the plate of scones he had brought her. There were at least a dozen questions burning on her tongue but she didn't dare open her mouth to ask them. Hayden was so absorbed by his reading that she didn't want to disturb him. She also didn't want him to change his mind about the invitation to his council meeting now that something was actually happening.

Karina was focused on braiding her hair when she felt Hayden press up against her back, wrapping his strong arms around her chest. He pulled her close and sighed, "Sorry, I didn't mean to be so stern with you."

"It's alright. Is it bad? Will you have to take your army north?" Will they not have more than a few weeks of peace? They'd just barely avoided one war, was Orellia now headed straight into another one?

Hayden didn't respond right away so Karina waited patiently. "I won't have to go unless it gets worse but..." he hesitated, "I just don't understand it."

"Weren't they always hostile toward Orellia?" Karina asked, remembering how he'd told her about the endless battles with tribes up north.

"They were." He grabbed her tighter and shook his head, Karina felt his hair tickling her neck. "But never to this magnitude. In the past, they attacked traders, stole goods, but usually let the people live. And they never dared to attack such a well-defended military target before. Ruthians are tribal and the tribes hate each other as much as they hate us. For an attack like this, at least a dozen of the bigger tribes would have to band together and it's just...it's not what they normally do."

Chapter 4

T he lords, gathered together in the tent around a large wooden table, seemed to be just as confused as Hayden was upon hearing the news from up north. However, not one of them wasted much time pondering over the reasoning, instead, they started planning retaliation strategies. Karina stood off to one side, ignored by most of them. They still didn't like her being there but apparently, as long as she kept her mouth shut, they were willing to tolerate her presence.

Karina moved closer to the table and examined the large map of the continent laid out in front of her. It didn't make any sense. The Kingdom of Orellia spread from one coast to another, its borders dotted by several smaller countries. Karina's eyes were inadvertently drawn to Levanta, a piece of land huddled between Orellia and the Western sea. It was so small in comparison. That didn't make sense either. What madness had possessed her father? How could he have thought that he could win a war against Orellia?

Karina knew all of the country names. Geography was one of the few topics she was taught, being a girl, but some stood out more than others.

Hayden had mentioned Orellia having feuds and even some open conflicts with other kingdoms in the recent past. Seeing it all laid out on the map made it all sound ridiculous. Yet another thing that didn't make any sense to Karina. Now the barbarians were attacking? Wasn't that a little too many coincidences?

"Which of these countries have you been at war with?" she asked quietly, lost in thoughts. All eyes turned to her, the sudden silence surprising her.

"My queen, it's admirable that you wish to learn about our history but now is hardly the right place or time," snarked General Warren. He'd been the biggest opponent to her presence at meetings and now he finally had his chance to ridicule her over something she'd said.

But Karina wasn't one to give up easily. "I'm well aware of the time and the place, General. Would you be so kind as to humor me for a moment, please?" The last word was as insincere as she could manage, without being overtly offensive.

The lords glanced at Hayden who raised his eyebrow in Karina's direction. Upon seeing the determination on her face, he nodded.

"Pekhan, Xandia," one of the younger men said. Lord Gaston was one of the few friendly faces Karina kept seeing around Hayden.

She raised a finger to pause him and turned to Lamar, quickly snatching his coin pouch. "Don't worry, I'll return it," she promised, stopping his protests, then nodded at Lord Gaston to continue. Pouring a mix of Orellian and Levantian coins into her hand, Karina placed one on each of the mentioned countries, plus one on the mountain range to the north, next to a red flag marker symbolizing the destroyed outpost.

"There were some border disputes with Kurasa, a short conflict with the Jakari Islands." More coins were placed on the map.

Other lords chimed in, throwing several more names her way. Karina marked each country, making a chain of silver and copper coins around Orellia. "And Levanta, obviously," General Warren added with a smirk, placing a large gold coin with Hayden's bust face up on the map.

"Obviously," Karina nodded, not really paying attention to his condescending remark, but rather hypnotized by the map. And she wasn't alone.

Some of the lords also leaned over the table and Hayden frowned as he watched on. After giving a quiet order to Markos, who immediately left the tent, Karina turned back to face the group, knowing she would have to choose her next words very carefully. "Before the conflict with Orellia, Levanta coexisted peacefully with all of its neighbors for decades. This," Karina added, waving her arm over the map, "is not normal."

That was probably not the right word choice since it seemed to bring out anger on many of the faces surrounding her. "Are you suggesting that we are such insufferable neighbors that we inadvertently force everyone around us to wage war against us?" Warren asked, eyebrow raised and contempt seeping from his words.

"No, General. I'm suggesting that none of this makes any sense. Why would any of these countries want to attack Orellia? They knew they had no chance of winning."

Markos returned, closely followed by another man. Oscar Huxley smiled at Karina, bowing his head in her direction. "My lady, you...summoned me?" He hesitated mid-sentence, noticing the crowd of hostile faces glaring at him. "Oh. I shouldn't be here."

"No, Lord Huxley," Hayden scoffed, "you most certainly should not be here. But it seems the queen has requested your presence for some reason." He definitely wasn't happy but he didn't stop her, curious as to what she was thinking.

Karina felt relieved that Hayden trusted her judgment, but knew his patience was limited. "Lord Huxley," she turned to her friend, "why did King Harold decide to attack Orellia? And don't tell me you don't know. You hear every whisper along with all of the gossip, there must be something. My father was a lot of things, but he wasn't stupid. Plus, you heard Dalton in court. He said, 'Should the invasion occur'." That was right before Karina had killed him. "Even with the king dead, our army defeated, twelve thousand enemy soldiers camped at our border, he still didn't believe that King Hayden would actually go through with the invasion. And Dalton was the mastermind behind my father's plans. What was he expecting to happen?"

The lords around them whispered quietly to each other but none of them dared to interrupt her. Oscar looked around nervously before his eyes found Karina again and he sighed. "There is something but it's more gossip than actual information, I haven't been able to verify it, that's why I never told you. Also, because Dalton is dead and all this," he waved his hand at the men surrounding him, "well...happened, I didn't think it mattered anymore.

"Lord Dalton had a guest every couple of months. The mysterious man came, stayed for a couple of hours, and within the next few days, the king had a new plan of action against Orellia. Fake trade deals, spreading rumors, diplomatic rifts based on false pretenses. At one point King Harold even ordered our soldiers to be masked as bandits and start attacking people along Orellian trade routes." The tent filled with not-so-quiet grumbling. "General Rand refused to take part in any underhanded tactics and your father didn't push it, but I don't think he abandoned the idea. He probably ended up paying actual bandits to do it."

"That is outrageous!" one of the lords blustered but both Karina and Oscar ignored him.

Lord Huxley spoke louder to make sure she heard him right. "Then the man came for a longer visit. After that, your father decided that the disputed swampy shithole along our eastern border belongs to us, not Orellia, and we needed to take it back. We tried to stop him, we really did. Rand, Otto, along with countless others argued with him. Gods, Jansen nearly got executed for calling the king crazy. But your father was adamant. And we all know how it ended." Oscar shrugged.

"That land belongs to us by the treaty of..."

"Oh, for fuck's sake!" Karina raised her voice, interrupting an elderly lord's rambling. "That is not the point of the story!"

"You think it's all connected." Lord Gaston murmured, staring at the map now instead of Karina. "That, behind each of these coins there is a mysterious man whispering in someone's ear." He was smart, Karina liked him more and more.

As Karina looked around, she saw distrust or bemusement on many of the faces but a few of the lords seemed intrigued by the idea. The look on Hayden's face was indecipherable. Still, he hadn't stopped her or kicked her out, so she continued, "Yes. I believe these men come from the same place and have the same goal. To keep Orellia in a state of constant conflict, without any real allies you can rely on." Damn, she should really learn to say 'we' instead of 'you' when talking about Orellia. "While the other kingdoms have had decades of peace to focus on their growth and prosperity, Orellia has gone from one war to another. This is too much to be just a coincidence." Her hand waved over the coins on the map.

"Wow." General Warren clapped mockingly slow and loud, turning the attention of the room to himself. "Our new queen has such a vivid imagination. It's incredible how you have managed to fabricate such a tale out of nothing while trying to justify the stupidity that caused Levanta to lose everything. But you've wasted enough of our time already. I think you should go back to reading fantastical romantic novellas or wherever you fished this idea from and leave the decision-making to people who actually have something between their ears."

What the fuck did that asshole just say to her?! "Excuse me?!" Karina fumed but before she could open her mouth to start yelling at the general she was interrupted.

"ENOUGH!" Hayden's fists slammed against the table, making the coins jingle. The whole tent fell deadly silent in an instant. The king wasn't looking at either of them, his gaze was fixated on the map. "If you don't know when to shut up, you do not belong here," he snarled.

Crap. Now Karina had screwed herself over by making him furious. "I'm sorry," she whispered, lowering her head.

"Not you." Hayden growled, his voice distinguishably softer as he spoke to Karina before gaining in intensity as he turned his attention to Lord Warren. "General, you are an excellent military commander and one of my most trusted advisors. But if you continue to talk to your queen in that way, you will not be welcome on this council. That goes for all of you." Hayden's narrowed eyes scanned the other men in the room. "You may oppose her and disagree with her opinions just as you are free to do with me. But you will do so with respect and you will not be insulting. If you are unable to accept that, then get the fuck out of here right now!"

Most of the lords lowered their heads. It might have been in shame or just in fear of Hayden's anger, but nobody sneered at Karina anymore. "I-I..." Warren stuttered, staring at the king in disbelief before turning to Karina. "I apologize, my lady," he mumbled insincerely.

"Apology accepted," Karina retorted in a similar manner, still pissed at what he'd said.

Hayden stood up and strode right up to Oscar, piercing him with a cynical stare. "Was that the truth, Lord Huxley? Or just another carefully fabricated lie?" The threat in his voice had even Karina shivering.

"As I said, it's unverified gossip." Oscar didn't seem to be unnerved by the danger dripping from the king's tongue, "But I do believe there is some truth to it. I'd never lie to my queen." The hint of a smirk twisted his lips before he added, "Or to my king, naturally."

Hayden scoffed. "Naturally." Turning back to the table, he glanced at Karina. "Continue."

Karina had no idea whether he believed her or just wanted to give her more of a chance to make an absolute fool out of herself, but it didn't matter by this point. What was started, now needed to be finished.

"I think we all know that there is only one person powerful enough to be behind all of this. The same person who already tried to poison King Hayden in order to destroy the alliance between Levanta and Orellia, thus dragging all of us into a long and bloody invasion." They all knew what she was talking about. Cchen-Lian, the mighty empire on the western continent and its emperor Odi. A cunning man with a long-standing hatred for Orellia who had recently sent men to poison Hayden and implicate Karina in his death.

"Look," Karina did her best to calm down and sound as conciliatory as she could manage. It was certainly not her intention to cause conflict between Hayden's lords. "I don't pretend to know anything about waging war. I am not saying you shouldn't react to this new threat," her finger pointed to the red flag on the map. "Nor am I suggesting you make a move against Cchen-Lian based on my unfounded theory. All I am saying is that you have been so occupied by solving individual conflicts that you have, quite naturally, lost track of the bigger picture. All I am asking is that you take a moment to consider what I've said. Maybe General Warren is right and this is just my imagination. But what if it's not?" Finished speaking, she exhaled slowly, her hands shaking from the nerves. What if she was wrong?

Hayden nodded, looking lost in thought. "I think that's enough for now, we'll talk more about it after we return to the capital. General, make sure the men we talked about are dispatched north as soon as possible. We need to solve this problem before first snow, we can't do shit there in winter. And try to send negotiators to the tribes that were previously friendly to us, maybe we can find out what the fuck is happening. I hope I don't have to remind you," his eyes narrowed as he inspected everyone in the tent, ending on Lord Huxley with a scowl, "that not a word that's been said here today leaves this room."

Oscar gave the king a polite nod and Karina hoped she hadn't gotten her friend into trouble by inviting him. Or at least, into even more trouble than he was already in.

Chapter 5

A s the lords dispersed, Hayden absentmindedly swept up the coins from the map back into the pouch and handed it over to Lamar. Karina smirked, realizing that Warren's large gold coin, which he'd mockingly placed over Levanta, ended up in the captain's pocket as well. But the general probably had lots and wouldn't miss one. Come to think of it, so did Lamar. Karina was certain that Hayden paid him handsomely.

She couldn't quite decipher Hayden's mood, which worried her. Angry, furious even, annoyed certainly, those she would expect. But he didn't seem to be any of that. If anything, he seemed sad. As he picked up one of the paperweights and played with it, the map immediately rolled up. Karina wasn't sure whether she should talk to him, or apologize maybe? Whatever he was thinking couldn't be good and it was certainly her fault.

He finally turned and headed out of the tent. "I need to go for a ride." His voice was strangely void of emotions and he barely even looked at her before moving outside.

"Can I come with you?" she asked hesitantly, joining him as he strode through the camp.

His eyebrow rose as he looked over her gown, which was certainly not meant for a saddle, then he shrugged, "If you want."

"I do. I'll be right back." As Karina hurried toward their tent to quickly change into her riding clothes, her insides turned and twisted anxiously. Over the last few weeks, she had become quite proficient in telling what mood the king was in, whether he was seriously angry or just teasing her. Now, she could tell nothing. What'd happened in that meeting had thrown him off and Karina had no clue as to what conclusion he would reach after processing it.

He was already in Demon's saddle, waiting in front of their tent when she walked out, despite Karina being truly lightning-quick at changing her clothes. Her riding boots weren't yet properly laced up. Seraphina's reins flew in her direction, Hayden moving away before she'd even mounted her mare, which was not a good sign. Normally, he would push her up into the saddle.

She quickly caught up, ignoring Markos and Lamar who were following them as they took the road east toward Ebris, riding in absolute silence. Under normal circumstances, Karina would enjoy the ride. It was another beautiful late summer's day and the sun was warming the air despite the soft easterly breeze. But now, she kept nervously eyeing Hayden and had to bite her tongue to keep quiet. It was his turn to say something and he clearly wasn't ready yet.

They turned down one of the side roads and headed into a forest, the path getting thinner and less distinguished with each passing moment. Karina was lost. She'd have no idea how to return to the main road but Hayden seemed to know where he was going. They were quite close to his home so there was a good chance that this was a place he'd visited before. As the path zigzagged up a slope, the trees became scarcer and smaller until they disappeared completely, replaced by thick green grass whose long blades rocked in the wind like waves upon the sea.

As they approached the top of the hill, Hayden dismounted, attaching Demon's reins to a low thorny bush before continuing on foot. Karina did the same, making sure Seraphina had enough room to graze.

Hayden disappeared between some rocks so Karina carefully followed him, climbing over a particularly large one. When she finally lifted her eyes to see in front of her, she gasped in astonishment. The other side of the hill ended in a sharp cliff and they were standing near the very edge of it. Just a few feet from Karina, the ground suddenly dropped away into a seemingly endless fall. It must have been well over two hundred feet, if not more. She was never very good at guessing distances.

The cliff overlooked a large valley that was dotted with tiny villages, lots of fields and pastures. A river ran lazily from east to northwest. Its size was significantly smaller than the one that ran through Vantia but even so, there were plenty of boats going up and down it. Even from this distance, Karina could see where the main road crossed the water via a magnificent stone bridge. The view was so breathtaking she forgot all about moody Hayden, wars, and councils. Instead, she just stood there, enjoying the peaceful scenery.

"Careful." Hayden's voice was so close to her ear Karina flinched and nearly stumbled. "It's a long way down," he murmured, still sounding strained, but he wrapped his arms around her before pulling her back to his chest, resting his chin on her shoulder.

Karina sighed in relief. So, he wasn't furious at her. Unless he'd brought her here to push her over the cliff, which didn't really sound like him. "Are you going to throw me off the cliff?" she teased.

"I'll think about it," he chuckled, which was exactly Karina's goal. After heaving a deep sigh, Hayden continued, "I'm sorry I was like that, I was just..."

"Lost in thought?" Karina finished his sentence. "I understand. Were you angry with me?" Hayden didn't seem angry now but back in the tent was another matter entirely.

"No," he breathed out. Karina thought he would continue but he kept quiet so she held her tongue and waited, watching flocks of birds soar over the harvested fields, looking for leftover grains.

Hayden brushed a stray lock of hair behind Karina's ear then kissed the side of her neck before saying, "I was angry with myself because you're right. I've been king for ten years and didn't notice a thing. You've been queen for how long? Less than two weeks? And you just waltzed in there and effortlessly revealed this huge plot to destroy me and the whole of Orellia. Perhaps you should be throwing me off the cliff."

Karina remembered their earlier conversation and how uncertain and insecure Hayden had admitted to being. This must have come from the same place. "Hayden, that's the point. You've been too close to the whole thing. Sometimes it takes a fresh set of eyes to provide a different perspective, an outsider. Besides, it's all just wild conjecture."

"No, it isn't. There is more to this than those idiots know. I've seen it before. People suddenly changing their opinions, deals getting altered, alliances revoked. I signed it off as the Burning Fury bullshit, that nobody wants to have any dealings with the mad king." His voice was bitter. "But I was too blind and too stupid to see there was more to it than just my fabulous reputation," he scoffed.

He didn't just believe Karina might be right, he was convinced of it. The revelation would be almost intoxicating if it weren't for the fact that it made him feel like an idiot. That was not Karina's intention. "Hayden, please stop underestimating yourself. You can't be everywhere, know everything, and consider every possible option, including the crazy and improbable ones. If one of your advisors had come up with the idea, would you be feeling like this? Because it is their job to advise you, provide different perspectives and think of every angle. Can't you think of me as just another advisor?"

"That would be difficult to do." His hand glided up to gently squeeze her breast. "You have certain...attributes that make it almost impossible."

Karina held her breath when his other hand slid down her thigh, rubbing her through the thin leather breeches. "Yes," she breathed out, "I can hardly imagine you and General Warren in this position."

"Don't remind me about him," Hayden growled. "I mean, he is an excellent strategist and is good with men, but around women he is an even bigger asshole than I am, which is quite an accomplishment. I would prefer to keep him around but I will get rid of him if you want me to."

What? Hayden would willingly kick someone out of his council just on Karina's word? A tiny, spiteful part of her mind found the idea of Warren being humiliated in that way very appealing but that was certainly not the kind of a queen Karina wanted to be. "Don't. You know me, I forgive everyone. Even though I still want to punch that bastard's face."

"I noticed," Hayden laughed heartily. "Actually, that's why I stopped your argument. I would advise you against violence, it's going to hurt your hand more than it would hurt him."

That wasn't really new information to Karina, which was ironic since she usually tried to stay away from violence. "I know. It's not like I was actually going to do it." Probably. "Thank you for standing up for me," Karina sighed, wishing things had gone smoothly enough that Hayden didn't have to step in, but was still eternally grateful he'd spoken in her defense.

"Of course." Hayden briefly kissed her neck. "I don't need your authority trampled into the dirt to boost my own. I happen to believe we can benefit from each other. As long as it doesn't get out of hand and you don't start your own shadow council to overpower mine." He sounded serious but from the way his lips curved as he kissed her shoulder, Karina knew he was grinning.

"I'll think about it," she giggled, repeating his words. There was a long pause as they took in the peaceful view in front of them. "What happens now?" That was the big question. How does one react to being the target of such a huge conspiracy?

Hayden sighed, "I honestly have no idea. We'll gain nothing by letting Odi know we've figured out his plan. So, we play along for now and try to find out more information. That doesn't sound like much of a plan, does it?"

"It sounds like a great plan," Karina corrected. She opened her mouth to say something more but decided against it. No, it was really not a good idea.

Of course it didn't matter that she hadn't said it, Hayden noticed. "What is it?" he asked. Karina shook her head but he insisted, "Come on, tell me."

"You'll just get angry."

"Hmm, is it that bad?" He paused to take in a deep breath. "I'll do my best not to."

Knowing it was the best he could promise her, Karina said, "If you need information, you could talk to Oscar. The man has 'friends' everywhere."

"Karina, I know you two are very close friends and I'm really trying hard not to freak out about it but I just don't like him." Hayden didn't sound angry, which was a good start.

"Hayden," she turned to face him, raising her hands to cup his cheeks, "I'm not asking you to love him and I don't expect you to become best buddies. All I'm suggesting is you use his skills and resources for the good of our country."

He grinned playfully. "I like how you said 'our country'. I'll think about it. Huxley is getting married the day after tomorrow, we should probably let him settle into his new role before dragging him into problems of the state."

"Oh, right!" Karina had almost forgotten. "We are going to the wedding, right? I mean, I am." There was no way she would abandon her friend on his big day.

"As much as I'd love to pass on such a wonderful opportunity, I can't," Hayden snickered. "As Clara's guardian, I actually have to give her away to that..." he swallowed an insult, "...man. So yes, we are going. Gods, I hope I made the right decision. I'd hate to screw up that girl's life, she's been through enough already."

Shaking her head over his lack of enthusiasm, Karina answered, "Don't worry. They will both be just fine." Hayden snorted, unconvinced. Truth be told, Karina wasn't convinced either, but someone had to stay optimistic, right?

Chapter 6

Clara had to admit she looked beautiful. Vanity was never her thing, but what woman didn't dream of looking like a princess on her wedding day? Still, Clara would rather look ugly than get married to a complete stranger.

The royal caravan had arrived late last night and with Clara being held hostage by a crowd of maids commanded by her mother since early morning, she still hadn't even seen Lord Huxley yet. Given her current situation, worrying over him being an ugly, fat old man should be the last thing on her mind, but Clara still couldn't help but wonder what her husband looked like. And, more importantly, what kind of a man he might be.

The memory of the tiny glass vial tried to sneak its way into Clara's mind but the girl promptly chased it away. She forbade herself from thinking about that today. Getting through her wedding was going to be hard enough without trying to come up with a plan to poison the king.

Her hand slid over the satin dress, white with green trim, the emerald color matching her eyes perfectly. The bodice was so tight that Clara could barely breathe but it did bring out her cleavage, making her breasts look much bigger than normal. Wasn't that considered lying to her future husband? Her mother had just rolled her eyes and shushed Clara when she'd dared to ask.

If Sophia was surprised by her daughter's sudden obedience, she didn't let it show, probably assuming that Clara had simply come to terms with the inevitability of the situation and given up fighting against it.

Clara's wild red mane was the hairdresser's worst nightmare. After several attempts at subduing the unruly curls, the poor woman just slapped a large hair net over Clara's head, attaching it with dozens of pins. Adding a simple pearl tiara, the result was surprisingly pretty.

It was almost time. Clara was standing by the window, watching a gardener pluck weeds from a flowerbed. She had barely gotten used to these chambers in the palace. It was a beautiful suite overlooking the gardens, which she shared with her mother. Now she would have to move into her marital suite with her husband.

She couldn't even hope to return home to the Redwood family mansion because that, by birthright, belonged to Sebastian, the eldest of the three siblings. And since Lord Huxley was a foreigner who owned no land in, or around the city, the newlyweds were going to stay in the palace until they found a place of their own. Clara was at least grateful that her husband wasn't going to drag her off to Levanta as soon as they were married.

A soft knock at the door interrupted Clara's thoughts. Her voice trembled as she answered and when King Hayden entered the room, she tried to mask her anxiety with a deep curtsy. The king seemed different from how she remembered him. Handsome, yes, that hadn't changed, but he looked more relaxed as if a large part of his anger had simply vanished.

He smiled at Clara. A real, sincere smile that brightened his expression even further. "Ready?" the king asked. Clara nodded even though she couldn't be any less ready. The king's smile widened. "You look amazing. Huxley is a lucky man."

"Thank you." Clara's voice was almost a whisper. "You are too kind, Your Highness." This was the man she was supposed to murder? No. She couldn't afford to think about that now.

Did the king just chuckle? "This is probably the first time somebody has ever accused me of being too kind." He offered his arm and Clara grabbed it, anxious to be actually touching the king.

The hallways were empty and oddly quiet as they headed toward the great hall. "Are you nervous?" Hayden asked, probably feeling her body tremble. "It's normal. I was too." The corner of his mouth curled up and Clara had to forcibly stop staring at him. Who was this man and what has he done with the Burning Fury?

They stopped momentarily in front of the large doors before them. Hayden glanced at Clara before saying, "Don't worry. He'll be nice to you."

If only Clara could be as sure of that. Just as she took in a deep breath, the door opened, revealing a beautifully decorated hall filled with people wearing their finest clothes. Most of the Orellian nobility had missed the royal wedding since it had taken place in Levanta, so this was the next best occasion to show off. Especially since both the king and his new queen were attending the event as well.

Clara could see her now, standing next to the low dais in the center of the room. Queen Karina was wearing a surprisingly simple gown and her brown hair fell across her shoulder in a long, thick braid. If it wasn't for the thin golden circlet around her head, Clara would have never guessed that this was the queen. Most women in the hall were dressed far more ornately in luxurious and noticeably expensive gowns. Including Clara's mother, who was standing beside the queen, looking like a scruffy peacock next to a graceful dove.

When she couldn't avoid it any longer, Clara's eyes slid past the flowers adorning the dais toward her husband. A tiny pebble was lifted from her heavy heart. He wasn't old, fat, or ugly. Quite the opposite, actually. Older than she was, naturally, Lord Huxley looked to be about the king's age, twenty-five, give or take. He was tall and slender. Not overly muscular like some of Hayden's warriors who were built like mountains, but there was no belly bulging over the edge of his breeches either. His dark brown shoulder-length hair was pulled back and tied by a leather strap, yet several strands escaped and were now framing his face. No, he most certainly wasn't ugly.

Huxley watched her with a nervous smile and Clara realized that it wasn't just the first time she was seeing him, it was also the first time he was seeing her. She straightened up and held her head high, trying to put a polite smile on her face. She probably failed on that front. Smiles simply hadn't been in her repertoire over the past few days but, hopefully, she didn't look like she was attending her own funeral. There was no need to antagonize her husband any further, he already had plenty of reasons to hate her. He didn't seem to be hating her now, though. Besides being nervous, he looked almost pleased by what he saw and his brown eyes shone with what she hoped was kindness.

As they walked down the aisle, Clara found herself clutching Hayden's arm tighter, terrified of stumbling and embarrassing herself in front of her husband and the whole palace. The king placed his free hand over hers before gently patting it, probably hoping the gesture would calm her down.

"And if he isn't nice to you," King Hayden added to his previous statement, tilting his head toward Clara and whispering conspiratorially, "just let me know. I'll be happy to have him whipped."

Clara's eyes darted to the king to see him smirking, but the wicked glint in his eyes told her that he wasn't entirely joking. Hayden didn't seem to like her future husband very much and Clara had to wonder why.

Hayden gallantly helped her up the two small steps and before she knew it, Clara was standing in front of the man with whom she was supposed to spend the rest of her life. Lord Huxley bowed deeply, offering his bride-to-be a warm smile. "Lady Redwood." In contrast, the bow he gave the king was barely more than a firm nod. "Your Majesty." He had addressed Clara first, even though according to formality, that honor should belong to the king. Was this a little rebellion against his new ruler or was he trying to impress Clara?

She made a perfect curtsy. "Lord Huxley." Gods, this was so weird. And why the hell was she blushing?

The king took Clara's hand, and glaring at the man in front of him, growled, "Take good care of her, Huxley." Anger flared through the king's expression for a brief moment. Yes, that was the king Clara remembered.

"I very much intend to, my lord." Clara's future husband didn't seem moved by the king's threats and looked straight into his eyes. His answer was polite and respectful but he stood tall and didn't cower in fear or grovel like men often did around Hayden.

Clara wasn't sure, but she may have heard a quiet snort coming from the king's mouth before he took her hand and placed it into Huxley's extended one. Her husband's skin was warm but not sweaty and Clara was surprised that the touch wasn't entirely unpleasant. She gave Lord Huxley an apologetic smile, knowing her own hand must have been ice cold.

The priest talked but Clara barely listened, stealing quick glances at the man beside her. Despite custom, he never let go of her hand, his thumb gently stroking her wrist. Startled, Clara glanced between his thumb and his eyes only to have him stop immediately, looking sheepish.

It was probably normal that he wanted to touch her. After all, they were getting married and quite soon he was going to be touching her a lot more. Everywhere. Clara shuddered and chased the thought out of her head. Another thing she couldn't deal with right now. No, she had to get through this day, one moment at a time.

She repeated her vows mindlessly. It felt strangely surreal. How could she swear to love this man? She'd just met him. Clara hadn't even talked to him yet and now she was condemned by the gods to eternal damnation if she didn't love him? The only kind of love Clara knew was from romantic tales, where the knight saves a maiden from a terrible monster then she immediately falls in love with him. There were no monsters here and her husband certainly didn't look like a knight. No, the man next to her could never be mistaken for a warrior. With embarrassment, Clara realized her fingers were more calloused than his, even though she hadn't touched a bowstring in over two weeks.

Huxley's vows sounded much more earnest than Clara's but she noticed his tone changed slightly when it came to promising love. Most likely, he was thinking the same as she was. Or maybe he felt ridiculous making an oath to love his enemy. That's what she was to him, Clara had no doubts about that.

There had been a war between their two countries and his side had lost, that was the only reason Lord Huxley was being forced to marry her. Was Clara a punishment for something he'd done to the king? It made sense, they seemed to loathe each other and if Huxley was such an important lord in Levanta, Hayden probably couldn't have him simply executed unless he wanted his new subjects to rebel. So, he chose to humiliate Huxley by making him marry Clara instead. That certainly wasn't going to make her life easier.

The ceremony ended and they were officially married. The young girl called Clara Redwood disappeared, replaced by Lady Huxley, a woman Clara barely even recognized. As they faced each other, Clara's new husband gently touched her cheek, making her look up at him. There was a kind and nervous smile on his lips. "May I?" he whispered as he leaned in.

Was he really asking for permission to kiss her? Clara nodded. It was not like she could refuse.

Tilting her head backwards with his hand, Huxley's lips touched hers. They were warm and soft and for reasons unknown, tasted like apples. The kiss was brief, innocent, and Clara found herself almost wishing it would last longer. Upon opening her eyes (when had she even closed them?), Clara saw her husband's happy face and knew she was smiling as well. Her first genuine smile in weeks. Alright, this wasn't as horrible as she'd feared. At least, for now.

Chapter 7

The feast afterward was truly magnificent but still, Clara barely ate anything, nervous of the man sitting next to her. Her husband. It still sounded strange, and despite so many people congratulating them on getting married, Clara found it hard to believe that it had actually happened.

The royal couple were the first to approach them. The king kissed the back of Clara's hand and the queen hugged her, a warm smile brightening her beautiful face.

Sophia Redwood didn't look happy. Clara doubted joy had ever appeared on her mother's face. Instead, Sophia looked satisfied, probably glad that her unruly daughter was finally someone else's problem. "Remember," she hissed into Clara's ear while hugging her, "the time for your stupid rebellions is over. If you want to live a content life, you obey this man's every command and fulfill his every wish."

Clara squirmed out of the hug, struggling to keep her composure as she fought against the tears filling her eyes. As usual, her mother was honest, brutally so. Clara knew exactly what Sophia was referring to. Her lecture on what happens during the wedding night hadn't helped calm the girl's nerves. Quite the opposite, actually. It was one of the reasons Clara was getting increasingly scared as the day progressed.

Sophia had managed to paint such a disgustingly frightful and painful picture that Clara dreaded the moment she would be left alone with her new husband. Sure, he seemed kind and gentle now but, according to her mother, every man quickly turned into a lustful beast when it came to sharing their bed with a woman.

"You aren't hungry?" asked Huxley. His voice was soft as he held out a small plate of apple pie in front of Clara.

Food was the last thing on Clara's mind. "Not really. But thank you, my lord."

"Well, I guess I'll have one more then because this is absolutely delicious," he grinned, skillfully separating a chunk of the pie with his dessert fork. As he put the pie into his mouth, his expression turned almost blissful. Clara chuckled at seeing him so happy over such a simple thing. "You sure you don't want to try it?" He held the fork up to her mouth this time. Clara hesitantly opened it, not wanting to offend him. "And please, call me Oscar," he added as she ate the little treat. "I don't really believe in formalities between a husband and wife. So, is it good?"

Clara paused, blinked, then realized he was talking about the pie, still surprised over his request to call him Oscar. As a child, she'd barely known her father's first name since Sophia had only ever addressed him as "Lord Redwood" on the rare occasions they actually talked to each other. Was that not normal?

The pie was great, but it was just apple pie, nothing as magically exquisite as Lord Huxley had made it sound. Still, Clara needed to be polite. "It's delicious... Oscar," she finally said, trying his name out on her tongue. She liked it. Using first names made it feel like there was an actual relationship between them.

"I know, I know," Oscar nodded, "it's just pie, nothing special. But I like apples and they rarely serve them on these formal occasions. Apparently, apples are not fancy enough for a wedding in the royal palace." Clara stifled a giggle and accepted the next bite he offered, this time without protests. He was right, she realized, upon thinking about other events she had attended. There were no apples in the ornate fruit bowls placed on the tables either.

So, Lord Huxley liked apples. Look at that. Now Clara knew one personal thing about her husband. It was so ridiculous to think that Clara only knew this one thing about him that she almost burst out laughing. She fought against the urge since it wouldn't be a good kind of laugh. No. There was hysteria looming in the back of her mind and Clara knew that outbursts of laughter would quickly turn into desperate sobbing if she wasn't careful. And even someone as inexperienced with men as Clara knew that they hated crying girls.

As she watched him prepare another bite for her, she murmured, "I prefer grapes." Her eyes were fixed on the plate in front of them, she was afraid to look up at him, knowing he probably didn't care what she liked.

"That is good to know," Oscar replied cheerfully and reached for the nearest fruit bowl to pluck a few grapes out, holding two in front of Clara. "Red or white?"

He did care. That was surprising. "I...it doesn't really matter, as long as they are sweet and crunchy." What an absurd conversation to have at their own wedding. But, what else were they supposed to talk about?

"Interesting." Instead of offering the fruit to Clara as she expected, he put both grapes into his mouth, first the white, then the red, rolling them over his tongue with a pensive expression, almost as if he was tasting priceless wine. After that, he reached into the bowl again, taking a whole bunch of grapes this time. "I think you will like the white better then." He smiled as he offered a couple to her.

Clara took them from Oscar's proffered hand, grateful he hadn't tried to put them directly into her mouth. That seemed a little too intimate in her mind. And not in a good way.

They sat together in silence for a while. It was not as uncomfortable as one would expect. Clara watched curiously as Oscar scanned the room, pausing on each wedding guest before his eyes moved on to the next. He didn't seem to be looking for anyone specific, just observing.

"I was worried there wouldn't be any pie left for me," Oscar said, interrupting the silence with a smirk, "since the lady in pink over there seems to be making sure there aren't any leftovers."

Clara followed his gaze to the woman being mentioned and chuckled, quickly averting her eyes so the lady wouldn't notice them staring at her. "Yes, that's Lady Umber. She never misses an occasion to satisfy her ample appetite." Damn, now Clara looked like a gossip girl.

"The wife of Lord Leopold Umber? The one with the vineyards? Is that the man beside her?"

"No, that's Master Serkan, the royal armorer. Lord Umber is standing over there by the roasted boar."

It turned out that Oscar Huxley was quite interested in palace gossip. He seemed to know a lot of names, especially considering he was a foreigner who'd just arrived in the city, not to mention several pieces of basic information about people. He just didn't know which name belonged to which face. Clara was happy to help him out with that because it meant having a normal, 'safe' conversation.

The musicians had been preparing in the corner for some time. One of them nodded at the wedding organizer and upon his announcement, Oscar turned to Clara and extended one hand in front of her. "Would you do me the honor of dancing with me, my lady?" There was a hint of nervousness in his tone, as if he expected Clara to refuse. Which she couldn't, even if she wanted. Much to her own surprise, she didn't even want to refuse. Not just because dancing together was expected but also, she was curious how good of a dancer her new husband would be.

Clara loved to dance but knew that many men didn't have the talent for it, her own father being one of them. He was great with a sword but hopeless on the dance floor. Her mother had flat-out refused to dance with him ever, claiming he trampled her feet. He'd never stepped on Clara's foot (although there were times when he'd been close) but other than that,

Clara had to agree with her mother. Lord Redwood was a truly hopeless dancer, unable to keep to the rhythm or remember the correct steps.

That left Clara at the mercy of the many young lords that flocked around unmarried ladies at formal gatherings like this one. Some were good dancers but most weren't. A few took dancing as an opportunity to grope women where they weren't supposed to. Overall, it was a very unsatisfying experience.

During the ceremony and reception dinner, Clara had noticed that Oscar's movements and gestures were quite graceful for a man. She hoped it was a sign that he would prove to be at least a decent dancer.

"The honor is mine. And you may call me Clara, if you'd like." Clara realized, with a tinge of guilt, that she probably should have invited the informality when Oscar had. Hopefully it wasn't too late to fix it.

As she placed her hand in his, Oscar's smile grew brighter. "It would be my pleasure, Clara." The way he'd played with her name on his tongue made Clara shiver, partly in excitement, partly in fear. She decided to ignore the fear for now and focus on the excitement. One moment at a time.

And what a moment this was. Clara felt nerves tingle up her spine as Oscar placed his hand gently at her waist then pulled her closer to him, knowing that everyone in the room was watching them. But her worries were soon forgotten after the first few bars of the music began to play.

Clara's silent prayer that her husband could dance better than her father was answered. In fact, her expectations were surpassed by so much she could hardly believe her luck. Oscar was an exquisite dancer and as he led her in circles around the dance floor, Clara felt like they were floating, fairly certain there was a dreamy smile on her face. Oscar looked equally happy but also very aware of their surroundings, especially during the second dance when they were joined on the floor by the king and queen. Neither of the newlyweds wanted to bump into the royal couple by accident.

They took a short break after that, standing at the side to watch the other guests dance, eat, drink, and gossip. Oscar handed Clara a glass of wine with a splash of water added, something the women usually drank on these occasions to quench their thirst without getting drunk. "I hope I didn't disappoint," he whispered, watching as the king and queen kept dancing and smiling happily at each other. Was that what had changed King Hayden? Falling in love with the Levantian princess?

"Disappoint?" Clara shook her head. "You are an amazing dancer, Lord Hu-I mean, Oscar."

"That's very kind of you, Clara, but it's you who was amazing. I'm a little rusty, I'm afraid. We haven't had many balls in Levanta lately."

Clara swallowed roughly, unsure what to say. They hadn't had any balls because they were at war with Orellia. Then their king was killed by Hayden in battle and the Kingdom of Levanta ceased to exist. Oscar's country was absorbed by Clara's. How could he not be mad at that? She opened her mouth to apologize but he interrupted, "I should probably ask your mother for a dance." He didn't sound very happy about that thought and Clara could hardly blame him.

Clara watched on as they danced, noticing that her mother never shut her mouth the entire time. Oscar smiled and nodded politely, occasionally saying a few words when Sophia paused to breathe. The topic of their conversation was obvious as they both kept glancing in Clara's direction.

Clara frowned when something Oscar said made Sophia giggle like a schoolgirl. Clara turned away, not wanting to give off the appearance of being jealous or anything like that. Because she wasn't. She just didn't like the idea of Oscar enjoying a dance with Sophia. Why didn't her stupid mother marry Oscar herself if she liked him so much?

"Will you allow me the honor of this dance? Or would you rather rest for a moment?" spoke a familiar voice behind her.

Clara quickly turned around and curtsied. "It would be my honor, Your Majesty."

"I'll remind you that you said that when I step on your toes," chuckled Hayden as he offered her his arm. Despite his modesty, he was a surprisingly good dancer. Not as graceful as Oscar but still better than most of the men Clara had ever danced with.

When the song ended, the king glared over Clara's shoulder before nodding begrudgingly, his brows furrowing. "It seems that your husband has stolen my wife," he said, "so, I'm afraid you are stuck with me." He certainly didn't sound happy about it but it didn't seem to be because of Clara. No, Clara could feel the king's tension rise as he watched Oscar dance with the queen. He was jealous.

'Your future husband is a very good friend of our new queen', Sebastian's kidnapper had said. Was there something more than friendship between them? Was that why Hayden hated Oscar? And why the hell did Clara feel uneasy? She barely even knew the man, it wasn't like he was her property. Quite the opposite, actually.

The king's smile was clearly one he'd forced into place as the song ended and he practically dragged Clara to the other end of the dance floor. Poor Clara had to take quick steps to match his long strides. "Lord Huxley," Hayden growled, "I hope you enjoyed dancing with my wife." The way he stressed the word 'my' left no doubts why he was angry.

"I have." Oscar smiled, ignoring the king's mood. He stepped away from the queen and extended his hand toward Clara. "But I do believe it's time we returned to our respective wives."

"You bet it is."

"Gentlemen!" Rolling her eyes, the queen interrupted the argument before it began. "Be nice."

Clara felt Hayden relax as if the queen's words were a magical incantation. He bowed politely to Clara before heading straight to the queen and pulling her into a tight embrace.

Clara took Oscar's hand. He pulled her closer to his side but made no attempt to hug or kiss her, for which she was both grateful yet disappointed at the same time. "What would you like to do now?" he smiled, his thumb stroking the back of her hand.

It was evening already. A timer was gradually ticking down in Clara's head to the end of the night. One moment at a time. But this moment was ending and the next one... Clara didn't want to think about it just yet.

"Could we dance some more?" she asked sheepishly, hoping he wasn't too tired.

"As my lady commands," he grinned.

Clara sighed in relief. The next moment could wait a little longer.

Chapter 8

I t was late evening and several of the guests were now noticeably drunk. Clara couldn't dance anymore since her feet hurt too much, but she still couldn't force herself to say the words which would end this particular moment. Her new husband had probably guessed she was just stalling but he didn't push her on it.

Standing by the open window, Clara enjoyed breathing in the fresh night air while Oscar went to bring her water. A sweaty hand suddenly grabbed her arm and forcefully spun her around. Clara came face to face with a very drunk Lord Umber. "Well, well, well," he slurred, his breath smelling of liquor. "What are you still doing here, young lady? Shouldn't you be in bed, pleasuring your Levantian husband?" He spat out the last two words out with contempt.

"No!" Clara squealed, her good manners not allowing her to scream out loud. "Let me go!" She tried to squirm out of his grip but he held her tight.

"No?" An evil smirk twisted his lips. "You are married now, girl, you better forget all about that word. Hmm, I believe this palace hasn't seen a proper bedding ceremony for decades! Hey!" he shouted at a group of men standing nearby. "Are any of you curious about what the bride of our Levantian 'friend' is hiding beneath that beautiful dress?" Most of them frowned at Umber but a few grinned and took a step closer.

Before Clara could react in any way, Oscar appeared next to her and shoved Umber, freeing her from his grip. "That is not happening." Lord Huxley's voice lost some of its smoothness but he still sounded fairly calm, especially given the situation. He wrapped his arm around Clara's shoulders in a protective gesture, for which she felt eternally grateful.

"You don't give the orders around here, you cowardly Levantian scum," Umber hissed, grimacing in pain as he rubbed at the elbow Oscar had shoved.

A raised eyebrow was Oscar's only reaction to the insult. It seemed that Lord Huxley didn't get angry easily. "When it comes to my wife, then yes, I do."

"And when it comes to my palace and my fucking country, then I give the orders around here," a snarl announced from behind them. Unlike Oscar Huxley, King Hayden didn't need much coaxing to blow up at someone. He appeared next to the suddenly pale faced Umber, a vicious smirk curling his lips. "And in case you hadn't noticed, you old, fat asshole, the lady said no. You better start paying attention to that word, unless you want to be screaming it yourself in the dungeons below the palace."

Lord Umber stammered a few unintelligible words then squealed in terror as Hayden grabbed the front of his shirt. "Get the fuck out of here before I really lose my temper," the king whispered in a voice so cold even Clara shivered. However, when he turned back to Oscar and Clara, he seemed almost calm, saying, "You two should go, unless you want your wedding to be remembered as a bloody one. The drunker these idiots get, the worse it will be."

"Yes, I think we should. Your Majesty," Oscar added, bowing his head a little deeper than before, a hint of respect in his words. He led Clara out of the grand hall and into an empty corridor before letting go of her shoulders and giving her a worried look. "Are you alright?"

Was she? Clara honestly had no idea. The shock from Umber's attack was fading away but what replaced it was even worse. The day was over. All that was left was the wedding night. "I'm fine," she managed to mumble, leaning down to take off her shoes. The ornate tiled floor was cold but she couldn't stand those heels any longer.

"I'm sorry." Oscar's voice was quiet and he didn't look her in the eyes. "It's my fault. He only attacked you because of who I am. I mean, I'm used to being the unpopular one but I never thought how that might affect you."

Clara shook her head. "That's not true. Umber is always like that around women. All the ladies know to avoid him when he's drunk. Don't worry about him."

Oscar didn't seem convinced but didn't protest either. He simply took the shoes out of Clara's hand and carried them for her. Their new chambers weren't far and they walked together in silence, each lost in their own thoughts. Clara desperately tried to control her breathing, willing her heart to stop pounding so hard as it threatened to jump out of her chest. The fear that had loomed at the back of her mind all day, now started to draw closer causing her feet to feel heavier, reluctant to carry her forward.

The door closed behind them as they entered the bedroom. The loud clunk it made sounded like a prison gate being shut. It was dark and as Oscar went around the room to light the candles, Clara stared at the large bed looming in front of her. Tall, ornate columns held dark, silky drapes which hung neatly around the sides. The sheets were plain white and some romantic soul had scattered red rose petals all over them, which reminded Clara of drops of blood.

She couldn't move an inch. Clara could do nothing but stare at that monstrous thing, every ounce of her willpower was focused on keeping her tears at bay. One moment at a time. Except that Clara had no idea how to get through this next moment.

Just keep your mouth shut. Do whatever he tells you to do. No hesitation. No debates. And, most importantly, no crying. Her mother's advice ran through her head. 'It's not pleasant but it's the price we have to pay to have a good life', Sophia had said. 'Don't anger him or he will make it more painful on purpose.' No, angering her husband was the last thing Clara wanted.

Just tonight. She only had to get through this first night. Then it wouldn't matter. Then Clara would be a murderer, the king would be dead and the country would delve into utter chaos. What the hell was she doing? How had her life turned into such a disaster in just a few weeks?

No crying. It seemed like an impossible task.

The room was dimly lit now and Clara sensed more than saw Oscar as he moved to stand behind her. Breathe, she had to remind herself. Breathe slowly.

Oscar pulled on one of the pins holding the net over her hair. "May I?" he whispered hoarsely.

Clara couldn't respond even if she wanted to, her throat was constricted from suppressing the tears. She did, however, manage to nod. As Oscar's fingers skillfully removed each pin, Clara could tell he was being careful not to pull her hair too much. He was certainly being gentler than her mother had ever been while performing the same task. Finally, Clara's hair was free to fall down her back, the long red curls springing wildly in all directions.

"You are so beautiful," Oscar whispered as ran his fingers through her long tresses.

To be honest, Clara was surprised that he liked her hair. She was never really happy with how unruly it was, impossible to put into any kind of shape or style. Certainly not as smooth and silky as Queen Karina's hair. There were no other redheads in her family and Clara's father always claimed that she got her hair (and nature) from his grandmother, who was Ruthian.

Oscar brushed the hair away from her neck. Clara bit down on her lip to stay quiet, her fingernails digging into the flesh of her palms from how hard she was clenching her fists. She knew what he was going to do and she didn't want it. Any of it.

Of course, she didn't want this total stranger to touch her, kiss her, and do all those other disgusting and frightening things to her! But, there was nothing she could do to stop it. Even if her body wasn't completely paralyzed by fear, she had nowhere to run. Nobody would answer her cries for help. Oscar would easily overpower her if she tried to fight him. Clara belonged to Oscar now and he could do whatever he wanted with her, even punish her for disobeying him. No one would raise their voice in her defense.

Yes, she knew what he was going to do, even before his lips touched the skin on her neck, and yet, she still couldn't stop the whimper from quietly escaping her throat. A few traitorous tears escaped the prison of her tightly closed eyes and ran down her cheeks. She heard Oscar sigh deeply and step away, circling around to face her.

No! Clara desperately fought against the rising panic. Now she'd made him angry. Why did her stupid body refuse to listen to her? "I... I'm sorry," she sniffled, still determined not to cry. She kept her head down, looking at his dark leather boots. "I know my duty. I will do whatever you want, just please, don't be angry with me." More tears raced down her face, spilling onto the floor.

"Gods, Clara, I..." Oscar's hand rose up and Clara flinched, certain he was going to hit her. Perhaps she deserved it. He had been so nice to her and she couldn't do this one thing right.

She winced when his palm touched her cheek but he was being gentle, his thumb wiping away her tears. "Clara, I am sorry," Oscar said, sounding almost desperate. "I was an idiot to think that... I just forgot how incredibly young you are, how innocent. Look at me, please?"

Reluctantly, Clara looked into his eyes, afraid of what she would see in them. To her surprise, there was no trace of anger in Oscar's face. He looked sad, embarrassed even, but not angry. His voice gained intensity. "I swear I will not touch you unless you ask me to."

Clara's eyebrows came together, she wasn't sure what he meant by those words. Did he want to humiliate her by making her ask him to do all those things to her body? To beg him? No, that couldn't be it. There was kindness and compassion in his expression, not malevolence.

Oscar shook his head. "I'm normally brighter than this. I should have realized you would be scared of me and hate me. Listen, I swear on my life, on my mother's life, that I will not hurt you. I will not do anything you don't want, not tonight, not tomorrow, not in a week, not in a month. Not ever. All I'm asking of you is one thing. Give me a chance to prove I'm not your enemy."

Had Clara really just heard what he was suggesting? No, she couldn't believe he would simply let her off the hook on their wedding night. But what else could he be after? "I don't hate you," she whispered. "But how can we not be enemies? We killed your king, took your country, King Hayden forced you to marry me to humiliate you. How could you not hate me?" Why was she saying all this? Was she trying to convince him to hate her?

"Clara, if I wanted to hate anyone for that, it would be Hayden." Oscar bent his head down to hers and for a moment, Clara thought he was going to kiss her, but he just rested his forehead against hers. "You had nothing to do with any of it. And, while I didn't exactly choose to marry you, I don't regret it at all. You are a sweet and beautiful woman and I promise to do whatever I can to make you happy." His fingers gently touched her hand and he took a step back, giving her space. "You don't have to be afraid of me," he whispered with a smile so sincere it pushed more tears into her eyes.

No, she couldn't screw it all up now by starting to cry. Her teeth grinded on the inside of her cheek until she felt a sharp pain and the coppery taste of blood spread through her mouth. Clara really wanted to believe what Oscar was saying and, when she thought about it, he had been nothing but nice and gallant to her all day. In fact, he had done nothing to make her fear him at all, but the doubts Clara's mother had planted into her mind were hard to overcome. "I... I don't..." She didn't know what to say. What did he want to hear?

"It's alright. You don't have to do or say anything. We can just talk or go to bed if you are tired," Oscar replied, his eyes tracing her startled look to the bed. He leaned down to swipe the petals of the sheet. "We won't do anything more until you are ready. Do you want to change into something more comfortable? I mean, that dress looks amazing but I can't imagine how you actually breathe in it." He chuckled, obviously trying to distract her, and Clara felt so absurdly grateful she managed to smile despite her obvious terror. "I promise I won't look," Oscar added with a wink.

Chapter 9

The room had a small balcony overlooking one of the inner courtyards. Oscar made his way out there before pulling the drapes shut
behind him.

Clara stood in the middle of the room, unable to move. What had just
happened? The bed was in front of her, still empty and unused. Oscar
hadn't hurt her. He'd promised not to do anything until she wanted to.
Why would she ever want that? Clara pushed that question aside, unable
to deal with it right now.

What was it Oscar had wanted her to do? Thoughts whirled around
Clara's mind, preventing her from focusing.

Her dress. Right, Oscar had talked about her dress. He wasn't wrong, the
tightly wrapped fabric around Clara's chest wasn't exactly comfortable,
and changing into a loose nightgown was tempting. Clara glanced toward
the balcony door. Nothing was moving there. The drapes were thick and
heavy and covered the entire passage. Oscar had said he wouldn't look and
Clara believed him. If he truly wanted to see her naked, he could have just
forced her to strip in front of him.

Clara forced her stiff arms to move, her trembling fingers reaching for the back of her dress. A long line of tiny buttons and hooks was holding the fabric on her back together and as Clara wrestled against them she was getting increasingly desperate. She couldn't undo it. She couldn't even reach all the way back there. No, the dress was clearly designed so that the woman had no chance of taking it off on her own.

Why did Clara always have to fight against customs? Why couldn't she just be an obedient wife like everyone else? Oscar had been so incredibly nice to her, he deserved better. Clara couldn't control the tears anymore and they ran down her cheeks in streams. Her shoulders twitched as a sob forced its way out of her throat.

No, she wouldn't cry!

Unhook the tiny piece of wire. Slip the button through the hole.

Clara's fingers felt too numb to perform such a delicate task. She sniffled and whimpered again. The harder she tried to fight against it, the worse it got, until she could no longer stand and slid down to her knees, covering her face with her hands and sobbing.

Never in her life had Clara felt so desperate. Abandoned by everyone who was supposed to love and protect her. Useless, as if her whole life had been one huge failure. And scared. Afraid of what was going to happen tonight, terrified of what she had to do in the next few days and what would happen if she failed.

When she felt a gentle hand on her shoulder, Clara flinched. She was sobbing so hard she didn't even hear her husband return. Another thing she'd failed at. Men hated crying girls.

Oscar sat down next to Clara and gently put an arm around her, giving her plenty of opportunity to pull away. She should have. Oscar Huxley was one of the reasons she was crying in the first place. But Clara felt so incredibly alone that even the touch of a stranger was better than nothing. So, even though she was afraid of the price she would have to pay for it later, she embraced his hold and didn't protest when he grabbed her tighter and pulled her into his arms.

It was almost absurd how safe she felt being hugged by a man she had just met earlier today. She knew nothing about him other than he liked apples.

Oscar didn't scorn her for soaking the front of his fancy wedding jacket with her tears. He didn't get angry when all her attempts at suppressing the sobs failed, didn't try to sneak out of the room looking nervous or embarrassed like Clara's father always had when she'd cried. Oscar simply sat there in silence on the cold floor in what must have been quite an uncomfortable position and held Clara in his arms, rocking back and forth lightly as he patiently waited for her to calm down.

Clara cried for a long time. She cried for her dead father, her heartless mother, her poor brother, who was probably scared and in immense pain. For the king who had to die so that Sebastian could live. For herself and all the tragedies that had to fall upon her head for some cosmic reason.

Eventually, there were no more tears left. Clara stayed in Oscar's arms, trembling in his firm embrace, afraid of what he might say. She breathed deeply in an attempt to calm herself. Oscar smelled nice. There was a gentle touch of perfume but for the main part, it was just him. To her surprise, Clara really liked the scent of Oscar Huxley. "I'm sorry." Her voice was barely a whisper and she didn't dare to move, afraid to break the moment.

"It's alright." Oscar's tone was soft and comforting and he raised one hand to stroke her hair. "If it helps, cry all you want. I just wish there was something I could do to make you feel better."

Could it be possible that Clara had just met the one man in the entire universe who didn't mind if a girl cried? "You did," she replied in a trembling voice. "Thank you. I swear I normally don't cry this much. It's just, since my father..." A sniffle interrupted her words and she chose not to finish the thought. Thinking about Admiral Redwood was still too painful.

"Did he..." Oscar started quietly and took in a deep breath before continuing, "Did he die in the battle against us?"

Us. The kingdom of Levanta. Must have been hard for him to start thinking about himself as an Orellian, which he now was.

Clara shook her head. "No. He was an admiral. Pirates lured his ship into a trap and killed everyone." She felt Oscar's body relax and his slow exhale sounded almost like a sigh of relief.

Upon trying to shift her weight Clara winced as a sudden wave of pins and needles ran down the leg she had been sitting on. Oscar felt her move and let go of her, groaning quietly as he picked himself off the ground and stretched out his limbs. Without his arms around her, Clara felt strangely abandoned, almost wishing he would embrace her again.

Oscar extended his hand toward Clara to help her up, gently holding her elbows until she could safely stand on both legs again. A tiny part of her wanted to pretend to falter just so he would catch her and she could enjoy his warm scent again. How childish.

They were standing right next to the bed now and as Clara stared at the clean white sheets, she realized something terrible. Oscar must have noticed her face losing color again because he touched the back of her palm to get her attention. "Clara, I told you, we don't-"

"No, you don't understand," Clara interrupted him, her thoughts racing as she was trying to figure out what to do. Eyebrows raised, Oscar waited for an explanation and Clara hesitantly continued, "If we don't..." Damn, she couldn't even say it. "If there is no proof we...consummated our marriage, people will talk. They will call me unchaste, they can have me put on trial for not being pure on my wedding night. You could get in trouble too."

Normally, it wouldn't even occur to Clara to think people would do that, but Oscar had enemies. And his enemies were now her enemies as well, as Lord Umber had clearly demonstrated earlier.

Oscar frowned as he thought about her words. "I didn't think about that," he admitted. "But it doesn't change anything. People will just have to take my word for it."

"No, it's too risky. You..." How to put it so she wouldn't offend him? "You're new here, you have too many eyes on you."

Oscar chuckled softly. "Very diplomatically said, my dear wife. However, you are right, everybody hates me here and will be looking for any reason to take me out."

"Yes. So...we should just do it, I...I feel better now. I can do it." Ironically, Clara really did feel better after crying for so long, as if the tears had washed away a part of her fears and worries.

"Clara, I admit I've been with lots of women. Some of them I have wooed with sweet words or empty promises, some of them I have paid. But, I have never taken one against her will and I'm certainly not going to start now, with you of all people."

Oscar's confession surprised Clara. Of course, she'd expected him to be more experienced but the way he admitted it out loud like this still made her feel strange. "I'm your wife, I can't say no to you," she muttered, avoiding his look.

"That doesn't make it any less of a rape, Clara," Oscar retorted, rolling his eyes as he moved to stand on the other side of the bed.

What he said wasn't true. Technically, a husband couldn't rape his wife, except for some rare cases when he forced himself on her shortly before or immediately after giving birth, and that was more about the welfare of the baby than the wife. Other than that, the woman had no right to refuse him.

Clara clenched her fists. She didn't need any extra eyes on her with what she needed to do to save Sebastian. "I want you to." That was what he wanted to hear, wasn't it?

"No, you don't," Oscar said dismissively. Of course she didn't, it must have been clearly written on her face. "Look," he gave her a soft smile, "if the woman isn't ready and doesn't truly want it, it gets quite uncomfortable for her, painful even. I don't wish that for you."

"Isn't it always like that? My mother..." Clara clamped her mouth shut in the middle of a word, feeling her cheeks turning red. She couldn't possibly talk to this stranger about those things!

Oscar's eyebrow rose up as he waited for Clara to continue. When she didn't, he walked over to her and grabbed her hand, kissing the back of it. There was an amused smirk on his face but it didn't feel like he was mocking her. "No, Clara," he said calmly. "It certainly isn't always like that. Under normal circumstances, it's more than enjoyable for both."

Clara blinked in surprise, not sure what to say. Was her mother lying to her? Or maybe Sophia didn't know any better? Maybe things were different in Levanta? No, that was nonsense. Perhaps it was Oscar who was lying to Clara to ease her fear, to prevent her from bursting into tears again. That sounded like the most logical option.

He moved back to his side of the bed and pulled the blanket aside. "There should be a long strap of cloth in that cabinet over there."

Oscar pointed toward one of the walls and Clara walked there, searching through the drawer until she found what he wanted, not even daring to guess why he needed such a thing. Upon turning around, she saw her husband with a dagger in his hand and before she could do anything to stop him, he ran the blade over his palm.

The cut wasn't deep, it was more of a scratch, but it filled with blood quickly. When Oscar clenched his fist and held it over the center of the bed, a few crimson drops fell down on the sheet, making a small, bright red stain. "Now there's proof," Oscar smirked as he returned to Clara, holding his bleeding palm out in front of her.

It took her a second to realize the implications of what he had just done. She was wrapping his hand but her eyes kept jumping to the stained sheet. She couldn't believe it. He'd just given her a way out and didn't seem to be asking for anything in return.

"Don't worry about it," Oscar said as he touched her cheek to make her turn away from the bed. "I probably overdid it, I don't think there's normally that much blood."

"You've never...?" Gods, why was Clara asking him about that? Not only was it incredibly personal but did she really want to know more about his past experiences?

Oscar blushed a little. "Proper girls don't willingly give their maiden-head to scoundrels like me." Scoundrels? Clara blinked in surprise. So far, Oscar seemed like the nicest, most gallant man Clara had ever met. He spoke before she could ask him about it, "The blood should dry up quickly if you want to go to sleep. Or we could stay up and talk a while."

While actually getting to know her husband was tempting, Clara could barely keep her eyes open any longer. "Could we talk tomorrow, please?" she asked. "I really want to but I'm exhausted." After he'd smiled and nodded in agreement, Clara nervously shifted her weight. "Oscar?" Gods, this was so embarrassing. "Could you please help me out of this dress? I tried but I just can't..." She almost sniffled again. Damn, why did the stupid dress make her want to cry?

"Of course, my lady." There was amusement in Oscar's expression but not the bad kind. Clara hesitantly turned her back to him and tried not to flinch when his fingers gripped the fabric of her dress. "Seriously, who invented these things?" Oscar mumbled as he skillfully removed the hooks and buttons.

Clara could feel him being extra careful not to touch her skin too much, but his fingers slipped a couple of times causing her to involuntarily shiver upon feeling them slide along her spine. Fortunately, Oscar was much faster than Clara (being able to see what he was doing probably helped a lot) and soon, the entire back of her dress was undone.

Oscar waited on the balcony again while Clara finally took that awful thing off, tempted to toss it into the empty hearth and set fire to it. It was not like she was going to wear the dress ever again. She put on her nightgown followed by a long robe before calling Oscar back into the room.

They stood facing each other, the large bed between them. Oscar scratched his head. "I know it would be very gallant and gentlemanly to offer you the bed for yourself but I would really prefer not to sleep on the floor," he said hesitantly.

Yes, after sitting on it for a while, Clara had to agree that it wouldn't be very comfortable. "It's alright," she replied. Oscar had been so nice to her she could never let him sleep on the hard floor. If anyone should sleep on the floor, it should be Clara. But the bed seemed large enough to accommodate both of them comfortably while still allowing them to maintain their personal space. "I think we can manage."

For some inexplicable reason, Clara trusted Oscar. And maybe even wanted to be close to him, no matter how ironic it sounded. Clara turned around, blowing the candles out as Oscar undressed. A small, curious part of her was tempted to peek at him but she was too afraid he'd notice. What would he think of her if she did?

Without the candlelight, the room was pitch black. Not wanting to stub her toe, Clara carefully walked over to the bed and removed her robe before crawling under the blanket. Knowing that someone was lying beside her, hearing his quiet breathing, feeling a soft pull on the blanket as his hands clutched it closer... It was beyond strange. Clara doubted she'd be able to fall asleep at all.

"Oscar?" she whispered upon hearing him wiggling to find a more comfortable position. "Thank you."

"Don't mention it," he whispered back. All was quiet for a while. So quiet that Clara thought he'd fallen asleep, when he suddenly said,. "Clara? You don't have to answer if you don't want to but...what exactly has your mother told you about intimate relations? Because it seems like you have a very, very wrong idea about the whole thing."

It was a good thing the room was so dark because Clara felt she'd gone red from her head to her toes. How could she possibly talk about these matters with a complete stranger? And did she really have the wrong idea? Knowing her mother, it was entirely possible..

Clara sighed, eternally grateful that Oscar couldn't see her. "Mother said it's something we have to suffer through to keep the man happy and have a good life," she whispered. This was just one of the many things Sophia Redwood had told her but it described the gist Clara had gathered from her speech the best.

"Ouch. Now I feel sorry for your mother. That's simply not true, Clara, and I hope one day I can prove it to you."

He sounded so earnest that a tiny seed of hope awoke in Clara's mind then started to take root. Until she remembered the glass vial and what she had to do with it. Now, the guilt she felt doubled. She was going to drag Oscar down with her and he certainly didn't deserve it.

Fortunately, Oscar couldn't read her mind, so he hadn't noticed her despair was no longer focused solely on tonight. "Don't worry about it now," he told her in a comforting tone. "Sleep, Clara. You are safe."

And for the first time in weeks, Clara really did feel safe.

Chapter 10

C lara was wandering through an unfamiliar garden. It was a hot, sunny day. The sun was hanging high in the clear blue sky. A scorching hot day, one might say. Despite wearing only a thin nightgown, Clara was lightly sweating.

She leaned down to pick a rose, carefully plucking it from the bush so she wouldn't be hurt by the thorns. But the flower didn't have any thorns, Clara noticed while raising it up to her face. It didn't smell like a rose at all. No, it smelled like apples and something else, something manly, but not in an unpleasant way. Something like...Oscar.

Smiling, Clara breathed in deeply, savoring that beautiful scent, wrapping her arm tighter around its source.

Wrapped her arm? Wait a moment, Clara thought, what was she wrapped around? Chasing the dream away, Clara's mind went over the events of last night. Her eyes widened in horror upon realizing that she was cuddled up to Oscar Huxley's back, one of her arms hugging his chest tightly. She'd just been sniffing the skin on the back of his neck like a creep.

Oscar was motionless except for his chest, which gently rose and fell as he took deep breaths. Perhaps he was still asleep? Clara carefully pulled her arm back, shuffling over to her side of the bed as quietly as she could manage. It was uncomfortably cold.

"Good morning," Oscar chirped as he rolled onto his back, stretching his arms and folding them under his nape. There was a grin on his face and he appeared to be wide awake.

Clara nervously clutched the blanket, pulling it closer to her chest, fairly certain her cheeks had turned scarlet by that point. She felt like a complete idiot. "Good morning." It felt rude not to respond even though she would have preferred the bed to swallow her up whole, taking her away from this situation completely. "I'm sorry, I... I think I was cold."

Yes, Clara remembered being unable to fall asleep, trembling from a combination of fear, exhaustion, and cold. But she certainly didn't remember crawling over the entire width of the bed to wrap herself around her new husband like a vine.

"You have nothing to be sorry for, Clara," Oscar smiled. "You can hug me as much as you want. I would have returned the hug to keep you even warmer but I'm a man of my word." He shrugged in a gesture of surrender before resting his hands back behind his head. "I didn't touch you." He was probably mocking her a little but Clara deserved it. After freaking out when he'd tried to touch her yesterday then spending the entire night cuddled up to him, she probably deserved to be made fun of.

It was late summer and the mornings were getting colder, especially since Clara and Oscar had forgotten to close the balcony doors last night. They hadn't even closed the drapes so now there was a soft breeze running through the room to add to the chill. Clara shivered, feeling goosebumps forming on her arms. Her slight tremble didn't escape Oscar's attention.

"It's still pretty warm over here," he smiled, lifting up the blanket. His tone was playful and Clara found herself drawn to him. Despite being a stranger to her, he made Clara feel safe. And it was quite cold.

She shuffled back over to him before she could overthink it and change her mind. Oscar looked surprised, but pleasantly so. At least Clara hoped that was the case. Hesitantly, she rested her head against his warm shoulder before wiping her unruly hair out of the way. It was one big curly mess. Clara had forgotten to braid it before bed and now she'd have to spend half an hour untangling it. But that could wait.

Oscar rested one arm around Clara's shoulders, checking to see whether she would protest. When she didn't, he added the other arm, pulling her closer before shifting into a more comfortable position. Her eyes closed, enjoying the warmth her husband emanated, Clara inhaled deeply through her nose to savor his scent.

"Oh, I'm sorry." Oscar sounded embarrassed upon noticing her sniffing him. Seriously, she had to stop doing that, it must have seemed so incredibly weird. "I'm sweaty from all the dancing last night. Hmm, my brother warned me that a young wife means a life of toil. I guess the asshole was right about something." Clara felt Oscar's shoulders twitch as he chuckled and she couldn't help but do the same. "I'll bathe as soon as we get out of bed," Oscar added.

Awesome, now she'd made him think he stunk even though it was quite the opposite. In an attempt to distract him, she said, "You are not that much older than me." Or was he? "You can't be more than twenty-five. Twenty-eight tops." Clara blushed. After a moment of hesitation, she added quietly, "And you smell great."

"Oh, my dear wife, now you have insulted me!" Even if Oscar wasn't laughing, Clara could tell from his tone he was just joking. "I'm twenty-four, actually. No gray hair yet. And thank you."

"So, you have a brother?" Clara asked curiously. It was infuriating. Were he an Orellian nobleman, she'd know at least the basics about him.

His fingers played with her hair, stroking it softly. "Yes, I have two older brothers, just like you," Oscar replied. It seemed he had gathered more information about her than she had about him. "They are perfect in every possible way, as opposed to me, who has always been more of the black sheep of our family. And even though they are assholes, we still love each other. I think you will like them when we go to visit."

It should feel strange how he'd already started planning their future but it didn't. If only Clara could have a future. The man holding Sebastian had given her five days. What hurt could it do if she spent one of them pretending to have a normal life? Getting to know her husband?

"Oh, and my parents," Oscar added, "they're going to love you. My mother especially. She'll be absolutely thrilled."

Clara blushed. "Well, you've already met my mother. I don't think being thrilled is even in the range of her emotions." Clara was unable to hide the slight contempt from her words and she regretted it immediately. Oscar seemed to love his family greatly, what would he think of Clara upon hearing her spout such ugly words about her own mother? "But she liked you."

"I'm not so sure she did," Oscar chuckled. "I think she was just relieved."

"That you weren't old, fat, and ugly?"

He playfully pulled on her hair. "No, my dear wife. I think she was relieved that I was indeed from a wealthy and important family. I take it, me being old, fat, and ugly were some of your worries?" Clara groaned quietly, covering her face with her hands, but before she could start apologizing, Oscar laughed. "It's alright. What do you think my first thoughts were? I mean, Hayden hates me so naturally I assumed he was going to marry me off to some mean, ugly hag who'd make my life a living hell. I contacted some people I knew trying to get more information about you because I didn't believe you were the perfect, young, beautiful lady that he'd made you out to be."

"Is that how you know about my brothers?"

Clara felt him shift uncomfortably. When he answered, he sounded slightly ashamed. "Yes. Karina called it spying but I only asked a few colleagues."

"No, it's fine, I think." Clara paused to think. He'd talked about her with the Queen? They must be really close friends. It made Clara feel uneasy but she couldn't exactly berate him for it. "I would have done the same if I'd had the opportunity," she replied politely.

His finger gently caressed her cheek before returning to her hair. "I'm sorry. You can ask me anything you want, I promise, I won't lie to you."

"What else have you found out about me?" Clara was quite curious about what other people had said about her.

"Uhm..." Oscar hesitated and when Clara lifted her head to look at him, he was biting on his lower lip. Damn, was it that bad? "I promised I wouldn't lie," he continued, "so I won't answer that question just yet because it would spoil a surprise I have for you."

Clara felt a wave of almost child-like excitement. "A surprise?" Who doesn't love surprises?

"Later." There was a smirk on Oscar's face and sparks of mischief in his eyes but, for reasons she didn't understand, Clara trusted it wouldn't be anything bad.

How did he do that? She hadn't even known him twenty-four hours and he'd already made her trust him. Not with everything, though. Nobody could be trusted with the secret of the glass vial that was safely packed among Clara's perfume bottles.

Oscar moved to sit up. "I'll go check if the bath is ready."

As he got out of bed, Clara noticed he'd slept in his underpants and a shirt. She wondered whether he did that normally or whether he was trying to avoid making her feel uncomfortable. A tiny, curious part of her mind wondered what he would look like without the shirt. Not that she would admit to it.

While Oscar didn't seem overly muscular, he wasn't gangly like some of the clerks in the palace who resembled spiders with their long, thin arms and legs and no defined chest to speak of. From what Clara could see of Oscar's legs (before she'd politely turned away to let him put on his breeches), his muscles were clearly defined and his arms had felt rather strong when he'd held her. Oscar Huxley might not be a warrior but that didn't mean that he was weak.

There were two doors at the back of the room that Clara hadn't noticed before. Oscar disappeared behind one of them. If he'd noticed her ogling his body, he hadn't let it show. There was a smirk permanently fixed on his face though, so he probably had noticed.

Clara shook her head, trying to clear her mind. What was she doing? She needed to focus on saving Sebastian, not thinking about how good this man's arms felt wrapped around her. Plus, Oscar wanted more than just to hug her and despite his proclamations, his patience wasn't limitless. He would grow increasingly annoyed with her prudishness until she gave in and did whatever he wanted. Sophia's descriptions ran through her mind again, sending a shudder down Clara's spine. Was her mother really wrong?

Hearing voices behind the door where Oscar had gone, Clara quickly got out of bed, reaching for a robe to cover her thin nightgown. Before she could decide whether to go see who her husband was talking to or not, the door opened and Oscar peeked inside the room, smiling. A tiny woman followed him into the bedroom, her long, gray hair gathered in a loose bun at her nape, a few smooth tresses framing her face. She looked so frail that the slightest breath of wind might break her in half but there was a wide, warm smile on her wrinkled face.

"This is Friska," Oscar announced, gently tapping the woman's shoulder before moving over to Clara. "She's my... I don't know, maid, I guess?" He chuckled, giving Frisca a warm smile. It was clear that they were very close.

The woman walked to Clara and made a clumsy curtsy, her gnarled hands lifting the skirt of her simple brown gown. "It's such a pleasure to meet you, Lady Clara," she announced, sounding so earnest in her greeting that Clara had no choice but to return her warm smile. Friska stepped closer and slowly reached for Clara's hand, bowing her head to kiss it. "Gods, you are so lovely!" she said in a shaky voice.

"Friska!" Oscar hissed at her, eyeing Clara worriedly.

As his wife, Clara had very limited control over her own life. But, as the new lady of his household, she controlled all of the servants they employed. If she wanted to have this old woman punished for her clearly inappropriate behavior, Oscar couldn't exactly object to it. Not that Clara would want to do that. The old maid was adorable and Oscar clearly loved her.

"Thank you, Friska," Clara returned, gently touching the woman's shoulders. "I have to say that your name is very unusual. Or is it a common one in Levanta?"

Oscar sighed, rolling his eyes before disappearing behind the bathroom door again. The maid chuckled, "Actually, my real name is Francesca, my lady. But when the young lord was just a small cub, he couldn't pronounce it properly. He'd call me Friska instead and it sort of stuck with me. You can call me however you wish, my lady." Friska bowed her head again, clearly nervous in front of Clara, especially after Oscar had snapped at her. "And I apologize," she added. "I didn't mean to offend you."

"It's quite alright. I'm not one to insist on formalities," Clara tried to calm the maid down. She dared to caress Friska's cheek, surprised by how warm and soft the wrinkled skin of the old lady felt. "You don't have to worry about offending me," Clara continued. "Or be afraid of me, for that matter. Did anyone else come here with Lord Huxley?"

Showing her incomplete set of teeth in a wide smile, Friska shook her head. "I'm afraid it's just my old hide. The young lord never really needed servants. But he did say you can employ other people if you want, some real maids to help you out with dresses and hair and such. I've only ever taken care of boys, I don't really know what a proper lady needs."

Neither did Clara. Gods, she was expected to lead Oscar's entire household. She wasn't even sure what that meant, let alone how to do it! Oscar was such a nice man, he really deserved a better wife.

"Go enjoy your bath, my lady," Friska beamed. "I'll set up breakfast for you and the young lord." Friska gave her another smile and scurried away to pick up Clara's dress from the floor.

Clara hesitantly walked over to the bathroom door, nervous, all of a sudden. Did Oscar expect her to bathe with him? It didn't seem like he'd force her to but wouldn't he be disappointed if she didn't want to? Or did she want to?

The door creaked as she pushed against it.

Chapter 11

Clenching her fists to stop her hands from shaking, Clara stepped through the door. Behind it was a spacious bathroom. A large mirror and washing basins were set on a table to one side, along with some toiletries. Clara's heart skipped a beat when she noticed the poison vial among her perfume bottles. Friska must have unpacked her things but fortunately didn't realize that one of the vials didn't contain perfume.

A large oval bath was placed in the middle of the room. As the steam rose from the hot water, a rich fragrance of expensive oils spread throughout the room. The bath was big enough for two and Clara shifted her weight nervously upon seeing Oscar sitting inside, scrubbing his arm with a washcloth.

"I'm almost done," he smiled. "I'll finish washing quickly, and then it's all yours to enjoy for as long as you want." There were no windows in this room, leaving it illuminated only by a couple of lanterns strategically placed around the room, but Clara still looked away to avoid staring at Oscar's naked chest. He chuckled at her modesty but his expression turned to one of seriousness as he said, "Sorry about Friska. She's-"

"Sweet?" Clara interrupted him. "I like her." Sighing, she turned her back fully to Oscar and rested against the wooden edge of the bath. "Oscar, I don't know anything about running a household," she whispered, feeling ashamed.

The water splashed as Oscar moved behind her. "Neither do I, Clara," he said. "That's why I dragged Friska across half of the continent. And, to be honest, I've never imagined myself having a huge mansion with dozens of servants. I mean, if that's what you want, we can talk about it, but... I'd be quite content just staying here in the palace for now."

"I have no idea what I want," Clara replied, she had never even thought about it either. "I'm sorry, I'm such a shitty wife." Clara slid down the bath and onto the ground, resting her back against the warm wood, heated by the water inside the tub.

Oscar rested his arms over the edge of the bath before looking down at Clara, smiling softly. "Honestly, my dear wife, if we were in Levanta, everyone would pity you for having such a shitty husband. Just because nobody knows me here, I haven't suddenly turned into ideal marriage material." He sighed and looked off to the side. "I'm not exactly a good guy, Clara. I'm more of a..."

"Scoundrel?" Clara finished for him, remembering what he'd told her last night. "Oscar, you've been nothing but kind to me." Way more than she deserved. "I don't care about your reputation."

"Thank you. I don't really know what I'm doing with this whole marriage thing either. So just tell me when I fuck something up." With that said, he slid under the water. When he reemerged, he gave Clara a mischievous smirk, adding, "Hayden certainly won't be thrilled if we stay here in the palace."

Angering the king didn't seem like such an amusing idea to Clara but Oscar seemed to know what he was doing. She glanced up at him to guess whether she could ask more questions. Curiosity was a dangerous thing but Clara's new husband was in a good mood, so she decided to give it a try. "Why does the king hate you?"

"Well, that's a long story. Could you please hand me a towel?"

Clara stood up and went to pull a large towel out of one of the cabinets lining the bathroom walls. As she was handing it to Oscar, she chastely looked away, turning around as he climbed out of the bath.

Oscar grinned over her flushed cheeks. "It's all yours. I can dress in the bedroom. And don't worry about Friska, she won't gossip." Towel wrapped around his hips, he took a step toward the door.

Even in the dim light, Clara could see that she was right on her assumptions over Oscar's body. While he wasn't overly muscular, everything was clearly defined, with not a pound of excess fat in sight. The front of his chest was lightly covered with short, curly hair and Clara found herself curious how it would feel to touch them. Seriously, what the hell was happening to her?

Tearing her eyes from Oscar's chest, Clara realized he hadn't answered her question. "You don't want to tell me?" she asked, unable to mask the disappointment in her voice. Why would he want to tell her, though? Women should stay out of their husband's business.

"What?" Oscar paused what he was doing, his brows coming together in confusion. "Oh, right, Hayden. Sorry, I got distracted," he grinned. "I'll tell you but you really should take that bath before the water gets cold."

Clara bit her lip, indecisively glancing between him and the steaming water.

Oscar smiled. "How about you bathe while I talk? I won't look."

Before Clara could think about the answer, Oscar turned away to grab another towel before raising it to dry his hair. The dark, wet locks reached just below his shoulders. Water was dripping from them, making puddles all over the floor.

Clara quickly shook off her robe and reached for the hem of her nightgown, hesitating only a second before pulling it up over her head. Keeping an eye on Oscar, she climbed into the bath, sighing in pleasure as her body submerged into the warm water.

Once Oscar heard the water settle, he hesitantly glanced at Clara. "Clara? I hope I can count on your discretion. I mean, you don't strike me as the gossiping type of girl but... I can only be honest with you if I'm sure that whatever I say will stay just between the two of us."

"Of course," Clara nodded, trying to look as serious as possible while deep inside she was actually bubbling with excitement that Oscar was willing to trust her with his thoughts and maybe even secrets.

Oscar smiled briefly before turning away to resume scrubbing his hair dry with the towel. "There are plenty of reasons why our beloved king hates me," he said in a cheerful tone. "First, I'm a politician. I spend my days talking to people, weaving nets of half-truths and pretty lies, whispering into the right ears and listening in to rumors, gossip, and complaints. My job is digging up dirt and secrets and swallowing down whatever insults people throw at me. There is actually huge power to be gained through information, and words can do a lot of damage, Clara, more so than any weapon."

Oscar sounded very passionate about his admission, causing Clara to frown. Did he really just confess to being a professional liar and manipulator, and to enjoying it? He did promise not to lie to her but what if it was just another lie? Maybe Clara should be more careful around Oscar Huxley. After all, he did admit that he was not a good guy.

"I wondered why you seemed so calm when Lord Umber insulted you last night," she said. "But what good are words when there's a blade at your throat?"

"You should ask the queen about that," he chuckled, sounding almost pleased with Clara's answer even though she was essentially disagreeing with him. "She and the king were attacked by a gang of rebels set on killing Hayden. He literally had a noose hanging above his head yet Karina managed to talk them down, using just her words, nothing more." Clara gasped, she had no idea someone had actually gotten so close to killing the king. Oscar turned, his eyes piercing her. "And that is NOT public information," he added.

A secret. Something she was definitely not supposed to know. Fear mixed with excitement inside Clara's mind as she nodded vigorously to let

Oscar know she understood. She had no one to talk to anyway, even if she wanted to talk about it.

Oscar's expression softened. "Would you like me to help you with your hair? It looks pretty tangled." Clara nervously wrapped her arms around her chest to cover her breasts. He'd seemed to like touching her hair last night so it would probably make him happy, but letting him touch her while she was completely naked? That seemed wrong.

"Just your hair," he smiled upon seeing the doubts written across her face.

"If you wish," she murmured, trying to sound confident but her voice trembled slightly.

Oscar shook his head. "It's not about what I want, Clara." His hair was almost dry now and he was sliding the towel over the rest of his body. Clara remembered how safe she'd felt when he'd held her as she'd cried. Maybe it wasn't such a bad idea.

"There is a bottle of hair oil over there," she said. "It needs brushing with the oil first. It's a really troublesome chore." Oscar smiled excitedly and headed for the cabinet while Clara dipped her head under the water to wet the tangled mess.

After surfacing, Clara sat with her back facing the edge of the bath. Oscar was very gentle, rubbing the oil onto his hands first and then spreading it over her hair. "Anyway," he continued, "Hayden sucks at politics and hates politicians in general. You know, people who prefer talking over yelling or stabbing others with a sword, are apparently just a bunch of sleazy worms, without a shred of honor." Oscar scoffed. "As if there was something honorable about killing people."

Clara forcibly kept her eyes down, not letting them wander toward the vial containing poison. No, there was nothing honorable about her. "A warrior's point of view," she noted quietly. Her father was the same as King Hayden in this manner.

"Yes, exactly." Oscar grabbed the brush and started to untangle her tresses. It was strange, he didn't seem to mind her disagreeing with him. "I'm not sure how much you know about international politics but there have been multiple feuds between Levanta and Orellia in the past few decades. And in the last few years, I've played an active role in many of them."

Clara knew little to nothing about politics in general, let alone international ones. "Why?" she asked, hoping she wouldn't come across as stupid.

"Our king didn't like your king," Oscar sighed. "It's more complicated than that but I can't talk about it. However, it means that I, along with a few others, have been making Hayden's life hell for years."

So, Clara's husband truly was an enemy to Orellia. The king had every right to hate him. And Clara? "Why didn't he simply execute you?" She blurted the question out without thinking about it. "I... I mean..."

Oscar laughed heartily, his fingers and the brush never stopping their smooth movements through Clara's hair. "Karina made him promise that there would be no retribution, that we would all start with a clean slate. If it weren't for that, then yes, I'd probably be dead."

"I'm sorry, I didn't mean to..."

"It's alright, Clara. I really don't get angry that easily. Plus, I did say you could ask me anything." He was quiet for a while and Clara relaxed a little, tilting her head back, enjoying his gentle touch. "There's more to it than that. I think Hayden is afraid of me. I have a lot of contacts all around the world and I know a lot of secrets."

"And information is power," Clara added. That was something her father used to say when she'd asked him why he'd sat examining maps and books and parchments all night instead of sleeping.

Oscar leaned forward to look into her face, sounding astonished as he said, "Hmm, looks like my wife isn't just beautiful, but also really smart." Clara blushed, her cheeks suddenly hot and not just from the warm water she was surrounded by. "I'm a lucky man," Oscar smiled and placed a fleeting kiss on her forehead before running the brush through Clara's hair a couple more times. "I think I'm done. Dip," he commanded.

A hand pressed on the top of her head and Clara giggled, taking a deep breath before letting Oscar push her underwater.

He used a delightfully scented soap to wash out the oil, rubbing it gently into her scalp. "There's one more reason," he said quietly, sounding almost sad. "I didn't want to talk about it, because this whole situation is weird and I didn't want to put you into an awkward position."

"The King is jealous about your relationship with the Queen," Clara finished for him. Noticing his raised eyebrows, she smiled. "I might not be a skilled politician but I'm not blind. I saw the way he looked at you when you danced with her."

Hayden hadn't been the only one looking at them. Clara remembered her own doubts. Close friends. Were they just that? Did she really want to know?

Some of her thoughts must have shown on her face. "We've never been anything more than friends, Clara," Oscar said calmly. "We grew up together, I'm like a brother to her. Plus, for reasons I don't understand, she's actually in love with Hayden." Clara nodded, unsure why he'd felt such a need to explain it to her. "Alright," Oscar announced, changing the subject, "I think your hair is perfect again." He stepped away to finish getting dressed while she rinsed out the soap.

Clara thanked Oscar as he headed for the door to the bedroom. "I'll go check on breakfast," he said, "take your time."

"I think I'll be quick. The water is great but I'm starving."

Oscar rolled his eyes. "Of course you are, you barely ate anything yesterday."

Clara sank under the water again, enjoying the warmth permeating her skin. It was far from hot anymore but it still smelled great. She noticed a small door at the back of the room, probably an entrance for servants. Of course, how else would they have been able to prepare this bath while Clara and Oscar slept?

Her eyes were inadvertently drawn to the poison vial. Maybe she could use this door to sneak out unnoticed? Sebastian's kidnapper said that the poison didn't have an immediate effect and if she was careful, she might get away with it.

It was tempting. To have a normal life. Be with Oscar and get to know him better. She might even let him touch her one day? The way his fingers had massaged her scalp just moments ago had felt amazing, making her wonder whether her mother's words weren't just a lie, a misunderstanding, or misinformation. But how could Clara possibly live with herself after murdering someone? Even if nobody ever found out. Even if Orellia didn't crumble into a bloody civil war or whatever was going to happen after Hayden's death. How could she ever look into a mirror and see herself as anything but a filthy, heinous murderer?

Chapter 12

C lara truly was starving. She kept stuffing her mouth with food, ignoring Oscar's amused grin. It wasn't just yesterday that she'd barely eaten anything. She hadn't eaten properly in weeks. Not since she'd gotten engaged. And now, since at least some of her nerves had disappeared, she found herself completely famished.

Friska had set a table for them in the corner of the bedroom, ordering a couple of palace maids around until everything was to her satisfaction. Then she'd sent them to clean the bathroom, giving Oscar and Clara some privacy.

Oscar talked about his family while Clara ate, most likely in an attempt to even out their familiarity since he knew a lot about her from his 'friends' and she only knew what he'd told her already. Even though he grumbled over how his brothers were perfect and always mocked him, it was clear he loved them. It was the same with his parents. Oscar absolutely adored his mother, his description and stories making her sound like she was the goddess of kindness incarnated into a beautiful woman. Clara felt a pinch of envy. She could barely say one nice thing about her own mother.

"Are you finished?" Oscar chuckled when Clara finally set the fork down and leaned back in her chair. "There is a banana peel left and of course, you could always start on the table. Just be careful, cedar wood is quite hard."

Clara rolled her eyes. "Very funny, my dear husband." She grinned at him, in a better mood than she had been in weeks. The vial was forgotten, for now. Clara had decided to have one last normal day before attempting anything. Hopefully, Sebastian could forgive her for that.

"I promised you a surprise earlier," Oscar said in a more serious tone, suddenly looking a little nervous. Clara's eyes brightened and she tried to hide her excitement, not wanting to look too eager. "I have a gift for you," Oscar continued as he put the napkin aside and stood up, extending his hand toward Clara.

She accepted it, her smile widening. Who doesn't like gifts?

Oscar kept hold of her hand as he guided her through yet another door which led out of the bedroom. It was a strange feeling. Clara had often watched couples walking in gardens hand in hand and wondered what that would feel like. As it turned out, it was so pleasant that her heart fluttered. She constantly had to remind herself to try to at least look calm and composed. She was a married woman now and she needed to act like one.

There was a spacious parlor behind the door. Two comfortable looking armchairs and a sofa were placed around a low tea table next to the now empty hearth. A couple of other chairs and a games table were strategically placed close to the large window, presumably to capture the best light. The walls were lined with bookshelves filled with various titles.

"It's not mine," Oscar commented upon seeing Clara admire the extensive library. "I didn't exactly bring many things over."

He didn't sound sad but it still sent a sharp pang through Clara's heart. She wasn't the only one who'd lost her home and had to leave everything and everyone behind. "How big is this place?" she asked, changing the subject.

"It's just these two rooms, the bathroom and a small study over there," Oscar pointed toward a door over by the hearth. "I have taken that room for myself, I hope that's okay with you."

Clara nodded absentmindedly, still amazed by the parlor. What would she need the study for? Women had no use for such rooms.

"Do you think you could endure living here for a while?" Oscar asked. "I know you are used to a mansion but..."

"It's perfect, Oscar." Just enough space for two people. Clara had no idea what they would do with a mansion, not to mention it would probably require her to do actual household management. Here, Clara could just leave everything to Friska and the palace servants. Maybe she could find one girl to help her with her hair and dresses and such like Oscar's old maid had suggested.

Clara's husband didn't seem entirely convinced. "Are you sure?" He was still holding her hand, his thumb gently stroked the back of it. The gesture and tone of his voice made her pause what she was doing to look at him.

"Yes, I'm sure," Clara replied. "I don't want to move again. I've just gotten used to staying here in the palace." Even if it was going to be less relaxed around here now that the king was back. Although, who knew? The new king didn't seem so scary anymore. "At least my mother can't live here with us," she chuckled. If Clara and Oscar owned a house, Sophia would definitely be there all the time, 'visiting' and sticking her long nose into everything.

Oscar smirked. "Yes, I'm sure she'll be very disappointed and displeased with me. It's a good thing I'm used to being glared at." Clara opened her mouth to start apologizing, ashamed of her mother's behavior, especially now she knew more about Oscar's mom but he shook his head to stop her. "It's alright. You don't get to pick your family. I mean, my sister-in-law is an obnoxious, self-centered prude, but I have to put up with her since my idiotic brother married her."

"So, about your gift," Oscar started. He was nervous again, cupping Clara's face and leaning forward to look into her eyes. "I wanted to give it to you yesterday but then I realized it might actually upset you, so I decided to

wait until you were feeling a little better and, hopefully, trusted me a little."
Now Clara was nervous too. "I wanted to give you something personal,
not just a random piece of jewelry or perfume. And I swear that's all this is.
Just a gift that is supposed to make you happy, alright? There is no hidden
agenda behind it, no manipulation, nor any threat. Could you please keep
that in mind?"

Clara blinked in surprise. Seriously, what could he possibly want to give
her that would require such a speech? That would make her think he was
threatening her? She nodded in response to his question, not entirely sure
she wanted to see the gift anymore.

Oscar let go of her face and smiled sincerely, "I promise, it's nothing bad.
Could you close your eyes for me?"

With her eyes closed, Clara heard Oscar leave the room, probably into
the study, but he returned quickly. Clara heard soft rustling as he sat
something down on the low table in front of the sofa followed by footsteps
as he came back to her.

"I'll take your hand," Oscar offered quietly, waiting for her nod of
agreement before gently guiding her over to the table. "Alright," he said,
drawing in a shaky breath, "you can look. Just remember, it's a gift, meant
to please you, nothing more."

Clara was afraid to open her eyes and look down but what else could
she do? She forced herself to do it then her heart skipped a beat. The gift
was long and thin and even though it was wrapped in a black cloth, it was
more than obvious what was hiding inside. Clara had to remind herself to
breathe and even when she did make a sharp inhale through her nose, it
didn't chase away the darkness that loomed in the corners of her vision.
Darkness caused by rising panic.

He knew. She thought archery was her well-guarded secret that nobody
outside of her family had any clue about. Yet somehow this foreigner, who
had just arrived in the city two nights ago, knew all about it.

Sophia's words resonated through Clara's mind. 'Do you have any idea
the dishonor and shame you could bring upon our family if anyone found
out?! I will not let you embarrass your husband in this way.' Clara had

somewhat come to terms with never touching a bow again. Just one of the many freedoms she'd lost by getting married. Yet now her own husband was giving her one.

What could he possibly mean by this? Was it a silent threat? Was he hinting that he knew what Clara was doing, that none of her secrets were safe from him? Was he mocking her? Giving her something she wasn't even allowed to touch? A constant reminder of the control he'd have over her life?

Her hands trembled as she reached for the cloth, carefully pulling the top layer aside. Clara blinked a couple of times, chasing the tears away from her eyes. The bow was beautiful. Unlike the bow Clara had received from her father, which was an ordinary weapon, standard military issue, Oscar's gift was an artistic masterpiece. The limbs were skillfully carved into the perfect recurve shape for her size, with exquisitely detailed markings along the length. Clara even noticed there were Redwood and Huxley crests carved and painted above and below the grip.

All the flare and beauty of the bow didn't make it any less dangerous, though. Clara assumed that it would have about the same draw weight as her old one.

She clenched her fists at her sides to prevent herself from touching it. She couldn't, not in front of Oscar. Was that what he wanted? To scold her for laying her hand on a weapon? Her head turned from side to side. No. No touching. Even though she wanted nothing more than to slide her fingers over the smooth surface of the yew wood, string it, then try out the draw weight. Her entire being begged to sneak out to that quiet corner of the training grounds, the one that was abandoned most of the time.

"Clara..." Oscar sighed.

She shook her head again. "No. I can't." The words were more of a reminder to herself than a response to him.

"Clara, please remember what I said." His voice was more intense now as he was trying to get through the layer of panic running through Clara's mind. "It's just a gift," he continued. "It's yours, you can do whatever you want with it. You can use it as much as you want."

Finally taking her eyes off the weapon, Clara gawked at Oscar. Use it? "I can't. It's... I've never seen anything so beautiful, but I just can't. How...how did you know?"

"The tournament," Oscar explained softly. "Someone recognized you there and when I was trying to find out more about you, they were willing to sell that information for the right price."

He paid people to spy on her, how very romantic. "I'm sorry," Clara said, looking down in shame, "I promise I won't do that again. I don't want people to drag your name through the mud because of me. I won't embarrass you like that."

"Clara," Oscar's hands cupped her cheeks and forced her to look at him, "I honestly couldn't care less about any of that. I told you, I had a bad reputation in Levanta and it's not going to be any better here. And since you are my wife, it's going to rub off on you as well.

"I'm afraid the main reason you will be invited to afternoon tea parties now is that you will be a curiosity, someone to take pity on and gossip about. To question you relentlessly over the evil mysterious foreigner you, poor girl, were forced to marry." He sighed, looking sad and apologetic. "I don't know how much you enjoyed being popular but I'm afraid you will be enjoying a different kind of popularity now, a very unpleasant one."

Afternoon tea parties? They weren't really Clara's preferred way of spending time. She momentarily forgot about the bow as she pondered over Oscar's words.

People were going to dislike her, Clara saw that clearly last night. Just because she married someone. And she didn't even get a say in that. How unfair!

Clara imagined walking down the palace halls, followed by the quiet whispers from ladies, both known and unknown, shushed conversations whenever she was within earshot, giggles after she'd left. No, she didn't love being popular. She never really was popular, in the true sense of the word. Yes, her family was rich and powerful, but she was always an outsider here in the palace and never truly fit in. But, she was tolerated, even liked by some people. And now, all of that would be gone just because she was forced to marry Oscar?

Would she change it if she could? Would she choose acceptance into the flock of vain, envious, self-centered women that moved around the court over marrying Oscar? Sure, Clara would have preferred not to be married at all but, given the circumstances, it could have turned out much worse. Oscar had been nothing but nice to her and, as far as she could tell, he'd been honest with her. That was more than Clara could say about most of the ladies she'd met in the palace.

Oscar watched Clara think, carefully scrutinizing her expression before continuing, "Since you are already in for all of that, why not enjoy the freedom it gives you? Trust me, when you are already seen as weird and unpopular, you get away with a lot of things that would be unthinkable in 'proper' society.

"As I said, this..." he waved his hand over the bow, "is yours. If you don't want to use it, that's your decision. But don't refuse it because of me. For all I care, you can walk around the palace hallways carrying it. It's a gift, no strings attached. Quite literally," he chuckled over his own pun, "apparently the string is only supposed to be on when you actually use it. Which, I gather you already knew. I didn't. I really don't know anything about weapons."

Clara didn't know what to say. Seriously, how much more perfect could this man get? "Thank you," she breathed out, still unsure whether this was all real. "I...I don't know what..."

"It's a gift, I don't expect anything in return," Oscar replied. Then, with a mischievous grin, he added, "You could give me a kiss, but only if you really want to. The bow is yours either way."

Chapter 13

A kiss? Before Clara could change her mind, she rose up on tiptoes and put her arms around Oscar's neck, pulling him closer. With barely a moment's hesitation, she leaned up and pressed her lips against his.

Oscar was taken aback but recovered quickly, placing one hand on Clara's head to hold her steady. The other arm wrapped around her waist, pressing her into his chest.

How different this was from their first kiss, that brief, innocent touch of their lips during the wedding ceremony. Clara didn't expect it to be so incredibly pleasant, or hot, simply breathtaking. She didn't protest when Oscar's tongue slipped inside, to gently play with her own and explore her mouth. Yes, Clara had seen people tongue-kissing before, but she'd always thought it would be gross. As it turned out, tongue kissing was a lot of things but, gross was certainly not one of them.

When Clara could no longer take all of the overwhelming feelings, she pulled away. Oscar let her, albeit reluctantly. Clara rested her head against his chest and tried to calm her wildly beating heart while taking quick, shallow breaths.

Why had she done that? And why had it felt so spectacular? And what was that pulsating desire she felt between her legs now? Where did that come from?

Oscar was holding her tightly in his arms and Clara could feel that his breathing was also ragged. Only now did she realize something hard was pressed against her hips. Clara squirmed uncomfortably upon realizing what it was.

"Sorry," he whispered shakily, letting her step away from him. "That was...unexpected."

"You asked for a kiss," Clara whispered.

Oscar's eyebrows shot up. "I was only joking, I didn't expect you to..." He shook his head. "You don't have to do anything I say."

"I know." Smiling, Clara looked up. Even though she wouldn't admit to it, she'd wanted to kiss him. Their first kiss had left her curious and now that she knew she could trust Oscar, she'd wanted to see whether the second one would be just as good. Turns out, it was better.

Clara's hand hovered over the bow. It still felt like sacrilege to actually touch it, especially in front of her husband. But Oscar gave her an approving nod so she carefully reached out and slid her fingers along the smooth wood, sighing in pleasure as she grabbed hold of the curved handle. It was a few inches shorter and a little lighter than her old one, making it a better fit for her height than the standard military issue.

Clara pulled her gown up to wedge the bow between her legs, the lower limb pressed against her left shin, the center resting against the back of her right thigh. Holding the string in her left hand, she grabbed the tip of the upper limb and pushed forward, grunting as she struggled against the resistance.

Oscar watched with great curiosity, looking astonished when Clara finally managed to set the string in the right place. "I guess I'll have to be careful around you, if I don't want you to strangle me with your bare hands," he chuckled.

Clara gave him a nervous smile. "You really don't mind?" Most men she knew would be at least uncomfortable around a woman wielding a weapon, some even furious. And yet, Oscar shamelessly admitted to knowing nothing about weapons while gifting her one. That was above and beyond Clara's comprehension.

"I really don't mind," Oscar shrugged, running his fingers over the bow. "I told you what I do. I realize talking to people isn't as exciting or sexy as halving enemies with a single swing of a broadsword on a blood-soaked battlefield. But, it's what I love. A passion."

"I was under the impression that this," he pulled on the wood and Clara tightened her grip, as if suddenly afraid he would tear it out of her hands, "was similar for you. Why the hell would I stop you from doing something you love? For the sake of my pride? I can assure you that my pride is fairly flexible, I have to swallow it down quite often."

A passion? Clara had never thought about it in this way but the word did seem to fit.

She couldn't keep the wide grin from her face anymore as her fingers plucked the string, testing the tension. Oscar nestled himself on the sofa, watching her with curious amusement. Ignoring him, Clara rolled her shoulders to stretch out her muscles and slowly pulled the string all the way back to her cheekbone.

The draw weight was just about right, maybe a little lower than her old one, but it didn't matter. As her father would say, she wasn't hunting elephants. The draw was more than enough to hit a target accurately from the usual distance. Since, without bracers it would be quite painful, Clara didn't release the string, slowly returning it to its original position instead. Only then did she glance at Oscar again.

There was something sparkling in his eyes that looked almost like admiration. "You look like a fierce female warrior from the southern jungles."

"I thought that was a myth," Clara replied, her cheeks burning so hot that she was sure her face was scarlet right now.

Oscar chuckled. "Most myths are based on a grain of truth. I have to admit," he said a little shyly, "I was not exactly thrilled at marrying a woman who was supposedly a perfect lady in every way. Mainly because, I'm far from perfect myself. I'd expected you to be a self-centered prude who only cares about dresses, jewelry, and perfumes. And I'd expected you would make my life a living hell, hating me for lowering your social status. But... When I found out about this little hobby, I actually started looking forward to meeting you."

Clara stared at him with her mouth agape. "You were pleased because I'm NOT a perfect lady?" That was so messed up. Clara had spent her whole life listening to how men only loved polite, timid girls with flawless manners. How anyone below that standard was discarded as unworthy of a good marriage and pretty much of life in general. Had her entire life been a lie?

Oscar walked over, taking one of her hands into his. "Perfect is boring," he soothed. "Plus, nobody is really perfect, everyone has dark, dirty secrets. They are just usually not as exciting as yours." That was a strange perspective. Grinning, Oscar continued, "I do have some arrows for you as well but I wanted to wait on giving them to you. Mainly to make sure that one of them wasn't going to end up inside of me." His tone was serious but there were sparks of joy in his eyes. "Am I safe, now?"

"Hmm," Clara faux-pouted, "I'll think about it."

They spent the rest of the day together, talking. Oscar had Clara show him the gardens, then in the evening, they walked to the abandoned corner of the training grounds where Clara had trained whenever she'd managed to sneak out. Clara was hesitant to go but Oscar had insisted. In fact, he carried her bow the whole way there. To a random observer, it looked like a cocky lord was about to show off his archery skills in front of a young girl, while in all honesty, it was quite the opposite. Oscar didn't forget to point that out.

Clara was incredibly nervous, certain that even if she managed to draw the bow with her shaky muscles, the arrow was going to fly past the target instead of into it. Gods, why did she agree to this? She didn't want to but her husband was such a skilled conversationalist that Clara found herself walking to the shooting range before realizing how it happened. Oscar was a charming companion but Clara was beginning to see how dangerous he could be. Not that there was anything she could do to stop it, she was powerless against his words.

Despite Oscar's assurance that he didn't care if someone saw them, Clara made sure their corner of the training grounds was completely abandoned before putting on a bracer and reaching for the bow. The arrows were held in a beautiful quiver that came with the bow. Clara put it on her back, the arrows nestled inside, the ends poking out from behind her shoulder. Her hair was plaited into a tight braid to make sure it stayed out of the way.

Oscar's gaze was distracting. He carefully observed her every move with genuine curiosity.

Clara closed her eyes and shook the cobwebs from her head, imagining shaking off the dozens of intruding thoughts, leaving her mind empty and crystal clear. Her breathing steadied, becoming slow and deep. Clara focused on the muscles in her arms, shoulders, and back. Her feet moved instinctively, finding the right spot. She adjusted her posture according-ly, making sure every part of her body was in the correct position.

A soft smile formed on Clara's lips. For now, everything was forgot-ten. Her anxiety and worries, the vial with poison, even her brother and her husband. A single heartbeat seemed to last for hours as her hand rose up to grab the feathered end of the arrow. Clara didn't need to think about the motions, she had repeated them hundreds of times over. Her body knew what to do. Five arrows hissed through the air in quick succession and flew toward the target. Her smile widened. She knew they were good shots even without looking at the target.

Clara blinked a couple of times to wake herself from the deep, meditative state she entered whenever she held a bow. Only then did she look at Oscar, surprised to find he'd been standing just a few steps away from her this whole time. His face was one of serious contemplation, he wasn't smirking or joking around now. It was the first time Clara thought she'd seen respect in his eyes.

"Tell me something," he murmured, tilting his head to the side before clearing his throat to continue, "During the tournament. Did you make a mistake in the last round on purpose because you knew the winner would be invited to the king's table, where people would recognize you?"

He really was an intelligent man, dangerously so. "Yes," Clara nodded. There was no point in denying it. Grinning, she added, "I was really tempted to win and then just yell at everyone 'Hey, look! I'm a girl!' But gods, my parents would have killed me. Even my father urged me to keep it a secret and I didn't want to disappoint him."

"Hmm." Oscar crossed his arms in front of his body, examining Clara with curiosity, as if she were an interesting artifact in a museum.

Clara shifted her weight, suddenly feeling nervous. "What?" She knew it, coming here was a bad idea.

"Nothing." A smile eventually appeared on his lips but it didn't feel entirely sincere. "You are an intriguing woman. And a dangerous one." Then, as if coming out of a trance, the smile finally reached Oscar's eyes fully. "I'm really gonna have to be careful around you. Come on, show me that again."

They stayed at the training grounds until dark. Oscar made Clara show him how to shoot an arrow, complaining that even drawing the string was too hard. Dinner was waiting for them when they finally returned to their chambers so Oscar continued regaling Clara with stories about himself as they ate. When it came time for bed (the sheet had been changed for another plain white one), Clara snuggled closer to Oscar without hesitation, falling asleep while feeling warm and safe.

Despite how awful it made her feel, Clara needed to move forth with the plan to assassinate the king. She'd had one good day pretending to be normal, just like she'd wanted. But now the memory of Sebastian being beaten kept creeping into her mind, poisoning her every waking moment. Oscar unwittingly solved the biggest obstacle in her plan – he gave her access to the queen.

It turned out that Queen Karina was dying to meet Oscar's new wife, so she invited them both for tea. The queen looked just as beautiful as Clara had remembered from the wedding. Once again, she was dressed in a simple gown, no luxurious or flashy accessories, just a warm, sincere smile brightening her face.

While the queen and Oscar talked like the good friends they were, Clara just sat there, trying to calm her shaking hands enough to not spill tea all over herself. It was torture. Karina was such a kind soul, and from the way she talked, she obviously loved King Hayden very much. Clara felt like shit. How could she do this to them? What right did she have to destroy the lives of these two people and possibly the whole country, just to save her brother?

She barely said more than a few words throughout their meeting, choosing to keep her head down instead, staring solemnly into her cup. The queen didn't seem to mind Clara's quiet mood, she was probably used to people being nervous around her. With a warm smile on her face, Karina chatted away, mostly to Oscar, attempting to include Clara in the conversation whenever possible.

It was during one of these attempts that without even realizing it, Karina gave Clara all of the information she needed to not only get the terrible deed done but to also, hopefully, get away with it. Now Clara just needed to work out how to sneak away from her husband at the right time without raising any suspicion.

When she couldn't handle the guilt any longer, Clara politely excused herself. Oscar offered to accompany her back to their rooms but she refused, worried that he would figure out that something was wrong. Besides, Clara needed some time alone to gather her thoughts and make the final decision, even though it was already obvious what that decision would be. There was no way she could let her brother die.

As she walked through the corridors toward their chambers, a young maid hesitantly approached her. Clara had never seen her before but there were dozens of servants employed in the palace, so it wasn't very surprising. "My lady." The girl's voice was shaky as she bowed down to Clara. "I...I was told to give you this." A small box with a red bow appeared in the maid's hand, extended toward Clara. As soon as Clara took the box, the maid ran away, not even waiting for a thank you. She was probably too busy to idle in the hallway.

Clara eyed the box curiously. What could it be? A misplaced wedding gift? Another surprise from Oscar? Excited to find out what was inside, Clara untied the ribbon. The smile froze on Clara's face as she opened the box, her eyes widening in horror. It was a good thing she was standing so close to a privy chamber. She jolted for the privy, vomiting violently before the door had even closed behind her, her coughing interrupted only by her desperate sobs.

The box lay open on the floor next to her and, after forcing herself to calm down, Clara took another hesitant peek inside, confirming what she already knew. There was a finger in the box, a human finger. There was a ring slipped onto it, the Redwood crest clearly visible even under a layer of dried blood. Sebastian's ring.

Chapter 14

O scar sighed, shaking his head. The movement caused a few strands of his hair to escape the band that was securing it at his nape. He tucked the wayward strands behind his ear, something he'd done so often it had become instinctive rather than intentional.

Oscar liked mysteries and his new wife was definitely a big one. However, he felt he was too closely involved in this particular mystery, lacking enough information to be able to enjoy it fully.

Most of Clara's emotional imbalance could be easily blamed on her young age and this strange situation they were both forced into. Oscar understood that and as such, he'd tried to be as cautious and understanding as he could possibly be. Much more so than he would have been with any other woman. He'd even tried being honest with her. Not because he'd had any particular feelings for her but mainly because he didn't need any more complications in his life.

It wasn't that he didn't like her, he did. But, since she'd been a punishment from Hayden, (as she, herself, had put it), Oscar had fully expected

Clara to be a self-centered, annoying prude. But Clara was nothing like that.

Despite being so young, she was surprisingly bright and charming. Once she'd stopped being so terrified of Oscar, she'd even proven to be an interesting conversational partner. Beautiful, of course. That was hard to miss. Her fiery red hair looked amazing and Oscar was left wondering, with more than a little lustfulness, whether it was true that real redheads were red everywhere. Even thinking about her firm body, perfect skin, and perky breasts, just large enough for his hands, made his dick swell.

Oscar paused to take a few deep calming breaths. Thanks to his evil hag of a mother-in-law, Oscar hadn't even gotten to enjoy his wedding night. Hayden would have a laugh over that, if he knew.

At least Clara seemed to be physically attracted to Oscar. That gave him hope that once she sorted through all the lies and poison her mother had put into her head, she would let him fuck her. Oscar just had to be patient for now. Luckily, patience was his strong suit.

It wasn't until he'd seen Clara in action at the training ground that Oscar realized his wife wasn't merely an adorable, scared little girl. No, this woman was definitely dangerous. Or useful. It all depended on how much he could get her to trust him. Gaining Clara's trust would allow him to manipulate her into doing his bidding without her even realizing it. Afterall, that's what Oscar was good at. It was the only way he knew how to deal with people.

Karina was the one exception to that rule, and even she sometimes fell target to his subtle manipulations. His last attempt had worked out quite well, he thought with a sudden bitterness, remembering how he'd convinced Karina to offer herself to the king.

Yes, Oscar had wanted Karina to marry Hayden, it was the only way to save their country along with all of their lives. But why the fuck did she have to fall in love with the asshole? Seriously, that man was a stupid brute who couldn't control his emotions to save his life. Of course, Oscar knew that most of the myths surrounding the 'Burning Fury' were just lies made up so that people would be frightened of the king. But the truth still remained.

The man was moody and imbalanced. Not unlike Clara, Oscar thought, chuckling.

Clara wasn't really that much of a mystery. No, Oscar's instincts were telling him that his young wife was keeping a secret. It was something dark and distressing, and despite the almost child-like trust she'd shown in him, she was too scared to talk about it with him. It wasn't exactly hard to guess what it might be, the simplest answer was usually right. And the simplest answer, in this case, was that Clara was ordered to spy on Oscar.

Somebody was forcing her to do it. Oscar didn't believe she was a good enough actress to play out the meltdown she'd had on their wedding night. No, that was real. But, Clara clearly had another mission. One that involved being more than just his polite and obedient wife. It was sad, really, but Oscar should have seen it coming. Hayden would never have given him such an amazing girl if there hadn't been an ulterior motive behind it.

Oscar had considered confronting Clara about her secret, certain he could pry the answers out of her. But it was risky. Especially without knowing who was behind it. Maybe Grodin, the king's Master of Whispers? Was it on Hayden's orders, or not? There were too many unanswered questions and even if Clara trusted Oscar enough to talk to him, she probably didn't have all the answers herself. So, Oscar chose to wait, watching her every move like a creepy stalker.

This morning, his patience was finally rewarded. Clara had secretly snuck out through the servants' entrance in the bathroom and was now walking through the palace service wing. She looked terrified and absolutely desperate, barely holding back tears. Had Oscar left such a strong impression that she felt this bad about betraying him? Or was the simplest answer wrong and there was something else going on?

Footsteps sounded from behind him so Oscar quickly hid behind a thick, long window curtain. A maid rushed past carrying a tray holding a goblet already filled with golden liquid along with a large pitcher.

Clara had also noticed the maid. She stopped by the window, leaning against the sill and began breathing heavily. The maid cautiously paused next to her, asking whether the lady was alright.

Clara certainly didn't seem alright. She turned to the maid then reached out for her hand, pretending to falter. The maid barely managed to balance the tray. The maid set the tray down on a small ornamental table next to the window before grabbing Clara's arms. They exchanged a few quiet words that Oscar couldn't quite make out, resulting in the maid nodding before running off.

Water, Oscar realized. Clara had asked for a glass of water. What was she up to?

As soon as the maid disappeared around the corner, Clara moved to the tray the woman had left behind. A small vial appeared in Clara's hand, reflecting in the sunlight as she held it over the goblet.

Oscar's heart skipped a beat. Alright, the simplest answer was indeed the wrong one. Clara was being forced to poison someone. But who? By whom? With a shudder, Oscar remembered the glass of water she'd handed him during breakfast. Was that poisoned too? He felt fine now but that hardly meant anything.

His first instinct was to stop her but he forced himself to stay still, curious whether Clara would actually go through with it. Her hand was shaking as she continued to hold the vial over the goblet but she hadn't spilled a single drop yet. She didn't have much time to decide, the maid would be back soon and what Clara was contemplating doing didn't have a good explanation. She needed to make her decision and, to Oscar's relief, she made the right one. Sniffling, Clara lowered the vial without emptying the poison into the goblet. She slid down the wall before hugging her knees and sobbing desperately.

Getting involved in whatever the fuck was going on was dangerous but Oscar felt himself being drawn out of his hiding spot by two different motives. The first was simple curiosity. He had a lot of unanswered questions that his wife could provide him with answers for, or at least point him in the right direction. Afterall, knowledge was a powerful weapon.

The second reason Oscar wanted to approach Clara surprised him. He actually felt sorry for the girl and wanted to comfort her. When had he become so soft to the plight of others? Still, Oscar couldn't ignore the fact that she had a lot of potential. His young wife was definitely growing on him and it would be a shame to see her executed for attempted murder.

Relying on his instincts as always, Oscar cautiously approached Clara. She was still sobbing so hard she didn't even notice him until he stopped just a few steps away from her. Some skilled assassin his wife was.

"Who was it for?" Oscar asked, His voice sounding rougher than he'd intended. Clara flinched at the interruption to her melt down. Ever since they'd met, Oscar had always been smiling whenever they were together, but he sure as hell wasn't smiling now.

Clara's eyes widened in terror when she realized he'd seen everything. Oscar half expected her to either run or attack him. She was skilled with a bow, surely she knew how to use a dagger as well? What Oscar certainly didn't expect was Clara raising the vial to her own lips.

"NO!" he cried out. He was too far away to reach her.

Chapter 15

C lara froze with her hand poised against her lips, tears rolling freely down her cheeks. She eyed Oscar with such desperation it made him want to step forward and hug her, which was not a normal reaction for him. "I-I'm s-so sorr-rry." Sniffles made her words almost unintelligible.

"It's alright," Oscar comforted. He was used to sounding calm in tense situations but his voice wasn't entirely steady now. "Nothing happened, Clara. You didn't do anything. Give me the vial." She shook her head rapidly and Oscar watched the liquid inside the vial rock back and forth, threatening to spill onto her lips.

"Clara, please. Give me the vial." Oscar made sure to sound authoritative. He needed to get through to Clara somehow, to break through the haze of terror and desperation clouding her mind. "If you tell me what's going on, I can help you." Whoa. The words came out of his mouth before his brain could engage. Why the hell was Oscar promising to help her? Rescuing damsels in distress was very much not his style, especially if it could get him into serious trouble. But, to his own surprise, Oscar meant it. He actually wanted to help Clara.

She closed her eyes momentarily, before shaking her head in remorse. "You can't help me."

"Not if you drink that, I can't. But, if you give me a chance, I'll fix this." Whatever 'this' was. How could he be promising her something he didn't have the slightest clue how to deliver? "Come on," Oscar urged, "have I given you a single reason not to trust me?" Excluding following her like a stalker today.

Oscar slowly moved forward until he was standing right above Clara. Without breaking eye contact, he crouched down so they were on the same level and extended his hand out to her. Just fucking do what I say, his eyes were screaming at her. And she did. Hesitantly, Clara put the glass vial into Oscar's opened palm, along with the tiny cork. Oscar immediately secured the cork before slipping the vial into his pocket.

Alright, one danger averted. Now, onto the next.

They were running out of time. It wasn't long before the maid would return with Clara's drink. Oscar needed to ask questions, to think and strategize, but this was definitely the wrong place and time.

He grabbed Clara's wrist firmly and eyed her with what he hoped was an authoritative stare. "Alright, listen to me. You will do exactly what I say, when I say it. Understood?" There was no time for coddling, there was work to be done. Thankfully, Clara nodded without speaking. "Great. Now, stop crying." To Oscar's surprise, she actually did stop crying. If only that trick would work all the time.

As they rose from the floor together, Oscar intentionally bumped into the table that was holding the tray and a vase of flowers. The vase and tray went tumbling onto the floor with a sharp bang, taking the goblet and pitcher with them. A huge wet puddle filled the hallway, joined by shards of glass. Oscar hadn't seen Clara put any poison into the goblet, but it was better to be safe than sorry.

Clara flinched at hearing the glass shatter but with Oscar still holding her wrists firmly, she couldn't move away. "Look like you are about to faint," he whispered into her ear as he pulled her into a tight hug. It shouldn't be too difficult to pretend, Clara looked as white as a sheet anyway.

The maid rushed around the corner only to freeze when she noticed the mess on the ground, Oscar and Clara stood right in the middle of it.

"Oh, thank the gods you are here," Oscar called to her. "My wife became dizzy and knocked this thing over. I am so incredibly sorry for the mess, we hate to be such a burden." He put on his best apologetic smile. "I think the stress from the wedding has gotten to her, plus, just between the two of us, we haven't been sleeping very much, if you know what I mean." The salaciousness of his prideful grin had the maid blushing. Some people were so gullible. "Here, please," Oscar reached into his pocket and pulled out a couple of coins, "this is for your troubles." Money always helped smooth things over.

Putting Clara's arm around his shoulders, he slowly maneuvered them past the puddle on the floor. The maid was still holding a glass of water for Clara so Oscar took it, giving the woman a grateful smile. "Thank you for this. If only there were more kind souls like yourself in the palace."

After half walking, half dragging Clara around the nearest corner, Oscar paused to gather his thoughts. Clara didn't move, paralyzed by fear, which was useful for now. But there was no way she'd make it back to their chambers without bursting into tears again.

Oscar peeked into the nearest doorway and then pushed Clara inside. The room seemed to be a storage closet for bed linens and other things, nicely smelling of fresh laundry. Lucky for them, it was currently vacant.

Clara retreated to a wall as far away from Oscar as she could, cautiously watching him as he closed the door behind them. Given her previous reactions to him, she probably expected to be yelled at or slapped around.

Perhaps Oscar should do just that. Whatever game Clara was playing had put him in danger as well. If she'd been caught trying to poison someone, who would believe that Oscar had nothing to do with it? Nobody. Karina, maybe, but certainly not the king.

"So." He breathed out slowly, doing his best to stay calm. "Who was the poison for?" That was still the most important question. Clara looked down but didn't answer. "Clara," Oscar insisted, "I told you I would help you. But I need to know what is going on."

"The king," she whispered eventually.

Oscar's eyebrows went flying up. The king? This game just became more interesting but also much more dangerous.

The goblet! Oscar suddenly remembered the contents had smelled like apples. The entire hallway was permeated by the scent now that he'd spilled it everywhere. It all began to make sense to him. Karina had mentioned Hayden liking apple cider so much he had a servant bring him some every morning. Is that how Clara had known it was for him? What a stupid girl! Going around poisoning Hayden's glass, she might have killed Karina too.

Perhaps Oscar should just stay out of this. Or better yet, tell the king himself. He could certainly use this opportunity to build a little credibility with that bastard. He could throw Clara under the carriage, let her drown in the mess she'd created. That would be the logical thing to do. Why should Oscar care what happened to her? She meant nothing to him. None of the women he'd ever been with meant anything to him. There was only one that mattered and Clara's actions today had put her in danger.

But...

A small part of Oscar's mind was horrified by those thoughts and desperately wanted to help Clara, to protect her. He cared for his young wife, more than he thought he should. The feeling was nowhere close to what he felt for Karina but then again, nothing ever would be. But, he couldn't have Karina. Even before the war she hadn't shown any interest in Oscar beyond friendship, and now...she was in love with someone else. Karina was happy with the king, happier than Oscar had ever seen her. Perhaps it was time he gave up and just tried to let her go.

No, he didn't love Clara. But he liked her and maybe in time that could grow into something more. Provided she wasn't executed for attempted regicide, or actually succeeded in murdering Hayden. As much as Oscar hated the man, his death would only solve one problem, yet cause dozens of others. It wasn't worth it.

"Alright," Oscar said, scratching his head, "that could be a little problematic. Why the king?" If Clara was trying to kill Hayden in revenge for forcing her to marry Oscar, he could hardly help her with that. Plus, it would mean he was likely to find poison in his own glass in the not too distant future as well. But it didn't seem like that was the case.

She shrugged and sniffled, "I don't know. They didn't tell me."

"What are they threatening you with?" Obviously, Clara wasn't doing it out of her own free will. Or for money, for that matter. Her family was wealthy enough. No, whoever was after Hayden must have had something on Clara to keep her in check. Something important enough to force her into taking such a risk.

More tears sprang from her eyes as she looked up at him. "They...they have Sebastian. I saw him, h-he was...he was tied up and covered in blood and they were beating him and the man threatened to torture him and..." The stream of her words suddenly paused and she had to force herself to continue. "Yesterday I received a gift box with...with a finger inside. Sebastian's ring was on it. And I just couldn't... He's my brother and I love him, I mean...I know I should love the king too and that I'm a horrible person and everyone should hate me and despise me but...he's my brother and I just can't..."

To his own surprise, Oscar found himself stepping in to Clara and pulling her into a tight hug, interrupting her desperate blubbering. "It's alright. I understand."

He might have been a cynical man who only saw people as tools to be used and discarded, but there were a few exceptions to that rule. Oscar did have people he would fight for even if it meant risking his own life. Karina, naturally, but also his mother, father, and even his brothers would be on that list. Somehow, Clara had managed to wheedle her way onto this list as well.

The question that presented itself was, why hadn't she told anyone? But Oscar already knew the answer. Who would she tell? Her heartless mother? Who only cared about her own gain and social status? Her husband? Who she'd known for the whole of three days? The king? Whose life she was supposed to take? That would actually make sense if it were anyone else, but with the Burning Fury it must have seemed like a suicide mission.

Clara had calmed down a little but was still trembling in his arms. "You're going to tell him." Her voice was solemn. It wasn't a question. Oscar didn't react immediately, his mind still mulling over the possible options. Clara took his silence as a yes and continued, "I know he will have me executed and I deserve that but..." Her shoulders twitched with suppressed sobs. "Please don't let him torture me."

Gods, Hayden really did have an abysmal reputation with his own people. What kind of a ruling style was that? A tyrannical dictator that everyone was scared shitless of? "Nothing will happen to you, Clara," Oscar soothed her, even though he was once again promising something he had no idea how to deliver.

The easiest thing to do would be to simply wait. The kidnappers would kill Clara's brother, the leverage against her would be gone and everyone could live happily ever after. Except Sebastian, of course. An acceptable casualty in the grand scheme of things. But Clara would never forgive Oscar if he let her brother die.

What other options were there, though? There was not enough time to track down the kidnappers. They could be hiding anywhere. The only way to get more time and draw them out would be to make them believe the poison had worked and that wasn't something Oscar could orchestrate. No, Hayden would have to be in on the plan as well and he would, quite reasonably, never agree to let the whole country believe he had died.

Even without considering the well-being of Clara's brother, she and Oscar were in a dangerous situation. Their little theatrical show was no doubt going to be a hot topic for palace gossip. If Hayden found out about the poison from another source, he or his spymaster would put two and two together. The Master of Whispers, Grodin, might be old and no longer in top shape anymore, but he wasn't stupid.

Clara was right. They needed to tell Hayden before he heard it some-where else, made up his mind, and acted before listening to their side of the story. Oscar needed to talk to the king as soon as possible and make him see reason, to save both Clara's life and his own. Because if he did go there and speak up in her defense, it would be his neck on the line too. Was he really willing to do all this for a girl he barely knew?

Oscar raised his hand to caress Clara's hair, running his fingers through the wild, unruly red curls. Clara nestled into his chest, looking for safety and protection. It was a strange feeling, knowing Oscar could provide her with that if he tried.

No one had ever needed Oscar's protection. Least of all, Karina, who was always so independent and strong. Clara was much more vulnerable. Granted, it was mostly due to her age and the pile of shit circumstances she had been dropped into. The sheer amount of stressors this girl had been dealing with would probably break anyone. But even so, the idea of taking care of her, helping and protecting her, made Oscar feel good. He felt strong, needed. Right.

He let out a deep sighing breath, reaching a decision. "Alright, my dear wife. I will fix this." He sounded so convincing that Clara stopped sobbing to listen. "I'll talk to the king and I promise to make this right. I just need you to trust in me now."

She nodded frantically. As she looked at him with desperate hope, a strange, warm feeling spread through Oscar's chest. It was strong and somewhat new, yet oddly familiar. Was it pride? Oscar knew pride. He was often proud of how he'd cleverly manipulated people to use them for his own gain. However, this sort of pride was different. Pride from being the good guy, the knight in the shining armor, one who protects his maiden from all harm was somehow stronger. Cleaner.

Oscar smiled at Clara, tempted to kiss her tear-stained cheeks, but now was hardly the right time. Her trembling arms wrapped tightly around his chest reminded him that he couldn't exactly bring her along to his meeting with Hayden. No, he needed to hide her somewhere so Hayden's initial wave of anger couldn't reach her.

There was nowhere in the palace where Hayden wouldn't quickly find her, but there was one place where Hayden would be forced to tame his anger. One person who could stand up to him. Oscar smirked over the irony. Where better to hide someone from the king, than with the queen?

Chapter 16

Sighing, Karina checked her reflection in the mirror. She didn't find anything wrong and yet, somehow, some people weren't pleased with what they saw. The castle was filled with whispers and gossip. Nobody dared smirk to her face and there were no quiet snickers where she could hear them. Everyone was too afraid of Hayden to do that. However, Karina often glimpsed contempt in people's eyes as she approached. The women especially, could be brutal and uninviting, and Karina was just too different to fit in.

If only she could say 'Fuck them' and ignore them all, but that was easier said than done. The number of people who despised her being here was in stark contrast to what she'd been used to at home in Levanta. All of those, more or less subtle hints of, 'you don't belong here,' were wearing her down and she had not one real friend to complain to.

Hayden was busy catching up on everything that had happened while he was away, and trying to figure out what to do about Cchen-Lian. Plus, he wouldn't understand. People laughing at her because she refused to wear pompous gowns or expensive jewelry was too much of a 'womanly' problem for him. He'd probably try to solve it by force, which would only cause more trouble.

Oscar would understand, but he was newly married and Karina couldn't run to cry on his shoulder just two days after his wedding. She had hoped she would become friends with his new wife, but Clara had been so terrified of meeting the queen that she'd barely even spoken a word to Karina. Hopefully, that would get better in time. But for now, Karina was left to drown in this mess all alone.

Well, not completely alone. Her loyal maid Laina had followed her to Ebris and for that, Karina couldn't be more grateful. At least there was one normal person she could talk to. Aside from Hayden, of course.

Hayden and Karina talked to each other a lot. Hayden took his time explaining everything to Karina about her new kingdom. They talked about the decisions he'd been making during the various meetings, treaties and trade agreements along with the thousands of other little things that were apparently required to run a country.

Karina had never truly realized how complicated ruling a country was. Her father probably hadn't even cared about half of these matters, leaving the basic decisions to Otto and the rest of his council. Hayden, on the other hand had a much tighter grip on the ruling, which gave him more control, but it also meant he had to spend much more of his time in endless meetings or buried under piles of parchment.

It was amazing how Hayden worked hard to make sure Karina was included in everything. He'd bring her along to meetings and glare at anyone who dared to object to her presence. Surely, it made people dislike Karina even more, but at least she felt that was a justifiable reason and not merely about her looking different. That was plain stupid.

A knock at the door interrupted her dark thoughts and replaced them with even darker ones. Today's disaster had finally arrived. Karina made sure Laina was present in the room with her before answering the door. There was no way she could face this on her own.

A tall, thin woman entered, immediately dipping into the perfect curtsy in front of Karina. Her gown was beautiful, ornate and perfectly matched by her jewelry. Damn, even the ribbon used to tie the woman's hair into an impossibly tight bun on the top of her head was the same color as the lining of her gown. The woman's hair was gray but there were no visible wrinkles on her face, probably due to her skin being stretched back by that bun. Karina's scalp ached just imagining having her hair tied like that all the time.

Karina stifled a groan as she saw two maids carrying large bags follow the woman into her chamber. "Lady Locke," she addressed the woman, forcing a smile on her face. "Welcome. I'm glad you could come." No, she wasn't. Parvati Locke was the Orellian royal dress designer and an absolute menace. This woman was the reason Karina spent half of her wedding day looking like over wrapped candy. At least, until she'd been kidnapped and forced Hayden to cut the stupid dress off.

"My lady." Parvati's smile was strictly polite and just as forced as Karina's. It looked like there was another battle ahead, one that Karina wasn't looking forward to at all. Parvati waved toward the maids. "I have brought you some samples of the new wardrobe we talked about. All simple pieces." The way she spat out the word 'simple,' with poorly hidden contempt, made Karina bristle.

Fighting to keep a calm expression, Karina nodded. "Let's see them."

Parvati had the maids unpack the bags they'd brought and lay the gowns over the large bed before sending them away. The queen suppressed a sigh. It wasn't as bad as she'd feared but it was still far from what she'd imagined.

Parvati noticed Karina's less-than-excited look and lowered her head, a hint of disappointment piercing through her stern expression. "My queen, I-" Another knock at the door stopped her.

A spark of hope fluttered in Karina's heart. Perhaps Hayden was coming to rescue her? Whoever it was, their timing was perfect. As Laina opened the door, Karina was surprised to see Oscar standing in the doorway. He quickly adorned his most charming smile upon noticing Karina wasn't alone. "My lady," he bowed his head, "might I please have a word with you? It's kind of urgent."

"Excuse me for a moment, Lady Locke," Karina muttered then quickly rushed out to meet Oscar in the hallway. She froze upon seeing Clara standing behind him, utmost desperation marring her tear-stained face. "Oscar?" Karina asked, not even bothering to hide the threat in her voice. She closed the door before continuing, "What did you do?"

He smirked. "Now, that is unfair. Why do you automatically assume it was me who did something?" The question was purely rhetorical. Afterall, this was Oscar. He was always up to something. Only now it seemed like he'd dragged Clara into one of his schemes as well, which was certainly not alright with Karina.

Oscar sighed at Karina's expression. "Yes, I know. Under normal circumstances it would be a fair assumption. But this time, I'm actually trying to fix something that's not my fault. Could Clara please stay with you while I talk to your dear husband?"

"Of course." Karina gave the young girl a reassuring smile but Clara's eyes only widened in fear as she tried to step back, shaking her head in silent horror. Wow. Was Karina seriously so repulsive that nobody wanted to spend time with her?

Oscar turned to his wife, gently grabbing her arms. "Clara, I promised you I would fix this, and I will. I just need you to stay with the queen. You will be absolutely safe here." Clara sniffled, barely holding back her tears, but nodded, giving Karina a terrified look.

"Trust me, please," Oscar whispered before pulling Clara into his embrace.

Karina stared in astonishment. This was not the Oscar she knew. She'd never seen him being this open and caring, not even when it was just the two of them. It seemed he was really starting to like his new wife. But what the hell was going on with these two?

"Are you going to tell me what's going on?" she asked. Oscar was always in trouble but this time it seemed more serious than usual.

Shaking his head, he nudged Clara into the room. "Sorry Karina, the king first." After Clara disappeared behind the door, Oscar leaned closer to Karina, whispering into her ear, "In the very rare case Hayden comes in here and tries to do something stupid, stop him. If there's already blood on his sword, well...it was nice knowing you," he smirked and turned away before Karina could react.

Seriously? What the fuck?

After taking a moment to regain her composure, Karina returned to her chamber. Whatever was happening, either Hayden or Oscar would tell her eventually. Now she needed to look strong and calm despite feeling quite the opposite. She was a queen and had to act like one.

Clara was nervously standing by the door, keeping her head down. Parvati watched on with a raised eyebrow but upon noticing Karina's return, she turned away, running her hand over the gowns laid out on the bed. Laina was nowhere to be seen which sent a flare of anger through Karina's mind. Where did the girl go now that she was actually needed?

"Would you like to sit down, Clara?" Karina pointed at the sofa in the corner of the room. Clara walked over without protests, quietly sitting on the very edge, hands folded on her lap, head down. She didn't seem to be in any condition to provide Karina with answers.

Laina returned, carrying a large cup filled with steaming hot tea, the strong scent of herbs permeating the whole room. So that's where she'd gone. Karina felt a little ashamed of being so angry at her maid a moment ago. Laina had just ran off to make a cup of her famous calming tea for Clara, who looked like she desperately needed it.

Needing to get rid of Parvati, Karina turned to her. "Lady Locke, as you see, there are some matters I must attend to. Let's make this quick." Karina paused, taking in a deep breath. This was not going to be pretty. "With all due respect, this is not what we talked about."

"My lady," a frown appeared on the woman's face, "this is the bare minimum considered acceptable for court. You have to consider the social..."

A quiet growl escaped Karina. She'd had enough of this. "I never thought I would say this," she started in a quiet, icy tone, "but here goes. I'm the fucking queen. I don't HAVE TO do anything." That's what Hayden had said, right? "If I choose to walk around the palace wearing a shirt and breeches, nobody can say a word in protest. I am done with people trying to force me to be something I am not."

Parvati blinked in surprise, taking a startled step back. "I...I apologize, I didn't mean to..."

"It's alright." Karina willed her temper down. She didn't want to take her frustration out on the woman who was just doing her job. "Honestly, the gowns are beautiful," Karina tried to sooth Parvati. "You are a truly talented woman. But I just wouldn't feel like myself if I wore them."

A sad sigh escaped Parvati as she grabbed one of the gowns and, to Karina's surprise, threw it on the floor. "I understand, my lady. I'm truly sorry, I got a little too excited to finally have a woman in the royal family, someone who might appreciate the years of work I put into these." She waved her hand over the gowns. There was no reproach in her words, only sadness. "But I guess I'll just toss them on the hearth and start over with something that would be more acceptable to you."

"What?" Dumbstruck, Karina stared at her. "Why would you do that? Why not just give them to someone else?"

Parvati's confusion equaled Karina's as she seemed to be at a loss for words.

"She can't." Clara's quiet words surprised them both. Karina had completely forgotten the girl was in the room. The queen turned to her, expecting some sort of explanation, which Clara provided, "There's a law that forbids it. The assigned royal dress designer can only make clothes for the royal family. She's not allowed to give or sell them to anyone else."

"Gods," Karina groaned. This was seriously fucked up. Had Parvati spent the past decade designing dresses in the vain hope that Hayden would finally find a wife? Because there was certainly not much need to design for the king. And now? Karina had just told Parvati she didn't want any of it? Poor woman.

Karina rubbed the bridge of her nose. "Lady Locke, I honestly had no idea about that. I mean, we had some idiotic laws in Levanta, but this would never have even crossed my mind. I promise to make the king cancel that law so that all of your hard work won't be in vain." It shouldn't be a problem, Hayden probably had no idea such a law even existed.

Parvati's eyes widened in shock. "My lady, I..." Her voice wavered. "I don't even know what to say. That would be amazing."

Yes, getting Parvati off her back would be amazing for Karina as well. "It's no problem. Look," she walked over to her wardrobe and pulled a small silky pack out of it, handing it over to Parvati, "this is my favorite dress. The king likes me in it too," Karina added, a blush creeping across her cheeks. "If you want to design something for me, use this as inspiration. Oh, and the string on the top has been cut. If you could fix that somehow, I would be extremely grateful."

"That shouldn't be a problem." Parvati nodded excitedly, leaning out of the door to call the maids back. While they were gathering the dresses, her fingers played with the silky fabric in her hands.

Karina stepped closer, lowering her voice to a whisper. "I hope I don't have to remind you that whatever you saw while in my chambers," she glanced at Clara, "is private and not a source for the latest palace gossip. Is that clear?"

"Of course, I would never..."

"Good," Karina cut her off, gently nudging Parvati out of the door. "Let me know when you have something for me. I'll talk to the king at his earliest convenience."

Finally, all the women were gone and Karina could start on finding out what the hell was going on with Oscar. "Clara?" She walked over, crouching down in front of Clara so they were eye level. The desperation hadn't disappeared. If anything, it had increased as Karina addressed her.

"I'm sorry," Clara sniffled. "I really am. I didn't know what else to do."

Karina suppressed an eye roll. How very enlightening. "It's going to be alright," Karina comforted, attempting to soothe Clara. "When Oscar promises to fix something, he does. Even if he has to move mountains to do it." It was true, which is why Oscar rarely gave out such promises. What had made him go out of his way for his new wife? And what the fuck was going on?

Chapter 17

O scar paused to take a deep breath before knocking on Hayden's study door. He still wasn't entirely sure what to say, something that was quite new to him. His normal approach wasn't going to work with the king, that was certain. Hayden hated people who played with words, preferring the straightforward approach instead. That was not something Oscar was used to but he would make it work to protect Clara.

A shadow of doubt lingered in the back of his mind. Was he really going to stick his neck out for Clara like this? The look of pure desperation on her face when she'd raised the poison to her lips helped chase any doubts away. Whether Oscar had wanted this or not, Clara was his wife and he'd sworn to stand by her side in good times and bad. Besides, a surprisingly large part of him actually wanted to protect her. Being in this country really was a bad influence on him.

Oscar brought his fist down on the wood before doubt could change his mind. The king's "Come in!" already sounded annoyed and his frown deepened upon seeing Oscar's face. What a great starting point.

The king's study was large. Lined with shelves that overflowed with various books, parchments and maps, an almost perfect mimicry to the large wooden desk Hayden was sitting behind, which also overflowed with the same. He put aside the parchment he'd been reading before being interrupted, then glared at Oscar. "Lord Huxley. What brings you here?" He wasn't even trying to disguise the hostility in his words.

Oscar, on the other hand, was quite used to being treated like dirt and didn't have a problem acting politely, all while being angry and annoyed himself. "My lord," he replied, bowing his head. "I hope you aren't too busy."

Hayden's eyes narrowed but, with a hint of amusement, he actually chose to respond, "Well, I'm trying to figure out what to do about the sudden outbreak of green fever in our mining stations along the southern border. It seems to be hindering our silver ore shipments."

Oscar fought back a smirk. "A report from Master Grodin, I assume?" he pointed at the parchment. "There is no green fever outbreak. The guy you appointed to oversee the miners is stealing part of the shipments for himself."

"And how would you know that, Lord Huxley?" Threat loomed behind the king's words.

Oscar knew he had to be careful now. It would be easy to make this idiot angry, but antagonizing him further was the last thing Oscar wanted right now. No, he needed to calm Hayden down and achieve at least a neutral tone with him. And for that, Oscar had to be honest, no matter how much he hated the idea. "Because I was the one who fed that lie to Grodin's people and encouraged the man to steal from you," he admitted shamelessly.

"Is that so?" Hayden growled.

"Yes," Oscar nodded, looking straight into Hayden's eyes. "Why don't you show me the report? Perhaps I can cast some light on other areas as well."

Hayden scoffed and leaned back, crossing his arms in front of his chest. "You expect me to hand you a top-secret report from my spymaster? Why are you here, Huxley?"

"Your spymaster is an old man who is losing his touch. I've played him so many times I stopped counting. I need to talk to you about something, so why don't you let me be useful first?" Oscar needed to gain Hayden's trust, which seemed like an impossible task given the relationship between them.

Fists clenched, Hayden leaned forward in his chair to snarl into Oscar's face. "If you think you can walk around this palace playing your little games and laughing behind my back, thinking Karina will protect you, you are gravely mistaken. Get the fuck out of here."

This was going worse than Oscar had expected. Quite an accomplishment since he'd expected it to go poorly. It was time to change strategy. Smooth words clearly didn't work with Hayden. "Listen. For once, I'm actually trying to do the right thing the right way. No games. So how about you stop being such an asshole and meet me halfway?" Wow, so much for diplomacy, Oscar thought. But, this was Hayden's style of communication, he should appreciate that, if nothing else.

"What exactly did you just call me?" Amusement sparked in the king's eyes. Oscar was well aware that the move he'd just made could help him just as much as it could totally screw him over. Now the king had something he could actually punish Oscar for. Hayden tapped on his chin, his dark eyes studying Oscar for the longest time. "Lord Huxley," he said eventually, "you surprise me. You do know if I show you this paper, there's a good chance you won't leave this room alive?"

Oscar rolled his eyes. "Well, Your Majesty," this time he didn't bother masking the sarcasm in his voice, "with you around, there is always a chance people won't leave the room alive. As if there was something in that report I don't already know."

Hayden grinned and reached for the parchment on his desk, pushing it across. Without a moment's hesitation, Oscar grabbed it then sat down on one of the chairs in front of Hayden's desk. He skimmed over the lines, knowing that the king was carefully scrutinizing his expression the entire time.

"The first two reports are true," Oscar said, his eyes still glued to the parchment. "Although, Grodin exaggerated the importance of those events. As far as I know, it was just stupid people doing stupid things, not a conspiracy against you." His brows knit together as he went over the next few lines. "The river pirates are a pure fabrication but not one of my doing. I've heard about this before but I have no idea where it came from, or what purpose it serves."

"Oh, I know the purpose very well," Hayden growled but didn't explain further. "What about the news from Kurasa?" He looked intrigued and despite Oscar's ability to read people, he had no idea what the king was thinking. Did he trust Oscar's words? Or was he merely amused by what he thought were intricate lies?

Oscar had been entirely honest until now but the urge to lie spiked after the king's question. After all, Oscar did say there was nothing on the paper he hadn't already known about. But he needed Hayden's trust and couldn't afford to be caught out lying. Not now, when he actually had a chance of accomplishing his goal and maybe even gaining actual political power in Hayden's court.

"I don't know," Oscar admitted, his gut roiling over admitting ignorance in front of the king. "I've never heard about it before. I have some people in place around King Simri, I can ask around." *If I'm alive.* Oscar didn't add that last bit since it was a fairly obvious condition. "You think it's connected to Karina's theory about Cchen-Lian setting people against you?"

"You are supposed to be the smart one around here, you tell me." Hayden's expression was still indecipherable.

Tucking a few strands of hair behind his ear, Oscar considered the possibility. "I think it's possible. But then again, Simri is an idiot. The trouble he's stirring could just be him making some stupid flashy move he thinks is smart." Oscar shrugged. "Without more information, I wouldn't jump to any conclusions." *While Kurasa making a move against Orellia* was an interesting piece of information, it wasn't why Oscar was here. He put the paper back on the table, hoping he had proven to be useful enough not to get stabbed as soon as the king learned about the poison.

"Well, Lord Huxley," Hayden smirked, "now that you have buttered me up, why don't you get to the point. Why the fuck are you really here?"

Oscar was still unable to read Hayden, which sent a tingle of fear down his spine. But, he'd already chosen his strategy and it was too late to back out. Taking a deep breath, he placed the vial on the table between them. Hayden's eyes narrowed as he watched it. "This was supposed to end up in your apple cider today," Oscar said matter-of-factly.

"Oh, really?" Hayden leaned back in his chair, a contemptuous smirk twisting his lips. "And you are such a loyal subject that you heroically saved me and came here to claim your reward?"

"No. I came here to make sure you don't do something stupid to the person who was supposed to kill you. Which was Clara."

Hayden burst out in laughter. "Gods! I was wondering what game you were playing. But, truth be told, I'm disappointed. I had expected a man of your reputation to come up with a better lie to cover up whatever it is you are trying to achieve here."

"My dear king," Oscar spat out, "despite my better judgment, not a single lie has crossed my lips today. Like I said. For once, I'm trying to do the right thing, the right way. But that clearly requires an actual king, not a self-centered prick like you." A dangerous move, but the direct approach was the only thing that seemed to work with Hayden.

The king's eyebrows shot up. "You really want me to believe that Clara, who has been nothing but a proper lady from a loyal family until you arrived here, suddenly decided to poison me two days after you were married? And that you have nothing to do with it? That's just absurd."

Oscar said nothing, looking the king right in the eyes.

A frown ran over Hayden's face. "Alright, let's just say for a moment that I'm insane and actually believe you. So, you stopped your wife from murdering me and ran straight here to rat her out? Just to save your own hide? Some man you are."

Oscar rolled his eyes. "Seriously, you should compile all of your stupid theories and publish them as a book. People would laugh their asses off. Now, will you stay quiet and let me talk or are there other treasures hidden in that empty space where normal people have brains?" Hayden's eyes narrowed and Oscar knew he was very close to the line. If he stepped over it, he'd be dead. This confrontational style of communication was seriously not his strong suit. "Please?" he added in a more conciliatory tone.

"Speak quickly, Lord Huxley. My patience is far from limitless."

It really wasn't a long story to tell. "Somebody kidnapped Clara's brother. They told her to poison you or he would die. She received a finger yesterday with his ring on it as a reminder to hurry up. She didn't have a choice."

"Nicolas?" Hayden's brows furrowed in confusion. "She should have just come to me."

Oscar snorted. "Yes, because you are such a kind and gentle ruler that you inspire loyalty and trust from your subjects. People are frightened of you. Do you really think someone would be crazy enough to come and tell you they were supposed to poison you?" Oscar knocked on his own forehead a couple of times, immediately regretting it. Damn, he was getting too worked up by this debate. Normally he was much more in control of such gestures. "And no, it's the other brother, the diplomat."

"Sebastian Redwood isn't even supposed to be back on the continent yet." The king ran his hand through his hair, his frown deepening as his eyes pierced Oscar, looking for any sign of deception. There was none for him to find. A hint of uncertainty broke through the king's scrutinizing gaze before he finally sighed, "She really did try to kill me."

Chapter 18

O scar stifled a relieved sigh. Hayden trusted him, at least to some small extent. Now Oscar had to steer Clara (and himself) away from Hayden's vengeance.

"She didn't go through with it. Listen." Oscar's voice gained intensity. He needed to make sure the king understood. "I watched Clara holding the poison over your glass but she didn't put a single drop in. And when I confronted her, she tried to drink the vial herself. I won't let you hurt her because of this." Oscar clamped his mouth shut, immediately regretting those words, but the damage was already done.

"You won't let me?" An evil smirk twisted Hayden's expression. "How cute. What authority exactly do you imagine you have over me, you sneaky, lying piece of shit?"

Damn, Oscar had gone too far. Now, he could either continue onward in the same direction, get punched in the face and thrown into jail or, he could swallow his pride, yet again, no matter how much it sickened him to grovel in front of the king. Especially knowing Hayden would definitely rub it in his face. However, as Oscar had told Clara, his pride was flexible.

"I do apologize, Your Majesty." Oscar made his best effort to make it sound honest but it was hard to push the words out through gritted teeth. "I didn't mean to say that."

"Oh, yes, you did." Hayden grabbed the vial, rolling it between his fingers. Oscar waited, silently contemplating why he hadn't poured the poison into the bastard's goblet himself. Eventually, Hayden's eyes found Oscar's again. "Why do you care so much about Clara?"

Oscar snorted. "Have you forgotten already? You made me marry her."

"Yes, she's been your wife for two whole days. And now you are sitting here, sticking your neck out for her? That's not your style, Huxley."

"I like her and she doesn't deserve any of this." That was the truth. "You don't know anything about me, my dear king. I think you, of all people, should understand that having a bad reputation doesn't necessarily mean you are a bad person. I mean, talk about disappointment. I haven't seen you eat even one newborn." Oscar was well aware that he should dial it down but he just couldn't help himself. The frustration at Karina choosing this idiot over Oscar was bubbling dangerously close to the surface now. And this was neither the time or the place to let it spill out.

Hayden chuckled. "You are too smart for your own good. So, you speak nothing but the truth now?" Before Oscar could respond, the king added, "You're in love with Karina."

"Seriously?" Oscar took in a deep breath to calm himself. "This is what you want to talk about?"

The king shrugged indifferently, his eyes drawn back to the vial. "The danger is averted for now. I need to take advantage of this rare opportunity to hear the truth coming from the lips of the infamous Oscar Huxley."

"You're an asshole." Oscar scowled at the smirking king. Hayden wanted the truth? Fine, he shall have the truth. "Of course, I love Karina. I've been in love with her for years, long before she ever met your sorry ass. But, for reasons I cannot fathom, she only loves you. And as long as she is happy, I will not interfere."

Oscar closed his eyes, feeling strangely lightweight after finally admitting the truth out loud. At the same time, icy dread settled in his stomach. He'd fucked up. The Burning Fury didn't share and he certainly wasn't going to share the love of his life with a man he despised.

The chair scraped against the floor as the king stood up. Oscar heard quiet footsteps move behind him but he didn't open his eyes. The thought of his impending death was bad enough, he didn't need to see the smirk on Hayden's face as he delivered it. It was stupid, really. Telling the truth was never a good idea. Oscar should have stuck to his normal strategy of lies and manipulations.

As the footsteps slowed beside him, Oscar swallowed his fear back, then opened his eyes, exhaling slowly. He'd expected a blade against his throat or, at the very least, Hayden dangling shackles in front of his face. Instead, Oscar saw a low cut glass filled with golden liquid. By the smell coming from it, this wasn't apple cider.

Hayden waited until Oscar took the glass before leaning back against the table, his arms crossed over his chest. "Drink," the king commanded, his voice ice cold. The vial with poison was nowhere to be seen.

Perfect. Oscar ground his molars together. This was just perfect. For once, he tried to do the right thing and his reward? Death. How fucking ironic.

Oscar briefly considered asking the king to slit his throat. Being poisoned seemed a little too painful, but he would be damned if the last thing he did before dying was beg that bastard for a favor. Oscar had played the game and lost. That happens.

He downed the glass in a few big gulps, coughing as the liquor burned its way through his throat.

Hayden seemed amused but there was respect in his expression as well. "It wasn't poisoned," he noted, reaching for his own glass. "You wanted me to trust you. That's why you came here and put on this show, right?" Sipping the liquor, he chuckled softly. "I wanted to see if I could trust you too."

"By making me think I was going to die? What the hell does that prove, Your fucking Majesty?" Oscar's fingers gripped the empty glass tighter as he contemplated throwing it at the king.

Laughing quietly, Hayden moved back to the cabinet and pulled out a large bottle before holding it over Oscar's glass. As he poured the liquor, Hayden watched Oscar with a poorly concealed grin. "Why don't you just call me Hayden? Perhaps you can manage to do that without all the sarcasm. And, Oscar," the king smirked, "the fact that you were willing to drink it proves that you have a spine. That is something I didn't expect."

For the first time in a very long time, Oscar was speechless. He had seriously underestimated the king's intelligence and nearly paid the highest price for it. However, it seemed that Oscar had somehow made a good impression anyway.

To give himself time to think of what to say next, Oscar took a sip from his unpoisoned drink, this time savoring the taste of the priceless brandy.

"If you are still interested," the king said as he moved back to his chair, leaving the bottle on the table, "I could actually use your help. Gods know, I can't afford to execute potentially useful people during this stupid Cchen-Lian situation. Karina suggested I ask you for your help. I wasn't thrilled about approaching you to ask for favors, so it's a good thing you so graciously offered it yourself." Hayden was grinning again, but this time it wasn't the evil grin from before. No, this one looked almost friendly.

So, not only was Oscar not getting arrested or killed, he was being offered a job. "What about Grodin?" he asked, curiosity overtaking his better judgment. The current Master of Whispers would hardly be excited to have Oscar meddling in his business. "Actually, you know what? It doesn't matter right now." While this was all nice and pretty, it wasn't the reason Oscar had come here. "What about Clara?"

"Of course, I'm not going to punish her for this. I'm quite offended you'd think that low of me. But, I guess I understand it."

"You don't exactly give off a merciful ruler vibe," Oscar said. "The worries were mostly hers, though. She begged me to convince you just to have her executed, instead of tortured."

Exhaling slowly, Hayden closed his eyes and tilted his head back to rest against his chair. "Fuck," he muttered.

Oscar could expand on the details but chose to keep his mouth shut. He'd already pushed his luck way too far today. "What about her brother?" he asked carefully. "I know you can't let the whole country believe you've died just to make them release him but, isn't there something you can do for him?"

Oscar watched as the king raised his glass to his mouth but noticed he wasn't really drinking, just taking the tiniest sip to wet his lips. "I'd love to help him out of this mess but right now, I don't quite know how," Hayden answered. "Maybe we can come up with something later." He let out a frustrated sigh as he ran his hand through his hair. "This is really bad timing for Clara. She doesn't even know about Nicolas yet."

A cold shiver ran down Oscar's spine. "What's happened to Nicolas?"

"I'm not sure, yet. He was stationed at the Blackwater outpost." Oscar's brows came together. Why did that name sound familiar? "The one that was raided and destroyed by the Ruthians," Hayden added upon seeing Oscar's confusion.

Well, shit, Oscar thought. So, Clara was about to find out she'd most likely lost both of her brothers? That was going to break her completely.

The king nodded. "Yes, you see what I'm saying? He might be alive. Some of the men survived the attack and are slowly making their way through the forests, trying to get back to our forces. Nicolas seemed like a capable man. But chances are high that he died during the raid and we may never even find his body."

This day was just getting better and better. "Don't tell her. Not now." She'd already tried to drink the poison, there was no telling what she would do when hearing this news.

"I wasn't going to. Not until I know for certain what happened to him." Hayden's eyebrow quirked. "But what about you and your new-found honesty?"

Oscar rolled his eyes. "This was a one time deal. Don't worry. I'll be back to my usual lying, manipulative self, momentarily."

Scoffing, the king shook his head before lowering his gaze to the glass in his hand. Oscar suddenly realized that his comment was a particularly bad move.

Hayden had trusted Oscar enough to offer him a job, to let him in on state secrets. It was a fragile trust at best, but trust, nonetheless. It would be stupid to throw it all away and, while Oscar was a lot of things, stupid wasn't one of them.

Oscar had always been ambitious. He'd wanted to be that someone who pulled on the important strings, who knew every secret. In this palace, he only had two choices – to be 'with' the king or 'against' him. Since the road against would lead straight to the gallows, there really was only one logical choice. To play on the king's team.

Oscar didn't particularly like Hayden but at least now, after passing the king's test, Oscar could respect him. That was more than he could have ever said about King Harold, Karina's late father.

"I'll be back to my lying self soon," Oscar repeated. "Except for inside this room. When we're in here, there will be no lies, you have my word on that. How does that sound?"

"A little too good to be true." Hayden's head tilted in thought as he stared at Oscar for a very long moment. "Alright. You have one chance, Oscar. Don't fuck it up because you won't get a second. If you cross me in any way, we will be having a very different conversation in a very different location. I can assure you that our torture chamber is much better equipped than the one in Vantia."

Oscar had no doubts about that. Feeling like he'd just made a deal with the devil, he raised his glass to Hayden. No more words were necessary. The king repeated the gesture, taking another tiny sip before nodding at Oscar. With the conversation now over, the king lay back in his chair. Lost in thought, he aimlessly stared out into space.

"Hayden?" Oscar asked, feeling strange to be using the king's first name only. Hayden was right about one thing – it was much easier to say without sarcasm than his royal titles. "You don't drink much, do you?"

Come to think of it, Oscar had never seen Hayden drink more than a glass or two, ever. Not during his own wedding, or Oscar's, nor at any of the dinners or banquets held in Levanta while Hayden was there. Even here, in Hayden's home, Clara was poisoning his watered-down apple cider, not wine or something stronger.

The king chuckled, giving him a side glance. "A bit of friendly advice. If you ever see me drunk, run. Especially you. I mean, I can somewhat control myself around most people, even when I'm drunk but... You're such a sleazy bastard, I'd fucking kill you with my bare hands." Hayden was laughing but Oscar could tell that he was being deadly serious.

"Noted," Oscar mumbled nervously. The legend of The Burning Fury might be just a bunch of made-up nonsense but the truth remained. The man in front of Oscar was dangerous in more ways than one. "So, what happens now?"

Hayden set the unfinished drink down on the table and Oscar did the same. He was already starting to feel the effects from just one glass and the day was far from over.

"I will talk to Clara myself, find out what she knows. Not that I don't believe you," Hayden added, his words laced with sarcasm.

"Suit yourself," Oscar shrugged. He didn't expect the king to suddenly have blind faith in him. "Just try not to freak her out even more than she already is."

"Well, look at you. A knight in shining armor, protecting his woman," Hayden scoffed. "Don't worry, I'll be nice. Where is she?"

Now it was Oscar's time to smirk. "Where do you think? I left her in the one place where you actually have to control your temper so you wouldn't simply run over and stab her."

Hayden frowned as he contemplated Oscar's words before realizing what he meant. He leaped from his chair, smashing his fists against the table. "Are you fucking insane?! She just tried to kill me and you left her alone with Karina?!"

"Hayden, calm down!" Oscar didn't move, guessing that it would only provoke the king to attack him. "Do you really think that if there was the slightest chance Clara would hurt Karina, I would leave them together in the same room? Or stick my neck out for her here with your insane Majesty? Trust me, she is harmless now. The only person she could possibly hurt right now is herself and I don't want that, which is why I couldn't leave her alone."

Hayden merely growled as he stormed out of the room. Oscar had to lengthen his stride to catch up. "Aren't Karina's chambers that way?" he asked as he realized the king was going in a different direction.

"There's somewhere else we need to stop by first. And Karina had better be safe, Oscar," Hayden snapped, giving Oscar a furious look. "Because if something happens to her, it won't be just your blood running down these halls."

Chapter 19

Clara couldn't take it anymore. The queen was being so nice to her but the more she tried to calm Clara down, the harder it was to hold back the tears.

How had Clara become such a horrible person? Trying to poison someone? Her father would be disgusted by her. She didn't even understand why Oscar wanted to help her, instead of just dragging her out in front of the king himself. He was going to get in trouble over this. Another life destroyed, all because of her.

Trust me, he'd said. And Clara did. There was something in his voice that made her truly believe he wanted to help her. Something different, that wasn't there before. Besides, what other choice did she have? Clara had nothing left to lose. Oscar, on the other hand, wasn't involved in this mess at all. It would be incredibly unfair if even part of her blame fell to him just because he was her husband. Clara should have gone to the king herself. If only she wasn't such a coward.

Even now, if Clara tried to muster up enough courage to actually go to the king, she wouldn't be able to. The queen wouldn't let her leave the room.

Karina was hiding her nerves well but Clara could feel them pouring out of her anyway. The questioning had stopped, fortunately. Oscar had told Clara to keep her mouth shut and that's exactly what she had been doing, even though it was eating her up on the inside. She wanted to apologize, to beg for forgiveness but Clara doubted there would be enough time for that once the furious king barged into the chamber.

The knock at the door was almost a relief. Clara was frightened of what was to come but the waiting felt even worse. Right, probably not worse than whatever torture they put failed assassins through.

Taking a deep breath to calm herself, Clara placed the empty teacup onto the small table. No matter what was going to happen, she had to protect Oscar. None of this was his fault and Clara simply couldn't bear the thought of dragging him down with her, not after how incredibly kind he'd turned out to be.

The queen opened the door and Oscar entered, an earnest smile brightening his expression. He unceremoniously pushed Karina into the hallway and closed the door behind her before walking straight to Clara. The relief she felt upon seeing him unharmed was almost tangible. When he wrapped his arms around her, Clara's entire body relaxed.

"It's alright," he whispered into her ear. "You are safe, nothing will happen to you. The king just wants to ask you some questions but he isn't angry and he won't punish you. Just tell him the truth and you will be fine."

Clara stared at Oscar, unable to comprehend what he was saying. How could the king not punish her? She'd tried to kill him, she was a despicable human being. Too weak to even take her own life. "But I..."

"You didn't do anything wrong, Clara. You are a desperate woman in a horrible situation and everybody understands that. Including the king." Oscar sounded calm and convincing, there was no trace of doubt in his voice.

The door opened again and a familiar voice hollered, "So, where is the little assassin?" Clara shuddered and tried to stand up but her husband pushed her back onto the sofa.

"Hayden, for fuck's sake," he sighed, moving to stand between Clara and the king.

"Hayden?" The queen raised an eyebrow. "When did you two become so familiar?"

Oscar chuckled. "Oh, we're best friends now." Clara stood up to grab Oscar's hand, desperately trying to figure out how to stop him from getting into even more trouble on her behalf.

"I didn't kill you, Oscar. Don't push it," the king snarled before sighing and closing his eyes briefly. When he spoke again, his voice was much calmer, almost kind. "Clara?"

Clara swallowed around the lump in her throat, fighting the urge to cry, or hide behind her husband like a frightened child. No, this was her mess. "Your Majesty," she murmured. Steadying herself, Clara squeezed Oscar's hand then let go before dropping down to her knees. "I just want you to know I am truly sorry for what happened and I will accept any punishment you decide for me." Somehow, she managed to keep her voice steady with only a few stray tears escaping her eyes. She quickly wiped them away before continuing, "I don't know what Oscar told you but I swear he had nothing to do with it." The king hated her husband and thus, when the new Lady Huxley had tried to poison him, his first thought must have been that it was Oscar's idea.

"Clara," the king addressed her gently. "Stand up, please." Both he and Oscar extended their hands and once Clara had hesitantly grabbed them, they helped her up. The king let go but Oscar pulled Clara into him, putting his arm around her shoulders in a protective manner.

By some miracle, there was only the kindest of smiles on the queen's face. She nodded when Clara looked to her. It didn't seem like either of them hated her. How was that possible?

Karina walked over to a door on the other side of the room, "Why don't we all sit down?" She led them into a spacious parlor, bigger and more luxurious than the one in Oscar and Clara's suite. Also, considerably messier.

Books and parchments overflowed from shelves lining the room. They also covered a large desk stationed over by the window, as well as several of the chairs and a large portion of the floor. "Sorry about the mess," the queen mumbled as she picked up a couple of scrolls from the sofa, adding them to an already dangerously stacked pile on the table. "I was just doing some research."

"And I thought my study was a mess," Hayden chuckled, squinting at a paper covered in tiny letters as he picked it up off the ground. Clara could see several similar ones. They seemed to be hastily written notes of some sort, numbers mostly.

Snatching the paper out of the king's hand, Karina frowned. "That's mine." She quickly collected the other ones as well, carefully putting them away into a desk drawer. "It's just an idea I had," she added, reacting to Hayden's raised brow. "I'll tell you more about it when I have something solid in my hands."

"Alright." The king shrugged before lowering himself into one of the few armchairs that wasn't covered in scrolls. Oscar led Clara toward another cleared sofa and sat down, his arm still tightly wrapped around her. She was grateful for his touch because she had no idea what was happening and her husband provided her with one safe point to hold on to.

"Clara, I'm not angry with you," the king said, leaning forward, studying her body language intensely.

Clara forced herself to withstand his scrutiny, concentrating on breathing and the warmth of Oscar's body next to her. As far as she could tell, Hayden sounded sincere.

"I promise you are safe," he continued, "I just need you to tell me exactly what happened. Every detail you can remember." Sensing Clara's confusion, he added, "How did they contact you? Was it here in the palace?"

Horror crept up Clara's spine, her face losing even more color. If she told the truth, they would know she tried to run away from the wedding. Oscar would find out that she only married him because those men had threatened her brother, otherwise she would be wandering alone through the eastern provinces right now. He was going to be angry, or at least disappointed. Would he leave her? Clara couldn't be alone, especially not now when her whole world was crumbling.

Reaching a resolution, Clara clenched her fists. She didn't want to lie but that didn't mean she had to tell the whole truth. "It was just a few days before the wedding," she said. "I went for a ride through the city. They followed me and waited until there was no one else in sight." There. None of it was a lie.

"You were alone? No guards or an escort?" Hayden frowned, his question making Clara shudder. No, she couldn't tell them.

While she was desperately trying to figure out what to say, Oscar came to her rescue. "She wasn't a prisoner, Hayden. Nor was she marrying someone super important to need extra protection. Why couldn't she leave the palace alone?"

"Hmm. True." Hayden shrugged and nodded at Clara. "Continue, please."

She told them everything about the kidnappers, the abandoned farmhouse they'd taken her to, about her brother, beaten and covered in blood. About the girl who'd given her the gift box. Every detail she could remember, knowing it was not enough. Nobody would be able to find her brother based on this information. Sebastian was going to die.

The queen's maid peeked into the room. "I'm sorry to interrupt but Doctor Shuen is here, asking to see the king."

"Already?" Hayden sounded surprised. "Send him in."

Clara had never met the royal physician but she knew he was from Cchen-Lian, so his darker complexion and distinctly shaped eyes didn't surprise her. Shuen hesitated in the doorway, looking over the messy parlor and the people inside before bowing his head in the king's direction. "My apologies, Your Majesty, but you told me to come see you as soon as I found something out. And I did." He nervously glanced at Clara before looking back at the king, clearly unsure whether he should continue.

"It's alright, you can speak freely here, Doctor." Hayden gave him a reassuring nod and gestured toward an empty chair.

Shuen sat down before pulling the damned vial out of his breast pocket and placing it on the table. Clara closed her eyes, unable to look at it anymore. "Very well," the doctor said, sounding almost excited. "This isn't poison."

Everyone stared at him in surprise. "But..." Clara started, not really sure what she was going to say. The man clearly said it was poison. Or did he? Actually, now that she thought about it, he didn't mention anything about poison or Hayden dying. He just said that the effects weren't immediate. But if it wasn't poison, then what in the Underworld was it?

"Well, I doubt those men would go through so much trouble to give me something to boost my health," the king scoffed. "What is it then?"

"It's not poison in the common sense. It's not designed to kill a person. However, that doesn't make it any less dangerous. More so, actually." Shaking his head, Shuen carefully picked up the vial. "I honestly never thought I would hold this in my hand. It's sort of an alchemical legend." He looked around the room, clearly enjoying the full attention of everyone present. "It's called Lunatic's Tears. It's a special potion, an extremely rare one. As far as I know, there is only one person alive who knows how to make it. I didn't even think he really existed, I thought this was just a myth.

"If you were to drink this," Shuen went on, turning to face the increasingly impatient king, "you would feel sick for a couple of days. Four or five, probably not more. Nothing serious, it would most likely seem like you ate some bad food, a poison would hardly even cross your mind. After that, you would look and feel absolutely fine again."

Shuen paused and Hayden leaned back into his chair, crossing his arms in front of his chest. "Doesn't sound very dangerous. What's the catch?"

The doctor noticed Hayden's patience was wearing even thinner so he stopped with the theatrics. "You'd go crazy," he said matter-of-factly.

Clara felt Oscar's shoulders twitch as he chuckled. "That'd be a big change."

The royal couple frowned at him and Shuen raised an eyebrow. "Trust me, Lord Huxley, it would. The tricky thing about this potion is that it works slowly. At the beginning, nobody even notices something is wrong. The person under its effect slowly starts making more and more irrational decisions, seeing enemies everywhere, and eventually they begin hearing voices, or seeing people that aren't real. Their memories become twisted and scrambled. They become convinced that everyone is deceiving them and betraying them. Even the people closest to them are in danger of being accused of made-up transgressions, if they aren't killed right away, as the potion also greatly boosts a person's aggressive tendencies."

"So, you are telling me..." Karina's voice was shaking as she reached for her husband's hand for comfort. "You are saying that this thing would slowly turn Hayden into an insane paranoiac, the real Burning Fury? And we couldn't do shit about it because anyone who would dare to oppose him would end up dead?" Her fingers tightly squeezed Hayden's. "That he would kill me because he would be convinced I somehow betrayed him?" she asked quietly.

Clara hid her face in her hands. What disaster had she almost brought upon this country?

"Yes, my lady," Shuen answered. "I'm afraid that in a matter of weeks, you wouldn't even recognize the king as the man you know today."

"Wow. That's a brilliant plan." Oscar sounded genuinely impressed and Clara wasn't the only one who turned to him with a scowl.

Chapter 20

"O scar!" the queen rebuked, anger twisting her beautiful face.

Oscar grinned. "What? Karina, you have to admit that who-ever came up with this, and I think we can all agree on who it was, is an amazing strategist. I truly admire the idea behind it, it's flawless."

"That's some seriously messed up perspective," Karina fumed. "You can't just-"

"He's right," the king interrupted her, sending an apologetic smile in her direction. "I can't believe I'm saying this, but the asshole is right. It is a brilliant plan. I mean, if they just killed me then you or someone else would take the throne. Yes, there might be some friction and unrest but Egmont would handle it. The Chancellor has spent more time ruling this country than me over the past few years. But to make me go insane and have me destroy Orellia from the inside? That's just..." He scoffed, staring at the vial in Shuen's hand. "Yes. Brilliant."

Oscar put a hand on his heart, pretending to swoon. "Oh, Hayden, such praise. It makes my heart flutter."

"Savor it, since I doubt I'll be repeating it again, my dear Oscar," the king retorted sarcastically.

Karina sighed, rubbing the bridge of her nose. "I think I liked you two better when you hated each other. So, what do we do now?"

"Don't worry, we still hate each other," Oscar teased. His expression grew more serious as he spoke again, "This is actually very good news. Obviously, you couldn't let the whole country believe you'd died just to save Sebastian Redwood." Clara flinched upon hearing the name. Oscar's fingers gently stroked her arm to comfort her. "But you can easily pretend to have a stomach ache for a few days to convince the kidnappers that Clara has succeeded."

It took a few moments for Clara to realize what Oscar was suggesting. No matter how much it pained her, she had come to terms with her brother dying, simply because she didn't see a way to rescue him. But, if those men truly believed she had given this mysterious potion to the king, they might let Sebastian go. The feeling growing in her chest dangerously resembled hope.

Hayden looked lost in thought for a minute. "I can pretend more than that," he said eventually, his eyes jumping between Oscar and Karina. Both of them seemed to understand what he was saying. Clara only felt more confused.

She shouldn't be in this room. They were talking about conspiracies, politics, and state secrets. What did Clara know about any of that other than being a pawn for their enemy?

"And here I was, afraid that you would punch me for even daring to suggest it," Oscar rolled his eyes.

"Oh, I can still do that if you desire it so much. It would certainly make me happy."

Clara closed her eyes, feeling totally stupid. What was wrong with her? She considered herself a fairly clever person but the thick fog of fear and desperation was clouding her mind.

Clara had a choice. She could remain a perpetually scared little girl that people had to comfort, pat on the back, and park somewhere in a corner with a cup of hot tea. Or, she could start acting like a grown woman, unafraid to think or speak for herself.

There was nothing to fear anymore. The king didn't seem to be interested in punishing Clara and neither he nor the queen hated or despised her. Oscar had helped her and protected her. He might be considered a shady, dangerous person by many, but he'd treated Clara with nothing but kindness. He had definitely earned her trust. Now there was even a small chance to save Sebastian. Everything had worked out better than Clara had hoped. There was no reason for her to cower in a corner, whimpering in despair, anymore.

Clara forced herself to calm down, determined to prove she wasn't just a stupid gullible girl, easily manipulated by the enemy. That she wasn't a weakness. Oscar's weakness. This was his playground. Like he'd told her before, words and secrets were his life, his passion. If Clara ever wanted him to truly respect her, she needed to step up and play his game.

For the first time in weeks, Clara felt her thoughts return to normal.

Good, she nodded inwardly. Now, what were the people around her saying? It felt like putting together a puzzle with several important pieces missing, secrets Clara had no clue about. But now that she could think straight again, she could at least get a rough idea.

"You want to pretend that you drank the potion and then slowly go crazy over the next few weeks. You hope to draw out whoever orchestrated this, so they unveil their plans." Her voice was quiet. She didn't even realize she was vocalizing her thoughts at first, not until all the faces in the room turned to her. Clara shifted her weight nervously, making Oscar drop his arm from around her shoulders.

Nobody interrupted her, so she continued along her stream of thought, "But there must be more to it than destroying Orellia. What would anyone gain from that? Except, maybe they don't want to destroy us, just weaken us so they can...attack?" With the highest military commander insane and the rest of the country's leadership in disarray, an invading force would have a much easier task. Even so, Orellia would be a formidable enemy, which didn't leave many options as to who might be behind all this. "Cchen-Lian?" Clara asked hesitantly, shooting a look at Doctor Shuen.

The king's angry growl had her flinching. "Seriously, why the fuck did I ever believe you could keep your mouth shut?"

Clara blinked in surprise, fear quickly creeping back into her mind. What the hell was she doing? She should have just kept quiet and stayed out of things she didn't understand.

Oscar gently touched her hand, intertwining his fingers with hers. When she reluctantly looked up into his face, he seemed astonished. Only then Clara realized that the king's words weren't aimed at her but rather, at her husband.

"Hayden, I didn't tell her anything," Oscar said, unphased by the king's outburst. A corner of his mouth curled up as he looked at Clara before turning to the king to calmly endure his stare. "She's just smart like that. Some women are. You should know, you married one as well." His praise made Clara feel better than she would dare to admit.

Hayden mumbled something angrily but as the queen grabbed his hand again he quickly calmed down. "Clara, I hope you realize that whatever is said here today is a secret, not meant for anyone outside of this room."

"I understand, Your Majesty. I will not disappoint you again." The Redwood family had always been loyal to the throne. Clara couldn't even imagine how ashamed her father would have been of her if he'd found out she'd tried to poison the king.

"So it's true?" Doctor Shuen sat the vial down on the table, visibly shaken. "Emperor Odi?" He stared at the tiny bottle with fear evident in his eyes.

Hayden sighed. "Yes, Doctor, it is. And I'm afraid you will have to choose where your loyalty lies."

Clara shivered. It was not like the man could decide to be loyal to the emperor now, not with all the secrets he knew. Would the king have him executed? Imprisoned? Clara didn't know much about Shuen, only that he had been a member of the court for a very long time. Still, he did come from Cchen-Lian. It was his home. It must have been difficult for him to choose between the two countries.

"Your Majesty," Shuen bowed his head to the king, "I made that decision a long time ago. I understand you questioning my loyalty in this situation but I'm not sure what I can do to alleviate your suspicions. As you know, I don't have any ties to the empire anymore and it has been a very long time since I considered Xi-huan my home."

The queen spoke before Hayden could respond. "I don't think that's what the king meant, Doctor. I believe what he was saying is that it is hard to go against your own country." There was sadness in her voice and Clara felt Oscar's fingers press down harder for a split second as he let out an almost unnoticeable sigh.

Of course, it made sense. Technically, both of them had betrayed Levanta by making a deal with the enemy. They might have done it to protect the people from war but it still must have left a painful pang in their hearts. In a clumsy attempt to comfort her husband, Clara ran her thumb over the back of his hand, earning a fleeting, yet sincere smile.

"Then there is no problem, Your Majesty." Shuen proudly squared his shoulders. "Orellia is my country."

Karina nodded at him then gave her husband a worried look. Hayden, are you sure you want to do this?"

"Of course I don't want to do this," the king sighed. "But what I want doesn't matter. You said it yourself Karina, it's not about us or what we want. These people have been so many steps ahead of us all this time. We finally have a chance to get ahead. I don't really see another option here." Shaking his head in resignation, he turned to Shuen, "So, how exactly does this thing work? How fast would I begin to lose my mind?"

The doctor took his time to answer. "Truth be told, I'm not really sure. Lunatic's Tears are considered a myth by most people, there aren't any scientific studies describing the effects. I could try to contact-"

"No," Oscar interrupted him harshly. "If you start poking around, somebody will surely notice, and we lose the element of surprise. No one outside this room can know about the potion. You'll just have to wing it," he smirked at the king. "Oh, and I want to hear it."

Hayden gave him such a furious glare Clara shuddered in fear. "Lord Huxley is right, yet again," the king gritted his teeth. "Gods, I really hope you will be as useful as you claim to be because I'm starting to regret not slitting your throat the moment we met."

Oscar seemed to be enjoying poking the king but Clara didn't like being caught up in the middle.

"Don't worry." Oscar's tone was serious now. Most likely, he realized he was dangerously close to crossing the line between friendly banter and actually making Hayden mad. "I might be an asshole but I gave you my word. Plus, Orellia is my country now too, isn't it?" There was a slight hint of sarcasm in his words but the smile he gave to Clara was honest and warm.

The king rolled his eyes but didn't respond, turning to Clara instead, "I'm afraid this goes for your brother as well, Clara. If those men truly release him, and you have to keep in mind there is a chance they won't, you will have to lie to him. You will have to say you gave me the potion. You can act surprised that I only got sick and didn't die but under no circumstances can you tell him what we've talked about today. Can you do that?"

Clara thought about it. Could she do that? She wasn't a great liar at the best of times, and deceiving her brother like that wouldn't be easy. Why did the king want her to lie? Wasn't Sebastian one of his most loyal people? He certainly wouldn't divulge Hayden's secrets.

Oscar gave her a reassuring nod and Clara nodded as well. It wasn't like she could say no to the king at this point. "I can do that," she said with a conviction she didn't feel.

"How are we going to know what they are planning?" the queen asked, clearly not happy with the plan. "I mean, Hayden pretends to go insane, fine, but how does that help us? If they truly intend to invade Orellia, the fact that our king is not really crazy won't do us much good when there is an army at our border."

Shuen scratched his head, clearly realizing just as Clara had, that he shouldn't be part of this discussion. "If I may?" he spoke nervously, waiting for Hayden's approving nod. "I know I can't be certain of this, but I believe there must be someone here in the palace who knows all about the effects of the potion. You see, a person under the effects of Lunatic's Tears becomes easy to manipulate. If someone was to stand behind the king and whisper the right words into his ear at the right time, they could somewhat control his actions. Especially, if the goal is to cause mayhem in Orellia. I imagine someone will try to carefully pit the king against his most trusted advisors."

"Are you telling me that when I start to 'exhibit signs of madness'," Hayden's fingers mimicked quotation marks to amplify the sarcasm in his voice, "someone will approach me and tell me to get rid of Lord Egmont or General Warren?"

The doctor nodded. "Yes, that would be the way to take full advantage of the potion. When your mind is clouded by its effects, all it would take is a simple seed of doubt. Say, if you heard a casual mention of the queen exiting someone's chambers, kissing the man goodbye..."

"I'd kill him." Hayden's eyes narrowed and Clara noticed him glaring in Oscar's direction.

Shuen sighed, avoiding the king's gaze. "I'm afraid, Your Majesty, you would kill them both. And that it would not be pretty."

The king swallowed roughly, visibly shaken by the idea. He pulled on Karina's hand, making her move onto his lap, then tightly wrapped his arms around her. "I'd never do that," he whispered, his voice shaking.

"It wouldn't be you," Karina soothed, gently stroking his hair.

Clara felt it inappropriate to witness such an intimate moment between them. Oscar tensed a little before forcing himself to relax again. Close friends? No way, Clara thought. There was more between Oscar and the queen than friendship.

"By the way," Karina smirked at the king, "if you are really willing to go through with this stupid plan, you are going all the way. I mean, you aren't drinking that," she frowned at the vial on the table, "but I'm certain the doctor can give you something that is actually going to make you sick for a couple of days, so you won't just be pretending."

Hayden groaned. "I hate you," he said, mock-glaring at her. "All of you. When I'm insane, I'm having you all executed."

Clara knew he was just trying to lighten the situation with his very inappropriate joke but even so, she shuddered.

Chapter 21

When the meeting finally ended and Clara and Oscar left the queen's chambers, she was relieved almost to the point of tears. Oscar never let go of her hand, even when they were out in the hallway, but he did loosen his grip just enough so that Clara could pull away if she wanted to. Which she definitely didn't. Despite her decision to stop being a scared little girl, Clara was so exhausted that she wanted nothing more than to cuddle up to Oscar and relax in his arms. How pathetic.

Now that she had seen Oscar in his usual environment, it became clear that a man like him would have no interest in a whiny girl. And what else had Clara been ever since they'd met?

She had to stop. Clara decided to be strong in front of Oscar from now on. His patience with her certainly had its limits and Clara dreaded being alone.

That was the main reason she agreed when Oscar asked if she would like to go for a walk in the gardens. Clara didn't really want to go for a walk. She would have very much preferred to return to their chambers, curl up in one of those big cozy armchairs in the parlor, wrap herself in a thick blanket, and get lost in a book from the library. After all the stress she'd been through, Clara wanted nothing more than to forget about the real world for a couple of hours.

Her husband didn't seem shaken or worried by the recent events. In fact, Oscar seemed almost excited. As if a powerful foreign empire attempting to turn King Hayden into a murdering lunatic was wonderful news.

Perhaps that was a harsh judgment. Oscar had struck some sort of deal with the king. That must have been the reason for his excitement. There was still some bitterness between the two men when it came to Karina, but other than that, they seemed almost friendly toward each other. It was that strange kind of friendship between two men where they keep bickering and constantly insulting one another, but it was friendship, nonetheless.

It was a warm, beautiful day. The alluring smell of flowers permeated the air, birds chirped, and leaves in the trees high overhead rustled in an occasional breath of wind. Much better than being chained to a wall in the dungeons, Clara thought to herself, smelling the putrid stench of gore while listening to screams of pain. Clara knew that. She realized she should be happy and grateful, but she was so tired all she felt was emptiness.

As they reached a small lake, Oscar headed straight for the secluded pebble beach. With a mischievous grin, he picked up a stone before skillfully skimming it across the water. The pebble bounced several times before finally sinking.

Clara chuckled, amazed by discovering yet another surprising facet of her husband's personality. A large log was conveniently lying sideways on the beach so Clara sat down on it, hugging herself in a vain attempt to stop her body from trembling.

"Is everything alright, Clara?" Oscar asked, crouching down in front of her. "Are you cold?"

Most of the shaking was probably caused by all of the exhaustion and stress Clara had been through, but there were a few goosebumps rising on her forearms. "A little," she admitted.

Oscar took off his jacket and gently draped it over Clara's shoulders. It was warm and smelled of him. Clara gratefully wrapped it around her body.

The pebbles creaked as Oscar walked back to the water's edge, picking up a couple of stones on his way. Clara watched on with a smile, surprised he was enjoying a children's game. The Oscar in front of her seemed like a completely different man from the one who'd praised the enemy's plan to turn the king into a madman. But which was the real Oscar Huxley?

"I know," he grinned upon noticing Clara's smile, "it's childish and immature. But it's what I do when I need to sort out my thoughts."

Another stone bounced off the water's surface. Once, twice. It sank on the fourth or fifth skip. Oscar pouted in discontent, causing Clara to sigh. He was distracted because of her. She was nothing but trouble.

Resting her elbows on her knees and her chin against her hands, Clara watched as Oscar continued to throw one pebble after another. The plopping sounds were so calming that Clara didn't even realize she was dozing off until her chin slipped off her palm and she jerked awake.

Naturally, it didn't escape Oscar's attention. He dropped the remaining stones. "You didn't really want to come here, did you?" he asked, smiling softly. Clara avoided his look, which was an answer on its own. "Clara," he said, crouching and grabbing her hands, "you are allowed to say no to me."

"I didn't want to cause more trouble," Clara whispered sheepishly, still not looking at him. She wanted him to hug her but was too afraid to ask. What a way to stop being scared. Sighing, Oscar rested his forehead against their joined hands without saying anything.

"I'm sorry," Clara said, tempted to kiss the top of his head. "Can I ask you something about the...about that thing?" Was she even allowed to talk about the secret plan?

After carefully checking their surroundings to make sure there was not another living soul nearby, Oscar nodded. "Of course."

"If those people already have someone in the palace, why did they need me?"

Clara was worried that Oscar would be annoyed by her stupid questions, but he just smiled at her. "You really are a smart one," he praised. "Firstly, the man on the inside is just Shuen's theory, which may or may not be true. The potion would work regardless, and planting an unwaveringly loyal person in the king's proximity is not an easy task, trust me on that.

"Secondly, you are the perfect scapegoat. Poisoning the king is a dangerous task. Whoever does it, is likely to get caught. You Clara, have not one but two possible motives. You hate the king for marrying you off to a creepy foreigner. And, if that wasn't believable enough, there's always me. I'm known to hate the king and I'm a known manipulator. Everyone would believe that I'd twisted your mind and convinced you to kill Hayden for me. Not a shadow of suspicion would be cast to the people who were really behind it."

Clara took a moment to think about his words. It sounded logical, albeit a bit cold. But, Clara had wanted an answer and Oscar had given her one without being condescending. In fact, he treated her like his equal.

Another question, unrelated to this secret conspiracy mess, was burning on her tongue, but Clara wasn't sure whether it was appropriate to ask. Or if she even wanted to know the answer.

Oscar gave her time to digest but when he noticed she had finished mulling his words over, he looked at her nervously. "Can I ask you something personal? You don't have to answer me if you don't want to but," he paused upon seeing her chuckling, "What are you laughing at?"

"Sorry, I was just thinking about whether I could ask you something personal as well."

"Well, my lady, I already told you, you can ask me anything you want." The stones creaked as he sat down on the ground in front of her. When he spoke again, his tone was serious. "Why don't you start? I think I have a fairly good idea of what you want to ask me."

Clara hesitated. "I don't have to..."

"Is it about Karina?" Oscar looked up at her through his long lashes. "Are you sure you want to know the answer?"

No, she didn't. "Yes, I do. You said you are like a brother to her and I thought it was strange. The normal thing to say would be that she's like a sister to you." It wasn't really a question but it implied one clearly enough.

Oscar scoffed as his eyes drifted up to stare at a few stray clouds in an otherwise clear blue sky. "How about that, twice in one day. Who would have thought?" His eyes found Clara's and there was pain in them, mixed with a hint of trepidation and sadness. Clara immediately regretted asking about the queen. Not because she was afraid of the answer but because she didn't want to hurt Oscar.

"It seems like you've caught me out on one of my half-truths. No, she's not like a sister to me. Maybe before, when she was a little girl, but for the past few years..." He sighed and shook his head, leaving the rest of the sentence unfinished. "But she never felt the same way and I've accepted that. Now she loves Hayden and she is happy." His eyes closed and he lowered his head. "Does that answer your question?" There was raw pain in his voice and Clara hated herself for that.

She slid down from the log to kneel in front of him, gently touching his hands, scared that he would pull away from her. "I'm sorry, I didn't mean to-"

"It's alright." He grabbed her hands, his thumbs sliding over her skin. "I'd gotten so used to being in pain every time I see her that I was really surprised to find it's not so bad anymore. Not since I met you."

Clara wasn't sure what to think about that. She only knew about romantic love from the fairy tales and stories she'd read. Her husband had just admitted to being deeply in love. Just not with her. Her first reaction was disappointment, pain, even anger. But how could she blame Oscar for that? He'd known Karina his entire life. He'd only met Clara a few days ago and so far, she'd been nothing but trouble. Her fingers found the nearly healed cut on his palm where he'd cut himself during their wedding night to 'prove' they'd consummated their marriage. He cared, even when he didn't have to. And, judging by his words, he clearly had at least some feelings for her..

His sad chuckle interrupted her thoughts. "Damn, sorry," Oscar looked almost ashamed, "that was a completely inappropriate thing to say to a woman, let alone to my wife."

"No, I asked. Thank you for being honest with me. And...for everything you've done for me, especially today."

He slid one hand out from hers and carefully placed it on her cheek. "I want to keep you safe. And happy. It seems like I will have to do a better job, on both fronts."

"You're doing an amazing job." Clara had to blink away tears. She was the consolation prize but it didn't matter to her, at least, not now. "What was it you wanted to ask me?"

Oscar shook his head. "It's not important."

"No, ask me." After him being so honest, and Clara had no doubt that what he'd said was the truth, it felt only fair to tell him whatever he wanted to know. Hopefully, it wouldn't be about sex.

A curious look settled across his face as eyed her thoughtfully, "Alright. What were you really doing alone in the city a few days before our wedding?"

Clara froze, swallowing roughly. She had almost forgotten about Hayden asking her that and how she'd struggled to answer. The king hadn't noticed, but of course, her husband had. He'd been holding her hand the whole time, feeling her shudder in fear. And he was so damn smart. She lowered her head, not sure what to say. She didn't want to lie, but if she told the truth...

"Were you trying to run away?" His voice was soft, his hand still on her cheek, thumb gently stroking her skin, but he didn't force her head up. Clara let out a resigned sigh and nodded, afraid that her voice would betray her if she tried to speak. Oscar didn't pull away as she'd expected, he didn't move at all. "Don't worry, I understand. Do you still want to?" His words were careful, hesitant.

"No!" She didn't have to think about that. Looking into his kind brown eyes she desperately tried to figure out what to say. "I...I was scared and I didn't know what to do. It felt as if…I wasn't in control of anything in my life, everything was decided for me by someone else. I just wanted…"

Oscar cupped her cheeks and wiped away the tears that escaped her eyes. "To be free," he finished her sentence. There was a sad smile on his lips as he looked at her with compassion. "I wish I could help you with that."

"Oscar, I have felt more free during these last few days with you than I have in the last few weeks. Maybe even years. No, I don't want to run away. I'm sorry that I tried." It wouldn't have solved anything anyway. How long could she survive out there alone?

His lips now curled into a playful grin. "That's good to hear. And really, don't worry about it, I absolutely understand." The pebbles under him creaked again as he wriggled uncomfortably, causing Clara to shift her legs as well. Oscar chuckled as he stood up, pulling Clara up with him. "Not the most comfortable place to have such debates. So, what would you like to do now, Clara?"

"I think I'd just like to go back to our chambers." She was more tired now than before. Dissecting her feelings like this was exhausting. "But…" A deep breath. No being a little girl anymore. "Do you think you could hold me?"

A pair of strong arms wrapped around her, pulling her closer to Oscar's chest. "Anytime," he whispered into her hair. "You aren't angry that I love someone else?"

"Angry?" Clara scoffed and rested her head against his chest, reveling in the heat that emanated from him, enjoying his scent. "It's not like you can control it. If it makes you feel any better, I don't think I love you either. I mean, I would know, wouldn't I?" She didn't really have a clue what love felt like, the tales she'd read always described it as a strong, beautiful feeling. It would probably be hard to miss.

She felt Oscar's shoulders twitch as he laughed. "Yes, you would know. And I think that as long as you don't hate me, we'll make this work, somehow."

Yes, Clara agreed silently. She closed her eyes, putting her arms around his body, instantly feeling calm and safe.

Chapter 22

C lara propped herself up on one elbow, watching her husband sleep. It was early morning, the sun had only just begun to lighten up the sky over the eastern horizon, but Clara was too restless to fall asleep again.

It had been three days since that secret meeting. Three days since the king had 'fallen ill'. It was the worst kept secret in the palace. Nobody spoke about it openly, but everyone knew and everyone avoided going anywhere near the king's chambers since he was, quite understandably, much more irritable than usual.

Three days and not a word from Sebastian's kidnappers. Clara didn't expect them to release him right away but it was taking so long she had begun to lose hope. Had it all been for nothing?

Oscar did his best to distract her. They spent a lot of time lying in bed or cuddling on the sofa. He even had Friska start a fire in the hearth to make the parlor feel cozier. They talked endlessly about everything and anything, getting to know each other better.

But, since Clara's husband had struck a deal with the king, he was often busy reading through scrolls and parchments and meeting up with people, mostly outside of the palace. He never invited Clara to any of those meetings, didn't even talk about them with her, but she respected it. The more people who knew about his secrets, the less power they had. And the more danger they brought.

When he was in town, or busy working, Clara filled her time with reading. However, thoughts of her brother kept intruding into her mind, distracting her. She didn't exactly have any friends she could talk to, especially not now. What would they even talk about? The girls would want to hear all about Clara's wedding, especially her wedding night. Or they might gossip about the king's sudden illness. Clara didn't want to lie, so she preferred to stay out of sight.

She also wanted to avoid her mother, who for some reason still lurked the palace hallways instead of returning home to the Redwood mansion. Clara suspected it was because Sophia wanted to talk to her, hoping to 'casually' run into Clara and get some information about her husband. Something to brag and gossip about, or maybe give her unruly daughter some more of her condescending, frightful advice.

Oscar wriggled in his sleep, mumbling something unintelligible, a smile appearing on his face. Clara wondered if he was dreaming about the queen. It would be foolish to think he'd dream about Clara, dangerous to let hopes like that take root in her heart. But it was enchanting to watch him like this, all the same, it almost felt as if she was intruding on his private moment. A couple of tresses of his long hair were covering his face so Clara carefully brushed them away so he wouldn't wake to them tickling his nose.

Ever since their wedding night, Oscar had been the perfect gentleman. He'd never tried to touch her in a sexual way, merely hugging her, holding her hand, or gently placing his palm on her cheeks or arms. He hadn't tried to kiss her and although Clara was grateful for his restraint, there was a hint of disappointment she didn't quite understand.

The kiss they'd shared after Oscar had gifted her the bow had made Clara think of her mother's words more often than she would care to admit. Truthfully, she had felt a lot of things when their lips had met, but none of them were bad. None of them had made her shudder in fear or repulsion.

Quite the contrary. It had made her want more, even though Clara wasn't really sure what 'more' would encompass.

She liked when he hugged her. His strong arms made her feel safe and protected. But, more and more, she found herself wondering how it would feel if his fingers (or even his lips) touched her skin in other places. The only thing she could base her thoughts on was the terrifying memory from their wedding night when he'd kissed her neck. But...the fear she'd felt back then had nothing to do with Oscar. It was all in her head, all those frightening images her mother had planted in there. Oscar had said it wasn't true and, unlike her mother, he had never lied to her.

Unfortunately, Clara had no idea how to test her new theory. If she asked Oscar to kiss her again, would he think...? He would want to do more and Clara certainly wasn't ready for that.

Perhaps she could kiss him again? Some place where she could move away if things got too... Too what? Gods, she didn't even know the proper words for these things! Oscar had admitted he'd been with plenty of women yet Clara couldn't even think about matters of sex, let alone talk about them.

Careful not to wake Oscar, Clara sat up in bed, still watching his handsome face. Her hand touched her own lips, the memory of Oscar's tongue in her mouth sending a strange tingling through her body. How does something so weird feel so good?

Her fingers slid lower, finding the spot on the side of her neck. That's where he'd kissed her, or at least he'd tried to, before she'd started crying. Clara closed her eyes, trying to remember what his lips felt like on her skin, but that memory was wrapped in such a thick layer of fear that it was useless right now.

She moved her hand down, tracing her collarbone to the small dip at the base of her neck. Would it feel good if it was his hand? His finger sliding down to the lace hemline of her satin nightgown? His lips, even? The idea was strangely enticing.

Her fist clenched. What the hell was she doing? She should be worried about her brother, her king, her country, not fantasizing about her husband touching her. No matter how intriguing that fantasy was. With a sigh, Clara opened her green eyes, finding herself staring straight into Oscar's brown ones. She'd been so busy with her own thoughts she hadn't even noticed him waking or sitting up beside her. A wave of shame washed over her, she felt as if she had been caught doing something highly inappropriate.

Oscar smiled warmly but there was a tiny spark of amusement in his eyes. No doubt, he had a fairly good idea what she'd been thinking about. Clara didn't think she could blush any harder, it felt as if all the blood from her body was running through her cheeks right now.

"Good morning," he greeted, the corner of his mouth rising up in a roguish grin. Clara mumbled something in response, it probably didn't sound like good morning though, her eyes quickly darting down to avoid his. Oscar stretched his arms out with a long yawn. "Gods, I'm hungry. I'll just wash up quickly before breakfast. Or would you prefer to stay in bed?" The twinkle in his eye clearly hinted that he didn't just mean to sleep.

Shaking her head vigorously, Clara jumped out of bed and grabbed her long robe to cover herself. Oscar chuckled behind her as he headed to the bathroom. "Clara?" he called out as he disappeared through the door. "Just tell me if you need my...assistance with anything."

He was gone before she could respond. Not that she was brave enough to say anything. What would she even say? 'Hey, I want you to kiss me, but just kiss me. I don't want anything more right now. Maybe ever.' Yes, she could see him being thrilled to oblige, not. But, maybe...?

Grabbing a brush, Clara tried to fix her hair into a presentable shape and chase her wayward thoughts from her head. Both, unsuccessfully. The spot on her neck where he'd kissed her was throbbing, aching for a new memory to replace the earlier, fear tainted one. Clara tapped her finger on the spot, examining herself in the small mirror.

Her wild mane was a mess, as always. Maybe a skilled maid could actually make it into a proper hairstyle, instead of the braid or bun Clara usually resorted to so that it didn't get in her way? Oscar had said she could get one if she wanted to, but now that Clara was privy to so many secrets, she was paranoid of letting anything slip in front of a stranger.

"You look beautiful." For the second time today, Oscar had caught her completely lost in thought. She was facing away but glanced at his reflection in the mirror.

He watched her expression as he moved behind her. His finger rose up to carefully rest next to Clara's, covering the strangely sensitive spot on her neck. She blinked in surprise but didn't pull away, lowering her hand to make space for his. Oscar's finger trailed up and down, gently sliding across her skin, sending shivers down her spine. Oscar stepped closer until Clara could feel her back resting against his firm chest.

The finger disappeared from her neck, almost prompting Clara to voice her disappointment. But she didn't need to, as she felt one arm being wrapped around her waist, gently holding her in place while Oscar's other hand brushed her hair to the side. He was being very clear with his intentions and kept watch in the mirror for any sign of fear or disapproval.

But Clara was too fascinated by what was happening to protest right now. Cautious anticipation was building inside her. Yes, there was a hint of fear, but also excitement and a whole lot of curiosity. So much so, that she felt herself smiling as she actually nodded, giving Oscar permission to continue.

Oscar smiled in return before lowering his mouth to Clara's neck. It was nothing like his first attempt. The touch of his lips to her skin was fleeting but, for some reason, felt like it was setting her skin on fire. He traced his lips up behind her ear and then back down, the trail of kisses ending at the crook of her neck.

Clara closed her eyes, the raw emotions almost overwhelming her. She focused on her breathing, as the short, shallow gasps didn't seem to be providing enough oxygen for her lungs. She drew in a sharp breath when his teeth gently grazed her skin, feeling more than hearing his chuckle as he lifted his head away.

"As I said before," he whispered into her ear, "it's more than enjoyable for both. Let me know if you need my help with anything else, darling wife."

Clara opened her eyes just in time to see Oscar grinning widely as he stepped away from her, probably heading out into the hallway to ask Friska to start breakfast for them. Which was something Clara should have already done as lady of the house, instead of indulging in her fantasies. He'd said he was hungry, hadn't he? Now he was forced to wait even longer for food thanks to her. Some wife she was turning out to be.

She should...what should she be doing? It was hard to concentrate as her neck still tingled and burned along the line where his mouth had teased and grazed. Not from pain but from something dangerously resembling desire. Worryingly, the pulsation was mirrored by a similar sensation somewhere deep inside her, lower down.

How silly was it that all she wanted now was to call him back in to do it again? And maybe not stop just at her neck this time? It was definitely more than just enjoyable, Clara thought as she had to sit down, her wobbly legs refusing to carry her weight a moment longer.

Chapter 23

Oscar was away for the rest of the morning, leaving Clara alone with her thoughts to torment her. She soon became claustrophobic in the confined space of their chambers and, since there was nobody here to vent to, she chose the next best thing. Dressed in old breeches, a simple white shirt, and a well-worn jacket, her hair tightly braided and pinned around her head, safely hidden under a flat cap, she grabbed her bow and used the servants' entrance in the bathroom, hoping to sneak out of the palace unnoticed.

As she rushed through the corridors she tried very hard not to think about the last time she had snuck out this way.

The shock of seeing Oscar standing in front of her while she'd been holding the vial of poison was carved so deeply into her soul that Clara doubted she would ever be able to forget it. It was the kindness in his eyes, void of any anger, that had stopped her from drinking the potion herself.

He didn't hate her. He'd helped her, cared for her, protected her. What did it matter if he didn't love her? Love was something so perfect and idealistic that it seemed unobtainable by normal people. Plus, going by the look on Oscar's face and the sound of his voice when he talked about the queen, love sounded quite painful.

Clara lingered around the training grounds, watching Hayden's soldiers. Some of them practiced the same movements over and over, sweating despite the rather cold breeze, an indication that summer was finally coming to an end. Others were busy sparring in groups or pairs, trying to hit each other with wooden sticks.

One might laugh at them for playing with children's toys, but the sheer brutality along with the aggressive determination in their movements left no doubt that this was not a game. This was the world of men she knew. Dominant and brutal, using sheer force to get what they wanted. Her father might have been kind to her but at his core, he was the same. A warrior at heart.

How different Oscar was from these men! Calm, even when being insulted to his face. Not grabbing for the hilt of his dagger at the first sign of trouble. Oscar had even openly admitted he knew nothing about weapons. He was kind and understanding where others would be annoyed, hostile, and aggressive.

Clara didn't even want to think what would have happened if Hayden had forced her to marry a man like that. Surely, there were some important generals in Levanta who would gladly take a young Orellian bride as a consolation prize for losing the war. She shuddered, moving away from the training soldiers. There was no need to torture herself with such ideas.

The main archery range was a much quieter place, even when busy like today. Clara liked to sit and watch the archers practice, guessing which ones would be any good, taking note of any mistakes made. She would never approach anyone to correct them, naturally, but it was useful seeing others do something wrong, a reminder not to repeat the same mistakes herself.

There were about forty men actively training and a couple more just idling about. One of the men who stood watching was leaning against a railing not far from Clara, his blond hair in stark contrast with the dark uniform he was wearing.

"OY! Levantian!" Clara flinched when a voice boomed behind her.

The blond man turned around and rolled his surprisingly blue eyes. "That's Lieutenant Levantian to you, you ugly bastard. What do you want?"

"The general wants to talk to you."

Just as the second man, who really was ugly thanks to a thick scar running across his face, walked past Clara, she quickly shuffled away, not wanting to attract any attention, especially from ranking officers. It wasn't forbidden for squires and other civilians from the palace to use the training grounds, but Clara wasn't a squire. And even though Oscar had said he didn't mind people finding out she was practicing archery, it still wouldn't be very pleasant to have these men scold her for being there.

Fortunately, the small abandoned corner where she usually practiced unseen, was still abandoned. Clara could finally clear her mind and forget about her troubles for an hour, or maybe two. She wasn't really sure how much time had passed when the trees at the side of her range rustled. Clara was just ready to fire an arrow but carefully lowered the bow down upon hearing the noise, not wanting to shoot some random passerby by accident.

"Larkin?" a quiet female voice called as a young woman exited from the tree line. The woman froze, startled to see Clara standing there with an arrow nocked before continuing, "Oh. I'm sorry. I was supposed to meet someone here."

She was wearing a very simple blue dress which had Clara guessing she was probably one of the palace maids. It wasn't the dress, or the girl's possible status that caught Clara's full attention, though. The maid seemed to have a rich mane of very curly dark brown hair, not unlike Clara's. But, unlike Clara's simple braid, this woman's hair was intricately braided into a complex, stunning hairstyle. A style Clara could never even imagine, let alone recreate on her own head.

She returned the arrow back into the quiver and smiled politely at the maid. "No problem. I should probably get going anyway." The muscles on her shoulders and back ached terribly. "Hey, can I ask you a weird question?"

"Of course, my lord," the maid bowed her head respectfully, blushing at the attention. She had no idea who Clara was, and there was always a chance that a random boy on the training grounds might be the son of someone important, thus the formal address.

Clara walked closer to get a better look. "Who did your hair?"

"Uhh..." The maid gaped at her. Clara realized, a little too late, that coming from a boy, it was indeed a very strange question. "I I did it myself, my lord." Strange or not, the servants could get into trouble for not answering a direct question and the young woman seemed to know that.

Before Clara could ask the maid's name, a voice she recognised from earlier sounded from behind. "Mina?" A warm smile appeared on the woman's lips as Clara turned to see the blonde officer she had seen on the training grounds earlier. It looked like Clara was interrupting a date.

"Don't mind me, I'll just collect my arrows and get out of here." She walked over to the target, carefully plucking the arrows out one by one, taking care not to damage any feathers. Before she returned to pick up the rest of her belongings, the two had already hugged each other and kissed goodbye. The young woman headed back toward the treeline. The officer, Larkin, that's what she'd called him, watched her with a sad smile. Clara hesitantly approached to pick up her jacket. "I'm sorry. I was just leaving, you didn't have to-"

He looked at Clara and shook his head. "It has nothing to do with you. I thought I would have time but I just got assigned extra work. I only came here to let Mina know I have to head back soon." Sighing, he gave the treeline one more longing glance and turned to face Clara, sizing her up properly. "You're pretty good for such a young fella. Ever considered a career in the military?" One of his brows quirked in amusement.

"No, that's not for me." Clara hid her own amusement over such an offer. "You are a Levantian, right?"

Larkin rolled his eyes. "Yes. I'm sorry."

"Why are you apologizing?"

The man let out a sad chuckle. "A lot of folks around here seem to have a problem with that, so I thought I'd save some time by apologizing up front."

His sadness was sincere,but Clara could tell he wasn't actually sorry for being Levantian. He seemed to be a likable man, for a soldier. "I don't really mind your nationality. I'm actually..." She managed to swallow the words 'married to a Levantian' before they escaped her mouth. What a way to keep her disguise. "I've been around one a lot lately. Lord Huxley?" Clara phrased the last words as a question to see if Larkin knew her husband, slightly ashamed. Was she really poking around to see what other people had to say about Oscar?

"Ah, Lord Huxley." The Lieutenant didn't sound overly excited. "I heard that sleazy bastard got himself a young and pretty wife. How fair is that? We bled on the battlefield and got nothing yet he caused the whole war and received a woman as his reward." His words were bitter. He sighed, shaking his head, "Please, don't tell him I said that, I don't want to get into trouble again." Clara nodded absentmindedly, thinking over his words. Oscar truly wasn't popular, even with his own people. "Well, it was nice meeting you..." Larkin hesitated.

"Alec." Clara promptly gave him the name she'd used in the tournament last year.

The Lieutenant grinned as he bowed his head. "Alec. Perhaps you can stop by some time and show those idiots under my command how it is done. Later." His fingers went up to his forehead in a parody of a salute and he turned to leave. A strange fellow, to be sure, but Clara liked him.

As vain as it sounded, she couldn't stop thinking about the maid's hairstyle, wishing she knew how to do something that pretty herself. Then again... The answer was so obvious that Clara didn't know how she'd missed it. She was thinking about getting a personal maid, wasn't she? If this woman was interested, perhaps Clara could hire her. But first, Clara would ask Oscar to check on the young woman's credentials. It would be quite ironic if she accidentally brought a spy into their home.

Home. This was probably the first time Clara had thought about their chambers as being hers in that way. It was different to the feeling she'd had growing up in her family mansion, but it was definitely beginning to feel like home. Her own place, where Clara could be herself, without being bothered by her overly controlling mother or nosy brothers. Where she could be free.

Of course, it wasn't just Clara's place as she shared it with Oscar, but that no longer bothered her. Her husband had proven to be a truly modest roommate. As long as he had a place to sleep, warm water to wash himself in the morning and food on the table, Oscar couldn't care less about where or how he lived.

The quiet footsteps approaching didn't interrupt Clara's thoughts. It was only upon hearing a familiar voice that she suddenly looked up. "I had a feeling I'd find you here."

Dropping everything she was holding, Clara leaped forward. "SEBASTIAN!" she cried out, throwing her arms around her brother. Sebastian groaned painfully as she pressed against his ribs but Clara didn't loosen the hug. She needed to make sure he was real and not just a figment of her tortured imagination.

"It's me, Clara," Sebastian soothed, gently stroking her back. "I'm alive, I... They let me go. Clara?" His voice was trembling. "Why did they let me go?" Clara shook her head, desperately wanting to avoid that topic, but there was no escape. "What did you do, Clara?" her brother whispered.

Until now, Clara hadn't fully realized that by following Hayden's orders, keeping this secret from her brother was going to make her an assassin in his eyes. Someone who'd truly poisoned the king. Could she really make her brother believe that? "I couldn't let them kill you," she replied quietly, hiding her face in the folds of his shirt.

"Oh Gods, Clara, you didn't... Is that why the king is sick?"

Sort of, yes, Clara cringed internally. She hadn't really thought this through. What should she tell him? "I think so, but...it didn't work, Sebastian. The king is getting better. I...nothing happened."

"Nothing happened?" he repeated slowly, pondering over the words.

Clara held her breath, dreading the conclusion he was going to reach. Sebastian had always been loyal to the king. It would be quite ironic if he was the one who dragged her in front of Hayden and accused her of an assassination attempt. However, it might solve the problem of her lying to him. The king would just tell Sebastian the truth and Clara would no longer have to lie. Still, she would feel betrayed. Shouldn't family come first?

Sebastian took a deep breath before repeating, "Nothing happened. If the king recovers and...nobody suspects you? You haven't told anyone?" Clara didn't trust her voice so she just shook her head. Being a liar was better than being a murderer. But only by a little bit. "Alright," Sebastian said, nodding to himself as if he'd just come to some internal agreement, "Let's just keep this between us. We will never speak about it again. The least I can do is protect you from any fallout, since I failed so horribly at everything else."

"Sebastian, you haven't failed at anything, you- Wait!" Clara paused upon realizing something, her hands reaching for his, "Your fingers!" Sebastian quirked his eyebrow as she checked both of his hands, touching each finger just to make sure. They were all there. Clara laughed in relief, "Thank gods! They...they sent me a finger with your ring on it, I thought..."

Sebastian frowned. "They did take my ring away but no one cut me, thank the gods. The finger must have belonged to some other poor soul." He placed his hands on Clara's shoulders, waiting until she raised her eyes to him. "But, you're wrong, Clara. I did fail you. I'm so sorry. I swear that if I'd known that Hayden was going to marry you off to that..." a snarl escaped him as he unsuccessfully searched for a polite word, "that 'man', I would have stopped him. Lord fucking Huxley, of all the stupid Levantians!" Sebastian stepped away, his fists clenched in anger.

Surprised by his sudden outburst, Clara didn't respond. She was still trying to understand how he'd so readily accepted her 'murder attempt'. But, perhaps he was just glad to be alive.

Sebastian glared in the direction of the palace before returning his gaze to Clara. "Did Huxley hurt you? Because if he did, then I don't care what the king says, I'll-"

Clara placed a hand on Sebastian's chest. "He didn't hurt me," she interrupted him. "In fact, he's been nothing but kind to me. I know the Levantians were our enemy but they aren't anymore. I mean, the king married their princess and we are one country now. Don't you think we should put this hostility aside?"

"He's been 'kind' to you," Sebastian repeated mockingly. "You are so young and naive, my little sister. That man is a snake. Every word that comes out of his mouth is a lie. You need to be careful around him. In fact," his face brightened up with a smile, "why don't you come back home for a while? Come for a visit and stay for as long as you want. He can't exactly drag you away from your family home."

Clara's excitement from seeing her brother alive and mostly unharmed, although he did look pretty beaten up, was short-lived. Yes, she was glad Sebastian was back. But, had it really taken less than an hour for him to start meddling with her life again?

The offer to take refuge in the mansion wasn't as tempting as Clara would have expected. Not anymore. She wasn't going to give up her first true taste of freedom only to be belittled by her brother and pushed around by her mother again.

"Sebastian," she replied calmly, "I'm married now. I can't exactly run away from my husband." She didn't add 'and I don't want to'. Sebastian didn't seem like he would understand that.

"Of course, you can," he growled, before heaving a relentful sigh upon noticing her determination. "I don't like this. Or that," he added, pointing at the bow Clara had dropped. "Sister, you need to be careful with this little hobby of yours. If Huxley ever finds out...it will give him more reason to put you through hell."

Clara's eyebrows shot up. Seriously? Bad reputation was one thing, but Sebastian seemed convinced that Oscar was some sort of devil incarnate. Clara should probably defend her husband's honor but, knowing her brother, it was a waste of energy. "Don't worry, big brother," she said instead. "I can take care of myself."

"Naive as always," Sebastian scoffed. "I have to go talk to the king right now. If anyone asks about these," he pointed to the bruises on his face, "our ship was kidnapped by pirates. That part is even true." Wearing a sad smile, he gave Clara a brief hug before turning to leave. "And Clara?" Sebastian glanced back after taking a few steps. "Thanks for saving my life."

Hmm, now that was new, Clara thought. Sebastian had rarely ever thanked her.

Clara felt a little guilty for choosing Oscar, a practical stranger, over her own family but could anyone really blame her for not wanting to go back to a place where nobody would respect her? Oscar might have been a villain in her brother's story but in Clara's, he was nothing short of a knight in shining armor.

Chapter 24

Karina deeply regretted forcing Hayden to drink whatever was in the concoction Shuen had prepared for him, to make him actually sick instead of just pretending to be. The poorly king hadn't complained, nor did he hate her for it. In fact, he'd suffered in surprising silence, even when he was throwing up or curled up in bed with stomach cramps.

He'd tried to send Karina away at first, but she'd swiftly refused, choosing to stay by his side the whole time. She'd made it her mission to help him with tasks such as washing himself, forcing him to drink at least some water and trying to distract him with talk about her childhood.

She'd made sure the maids came into their chamber often. A different one each time. Word needed to get out that the king was very sick. And soon it did. Karina found herself watching the people around them, often wondering who might be the spy sent to direct Hayden's upcoming insanity toward the right people. Honestly, she was turning into a crazy paranoiac herself, feeling like there were very few people she could trust.

Hayden was asleep for the moment, his greasy hair stuck to his sweat laden forehead. The effects of Shuen's mixture were slowly wearing off, but he was exhausted by it all. Now that he'd finally managed to fall into a light sleep, Karina didn't dare move, staying completely silent and still so as not to wake him up. She knew why he hadn't complained and it made her feel even worse. He was taking it as a punishment. From her.

Karina had disagreed with the plan. It was a good plan, there was no doubt of that, but she was worried what it would do to Hayden's mental well being. He already hated how people believed him to be the cruel and evil Burning Fury. It was a necessary lie but one that Hayden struggled not to believe himself, sometimes.

Now that it was no longer just about spreading rumors or looking fearsome, but actually becoming the crazy and aggressive man people already thought he was, Karina was worried. The problem was not that Hayden would suddenly enjoy his new found role as a cruel and crazy ruler. It was that the guilt of having to behave so irrationally would slowly eat at him from the inside, turning Hayden bitter and angry at himself. Desperate.

Karina clearly remembered their wedding night fiasco. Hayden had been so laden down with the guilt of his perceived crimes against Karina that he'd spiraled out of control. His intense self loathing and despair that was buried just under the surface was still fresh in her mind and she certainly didn't want a repeat of that night.

Hayden knew Karina was against the whole plan from the start. He thought she was mad at him for agreeing to go through with it and because of that, he believed she was taking out her anger on him by making him suffer for days with a real illness, instead of just pretending to be unwell.

Did he really believe Karina would be so mean and vengeful? That hurt. Sure, initially she was angry at their plan and *maybe* her original intention, when she'd blurted those words out, was partly due to a petty desire to punish him. But then, it quickly became all about making the whole story as believable as possible. If they were intending on going through with this ludicrous plan, then they'd better do it properly.

If only Karina could convince Hayden she wasn't still angry at him. But, every time she tried to talk to him about it, he just smiled, closed his eyes and rolled over, looking so weak and fragile she kept her mouth shut.

The door creaked quietly before a head peeked inside the room. Karina, immediately recognizing the familiar features of Captain Lamar, head of Hayden's guards and his best friend, gestured for him to be quiet. He nodded and waved for her to come outside.

"Someone's here to see Hayden," he announced as she entered the large parlor, closing the bedroom door behind her.

There was always someone wanting to see the king. "He just fell asleep," she shook her head.

"Those clams hit him pretty bad," Lamar smirked. "Why did he even eat them? He hates those things."

Karina shrugged, not wanting to add more lies to the pile. Lamar knew nothing about the plan, which was another thing she'd deeply disagreed with. Yes, she understood the need for secrecy, but Lamar was Hayden's closest friend, they'd known each other since they were kids and he was loyal to a fault. Plus, as Hayden's personal bodyguard he was going to be one of the first to deal with the consequences when the king 'went crazy'.

The captain sighed. "I think he would want you to wake him up for this. One of his ambassadors is back from the eastern continent. It looks like he took one hell of a beating on his way home," Lamar chuckled. "Just ask Hayden if he wants to see him. His name is Sebastian Redwood. He's actually the brother of Huxley's bride."

Karina barely managed to hide her surprise. The plan was working. The men who'd given Clara the potion must believe that the king had drunk it and let their hostage go. She already knew Hayden was going to talk to him, but she had to play her part as the unsuspecting wife in front of Lamar. Nodding her reluctant consent to his request, Karina headed back into the bedroom.

Hayden looked so peaceful as he slept that Karina had half a mind not to wake him and send Redwood away until later. But Lamar was right, even though he didn't know the real reason. Hayden would definitely want her to wake him up. She sat down on the bed next to him and gently brushed the hair back from his forehead.

He groaned painfully, squinting in her direction before his features softened as he recognized her. "Waking up to your beautiful face is just as lovely this time as it was the first time," he smiled, his eyes closing again.

"Ah, then you aren't fed up with me yet? That's good to hear," Karina chuckled. "Hayden," she touched his shoulder to stop him from falling asleep again, "Sebastian Redwood is here."

It only took him a second to shake the sleep off after realizing what those words meant. "So, it's working," he whispered, eyes widening in surprise. There was relief in his expression, one that suggested that all the suffering he'd just gone through wasn't in vain. There was also fear because now he had to keep up the ruse.

"It seems so," Karina replied quietly. "Do you think he's going to tell you?" She was quite curious about what Redwood would say to the king. Everybody claimed he was loyal but was he loyal enough to the king to betray his own sister? To have her imprisoned or executed for poisoning Hayden?

Hayden shrugged and scrambled out of bed. "I honestly have no idea, but I can't wait to find out." He had to lean against the bedpost to keep his balance but there was determination in his eyes. "Take him to the parlor and call Naa'ri in here, please, I need to put on some clean clothes."

After summoning Hayden's dark-skinned elderly slave, Karina left their chambers to greet Sebastian Redwood. He truly looked like he'd been in a terrible fight. Although, based on what Clara had said, it was more of a beating than a fight. No fingers were missing though, it seemed that was just a ruse from the men who'd taken him.

"Your Majesty," he addressed her politely, bowing deeply then wincing in pain as he bent forward.

Karina invited him inside and they exchanged a couple of pleasantries, but he was clearly not interested in talking with her. Most likely, he considered her just some pretty little thing Hayden had brought home from his travels, like a potted plant one puts in a corner to admire. He seemed to know his way around Hayden's parlor pretty well. He must be quite a frequent and welcome visitor, Karina realized upon seeing him holding up a glass he'd just poured himself.

"Sebastian." The king walked into the room, still looking pale and tired, but at least he was able to stand on his own two feet unaided. He smiled at Redwood and gestured for him to sit down in one of the chairs.

Sebastian bowed to Hayden before sitting, sighing in relief when he found a comfortable position. "I do apologize for disturbing you, my lord, I heard you have fallen ill. But you did order me to come to you the moment I returned."

"It was just some bad food," Hayden dismissed with a wave of his hand. "I'll definitely be staying away from clams from now on. What happened to you? You look like you've been in quite a fight."

Karina studied Redwood's face as Hayden mentioned the 'food poisoning'. There was no reaction. The man was a perfect actor. And it was clear he had decided to lie to the king to protect his sister. Karina wasn't sure whether she should admire or despise him for that.

"I'm afraid I have some bad news, my lord. The Seagull was attacked by pirates on our way back. I was the only survivor. They probably intended to ask for a ransom. It took me a while, but I managed to escape their captivity and return home." A pretty lie, somewhat believable. Some of it might have even been true.

"Damn," Hayden growled. "Those pirates are really becoming a problem. We're going to have to do something about them soon. What about the negotiations in the east?"

Sebastian hesitated, glancing at Karina with a slightly raised eyebrow. Yes, in his world a woman probably had no place being in the room while important things were discussed. Asshole.

Some of the bitterness must have shown in Karina's expression because Hayden smirked at her before turning back to Sebastian. "You can speak freely in front of the queen." Redwood was a skilled diplomat but there still was a trace of surprise on his face before he quickly masked it with a polite smile.

Hayden called for Lamar and gave him a silent order, after which the captain swiftly left the room. Karina frowned, having no idea what was going on but quickly schooled her expression, not wanting Sebastian to know she wasn't clued in. He and the king discussed the situation on the eastern continent for a few minutes. Although the topic wasn't very interesting to Karina, she listened and occasionally engaged in their debate, just to piss off Redwood. She really didn't like the man and it looked like the feeling was mutual.

The conversation was interrupted by someone knocking on the door. Clara and her mother entered the room at Hayden's invitation, making polite curtsies, both looking surprised to see Sebastian, startled even. Clara fell short of looking truly shocked to see her brother in the room so Karina guessed he had probably already visited her to corroborate their versions of the crime before going to the king.

"Ladies, thank you for coming," Hayden smiled at them, pointing to the sofa. He waited until the women sat down before continuing, his tone turning solemn and serious. "I need to tell you all something and I'd hate having to repeat myself."

Karina tried not to let confusion show on her face, yet again. What was this about? It couldn't be something very important, Hayden would have told her.

Hayden sighed, running a hand through his hair. "Look, I'll just say it how it is. We are having problems with the tribes in the northern mountains and one of our bigger outposts there was completely destroyed. It was the one where Nicolas was stationed." He paused to let his words sink in.

Sebastian caught on first, leaning forward, his brows furrowed. Then Sophia Redwood gasped, her hands flying up to her mouth. And Clara... Clara wore a similar tortured expression to the one she'd had when she was waiting for Hayden to cast his judgment over her assassination attempt. She was shaking her head in disbelief and fear. Karina could almost hear her thoughts, *No, this is not happening. Saving one brother only to find out the other one is missing, possibly dead?*

A sharp pang of pain pierced Karina's heart. She wanted nothing more than to rush to the girl and hug her, but Clara was still afraid of Karina and probably wouldn't accept it. Karina expected her mother to console her, but Sophia ignored her daughter completely. Instead, she threw herself at Sebastian, leaving Clara alone on the big sofa, looking every bit a lost, frightened child.

Unable to bear it, Karina sat down next to the girl and gently touched her hand, letting Clara decide whether to accept comfort. Clara sniffled, peeking up into the queen's face. Whatever she found there, and Karina made sure there was nothing but a kind smile for her to find, convinced Clara that it was alright, so she grabbed hold of the queen's hand, squeezing it tightly. Karina sighed, putting her free arm around Clara's shoulders, feeling her tremble. At least, this was something tangible she could do in this horrible situation.

Hayden nodded to her in appreciation and took a deep breath before continuing. "We don't know for sure what happened to Nicolas, yet. There are survivors scattered in the woods around the outpost that are still trying to make their way toward our forces. They're moving slowly, having to avoid the enemy. It's quite possible Nicolas is alive. But..."

"But it's more likely he died in the battle," Sebastian finished the sentence, patting his mother on the shoulder. Clara drew a sharp breath and moved in closer to Karina who hugged her tighter.

"Damn. That's not the news I was expecting to come home to," Sebastian sighed before standing up, pulling his mother up with him. Sophia looked like only the presence of the king prevented her from wailing in despair. "Come on, Mama, I'll take you home. The king will let us know when there is news." Hayden nodded and Sebastian turned to his sister, his tone losing any hint of sincerity. "Come, Clara."

Karina bristled. Did he seriously just command his own sister like a dog? Clara herself, didn't seem to be very appreciative of his tone, frowning at him while trying to hold back the tears.

"Clara?" The queen spoke calmly and sincerely, "Would you like to stay here with me for a little while?" These people might be the girl's family but Karina didn't like either of them one bit. From what she remembered of Sophia at Clara's wedding, the woman wasn't exactly the epitome of motherly love. Quite the opposite. And Karina had already decided for herself that Sebastian was an asshole.

Clara shook her head. "I just want to go home."

Karina sighed. She couldn't exactly stop her from going with them.

"Come then," Sebastian commanded. "I'll have the carriage readied." He was gently holding his mother around her shoulders, supporting her as she weeped. As they headed toward the door, neither of them spared a look in Clara's direction.

Clara stood up. For a moment, Karina considered ordering her to stay just so she wouldn't go with them. Then she realized the girl wasn't following but rather, standing with her arms crossed in front of her chest, frowning at her brother. "That's not my home anymore, Sebastian. You take care of Mother, I'll be fine here."

Sebastian's face flashed with anger. Karina could have sworn he was about to snarl at his sister, but he quickly curbed his temper in front of Hayden. "As you wish," Sebastian returned through gritted teeth.

Seriously? Clara had one fucked up family. How did she grow up to be so normal? Sebastian and his mother left without another word, causing a raised eyebrow even from Hayden. Karina waved him back to bed. He'd done enough damage to the girl for one day.

"If you really want to go home, I'll walk you," she offered sincerely.

Clara lowered her head in respect, maybe even shame. "You don't have to, Your Majesty."

"I know I don't have to," Karina quipped, grabbing the girl's hand and leading her to the door, "but I want to." They walked through the hallways, side by side. Clara was lost in her thoughts while Karina tried to figure out what she should say to her. "I really hope your brother will be alright." Her choice of words wasn't ideal but it was better than nothing and the sentiment was there.

Clara sighed, stopping by one of the large windows to lean against the sill. From this vantage point, they could see one of the beautiful inner courtyards laid out in front of them. In the center, a large fountain show-cased sculptures of mythical water creatures, each one sprinkling out wa-ter. Skillfully cut rose bushes surrounded a couple of comfortable benches and several luxuriously dressed people strolled idly, chatting. Gossiping probably.

"He was always an excellent fighter," Clara said after staring out of the window for a while. "If anyone could survive something like that, it would be him. It's just..." She trailed off, hiding her face in her hands.

"Too much to handle for one woman?" Karina finished Clara's sentence and stepped closer to put a hand on her shoulder. Poor girl, being struck by one disaster after another. "Clara, if you ever need to talk to anyone, you can always come to me. And I'm not saying that as your queen but as a woman who has had her own fair share of disasters."

"Your Majesty, I couldn't possibly..."

Karina rolled her eyes then interrupted her. "Yes, you could. I'll order you to, if it makes you feel better." She smiled, letting Clara know it was just a joke. A frustrated sigh escaped Karina's lips at the girl's continued hesitation. She didn't want to come off desperate but it looked like she was going to have to admit to needing a companion herself. "I would actually appreciate it. Gods know, I could use someone to talk to myself. And please, just call me Karina."

Clara looked astonished by Karina's frank confession, before smiling through the tears filling her eyes. "I'd be honored, Your Ma-Karina."

Chapter 25

O scar looked forward to returning home. He was surprised at realizing how quickly he'd started calling those few small rooms he shared
with Clara, his home. And more surprisingly, it wasn't the opportunity
to finally have a few moments alone to gather his thoughts that Oscar was
looking forward to the most. No, he was actually looking forward to seeing
his young wife.

Clara had allowed him to kiss her neck this morning and it seemed that
she was interested in doing more. It was a real struggle not to push her, but
Oscar's patience was finally starting to pay off and he wasn't stupid enough
to let his lowly desires screw it up.

In truth, Oscar could have her right now if he wanted. She wouldn't
fight him. He could even make her enjoy the act. If it were any other
woman, one of his numerous short-term acquaintances, Oscar wouldn't
hesitate. But, he was supposed to be with Clara for the rest of their lives.
That seemed like a very long time, especially if he were to spend it with
a woman who was angry with him over forcing her into something she
wasn't ready for.

More importantly, Clara was different. She meant something more to Oscar. What it was, he wasn't entirely sure, but it made him extra protective of her. He didn't want her to get hurt. It was a good thing that Oscar had a ton of self-control which he'd earned during his many years of crawling through the mud and shit of politics and espionage.

He was bringing her a rose, had stolen it from the gardens, actually. Oscar felt silly carrying a flower through the palace hallways but Clara looked like the type of romantic soul who would love such a gesture. It was a small price to make her happy, he thought as he removed the thorns from the long stem, occupying his hands while he sorted through the day's thoughts.

Something strange was going on in this city. Someone was keeping tabs on Oscar, and not very discreetly. Often, Oscar found he'd picked up a shadow as he walked through the streets of Ebris, engaging with random people and scouting for information. Oscar didn't feel threatened by the unknown player's actions as they hadn't made any aggressive moves, yet. It felt more like a cautious 'hello' to a new colleague.

Oscar let it be, certain that the local player would contact him whenever they were ready. He was curious whether they were connected to the plot to poison Hayden and whether Oscar could somehow use this connection to his own advantage, but he had to wait. These things couldn't be rushed.

He entered his chambers through the parlor, expecting to find Clara curled up in an armchair, wrapped in a blanket and reading one of the many books from the library.

Clara was there, but before he could charm her with a smile or present his oh-so-precious gift to her, he noticed something was wrong. Instead of a book in her hands, Clara was standing by the fireplace, holding a glass containing the remnants of a dark brown liquor. Her eyes and nose were both red and puffy, indicating she'd been crying earlier. No tears were rolling down her cheeks now as she stared blankly off into space and continued to sip from the glass.

Oscar dropped the rose on a table as he rushed over to his wife. "What happened?" he asked, concerned. After gently prying the glass out of her ice cold hands, Oscar pulled Clara into his arms.

"Sebastian is back," she sighed. Her voice lacked emotion and her body was stiff but she leaned into his embrace when prompted and rested her head against his chest.

That was good news, it meant their plan was working. But Clara didn't seem to be happy about having her brother back. Confusing. "Isn't that a good thing?"

"It is."

Clara had mentioned she didn't exactly like her brothers but still, Oscar would've expected a little more excitement over the news. There must have been more to her melancholy mood. He waited patiently, Clara trembling in his arms.

"Nicolas is probably dead," she whispered, fresh tears soaking into Oscar's shirt.

Oh, fucking perfect, Oscar thought. "Hayden told you?" he growled. What an asshole. They'd agreed not to tell Clara anything until they knew what had happened for certain. However, as Oscar thought about it, the king probably hadn't had much of a choice. While he could easily keep secrets from Clara and her mother, he couldn't withhold such an important fact from Sebastian, the current Lord Redwood.

"Yes, he..." Clara paused. "You knew about it?"

Oh, crap. Oscar had let his guard down for a moment only to screw himself over. "Yes." He had promised not to lie to her, hadn't he?

Her eyes narrowed and she stepped back. Oscar didn't try to stop her. Her voice broke as she asked, "You didn't think about telling me? You said you weren't going to lie to me and I trusted you. Sebastian was right, I'm just a naive stupid girl."

Oscar had expected the anger but the pain he felt from her words was clawing its way through his chest. "Clara, I wanted to protect you." Gods, the way she looked at him, all that pain in her eyes...

It wasn't the first time a woman had looked at Oscar like this, it actually happened quite a lot, but this time it almost caused him physical pain. It was seriously unfair. He really was just trying to protect her. A tiny spark of anger over that fact flared in his soul and he grabbed onto it. Anger was better than pain.

How dare she make him feel like this? For once, he was trying to do the right thing and this is what he got in return?

Clara must have noticed the change in his expression because she flinched, looking afraid. She moved toward the door of the bedroom but Oscar stepped in her way. Startled, she stepped out of his reach. "Leave me alone," she whispered.

Oscar froze. What the fuck was he doing? This wasn't him. He didn't get angry easily, he'd even told her that. So, why the hell was he blocking her in right now? Yes, anger was better than pain. For him. Not for her.

"I'm sorry," he murmured, forcing himself to calm down. Wow, all that desire to be the 'perfect man' for his woman and he'd kept it up for how long? Five whole days? Such an achievement. "Clara, will you please hear me out?" It was difficult not to sound desperate. "I promise, I will leave you alone after this." He needed to at least explain himself.

Her eyes followed him cautiously as he moved away from the door to give her the option to leave if she really wanted to. Her expression was stern but she nodded in response to his question. That was a start.

"I only found out about Nicolas when I spoke to Hayden, after you..." Oscar paused. It was probably not the best time to remind Clara of how she'd tried to poison the king. "You were in a bad place and I didn't want to make it worse by telling you that your other brother is missing. I mean, you nearly drank the poison, I was worried that..." Gods, how stupid was he? This was not a good topic either.

Oscar pinched the bridge of his nose. "Look, I swear it was not my intention to deceive or manipulate you. I was only trying to protect you." He felt a strong desire to smack himself. So much for his gift of the gab. This could go down as the worst speech he'd ever made.

When Clara didn't respond, Oscar sighed, "I'm sorry I didn't tell you. And for scaring you just now." That was something he regretted deeply. He didn't usually get this emotional. "Thank you for hearing me out. Don't worry, I'll sleep somewhere else tonight." Even though he had no idea where.

He grabbed his cloak before heading for the door. The rose on the table sent a pang of sadness through his heart. This evening certainly hadn't worked out as he'd hoped.

Seeing Karina right now would only add to the pain Oscar already felt, but where else was he supposed to go?

She joined him on one of the balconies overlooking the gardens. "So, what did you do this time?" she asked before Oscar had even opened his mouth.

That was a good question. What had he done? "I don't know. Clara is angry with me for not telling her about Nicolas. But I was just trying to keep her safe."

This was all way too complicated. The problem was, Oscar had no idea how to deal with conflict in relationships. In the past, he would just wave the woman goodbye and move on to one that wasn't angry with him. He couldn't exactly do that with Clara. Nor did he want to.

"And you blame her for being angry?" Karina's eyebrow shot up. "You lied to her. Of course she's angry."

Oscar could point out that technically, he hadn't lied since they'd never spoken about that topic but he knew to keep his mouth shut. Karina could see through his bullshit.

Leaning against the balcony railing, she shook her head. "Why are you here with me when you should be at home comforting her?"

"I don't think she wants me there." No, Clara certainly hadn't looked like she'd wanted Oscar around.

To his surprise, Karina laughed. "Are you sure about that? Do you know what she said after Hayden told her about Nicolas? She said she wanted to go home."

A deep sigh escaped Oscar. Of course Clara would want to go home. Was she even going to be in their chambers when he returned?

Karina noticed his expression and nodded. "Yes, that's what I'd thought too, but when that asshole brother of hers tried to drag her away, she insisted on staying. Because that wasn't the home she meant."

Oscar's brows furrowed as he tried to decipher the meaning behind Karina's words. Did Clara really consider their modest chambers her home? Did that include him as well? But Oscar had screwed up. Everything he'd been trying to do was swept away in one moment of anger. Clara didn't trust him anymore and Oscar wasn't sure whether he had the strength and patience to start over.

"Oscar," Karina addressed him, "relationships are not a one-time thing. They are very much repairable. No matter what you said or did, you can work through it together. If you swallow your pride. And I'm sure you could, if you wanted to."

His pride? That was never the issue. "I don't want to hurt her," he admitted.

"Then don't hurt her, dummy." Rolling her eyes, Karina punched his shoulder. "Goodnight."

She turned to leave. "How about some advice?" Oscar called after her.

"Go to your wife, you idiot!"

That was easier said than done. Oscar didn't think Clara wanted him around right now. Plus, it was really late. She was most likely already asleep.

Since Oscar was homeless for the night, he decided to spend some time in the library and do some research. He didn't want to disturb Clara but needed a particular notebook from his desk, so he quietly crept through the parlor to his study.

After finding what he was looking for, he glanced up, freezing on the spot. Clara was standing in the door, wrapped in a thick warm robe, her eyes red. She had been crying again, this time probably because of him. Some husband Oscar was. She didn't look angry anymore, just sad and sort of lost.

Oscar held the notebook in front of himself as a shield. "I'll just take this and go. I didn't want to-"

"I'm sorry," she interrupted him, her voice shaking.

It looked like she was about to start crying again and Oscar had no idea what to do. Did she want him to hold her? Or was she still afraid of him? How the hell was he supposed to know? He took a few cautious steps toward her. "You have nothing to apologize for, Clara. I was the one who screwed up."

"No." Clara shook her head and Oscar stopped, unsure whether she was responding to his words or his attempt to move closer. "You were trying to protect me, I understand that. I'm still disappointed that you didn't tell me but...I shouldn't have gotten angry. I'm sorry. Will..." she swallowed roughly and blinked a couple of times, "will you please stay with me?"

Gods, Karina had been right. Oscar was such an idiot to leave Clara earlier. He quickly crossed the distance between them and pulled her into a hug, hugely relieved when her body relaxed into his arms. "Of course I will," he whispered into her hair, furious with himself. "Clara, I didn't leave to punish you, or whatever it is you are thinking right now. I thought that was what you wanted."

"It was." She sighed. "And it wasn't."

How very helpful. "Alright, I'm not going to pretend I understand." Women were such complicated creatures.

"I don't really understand it either," she chuckled, hiding her face in the folds of his shirt. "But that's how girls work."

Oscar still felt an intense pang of guilt in his chest as he remembered the look of utter betrayal in Clara's eyes upon finding out he'd kept her brother's misfortune a secret from her. This feeling was new to Oscar and very uncomfortable. He silently vowed to learn from his mistake and be upfront and honest in the future.

Chapter 26

C lara didn't think she had any tears left but apparently her supply was unlimited. She'd cried over Nicolas being missing. She'd cried over Oscar betraying her and then again over him abandoning her when she needed him. And now, more tears were streaming down her cheeks as he held her in his arms. Yes, she'd wanted him to leave earlier. She'd been so damned angry upon finding out he knew about her brother's disappearance and hadn't told her. Is that how he imagined honesty worked?

When she'd seen that flash of fury in his eyes, her anger was quickly replaced by fear. Oscar Huxley didn't get angry easily. He didn't bat an eye when being insulted or threatened, not even by the king. And yet, Clara had managed to make him mad just by saying a few words.

It was the rose.

After Clara had watched Oscar leave, standing in the middle of the room, angry, lost, and abandoned, she'd looked at the table and found it there. He'd brought her a rose. Not for a special occasion, just because he'd wanted to. He'd even made sure to remove the thorns. Only then, Clara truly thought about what he'd said and realized how unfair she had been to him.

Clara remembered how desperate she'd felt after everything had happened with the king. She was sure Sebastian was going to die. If someone had told her back then that her other brother might be dead as well... No, she wouldn't have been able to handle it. Oscar had known it, tried to protect her, and all he got from her in return was ingratitude. And then he was gone.

Being back in his arms was a huge relief. They were both quiet, neither of them wanting to break the silence first. "Thank you for the rose," Clara whispered eventually, feeling like she should be the one to say something. "It's beautiful."

"You're welcome." His voice sounded strangled. "I'd give you a hundred more, proper ones not stolen from the gardens, if it would fix this mess."

Clara shook her head. It wouldn't be the same. "I don't need you to give me anything."

"Then what should I do?" His shoulders twitched in a desperate chuckle. "I told you, I have no idea what I'm doing. I've never been in this situation before."

That was interesting. Hadn't he said he'd had lots of women? "You've never had a fight with one of your girlfriends?" Perhaps this was all Clara's fault. Maybe she was simply insufferable.

"Of course I have. I just..." He wriggled uncomfortably and Clara looked up to see his face. He seemed ashamed. "I never tried to fix it. If the woman was angry with me, I simply...found one that wasn't."

"Oh. And you can't do that now."

Oscar gave her a tender smile. "I think I could. But I don't want to."

Sure, he could. Clara hadn't even considered that. While it wasn't exactly gentlemanly for a man to have a mistress, it wasn't uncommon and it certainly wasn't something he'd be scorned or punished for. But, he said he didn't want that.

"Karina said that relationships are repairable but...I don't know how to repair things. I've always been the type of person who gets a new toy when the old one breaks."

Yes, Clara remembered him saying he wasn't a good guy. "A scoundrel," she smirked. It made a lot more sense now. "You went to talk to the queen?" Clara wasn't sure how to feel about that bit of information.

"I..." Oscar paused, biting on his lip. "It's not what you think." What exactly did Clara think? "I just don't have anyone else here to talk to. I didn't go there to complain about you or anything, I... Crap," he sighed, "I fucked up again, didn't I?"

Clara took a moment to organize her feelings before shaking her head. "Don't worry about it. She's your friend, I don't have a problem with that. Actually, I think she's my friend now too. I'm not really sure how that happened."

"Yeah, she does that," Oscar laughed and lowered his head to Clara's. It looked like he wanted to kiss her but stopped himself at the last moment, resting his forehead against hers instead. Clara knew he was just being careful with her, not wanting to force her into anything she didn't want to do but still, she felt a tiny pang of disappointment.

She wanted to stop being a scared girl, didn't she? Without second guessing herself, she rose up on tiptoes, tilted her head back and let her lips briefly touch his. She pulled away before Oscar could react, leaving him a little stunned. "Uh..." His expression was one of total confusion. "It's probably a stupid question but...does that mean we're alright?"

"Yes." Clara wasn't exactly a relationship expert either but she was tired of the tension between them. This seemed like an almost too simple method to end it but it was worth a try.

Oscar squinted at her with suspicion. "Really? Hmm. I was expecting something much worse." A playful grin formed on his lips. "If I get a kiss every time I make you angry, maybe I should do it more often."

"Next time you'll get an arrow," Clara mocked him.

"I'll try to keep that in mind," he chuckled before his tone grew more serious. "Did your brother really call you naive and stupid?"

Clara sighed. "He didn't say stupid." But it was quite clear from his words.

"Wow, I don't even know the man and I already don't like him."

What a coincidence. "Sebastian doesn't know you either and seems to hate you with a passion." Oscar quirked his eyebrows in amusement and Clara continued, her smile matching Oscar's, "Yes. He seems convinced that you are going to make my life a living hell. He even offered me shelter in the mansion and suggested I ran away from you. Can you believe he actually apologized for letting Hayden marry me off to you? He's never apologized to me for anything!"

"You didn't want to go home?" Oscar was smiling but his tone was slightly nervous.

Clara shrugged and rested her head against his chest again to savor his scent. "It doesn't feel like home anymore. I got a hint of how they'd treat me there today and... Let's just say, you've spoiled me with all the respect and freedom." She looked up at him with a warm smile. "I don't want to go back to being nothing."

"Clara, you aren't nothing..."

"Fine, maybe not nothing." She couldn't find a better fitting word. "But I'd just be a child there. Ordered around, patronized constantly and barely tolerated by either of them. This," she gestured to the room, "might not be a true depiction of a home but...I feel safe here. Like I can be myself, not just someone's idea of who I should be. Sorry," she chuckled awkwardly, "I'm not making much sense again, am I?"

Oscar caressed her cheek. "I think I understand you perfectly. I feel the same way. I've never been so open with my thoughts and feelings to anyone before."

Clara wanted to ask whether that included Karina, but decided to keep her mouth closed. Some things were better left unsaid.

"I do consider this my home," Oscar continued, "and if there's anything I can do to help you feel the same, just let me know."

"I think I just need some time. But I'm happy here. With you." The last two words were barely more than a breathless whisper. Clara didn't even mean to say them out loud but they didn't escape Oscar's attention, his face lighting up in a boyish grin. "We should really go to bed," she said before he could respond.

Oscar nodded. "Go ahead, I'll just wash quickly then join you."

After Oscar had disappeared into the bathroom, Clara let out a long sigh of relief. Neither of them knew what they were doing when it came to relationships but they'd managed to work it out between them. If this whole situation wasn't so painful and frightening, it would be laughable. Oscar was the one with all of the experience with women and yet, he'd expected her to know how to resolve their fight.

Clara actually felt calm enough to revisit her thoughts from this morning, remembering how she'd stood in front of her mirror and let Oscar kiss her neck. Sure, her world might have been turned upside down a couple of times since then, but shouldn't she be used to it by now? Her feet started moving of their own accord, taking her to the bathroom door. She knocked this time, not wanting to intrude on his privacy, then hesitantly peeked inside upon hearing his invitation.

Oscar stood shirtless with a washcloth in hand. His chest and arms were wet, the skin glistening as it reflected light from the single lantern in the otherwise dark room. His brows shot up at the sight of Clara stepping closer but he didn't move away as she slowly ran her fingers through the light dusting of dark hair covering his chest. His skin felt surprisingly soft under her fingers, but also icy.

"You're cold," Clara whispered, resting her palm over Oscar's heart, feeling the beats grow faster.

Oscar pointed to the washing basin. "No warm water." He seemed perplexed. Clara assumed he didn't know how to react to her sudden appearance. Neither did she. What was she doing?

"I just want to test something but..." She looked down at the bulge forming in his breeches. At least one part of him knew how to react, even if it wasn't exactly the reaction Clara had been looking for.

After following her gaze, Oscar shook his head and gave an apologetic smile. "That is beyond my control. I promise, I'll behave." He raised his hands in a gesture of surrender. His words sounded earnest and even though his eyes held sparks of mischief, Clara trusted him.

She handed him a towel, grinding her lip between her teeth as she watched Oscar dry himself. Getting her nightgown wet was not part of the plan. Yes, there was a plan. Clara didn't want to think about it too much because it was silly, and the most likely outcome would be a rather frustrated Oscar.

As soon as his chest was dry, Clara moved to him. Oscar was a few inches taller than Clara so, wrapping her arms around his neck, she pulled him down to her level as she rose onto her tiptoes. Oscar reciprocated by wrapping his arms around her waist. Clara didn't protest. Being held like this was pleasant, plus it gave her extra stability. Oscar probably thought she wanted to kiss him again because he smiled and lowered his lips to hers but that was not part of the plan.

Tilting her head to the side, Clara pulled Oscar even lower, before pressing her lips against his neck. Clara tried to repeat what Oscar had done earlier that day by making a trail of kisses up under his ear and then back down to the crook of his neck. When she carefully used her teeth during the last kiss, Oscar drew in a sharp breath. He pulled Clara closer, his fingers burying themselves into her flesh. Satisfied by his reaction, Clara stopped kissing and rested her head against his chest, listening to his ragged breathing.

When he realized she wasn't going to continue, Oscar loosened his grip but he didn't let go. "What was that supposed to test?" he chuckled into Clara's hair. "Whether I would turn into an uncontrollable monster and ravage you right here on the floor?"

"No."

Every man turns into a lustful beast when it comes to sharing a bed with a woman, Clara remembered her mother saying. A lie, obviously. Clara had shared a bed with Oscar for several nights already and he hadn't touched her against her will. And now she was literally provoking him and he still seemed as calm as if they were having a casual conversation over breakfast.

"If I thought that would happen I never would have done anything. I just..." Clara hesitated. "You said it was enjoyable for both. And, obviously, it's pleasant to be kissed but...I wanted to see what it feels like to be the one kissing." Her cheeks burned and she really hoped he wasn't going to laugh at her. Why did she even tell him all of that?

His shoulders did twitch in suppressed laughter but his voice wasn't condescending. "Ah, a thorough scientific method." Humor laced his words, not unkindly. He was being playful. "And? What are the results of your experiment?"

"You weren't lying." He certainly wasn't. Clara had always liked his scent and, no matter how incredibly weird and awkward it sounded, he tasted nice too. Oscar was grinning but Clara wasn't entirely convinced he was okay. "You aren't... frustrated or angry with me?" she asked quietly, avoiding his look. It probably wasn't the best way to phrase the question but it was something she needed to know.

Oscar chuckled again, cupping her cheeks so she'd look at him. "Clara, if we'd had the luxury of choice and had met under different circumstances, I would have spent days or even weeks trying to woo you and then seduce you. You wouldn't find that strange at all. So, why don't you stop worrying about my feelings and let me do something I'm actually good at?"

"We're married," Clara frowned as she thought about his words. "We can't just pretend we are...dating." Was that what he was suggesting?

"Why not?"

Clara opened her mouth to respond only to find she had no idea what to say. Why not, indeed? There was the ever-present question of what would her mother say, but why should Clara care about that anymore?

Seeing her obvious confusion, Oscar smiled warmly. "I promise to tell you if I'm ever feeling uncomfortable or overly frustrated. If," he raised a finger and waved it in front of her face, "you do the same."

"Alright." Something akin to excitement took root in Clara's soul, making her grin happily as she blurted out a question that had been bugging her since their first night together. "Do you always sleep in your shirt and underpants?"

Oscar laughed. "No. Actually, I'm used to sleeping naked but I didn't think you'd appreciate that."

No, she definitely wouldn't. Although... "You don't have to wear the shirt." The way the hair on his chest had tickled her cheeks when she'd leaned against him had felt strangely pleasant. Her cheeks heated at the thought. "Oh, I almost forgot," Clara added quickly, eager to change the topic. "There is a woman named Mina, I think she's a maid in the palace. Could you...umm, check on her?" Was that the right word?

"You think she's a spy?"

"What? No!" Clara certainly didn't want to get the woman into trouble. "No, I just wanted to talk to her about the personal maid thing. If...if that's still something I'm allowed to do?" she whispered hesitantly, nervous about spending his money in such a stupid and impractical way.

The Redwood family was wealthy. No doubt, Clara had been given a dowry but since they were married, Oscar had control over all of their finances.

Oscar's fingers softly traced the outline of her cheek. "Of course. You can have whatever you want, Clara. I'll ask around tomorrow." Oscar ended his sentence with a long yawn. "Sorry," he grinned sheepishly, "I'm really tired. Why don't you go and warm my bed for me, wife? I'm freezing."

Despite it being absolutely childish, Clara stuck out her tongue at him and followed it with a perfect curtsy. "As my lord wishes." She was giggling as she left the bathroom.

Chapter 27

K arina was itching to leave the palace and go out for a ride but Hayden was extra busy catching up on important matters after recovering from his 'illness.' She'd spent the last two days either by his side or hiding in the parlor of her chambers, which she'd reorganized into a makeshift study. Apparently, the queen needed a large room to drink tea and gossip, but not a proper desk.

Karina's little research project, as she'd called it in front of Hayden, was finally starting to show some results. She didn't have anything solid she could bring in front of General Warren and other lords without being laughed at, but Karina was patient. She had a feeling she was onto something important and wasn't going to give up now.

"Still working?" Hayden asked as he peeked into her room, curiously eyeing the mess inside.

Karina knew he was keen to see what she was doing but respected her privacy and didn't pry for answers. She probably should have given him more details, it was connected to the Cchen-Lian situation after all, but the last thing she wanted was to come up with another unfounded theory. "It's not really work, it's just-"

"Research, I know." Sighing, Hayden entered the parlor, taking care to avoid the parchments on the floor. "I need to talk to you about something and you probably won't like it very much."

Karina crossed the distance between them before putting her arms around his chest. "About the potion?" she asked quietly.

Hayden shuddered at her words then shook his head. "No. I need to go north."

"North?" Karina frowned. He couldn't just leave now. "But the plan..."

"The plan is on a very vague time schedule," Hayden interrupted her. "I have enough time to go there before people start expecting me to 'go crazy'." He didn't seem happy about it. "The situation with the Ruthians is getting worse. They've started to attack the caravans. A large group of tribes remained neutral but they refused to talk to my ambassadors. Apparently, they will not talk to 'just a man'. Let's hope they'll talk to a king'. We need information about what is going on there."

It made sense. If someone was pitting the Ruthians against Orellia, they'd probably talked to these neutral tribes as well. "Alright," Karina conceded. "When do we leave?"

"We?" Hayden sounded genuinely surprised.

Karina cocked an eyebrow. "Did you really think I'd let you go alone?" Hayden opened his mouth, no doubt to argue with her, but Karina put her finger over it to silence him. "No. I'm going."

"Karina, it's a warzone. Those woods are dangerous. They just destroyed an outpost with six hundred soldiers in it, I couldn't possibly..."

Yes, Karina was aware that going north was dangerous. But was it more dangerous than staying in a palace where everyone hated her and Cchen-Lianese spies roamed its halls? "Hayden, this is not up for discussion," she said sternly. "I'm going."

Karina did her best to sound confident and not let a shadow of doubt show in her expression. Of course, it wasn't up for discussion, but not because Karina said so. It was Hayden's decision and if he ordered her to stay, there was nothing she could do about it other than be angry with him.

"There's no way to guarantee your safety, I..." Hayden trailed off, looking pained. "I can't lose you," he whispered, desperately capturing her lips in a kiss.

Karina kissed him back, patiently waiting for him to calm down. "I can't lose you either." Just the thought was unbearable. "Which is why I'm going with you to make sure you don't do anything stupid." She grinned, letting him know it was a joke. "And you will be right next to me with that big ol' sword of yours. If someone tries to kill me, you have my permission to cut them in half, or whatever it is you warriors do to people."

"Karina..." Hayden's voice still sounded strangled but a smile was forcing its way out, which was Karina's intention. "Gods," he sighed in defeat. "I suppose I could bring the whole king's guard along but... We will have to move fast. It's not going to be a pleasant journey."

Relief flooded Karina. "I can manage," she proclaimed confidently. She hadn't expected Hayden to agree so readily but now that he had, she wouldn't say anything to make him change his mind.

"Pack some warm underwear then," Hayden smirked. "Even the summers are cold in the mountains. We're leaving tomorrow morning."

"Yes, sir," Karina chuckled, her mind already compiling a list of what she was going to need and how much her horse could carry. This time, there wouldn't be wagons packed with her clothes wobbling along like during their journey to the capital. A sudden thought popped into her mind. "Hayden? Could I bring someone along?"

Hayden rolled his eyes, probably regretting his decision already. "I don't think Laina would be thrilled to spend several days straight in the saddle."

No, Laina most definitely wouldn't. But someone else might. "That's not who I meant." Seeing Hayden's eyes narrow, Karina quickly added, "It's not Oscar either."

"I should hope not. He's promised to make himself useful. I can't see how he'd manage to do that in the middle of nowhere." Hayden let out a resigned sigh. "Look, you are the queen, a grown woman, you know what you are doing. I trust you. If you do bring someone along, and I honestly have no idea who or why, they're your responsibility. If they get killed, it will be on your conscience."

Feeling a little embarrassed, Karina lowered her head. "I'm sorry. I didn't mean to sound like a spoiled child. I swear I'm taking this seriously."

"I know you are, otherwise I never would have agreed to bring you along, no matter how furious you'd be with me." Hayden pulled Karina closer before placing a kiss into her hair. "I'm just tired and frustrated. I thought we would have some time to ourselves instead of dealing with a conspiracy and yet another war."

"We still have some time."

"How much? Half an hour? I need to talk to Warren, get the men ready, and-" He paused when Karina cupped the front of his breeches.

A mischievous smile playing on her lips, she whispered, "A lot of things can be accomplished in half an hour."

Hayden groaned before roughly grabbing her by the hips and kissing her. "Some of them, several times," he chuckled when their lips parted. "Turn around."

Karina let out a shaky breath and turned around, letting his hands guide hers to the back of one of the armchairs. "Hold," he ordered, reaching to lift the bottom of her dress.

His hands were ice cold, making Karina squeal in surprise when he slid them up the full length of her legs to her buttocks, sliding the layers of fabric out of the way. She gripped the edge of the wooden chair tighter as Hayden pushed her underpants to the side and slid his fingers to her core. She spread her legs to give better access, making him laugh. "Eager, my queen?" he teased.

"Always, my king," she breathed out.

One of Hayden's hands disappeared from her body as the sound of rustling fabric took over, Karina guessing he was undoing the front of his breeches. It had been weeks since they'd had sex for the first time yet Karina still felt the same burning desire every time he was near her. In moments like this, it was almost unbearable.

Hayden wrapped the end of her braid around one of his hands and roughly pulled on it, forcing Karina's back to arch. His other hand held her hips steady as he drove inside her in one strong motion, forcing her to release a loud moan.

It was true. A lot of things were accomplished in half an hour.

Karina was in a great mood as she walked the palace halls to talk to her potential travel companion. Her riding clothes caused multiple raised eyebrows and one or two surprised gasps but she couldn't care less.

A familiar wrinkled face appeared in the door after Karina knocked. "Friska!" Karina exclaimed happily.

"Lady Karina." Friska made a clumsy curtsy, a smile playing on her lips. "It's great to see you but I'm afraid Lord Oscar isn't here right now."

Karina wasn't surprised, she'd expected Oscar to be out in the city streets at this time of day. "Actually, I'm here to talk to Clara."

"Right, of course." Friska exchanged a few words with someone inside and stepped aside to open the door for Karina.

Clara was just rising from a sofa, placing a large book down on the table. "Your Majesty," she curtsied.

"Clara..." Karina raised her eyebrows and put a hint of warning into her voice.

"Right. Karina," Clara corrected herself, blushing. "I'm sorry, it takes some getting used to. What brings you here?"

Pointing to her obviously inappropriate clothing, Karina said, "I was wondering whether you'd like to go for a ride with me? Hayden is busy and I don't know any nice places around here yet."

"Oh. Uh..."

Seeing Clara's anxious hesitation, Karina wanted to smack herself. Of course, the girl was still afraid of being around the queen. The fact that

Karina had basically coerced Clara into being her friend hadn't suddenly made all of the tension disappear.

"It's alright, don't worry about it." Karina waved her hand lightheartedly, making sure there was no sign of disappointment in her voice. "I just love riding and didn't want to go alone, but it's no big deal."

Shifting her weight, Clara sighed, "I used to love it too but I just can't stand the sidesaddle."

Was that really the issue? "Do I look like someone who uses that torture device?" Karina asked, feeling hopeful.

"Well, my mother..." Clara stopped herself and frowned.

Ah, so Sophia Redwood wanted to mold her daughter into the perfect lady by taking away all of the fun things in her life. Except for archery. Clara had somehow managed to hold on to that in spite of her mother, Karina assumed.

Karina patiently waited until the girl's face brightened as she realized, "I don't have to care about that anymore, do I? Gods, I keep forgetting that she can't tell me what to do now."

"No, that honor belongs to your husband now." Karina suppressed an eye roll. "It sucks being a woman in this world, doesn't it? Anyway, I'm fairly certain Oscar doesn't care what type of saddle you use."

Clara grinned. "No, I don't think he does. Just give me a moment to change."

As it turned out, Clara also owned a set of riding clothes that were, without a doubt, highly inappropriate for a highborn lady. The number of brows raising as they walked to the stables hadn't increased since Karina had first ventured to find Clara, but the height to which they rose had definitely grown. One elderly, distinguished lady had such a funny looking 'offended' face it sent Karina and Clara into several rounds of unstoppable giggles, leaving Karina feeling like a fifteen-year-old girl.

Karina's mahogany bay mare, Seraphina, was already saddled and ready to go. After sending a thankful look to Markos, Karina's personal captain of the guards, Karina went to help Clara. The girl was busy putting a saddle on one of the brown mares in the common section of the stables. "She's not mine," Clara said, gently patting the horse's nose, "just one of the horses anyone from the palace can borrow. But I used to love riding her." The mare nudged her hand. Clara chuckled, "Yes, yes. Wait a minute."

It felt as if Clara was a completely different woman as she rode next to Karina. Smiling and chatting, this relaxed version of Clara on horseback looked nothing like the timid, frightened girl Karina had kept seeing during the past few days.

Clara dutifully offered to show Karina where the best shops selling perfumes and jewelry in the city lay, something a proper lady would probably want to see, but Karina quickly cleared the confusion by asking for the fastest route out of the city.

They ended up riding along the river, following a narrow path through the long grass, watching fishermen sit along the riverbank or rowing their small boats. Larger boats carefully followed the river channel, not wanting to get stuck on one of the shallow sandy patches that lined the shores.

Karina sighed. She missed home, watching the huge sailing ships that docked in Vantia and feeling the fresh sea breeze that cleared the air. This river flowed much slower, even becoming stagnant in some areas, and the odorous smell coming off the water was nowhere near pleasant.

Despite the remaining threads of Clara's anxiety, the women freely chatted about trivial, almost silly things, carefully getting to know each other without revealing too many personal details. Karina respected that. Making friends was a slow process that couldn't be hastened by an order from the queen. Still, there was something important she needed to ask Clara.

Karina hadn't found a way to seamlessly transition from their previous topics of conversation so she used one of the many moments of comfortable silence that spread between them. "The king is heading north to find out why the Ruthian tribes are attacking our forces."

Clara looked over, concern marring her features. It was quite obvious what she was thinking about.

"Yes," Karina nodded, "that's where Nicolas went missing. I'm going with the king." Clara's eyes widened. Karina smiled before continuing, "And I was wondering whether you'd like to come with me?"

Clara's eyebrows shot up. "Me? Why would the king want me there?"

Karina hesitated before answering, "The king has no idea I'm inviting you. But I was just thinking that, maybe...you'd want a chance to do something more with your life?" Karina slapped her hand over her mouth when she realized how incredibly rude her words must have sounded. It didn't even make any sense. Why would Clara want to go off into some northern wilderness when she had a safe new home in the palace? And a new husband. Crap, Oscar was probably going to be very unhappy about this offer.

"Gods," Karina rubbed her forehead, "I'm so sorry, Clara. I didn't mean to offend you or suggest that your life was anything less. Of course, you are free to do-"

"Karina," Clara still sounded hesitant using the queen's name, especially now when she was interrupting Karina's blabbering, "I'm honored, I...I'd love to go but I'm not sure if I can."

Clara actually wanted to go. That was a promising start. Karina continued, "If you are worried about the king, I promise he won't make any problems. I mean, he might roll his eyes or grumble a little, but nothing serious. But I'm not going to lie to you. It's going to be a rough ride. Several days in the saddle at quite a swift pace. And it's very dangerous."

"That's not the issue I'm worried about. I'm the daughter of an admiral, I can handle discomfort. It's just..." Clara sighed, grinding her lower lip between her teeth. "I'm not sure Oscar would agree."

The statement had Karina bristling, though she knew Clara was right. A husband could forbid his wife from going anywhere, let alone on such a crazy, totally inappropriate journey. And while Oscar was open-minded about a lot of things, not even Karina was sure whether he would condone this expedition. And even if he did, he would be angry with Karina for stealing his new bride from him just a few days after their wedding.

Karina found herself sighing now, scratching Seraphina's neck. "Whether you want to discuss my offer with him is up to you. The invitation stands. I just thought I could use a friend on the road and perhaps another skilled bodyguard." Clara raised her eyebrow before looking back at Markos and several other guards following them at a safe distance. Karina chuckled, deciding to show all of her cards. "Captain Markos might be extremely talented with a sword but sadly, his skills with a bow leave much to be desired," she grinned.

"Oscar told you." Clara's words were but a quiet sigh as she avoided the queen's gaze.

That was not the reaction Karina had expected. It seemed that Clara knew about the complicated friendship between the queen and Oscar and wasn't happy about it. "He did," Karina admitted, "but it was way before he'd met you. We talked about you before we even left Levanta." The last thing Karina wanted was to somehow muddy the relationship between Oscar and Clara. Even the other night, when Oscar had come to her for advice, she'd tried to stay out of it as much as she could. "And, I think it's absolutely amazing," she added, trying to steer the conversation into safer waters.

"Thank you." Clara blushed, clearly uncomfortable with being praised for such audacious rule-breaking. She squinted against the sun that had long since reached its peak and was now about halfway down to the horizon. "I'll think about it. I need to head back now, I have...something planned for the evening." Her words came out as an annoyed growl and Karina decided not to ask why. If Clara wanted to tell her, she'd do so in her own time.

"Think fast, we are leaving in the morning. And I've been told it's quite cold there, so keep that in mind when you pack," she winked, making it look like a sure thing Clara would come along.

The girl was lost in her own thoughts the entire way back so Karina stayed quiet, letting her think, hoping she'd reach the right decision. A decision that Oscar was hopefully not going to fuck up.

Chapter 28

Oscar was waiting for Clara in the parlor, sipping brandy from a low cut glass. Under normal circumstances, he wasn't one to indulge in hard liquor. Tonight, however, he was going to need every bit of help to keep calm. He had to remain the smiling, polite gentleman. Today, more than ever. For Clara. No matter how awkward dinner with her mother and brother was going to be.

Friska did her best to help Clara get ready but her gnarly fingers simply couldn't handle the tiny buttons on the back of Clara's beautiful gown. In the end, Oscar had to dutifully help his wife into her dress, even though he would've much rather been taking it off. He kept his heated looks and smart remarks to himself. Clara already looked incredibly nervous and Oscar didn't want to make it worse.

"You look amazing," he whispered into her ear after the last button was secured. "We don't have to go if you don't want to. I could say I'm too busy doing something for the king. I'll take the blame for canceling." Her brother already disliked Oscar, so it wouldn't make any difference.

Clara sighed, closing her eyes briefly before turning to Oscar with a determined look. "No. I can't keep running away from my problems. Just...don't leave me alone with my mother for too long, please?"

"Don't worry. I won't." Oscar was already determined to prevent the hag from spewing more poison into Clara's ears. He wasn't even done fixing the damage Sophia had made with her bullshit wedding night talk.

For a brief second, Oscar imagined a more vengeful version of Hayden forcing him to marry Sophia Redwood instead of her young daughter. A shudder ran through Oscar's entire body over the mere thought. Clara's eyebrow raised in silent query but Oscar just shook his head, forcing the smile back in place. "It's nothing. Just a weird thought." Very weird. "Are you ready to go?"

After glancing in the mirror one more time and fixing her already perfect hair, Clara nodded. "I'm ready."

A true gentleman would offer Clara his arm but Oscar held her hand instead, intertwining his fingers with hers. It felt more intimate. This way, he could stroke the back of her hand with his thumb and enjoy the little blushes that simple movement caused.

When he went to help Clara into the carriage, she motioned for him to wait a moment as she approached the front of the carriage, exchanging a couple of quiet words with the coachman. The coachman nodded his understanding before Clara returned to Oscar and allowed him to assist as she climbed inside.

As the carriage wobbled along the road, Clara avoided Oscar's eyes, looking nervous yet somewhat excited at whatever she'd planned with the driver. Oscar's curiosity was piqued, but he decided to wait and see what she was up to.

Maybe she'd told the coachman to go somewhere else to avoid the dinner altogether? And if so, was she ashamed of it? It seemed like the most plausible answer but as Oscar had already learned, the simplest answers weren't always the correct ones when it came to his wife.

The ride wasn't very long. A small blessing since Oscar had the urge to pull Clara onto his lap and start kissing her.

The carriage stopped. Even without looking outside, Oscar knew that they hadn't yet arrived at the Redwood mansion. "Are you trying to kidnap me, Lady Huxley?" he teased, trying to get a smile out of Clara.

"For a few minutes," she replied coyly. Her smile was beautiful yet she still seemed nervous.

Oscar helped Clara down from the carriage and cautiously looked around. The city was still new to him but it seemed that they weren't far from their destination. The road lazily zigzagged along a mild slope, locked between high walls and fences concealing luxurious mansions within. When Oscar turned to survey the area, his breath caught.

The entire city of Ebris lay out in front of him. From this position, he could see the royal palace high up on the cliffs overlooking the river, the stone houses surrounding the central squares, and the cramped little alleyways that made up most of the lower city. Cranes hovered over ships docked at the piers, moving sacks and crates back and forth. Carriages, horses, and people poured over the many bridges spanning the wide, lazy river. Oscar even caught a glimpse of some of the mansions further downhill that were partially hidden behind the trees of their own private estates.

"Wow, that's..." For once, Oscar was speechless. Clara gently took his hand but stayed quiet, giving him time to absorb the astonishing view.

After gazing his fill, Oscar turned his attention to his immediate surroundings. He noticed an old wooden shrine of Venir, the god of love, sex, and pleasure, standing just a few feet from them. He smirked over the irony but, since he knew Clara wouldn't appreciate him joking about it right now, he kept quiet. It took all of his restraint not to kiss her, though.

Clara fidgeted nervously, glancing at Oscar from beneath her lashes before seeming to come to a decision. Sighing, she said, "I want to talk to you about something. I thought I'd wait until after dinner but I can't stop thinking about what are you going to say and worrying you'll be angry with me, so... Let's just do it now so I can focus on the upcoming horrors of spending time with my mother."

The smile on Oscar's face didn't falter even when his heart did. Whatever she wanted to talk about was serious and she expected him to dislike it. His mind offered a few possible ideas he did not like at all.

Had Oscar really screwed up so badly that Clara didn't want to be with him anymore? Had she gone over everything that had happened between them and decided she wasn't going to give him a chance? It wouldn't be such a big surprise. Oscar did tell her he loved someone else, afterall. How's that for winning a girl over?

"I promise I won't get angry," he replied. "Just say what you need to say." He pushed the wild vortex of feelings swirling inside him away. Oscar was used to being treated like vermin, he would sure as hell take whatever Clara was going to tell him while keeping at least a semblance of a smile on his lips.

Clara faced him, holding both of his hands in hers. It felt better than a lowlife like him deserved.

"The king is leaving to go north tomorrow," Clara started hesitantly, making him frown. That was not something he'd expected her to say. He nodded. He'd known about Hayden leaving. "The queen is going with him," Clara added.

Oscar rolled his eyes. It was just like Karina, convincing Hayden to bring her along to what was technically a war campaign.

Clara bit on her lip before continuing, her voice had lost any signs of confidence. "She's invited me to come along."

Oscar took a second to mull that information over. "Are you telling me you're leaving home to go to war? Tomorrow?" he asked, chuckling over the irony of their situation. The simplest answers were never the correct ones when it came to Clara.

"I... You're right." Suddenly sounding ashamed, Clara stepped back. "It's ridiculous. I shouldn't have even mentioned it. I'm sorry." She slipped back into being that timid, anxious, and perpetually afraid girl Oscar hated so much.

He had noticed she did that whenever she felt nervous or insecure, especially around him. It was most likely a defense mechanism her mother had implanted inside Clara's mind – be a quiet, polite girl. Men will like you if you are so they won't yell at you, beat you, or rape you. Because apparently, that was all men were capable of according to Sophia Redwood. Gods, Oscar hated that woman! He didn't even understand where her hatred came from. Judging by what Clara had told him, Sophia's late husband was a very kind man.

Oscar slowly crossed the distance Clara had put between them, gently lifting her chin. He still had no idea what to do when Clara retreated like this, he was merely following his instincts. If there was a better solution than staying calm, smiling, and patiently waiting for Clara to come out her shell, Oscar was yet to find it. This method worked, although it required a lot of patience. It was a good thing that Oscar was a very patient man.

He took a moment to consider his next words before saying, "Clara, it's not ridiculous. It's surprising, and if you really think about it, extremely ironic, but not ridiculous." A sigh escaped him. "I won't pretend I'm excited over the prospect of not seeing you for weeks. And of course, there's the whole war and mortal danger thing. But you are not my slave. If you want to go, then go."

Oscar could forbid her from leaving but what good would it do? He only wished he'd had more time to woo her, to make her fall for him. To make sure she would come back to him.

There were dozens, if not hundreds of handsome, muscular warriors in Hayden's army and Clara would be a lone girl among them. Oscar was sure nobody would dare to attack her but they were definitely going to be fawning over her. Who was to say one of them wouldn't steal Clara's heart.

Wow, was Oscar actually jealous?

"You really mean that?" Clara frowned as she scrutinized his expression for any signs of malice or mockery. "I didn't think you would..." She trailed off, shaking her head in disbelief. "There are so many reasons I shouldn't go that I feel bad for wanting to."

Her supply of self-doubt was apparently limitless. Oscar barely stopped himself from rolling his eyes.

What did she want him to say? Oscar followed his instincts again. Clara was worried he would be angry, so he needed to convince her that he wasn't. Feelings. Women loved to talk about feelings, didn't they?

Oscar had always tried to avoid these conversations but with Clara, it wasn't hard to open up and share some of the messiness that was going on inside of him. Maybe, since she was a little bit broken in her own way, Oscar could trust her not to use his feelings against him. It was the same child-like, irrational trust she seemed to have in him. They weren't so different after all.

Oscar sat down on one of the benches in front of Venir's shrine, gently tugging Clara's hand, hoping she would take the hint and sit on his lap. To his surprise, she did. Wrapping Clara in his arms, he looked into her beautiful, soulful eyes. Her smile was still anxious but she rested one arm around his neck and relaxed into his shoulder. A promising start.

Oscar silently cursed Karina. Her offer came at very much the wrong time. Just a few more days and he would have worked through Clara's defenses and finally convinced her to do something more in bed than just sleep. After one night with him worshiping her, she wouldn't be thinking of disappearing into a cold wilderness for gods know how long.

"I'm not angry, Clara." He rested his head against her shoulder, enjoying the soft scent of her perfume. "I'm actually relieved," he chuckled, feeling stupid for bringing the topic up. Clara tilted her head, confusion evident. "Not that you are leaving," Oscar explained quickly, realizing a little too late that his words might have come out insulting. "But...because I thought you wanted to talk to me about leaving me, for good." Oscar wasn't used to admitting his fears like this, but with Clara, it was easy.

She played with a lock of his hair which had fallen out of the band. "Why would you think I wanted to leave you? I mean...I do want to go, but not because I want to leave you. Which I couldn't, even if I wanted to...And I don't," she added quickly.

"Of course you could leave me. If you decided to stay with your family after dinner tonight, I could hardly drag you out of there by force. And it's not like I can chain you to a bedroom wall to prevent you from running away. Although, come to think of it, that does sound like a fun idea," he grinned in an attempt to lighten the situation.

Clara smacked the back of his head playfully before going back to stroking his hair. Her whole presence was so soothing, causing all of Oscar's worries to melt away. Ironically, he was the one being insecure now.

"I like you, Oscar," Clara sighed. She didn't sound very happy about it. "A lot. More than I should, given the circumstances." Yes, Oscar could see how him being in love with someone else was problematic. "But there was something Karina said that I just can't stop thinking about. She asked me whether I wanted to do something more with my life. And I think I do. I mean, not that-"

Knowing she was in for another round of apologies, Oscar interrupted her, "Clara, this is probably the most mature thing I've heard you say. I absolutely understand that and I will support you if you choose to go." If only it didn't have to be so soon. But how could Oscar object after what she'd just told him?

She lowered her head so that their noses were touching. "I'll miss you."

And you have no idea how I will miss you, girl, Oscar wanted to say but kept his mouth shut, hoping she would kiss him. She did and it was a rough, desperate kiss.

Clara instinctively tried to reposition herself astride Oscar's lap to gain a better angle but her long gown kept getting in the way. With an exasperated sigh, Oscar pulled it over her knees in one swift move before quickly returning his hands to her back before she could get nervous about him doing something so inappropriate. Clara gasped but didn't protest.

Oscar tried very hard not to think about her naked legs and how they were wrapped around his thighs. He briefly considered ditching the stupid dinner altogether and just dragging his wife back home and into bed, but it was a silly idea. She wasn't ready to have sex with him yet. Oscar could feel the tension in her body growing as the kiss continued but it was not the good kind of tension. Clara was enjoying their kiss but she was still afraid of going any further.

Oscar settled for just having her body flush against his and her lips parted for his tongue. He put all of his ferocious desire into the kiss, wrapping his arms around her so tightly she could barely breathe.

When he felt her gently pulling back ever so slightly, Oscar forced himself to stop, resting his head against her heaving chest. He was also gasping for air, trying to control his thoughts and rid himself of the raging hard on that was poking into Clara's thigh. He knew it would make her uncomfortable.

Clara wriggled a little, her eyes widening as she realized what she was sitting on. Before Oscar could apologize, she giggled. "Don't worry, I..." Her breath was still ragged. "It's like a compliment, right?"

"Yes," he laughed at her words. "Finally, you are beginning to understand."

Chapter 29

N either of them wanted to break their intimate moment, but if they were to make it to dinner with Clara's family in time, they should probably head back to the carriage soon. Which meant that Oscar needed to remove his beautiful wife from his lap and force his rock-hard dick into a less embarrassing form.

"We need to get going, don't we?" Clara sighed, tightening her hold of his neck and pulling him even closer to her chest. Having his mouth so close to her breasts was certainly not helping with Oscar's 'situation'.

"Yeah." Oscar didn't want to move. He wanted to fuck Clara right here on this wooden bench, next to an old shrine to the god of love. He desperately wanted to make her scream in pleasure for everyone to hear. Let everyone know that she belonged to him.

Oscar wanted her. He had finally admitted it to himself, even though it made him feel strange. Not just because he wanted to have sex with Clara, but because he wanted to make her a permanent fixture in his life.

There wasn't much in Oscar's life that he considered permanent. He had a great family he could always rely on but, other than that, his life was a parade of fleeting sensations. People came and went without leaving a mark. Of course, there was one exception. Karina. She had always been Oscar's solid point, the center of his universe. But Karina was like a colorful shard of glass. Beautiful to look at, alluring to dream about, but try to touch it and you'll end up hurt.

Clara was completely different. She was soft and warm and Oscar felt safe around her. While her vulnerability might have seemed like a downside, it actually made Oscar feel needed. Useful. As if his otherwise pointless existence, where he only brought grief, pain, and disappointment to everyone around him, suddenly had purpose. Because he was brought here to protect Clara, help her, and care for her. To make her happy.

Oscar wasn't entirely sure what to make of these feelings. Normally, he wouldn't bother dissecting them into such depths. He pushed his thoughts away for another time. He would have plenty of opportunity to go over them once Clara leaves. Right now, Oscar just wanted to enjoy her presence. Even if it had to be spent in the company of her family.

"If you still want to go to that dinner, then yes, I think we should get going," he finally responded to her question.

With a sad sigh, Clara got off his lap and straightened her gown. "No, we should be there. Especially since I leave tomorrow. Oh, gods!" Her hands flew up to cover her mouth. "My mother will go crazy when she finds out!" She let out a hysterical chuckle, clearly not sure whether she should be laughing or panicking. After taking a few steps toward the carriage, she noticed Oscar wasn't following her and gave him a questioning glance.

"I just need a moment," Oscar mumbled. The memory of her hips grinding against his were still too fresh in his mind. Since Clara still didn't seem to understand, Oscar pointed down to his bulging breeches. Her eyes widened before she burst into giggles. "I'm happy you find me so amusing, my dear wife," Oscar teased.

"Sorry," Clara grinned, unsuccessfully trying to control her expression. "How does that work?" she asked, pointing to his crotch.

So innocent, Oscar thought. "I just need to take my mind off...well, you, for a few moments."

"Oh. Should I leave?"

Oscar shook his head, crossing the distance between them before taking her hand. Clara smiled cautiously, clearly unsure what to do so as to not aggravate the situation further, which was somehow hilarious and annoying at the same time.

"Oscar?" She sounded anxious again. "Are you really alright with me going even if...some people might...make fun of you because of me?" Her words faded into a sheepish whisper.

"Oh, I bet they will," Oscar grinned. "Am I such a horrible husband that my wife flees to the northern wilderness just a few days after the wedding? Or, better yet, am I such a coward that I send my wife to war instead of going there myself?" he chuckled, a hint of sarcasm in his tone.

Clara tilted her head to the side, studying his expression. "You don't seem bothered by that."

"Because I'm not," Oscar retorted with a smile. "Sometimes it's a good thing to be laughed at."

Clara clearly didn't understand what he meant by that but Oscar decided not to explain. She was smart, she could figure it out on her own.

When she realized Oscar wasn't going to continue, she let go of his hand to cross her arms in front of her chest. "Most men would take laughing at them as an insult to their honor."

"Honor is overrated," Oscar scoffed, rolling his eyes, curious whether Clara would follow his line of thinking.

"That's a very cynical point of view," Clara smirked but there was only light humor in her tone. "If you are considered to be without honor, you are free to do whatever you want. People won't have high expectations from you. And if they laugh at you, they...underestimate you?" She hesitated on the last two words, making them more of a question.

Oscar nodded with a bright smile. He truly had a clever wife. "Sometimes appearing weak is just as useful as looking strong." He paused, suddenly worried how his words would make her perceive him. After all, she was from an honorable family. Her father was a true warrior and

Clara adored him. "Does that disgust you?" he asked before he could stop himself. What the hell was wrong with him?

"Disgust me?" Clara quirked a brow as she realized Oscar's question was serious, her expression softened. "Of course not. It's just very different from what I know. Very...pragmatic. But not in a bad way." She glanced at his normal-looking breeches again. "Ready to go?"

Their conversation was truly an arousal killing one so Oscar nodded, taking Clara's hand before leading her to the carriage.

T he mansion was magnificent and Oscar's doubts returned tenfold. How could Clara want to live in their modest palace chambers after growing up in a place like this?

The two-story building was surrounded by a spacious garden. As the carriage drew closer, Clara grew increasingly nervous, tightly clutching onto Oscar's hand. Dozens of lanterns were placed along the path to the mansion entrance, slowly taking over the job of illuminating the scene from the setting sun.

Their hosts were waiting for them. Sophia Redwood was dressed in a ridiculous purple gown, wide and frilly, reminding Oscar of the monstrosity Karina had worn on her wedding day. Sophia's cleavage was a little too revealing for a lady of her age and her hair was twisted into an overly complicated style. No doubt the latest fashion at court.

Clara's mother had clearly put in an effort, as opposed to Sebastian, who was wearing a simple black formal suit with the Redwood crest embroidered on one side of his jacket. His condescending smile left no doubt that this family get together was not his idea.

Oscar gave them his best and brightest smile as he exited the carriage before helping Clara out. "It's alright," he whispered into her ear upon feeling her tremble. "Hey, can I kiss you right now?" he asked in an attempt to distract her. It might have been an odd question to ask his wife but he was careful not to do anything without her consent.

"You can kiss me anytime you want." Clara whispered in return, her voice shaky but she was smiling now. Clara probably realized Oscar was trying to distract her but what she most likely didn't realize was that this kiss would mark her as his 'property', thus expanding his protection over her.

While removing kissing from the list of forbidden activities offered a plethora of options Oscar could use later, for now he just lowered his head until his lips briefly touched hers, still slightly swollen from their passionate kiss earlier.

Intertwining their fingers, Oscar turned to face the menace that was Clara's mother. "Lady Redwood," he bowed deeply in front of the ridiculously dressed woman. Maintaining his firm grip of Clara's hand, he kissed the back of Sophia's. Thankfully, no signs of his insides churning over such a gesture made it to his expression. He had kissed worse hands and still managed to smile. "Lord Redwood." Oscar gave the asshole a firm short nod.

Clara let go of Oscar's hand and approached her mother like she was headed for the noose. Hands rested on her mother's shoulders, Clara leaned in to kiss the air on either side of Sophia's earrings in an awkward parody of a hug. She then embraced Sebastian sincerely, even though it still felt a little too formal to Oscar's mind.

Oscar reclaimed Clara's hand after the formalities were over then the Redwoods led them through their luxuriously decorated home to the spacious dining room. Clara smiled warmly at the maids and servants, earning sincere smiles in response. She was certainly liked by the common folk.

The large dining table was set for four. Oscar dutifully held out a chair for Clara to sit then waited until Sebastian had done the same for Sophia before sitting down himself. He was going to be nothing if not a polite and noble gentleman tonight.

The food was delicious. Oscar had to remind himself to eat only small bites at a time, as was custom for such a formal setting, as he listened to

Sophia's excited jabbering, nodding and responding in all the right places. Oscar found stealing the occasional quick glances at Clara across the table was much more exciting than the conversation. Their eyes met a couple of times, coy smiles on both their lips.

Sebastian stayed silent, sizing Oscar up with poorly hidden contempt and hostility. Honestly, the man must be a pretty shitty diplomat, Oscar concluded, especially if he couldn't even control his expression over a simple family dinner.

Sophia demanded Oscar talk about his family, her questioning focused on their wealth, social status, and influence. She voiced her excitement and hopes that she'd be able to meet with Lady Huxley soon. As if Oscar would ever allow this spiteful hag anywhere near his mother.

After the last course, they moved to the parlor where Oscar could finally hold Clara again. She seemed relieved when he put his arm around her then blushed like a ripe tomato as he pecked her cheek lovingly. Sophia scowled at them. Such open displays of affection probably didn't belong in her world.

Oscar barely concealed his devilish smirk. Oh, she was going to get a lot more uncomfortable tonight, he would make sure of it.

"I forgot to mention," Sophia started excitedly, leaving no doubt that she hadn't forgotten anything but was rather saving this information for the proper moment, "the Auburns are getting rid of some of their properties, after that unfortunate incident."

Oscar knew the 'incident' Sophia was alluding to. The honorable head of the Auburn household had encountered some problems paying his wayward son's gambling debts. A few too many visits from his debtors had left the son in dire condition, with one of his legs rumored to be permanently lame. An interesting tale, but not something to pique Oscar's radar beyond mild curiosity.

He and Clara were currently seated on the sofa, Oscar's arm wrapped around her shoulders and one of Clara's hands casually resting on his thigh. This was new for them both and Oscar loved the feeling, he just had to be careful to not let his imagination wander too far, avoiding any potential embarrassment caused by his overly eager dick.

Clara's mother continued in her conspiratorial tone, "They are selling that beautiful residence just down the road. Wouldn't it be wonderful if we were neighbors, Clara?"

"Erm...yes, wonderful." Clara's voice suggested she couldn't imagine suffering from a worse fate. "But we aren't looking for a house, mother."

Sophia's eyes widened in surprise. "Have you already found something? So fast? Tell me, I want to know all about it! How big is the garden? How many rooms for children? How many servants are you going to hire? Loyal and capable people are just so hard to find these days."

Clara gripped Oscar's leg tighter at the mention of children. Great. More bullshit reasons for Clara to be afraid of having sex with him was exactly what Oscar needed, not. "Actually, we've decided to stay at the palace for now," he replied, supporting Clara.

"But..." Sophia clearly didn't want to oppose him but couldn't hide her disappointment. "Are you sure that's appropriate for someone of your wealth and status, Lord Huxley?"

Again with the wealth. As if Oscar truly owned anything. He was entitled to a share of his family's wealth and there was also the hefty sum of Clara's dowry, but none of that was really his. Whatever Hayden decided to pay Oscar for his services certainly wasn't going to make him anywhere near rich enough to match what Clara's mother had in mind. Of course, Oscar could afford a fucking mansion. But what the hell would he do with it?

"You are the one being inappropriate now, mother," Clara said quietly before Oscar could think of a polite response. Look at that, his wife had found her courage. Oscar hoped it was at least partially thanks to his support. "Where Lord Huxley and I live is our decision."

"Clara!" Sophia scowled at her daughter. Oscar could almost hear the unspoken order to shut her damn mouth and behave. Clara shuddered but did not lower her head. Sophia grew angrier, spitting out, "Well, I apologize for being curious about the life of my only daughter. Considering I've been distraught lately, with my poor Nicolas..." she sniffled, dabbing a napkin over her dry cheeks. What a shitty actress.

Clara hesitated. Her mother's dirty tricks seemed to be undermining her fragile, newfound self-confidence. Oscar decided to pull out something that would surely make the mean hag step back. Casually, he kissed Clara's cheek before noting, "Getting a large residence right now wouldn't be worth it anyway, since Clara is leaving for a couple of weeks."

Clara's grip on his thigh grew painful now. Obviously, Clara wasn't happy with what he'd just revealed.

Sophia's brows furrowed as she thought over his words. "Oh, you're going back to Levanta to introduce Clara to your family? That's lovely," she rushed in with the first solution that came into her mind.

"No." Oscar waited for a few moments, giving Clara the chance to flaunt her new opportunity at her mother. But, to Oscar's dismay, she stayed quiet. He realized that Clara probably didn't understand that being invited to accompany the king and queen on such a dangerous and important mission was something to be proud of, not embarrassed by. "The king and queen are heading north tomorrow and Clara is going with them."

The dead silence that followed his words was finally interrupted by Sebastian's chortle.

Chapter 30

C lara couldn't believe that Oscar had just casually mentioned her leaving in front of her mother. It almost sounded like he was bragging about it.

Sophia gawked in disbelief while Sebastian continued to chortle, laughing so hard he nearly spilled his drink. "Seriously, Huxley, I'd expected you to be a lot of things but a jester wasn't one of them. Still, you should have started with something more plausible."

Clara frowned at her brother. Was her going away on a diplomatic mission really such an inconceivable idea? "It's true," she declared.

"Of course it is, sister," Sebastian chuckled, his tone infuriatingly condescending. Turning his back to Clara, he blatantly dismissed her as he addressed Oscar again, "I mean seriously? Even just the thought is ridiculous. Why would the king bring a silly little girl on a war campaign?"

For the first time tonight, maybe even the first time ever, Clara felt Oscar's body tense. Since he was renowned for being perpetually calm and composed, this was the equivalent to another man jumping up and screaming profanity. Clara softly stroked his thigh to calm him down. She suddenly understood why he'd brought up this topic and it was about time she stood up for herself.

"Actually," she interrupted before Oscar could even open his mouth, earning a surprised glance from him, "it was the queen who invited me." Sebastian finally looked at Clara, his eyebrow cocked in mild interest. Smirking, Clara continued, "Yes, since she is going as well, she asked me to come along as her companion." Clara paused, considering her next words. Did she really want to go there? Oscar's encouraging smile was all the convincing she needed to defiantly add, "And bodyguard."

Sebastian's expression hardened but it was Sophia who reacted first. "CLARA! You did not bother the queen with your disgraceful hobby, wasting her time with your nonsense, did you?!"

Shuddering, Clara remembered another time when her mother used the word 'nonsense'. 'You will stop with this nonsense,' Sophia had yelled right before destroying Clara's bow. But this time, Clara was no longer a frightened, meek little girl. This time, she wasn't alone. She glared back at Sophia with equal force.

Sophia took in a deep breath, contorting her features into a strained smile before turning to Oscar. "You'll have to excuse her, Lord Huxley, she is young and stupid. But she knows her duties well."

"I don't *have to* do anything, Lady Redwood," Oscar bristled at Sophia's last sentence and, while his words were still civil, his tone was not. A silent threat. "I will not excuse your daughter," Oscar continued coldly, "since there is nothing she should be apologizing for. Instead, I will do something I would expect any mother, or brother for that matter," he briefly glared in Sebastian's direction, "to do automatically. I will respect and support her. I'm sure you've heard those words before, Lady Redwood."

Flabbergasted, Sophia just stared at him. Even Clara was taken aback by Oscar's words, knowing that such open confrontation was not his style. Judging by Oscar's tension, Clara guessed this situation was about to take a very wrong turn. Her brother was scowling and Clara knew that sooner rather than later, Sebastian was going to say something that he couldn't take back. Oscar wouldn't get angry, but he wouldn't forget. Nor would he forgive.

Clara stayed away from palace gossip but even she couldn't miss hearing about Lord Umber being assaulted. The masked men had beaten him before leaving him lying in the middle of the street, naked. The man who'd so rudely attacked Clara during their wedding, was suddenly attacked himself. In broad daylight, no less. And for no apparent reason.

It could have been a coincidence. With Lord Umber's reputation, he must have lots of enemies. But Clara couldn't shake the feeling that Oscar had something to do with it. And while she could understand his motivation, could even be grateful for him avenging her honor, she surely didn't want something similar happening to her brother.

"Are the celosias in the back garden still in bloom, mother?" Clara asked with what she hoped was a pleasant smile. She stood up, tugging on Oscar's hand to follow. "I promised Oscar I'd show him the gardens. We should go while it's still light. We'll be back soon."

For a second, she worried that Oscar was too vested in defending her honor to leave with her but this was Oscar Huxley. His mind always won over his emotions. Or so it seemed.

He gave Sophia a forced smile before following Clara out of the room. She led him out into the garden, taking a deep breath of fresh evening air. The sun had disappeared below the horizon but there were still some lingering traces of light illuminating the countless flowers.

As Clara and Oscar continued to explore, tall rose bushes rose up around them, shielding them from view of the mansion. Hopefully, the distance was enough so that their words wouldn't be overheard either. Unless Oscar started yelling but Clara didn't expect that to happen.

She wasn't sure what to say. Was Oscar angry with her? Had she overstepped her boundaries by interrupting their terse conversation?

Sighing, Oscar pulled her into a tight embrace. "I'm sorry," he whispered. Clara rested her head against his shoulder, enjoying the warmth and safety she felt every time he put his arms around her. Oscar shook his head. "I normally have more control over my emotions. I'm sorry for going against your mother like that."

"No, you aren't," Clara chuckled. That much was obvious.

A quiet grumble escaped him. "Alas, you know me too well, my dear wife. I'm not sorry for what I said. But I am sorry I did it in front of you and your brother...and that I lost my composure."

"I think, given the circumstances, you were almost too composed. Sebastian's response would have probably been much worse. And...he's been through enough, I wouldn't want him to end up beaten by mysterious thugs," Clara teased, even though her voice was a little strained. Maybe bringing up this topic hadn't been the best idea.

Oscar stiffened before heaving a deep sigh. "I keep forgetting how smart you are. The thing with Umber... It was a momentary indulgence on my part. I'm not saying I regret it, but it's not something I do on a regular basis. And no matter how annoying your brother is, I would never hurt him," Oscar spoke with intense fervor, desperate for her to believe him. When Clara didn't respond right away, he continued on in a more subdued tone, "Are you angry with me?"

Clara scoffed. "No. Umber had it coming. I was just wondering what else you haven't told me."

Oscar liked secrets. But how could Clara live without knowing what's really happening, permanently worried about what else he was keeping from her and how it would affect her life? No doubt Oscar would always have a good reason to not tell her everything, like with Nicolas. But Clara's trust in Oscar shook every time she discovered something he decided to withhold from her.

"Clara, there are dozens of things I haven't told you," Oscar said quietly. "Even if I told you everything I can think of right here, right now, and it would probably take hours, there is always going to be something else. Tomorrow, in a week, in a year. I collect secrets. That's what I do, who I am. Until I met you, I didn't have to justify myself to anyone. Or...share."

Oscar sounded frustrated. Clara could tell a part of him wanted to push her away and end this stupid discussion once and for all. But he was desperately fighting against it and the mere fact that he would even try, filled her with hope. And a little shame. "I'm sorry," she apologized. "I guess, I feel so good around you that I forget that we've only known each other for a couple of days. I don't want to push you into being something you aren't." Which is what Clara's mother had been doing to Clara her entire life. Gods, was Clara slowly turning into a younger version of Sophia Redwood? The mere thought made her shudder.

"The only thing you've been pushing me to be, is a better man," Oscar smiled at her before rolling his eyes. "It's just a really complicated process with someone like me. And I'm not sure if it can be fully accomplished."

Clara gently traced the outline of his chin. "You already are a great man, you just don't see it. I don't want you to change who you are. I don't even want to know all your secrets. I just want to know about the ones that have something to do with me. Or you, for that matter. I want to be sure you are safe."

In the final remnants of dying light, it almost looked as if Oscar was blushing. But, since that didn't really sound like him, Clara concluded it was probably just the soft shadows moving over his face.

He nodded. "Alright, that sounds...reasonable." He paused for a few moments before saying, "I don't think there are any more that concern you. There are plenty of secrets that have something to do with me, a lot of which are incredibly embarrassing. I'll tell you later," he grinned. "There is one thing you might want to know. I think. I mean, a proper lady shouldn't concern herself with these matters, but it seems like my wife is hardly a proper lady, is she?" His grin grew wider.

Clara playfully smacked his chest. Not even a few hours ago, she wouldn't have dared but now she felt no fear. The events of this afternoon, even this difficult discussion, had brought them closer together. "I think it's only fitting," she mock-glared, "considering the fact that my husband is hardly a proper gentleman. Spill it, scoundrel!."

"Ah! I thought spousal abuse was supposed to work the other way around!" Chuckling, Oscar raised his arms as if to protect himself. Frowning over the sudden distance between them, Clara wrapped her hands behind Oscar's neck and raised up onto her tiptoes to kiss him. "Mmm," he murmured into the kiss with a dreamy smile. "Much better. Anyway, about this secret of mine. There is another potential player here in Ebris. Definitely a person of influence and power but not connected to the king."

A player? Clara cocked an eyebrow over the term. She had a vague idea of what it meant, and knew that it had nothing to do with playing games. At least, not the type of games she was used to. "And they don't like you sniffing around?"

"Ever the vocabularian, my dear," Oscar teased, rolling his eyes. "I'm not entirely sure yet. They've sent people to follow me, but I think at this point they are just checking me out to see whether I'm a threat or a potential asset."

That sounded really sketchy. "Didn't you just swear your loyalty to the king?"

"I...Well, I swore I wouldn't make a move against him and that I wouldn't lie to him. And that I'd make myself useful." Clara frowned, not liking how he deliberately played with words. Oscar, noticing Clara's displeasure, was quick to proclaim, "I'm not going to betray the king, Clara. But it's useful to know who all the players are and it never hurts to have powerful acquaintances."

His words were earnest so Clara decided to trust him. "Aren't you afraid that this 'player' will decide you are dangerous and try to remove you from 'the game'?"

"That's always an option," Oscar shrugged, apparently unconcerned by the possibility of being murdered by a mysterious crime lord. "I tend to rely on my instinct in these matters and those instincts are telling me I'm not in danger right now. I think this person is somehow connected to the poisoning situation we're in."

This great game of outsmarting the emperor of Cchen-Lian and his army of spies was focused a little too close to Clara's home for her liking. She looked around to see if they were alone but it was impossible to tell due to them being surrounded by thick rose bushes. "Are they with us, or against?" she asked, hoping Oscar would understand the question.

He did. "I think right now, it's safe to assume that everyone is against us, Clara," he sighed.

That was not very reassuring.

Chapter 31

C lara wanted nothing more than to stay in the garden and make out with Oscar like they'd done earlier that afternoon. It might sound silly or immature, but it had felt amazing and Clara desperately wanted more. Unfortunately, they'd already been away from their hosts for much longer than was considered 'socially acceptable'. It was time to head back to face her mother and brother again. Hopefully, they could smooth out some of the tension from earlier.

As they made their way back into the mansion, Clara was suddenly plagued by thoughts she hadn't considered earlier. After this, they would be going home. Tomorrow, Clara would be getting up early, to leave Oscar, for weeks. A torturous thought, especially now, with their newly-found closeness.

Hand in hand, they walked through the brightly lit hallways of the Redwood mansion. "Will you show me your room?" Oscar asked with a lopsided smile. Clara paled. Oh no. She didn't want him to see how childish her room was. "Come on, I'm curious," he nudged her.

"Oh, gods. Fine," she relented, "but don't laugh."

Leading a man to her bedroom felt strange, as if Clara was doing something unimaginably forbidden. The wild mixture of fear and trepidation running through her veins had her trembling.

Clara grabbed a lantern from the corridor before opening the familiar door and stepping into her childhood bedroom. The room where she'd spend most of her life. It had only been a couple of weeks since she'd left the mansion, but so much had changed since then that Clara was like a completely different person.

Oscar whistled in surprise as he surveyed the room. Clara groaned, fighting the urge to run away and hide. "You promised not to laugh."

"I'm not laughing. I just didn't know you liked dolls this much," he noted as he took in the silent army of dolls occupying several shelves along one wall.

Clara groaned, gently running her fingers through the soft yellow curls of the doll closest to her before leaving it in place and turning away to sit on her perfectly made bed. "I don't, actually. I used to, when I was a child. What girl doesn't? But these," she gestured at the shelves, "are sentimental."

Oscar didn't push Clara to continue. Instead, he gently sat down next to her, resting his arm around her shoulders in a welcomed gesture of comfort.

Did Clara want to share this with him? It was silly, but important to her, nonetheless. Seeing him laugh or even smirk would hurt. But, Oscar had dared to be vulnerable with her earlier, sharing some of what he thought were his own personal weaknesses, thoughts and feelings with her. And after all that had happened between them today, Clara felt like she was ready to do the same.

"The dolls are from my father," she said with a sad smile, adding, "Every single one. He'd often be gone for months at a time and he always brought back gifts from every port he'd visited. My brothers got daggers and swords. I got dolls. I loved the first few. I was like...five or six years old back then, I think. My father was always so excited when bringing them to me that I never told him I didn't want them anymore. Or that I would have preferred a dagger as well."

Clara blinked away the tears welling up in her eyes. She didn't want to cry. Not here, not now. Not because Oscar would see, but because her mother was no doubt lurking somewhere around a corner, ready to scorn Clara for acting like a child. "There were so many things I didn't tell my father and now I never will," she sniffled. "And, since my mother broke the bow he gave me, all I have left to remind me of him are these dolls."

"She did what?" Oscar growled.

"It doesn't matter anymore." Clara didn't want to talk about the bow incident but Oscar kept on staring at her, determined to get an answer, so she relented. "It was a few days before the wedding. We had an argument and she just took the bow and..." A shudder ran through Clara's body as she remembered the sharp cracking sound. "She was making sure I'd be a proper wife for you." Clara gave a strained chuckle. "It was one of the reasons I tried to run away. And why I was so freaked out by your gift."

Oscar kissed her temple. "Yes. It all makes a lot more sense now. I'm sorry you had to go through that. Do you want to take the dolls back home with us?" He wasn't overly excited about his proposal and to be honest, neither was Clara. The dolls were a part of Clara's past. Having them displayed in her new home would feel like she was still a little girl.

"That one maybe," Clara said, pointing to a blond doll in a beautiful red dress. "If it's okay with you. It was the first one my father ever gave to me."

"Of course." As Oscar looked around the room, a mischievous grin appeared on his face. "Can I take one too?"

Clara's eyes narrowed. "Sure," she said cautiously. What was he up to?

Instead of picking one of the beautiful porcelain dolls, Oscar went over to the comfortable armchair and pulled a simple redhead ragdoll from beneath the cushions. "This one?" he asked with a cheeky grin.

"Oh, gods, this is so humiliating." Clara hid her face in her hands again. "Ally was not a gift from my father. My old nanny made her for me."

"I figured. But it looks like the only one that has ever been played with. And, she looks like you. She smiles a little more, though." Oscar wiggled the doll from side to side in front of Clara's face, making the two long red ponytails tickle her cheeks.

Clara scowled at her husband as he played with the ever-smiling doll, its simplistic features hand embroidered with coarse thread, but Oscar's grin was too contagious. She found herself grinning back at him, grateful for the obvious attempt at distraction from her dark thoughts. Once again, he'd managed to improve Clara's mood with just a few words.

"I'm being serious, though," Oscar said, cradling the doll in his arms. "I'm bringing Ally home with me. Perhaps she can warm my bed while my wife is freezing her ass off in a tent somewhere in the northern wilderness."

Even though Clara didn't sense any reproach from his teasing words, she felt bad about leaving Oscar. "I won't go if you don't want me to."

"Of course you'll go. Don't throw away such an exciting opportunity for a man you met a week ago. I will be here when you come back." Oscar kissed Clara briefly before standing up. "We should go downstairs before someone starts suspecting me of doing something...depraved with you."

The way he said the word, running his tongue over his lips in the short pause beforehand, made Clara's breath hitch. She'd been distracted once again, completely forgetting they were still in her old home and that her mother and brother were waiting for their return.

"Right," she cleared her throat. "We should probably head home soon anyway. I need to get some sleep tonight."

Oscar nodded in agreement. Neither of them wanted to spend any more time in the Redwood home than absolutely necessary. He grabbed the two dolls before leaving the room. Clara immediately reached for his free hand as they entered the hallway.

"Clara?" Her mother called out, having just reached the top of the staircase. As she looked between Clara and Oscar, her brows tipped in disapproval. "There you are. We were getting worried."

Doubtful, Clara thought. "I was showing Oscar my room."

"Ah. You're taking Ally with you?" The smile that crossed Sophia's face was almost genuine. Almost. Clara nodded, subconsciously squeezing Oscar's hand tighter. "Clara, I was wondering whether we could have a little chat before you leave? Just the two of us?" Sophia glanced at Oscar, whose features hardened ever so slightly.

"I think it's better if we go now," he said in a strictly polite tone. "Clara is leaving early tomorrow," Oscar added as a final nudge into Sophia's obvious sore spot.

"Is she now? You won't spare even a moment to talk to your own mother?" There was that contemptuous tone Clara knew so well.

Determined to stop being afraid of her mother, Clara swallowed down her nerves. This woman had no power over her anymore. Oscar had come in with his shining armor and taken it all away. "Of course, I will," Clara said, doing her best to sound confident. Oscar gave her an inquisitive look and Clara smiled at him. "I'll be fine, Oscar."

"If you say so," he replied, eventually. It was obvious Oscar wasn't happy about Clara talking to her mother. To be honest, Clara wasn't entirely happy about it either. But Sophia was her mother, nothing would ever change that, and Clara couldn't exactly go through life completely ignoring her.

Oscar let go of Clara's hand to caress her cheek before leaning in for a kiss. The kiss was far from innocent. He didn't use his tongue but clearly, he was marking Clara as his in front of her mother. The look he gave Sophia before heading downstairs carried a clear message – *Clara is mine. If you hurt her, you will have a problem with me.* It felt strangely flattering to be the object of such a warning.

Shaking her head in disapproval, Sophia led Clara into a small parlor. Clara loved this room. The large parlor on the ground floor was more formal, used to entertain important visitors and discuss important things. The one upstairs was a family room. This room was where the Redwoods gathered from time to time to play board games, chat, read, or tell stories while sitting around the fireplace. No fire was burning here tonight, naturally, and the room felt abandoned. It was sad how nothing around here truly felt like home to Clara anymore.

"So, it's 'Oscar' now?" Sophia sneered, going around the room to light lamps.

How was that any of her business? "Yes. Is there something you wanted, mother, or are you going to chastise me for life choices I didn't make? As far as I remember, you were the one who accepted King Hayden's proposal to marry Oscar in my name."

"Sebastian has told me a lot about your new husband. You should be careful around him."

Seriously? First, Sophia forced Clara to marry Oscar, literally against her will. And now she's against it? It was ridiculous. "Yes, Sebastian already warned me. Anything else?" What a waste of time this conversation was.

"Clara, I know you probably hate me," Sophia sighed as she walked over to the window. "Gods know, I haven't been the best mother under the sun. But I've always wanted the best for my children. Including you."

Clara frowned. Was this some sort of new game? A sick theatrical show her mother was putting on to guilt trip Clara back under her control? It was impossible to tell.

Sophia's words sounded sincere. How the hell was Clara supposed to respond to that? "I don't hate you," she said. Clara's relationship with her mother was complicated but there was more fear and anger present than hate. "I can't say I love you, though," she added, quietly ashamed of herself. Shouldn't a person love their parents, no matter what?

"Understandable," Sophia conceded, lowering her head. Was there a tear sparkling in the corner of Sophia's eye? It was gone a moment later, as if it were an illusion all along. "Everything I did, everything I told you, everything I tried to teach you was so you would be able to protect yourself."

That didn't make any sense. "Protect myself? The only thing you ever taught me was how to pretend to be something I'm not. Oh right, and to be afraid of men. How does that protect me?!" Clara shouted. So much for staying calm.

"No, child," Sophia replied, narrowing her eyes. "I taught you how to be strong on the inside. So you wouldn't break whenever a pile of shit is dumped on your head. And gods know I tried to teach you to be invisible. To stay out of trouble just so you would have a slightly easier life. But apparently, that was never in my power. I did all of that because I didn't want you to suffer what I went through. Being a woman sucks, Clara."

Clara hesitated, remembering how Karina had told her the same thing. But Sophia's life was perfect, what did she have to complain about? "What did you *have* to go through?" Clara asked, not without contempt. "Dad was-"

Sophia's scoff interrupted her. "Don't even mention that bastard in front of me!" The raw hatred in Sophia's voice made Clara step back. "You were his precious little girl, of course you admired him. He would have brought you the world and let you get away with anything just so you would see him as the perfect father.

"I didn't want to be the one to take that away from you so I kept my mouth shut all those years. But you aren't a child anymore, Clara, so here's the truth. Your father was an asshole. I suffered through years of our marriage without complaining because, what else was I supposed to do?

"Nobody gives a shit if you are happy. Nobody cares that your husband fucks filthy prostitutes and then comes home and forces himself onto you as if you were just another one he didn't have to pay. Do you want to know the difference between a whore and a wife? The whore can say no.

"I tried to teach you to be strong, to survive. Because that's what women do. We don't break. We take the little we are given in this miserable fucking existence and we do our best with it. Despite those monsters with cocks getting in our way the whole time."

Clara couldn't speak, move, or even breathe. She had never seen her mother like this. So furious, so spiteful, so...earnest? Brutally honest, as usual, but it didn't seem like Clara's mother was lying. Still, Clara refused to believe her words. Hell, she refused to even think about them, let alone acknowledge them.

"And just when I thought you couldn't stoop any lower, mother," Clara spat out the last word like an insult. "What are you hoping to achieve with these filthy lies? Did you think that I would run back to you, so that you could continue to control and torment me for the rest of my life? That's not going to happen. I'm free now and you aren't taking that away from me."

"Right," Sophia scoffed. "Go then, daughter. Be free, be happy. Enjoy it while it lasts. Because all men are the same and your charming husband is no exception."

Clara wanted to scream. To tell her she was wrong. But was she, really? Oscar had hurt a lot of women in his life. Not physically, of course. But hadn't he admitted to having been with lots of girls, seducing them with sweet lies? Then leaving them at the first sign of trouble, or even just the first disagreement? There must have been quite a number of broken hearts in his past.

But could Clara hold Oscar's past against him like that? He'd been nothing but good to her so far. He'd trusted, respected, and supported her. Did it really matter who he'd been before? Some small, logical part of her brain kept trying to tell her that people don't change that easily but Clara decided to ignore it. Oscar deserved a chance. That was all he'd asked for during their dreadful wedding night, wasn't it? For Clara to give him a chance.

"You are wrong, mother," Clara replied coldly, with determination that surprised even herself. "Oscar is different. Goodbye."

Sophia didn't try to stop Clara from leaving but there was an ocean of sadness behind her final condescending smirk.

Even when she was no longer in her mother's presence, Clara couldn't stop thinking about what she'd said. Was what Sophia had said about Clara's father true? And did Clara even want to know?

Chapter 32

Oscar had trouble masking his tension. Leaving Clara alone with her mother was a terrible idea. Nothing good could possibly come from it, only a shitload of bad. Oscar didn't think Sophia would convince Clara to stay in the manor instead of returning to the palace, but another dose of poison in the girl's ears wasn't going to help Clara either.

He set the dolls down on a small table next to the main entrance so they wouldn't be forgotten on the way out, grinning over the redhead ragdoll again. Ally, that's what Clara had called her. Imagining Clara as a young girl, cuddled under a blanket on her bed with such a simple toy, was interesting. How many whispered secrets had Ally heard? How many tears were soaked into her stuffing? And why the hell was Oscar getting all soft and mushy over a stupid doll?

The answer was simple. Because the doll belonged to Clara and at some point, it was an important part of her life. And Oscar wanted to know every little thing about his wife, no matter how insignificant. Information was power.

Actually no, that wasn't the reason. Oscar wanted to know everything because he wanted to make sure Clara was happy. He wanted to avenge every injustice that she'd ever suffered from her stupid family. He wanted to make the people who'd hurt her pay for every single tear she had shed.

Smirking, Oscar forcibly stopped his train of thought. He was getting himself into dangerous waters. His revenge against that bastard Umber had brought him very little satisfaction and earned him a very much deserved distrust from Clara. Oscar had stupidly made himself look like an evil crime boss in front of her. Plus, the king probably wouldn't be happy if he found out who'd really paid for the attack.

Being so irrationally emotional when it came to Clara, was becoming inconvenient for Oscar, dangerous even. He had to get himself under control.

"Lord Huxley," Sebastian Redwood addressed Oscar with his ever present, contemptuous smile. "Would you like to join me for a quick game?" He pointed to a Citadel game table.

Not having to pretend to like the asshole anymore, Oscar smirked at Sebastian. "I'm not sure I have time for a whole round, but why not?" Oscar hadn't played in ages, mostly because nobody wanted to play against him anymore. People didn't like losing over and over.

"I'm not very good, so it should be quick," Sebastian shrugged. Somehow, Oscar knew he was lying. "Defend or attack?"

"You're the host, your choice."

Sebastian chose to defend and started picking his pieces. Oscar waited with his arms crossed in front of his chest, trying to figure out what had caused this sudden outburst of hospitality.

The game's rules were simple. One player was defending the Citadel, the other was trying to conquer it. They were each given a certain amount of credit, which they used to build their armies. Over two dozen figure types were available, some weaker and cheaper, some strong and therefore more expensive. The king was the most powerful and the most costly piece in the game, leaving the player who picked it with very limited options for the rest of his army. But as a defender, the king was practically immortal.

It was the reason he was almost always taken by the defending player and also the reason the defenders usually won.

"No king?" Oscar asked, quirking his eyebrow as he looked over Sebastian's army.

"Who needs a king?" Sebastian's expression turned cryptic. "I find it boring when he's around."

Was that meant to be a joke? Or some sort of test? Oscar's instincts were telling him there was more to this situation than just the game. "I think Hayden would disagree," Oscar noted as he quickly picked the pieces for his own army.

Sebastian chuckled. It was an annoying sound that grated on Oscar's nerves. "I meant in the game. No elephants?"

"Not a fan," Oscar shrugged, setting his pieces on the board. Sebastian wasn't wrong, taking elephants would be a smart move, but Oscar didn't want to win the game. He had a feeling that losing might serve him better. Oscar just needed to make sure it didn't seem like he was trying to lose on purpose.

They made the first few moves in silence. Sebastian set up his defenses while Oscar's army drew nearer. "You seemed to have wrapped my sister around your finger," Sebastian smirked, sending the archers to a ledge overlooking the battlefield. A common move. An odd one, considering he had several smarter options. But Sebastian either didn't see them or chose to ignore them.

"She's my wife. Some people might argue that makes me the one wrapped around her finger." A couple of Oscar's barbarians climbed the ledge to massacre the archers, only to be swallowed by a fire trap in the next turn.

"It certainly doesn't look that way," Sebastian retorted. His ballistas started to thin out Oscar's approaching army. Unfortunate but inevitable. Grinning smugly, Sebastian moved his knight, adding, "She's an extremely naive girl, but I guess that would be exactly your usual prey, wouldn't it?"

Oscar hated how Sebastian kept talking about Clara as if she was just a stupid, helpless child. "She's a smart woman," he countered, choosing not to react to Sebastian's question. Sadly, Redwood's statement wasn't entirely wrong. Naive girls had been Oscar's usual type in the past.

Oscar shook off his dark thoughts, focusing on the game instead. What the hell was Sebastian doing? There were ladders at his walls but he didn't use the hot oil. How was Oscar supposed to lose the game? It was like every time Sebastian could choose between two options, he always chose the wrong one. He was either really bad at the game or...

Of course. Oscar should have realized it earlier but he was distracted by the insults on Clara's behalf. Sebastian was doing the same thing as Oscar – he was trying to lose. But, for what purpose?

"You should have taken the king," Oscar quipped as his units destroyed the Citadel's flagpole, thus winning him the game.

Sebastian smirked. "Like I said, it's not much fun when he's around."

It was the second time he'd said that. It had to have deeper meaning. Was he testing Oscar's loyalty, trying to see whether he could catch him insulting Hayden or saying something that could be considered treason? Had Hayden set him up to this? Oscar didn't think so.

Having no idea what Sebastian's true intentions were, Oscar tread carefully. "I think the king's loyal subjects who just died defending your Citadel would disagree. He might not be fun, but it's safer with him around." Did that count as expressing loyalty?

"If you say so," Sebastian shrugged. Neither his expression nor tone gave any hints as to what he truly meant.

Under normal circumstances, Oscar enjoyed these games of wits but right now, all he wanted was to rescue Clara from her mother's clutches and leave this house of horrors. "What exactly is your point, Redwood?" he snapped. Damn, Hayden's straightforwardness was contagious.

"Oh, so this must be your suave demeanor and shrewd cunning, I keep hearing about? Talk about disappointment." Sebastian moved to pour mead into two glasses before offering one to Oscar. "Have it your way, then. I don't like you. After Hayden finally agreed to invade that shithole country of yours, I'd hoped to see you hanged. Then I return home to find that, not only are you not dead, but you're now my fucking brother-in-law. I will not let you screw up Clara's life with your filthy little games.

"From now on, you are to stay out of palace business. Get a house somewhere in the countryside. Buy a fucking vineyard or an orchard, I don't care. But stay away from the king. It's not like he trusts you anyway. He asked me to keep a close eye on you. You don't belong here and the sooner you accept that, the sooner you can start building some other life, far away from the capital."

Oscar masked his satisfied smile with a furious glare, because that was the reaction Sebastian expected to see. Internally, his stomach fluttered with excitement. Whether he realized it or not, Sebastian had just given himself away. He knew nothing about the deal Oscar had made with Hayden, which meant that he was lying about Hayden having asked him to spy on Oscar. Sebastian's righteous indignation was clearly an act. But what was his goal? Was he really just trying to protect Clara?

Oscar didn't think so.

The most likely answer? Sebastian was simply an eager loyal supporter of Hayden misguidedly trying to protect the king from Oscar's bad influence. It would make sense. Hell, it would be an absolutely perfect answer to the riddle.

However, when it came to Clara, the most likely answer usually turned out to be the wrong one. Did this apply to her brother as well? Because there was another option that popped into Oscar's mind. It didn't make much sense yet. He'd have to think about it some more. Plus, it was *wrong*. So wrong and fucked up that-

"Ready to go home?" Clara's question interrupted Oscar's thoughts. As he saw her face, a vicious snarl almost escaped him. Clara wasn't crying but she looked paler than the walls and seemed to be in a state of shock.

Seeing her standing in the doorway, looking so lost and desperate, made Oscar forget all about Sebastian bloody Redwood and his stupid games. He quickly crossed the distance between them to pull her into a tight hug. Clara hesitated, sending shivers of dread down Oscar's spine, but eventually leaned into him. She'd said she wanted to go home. That must count for something.

What had that poor excuse for a mother said to her? Damn, Oscar knew it was a bad idea to leave Clara alone with that witch. "Yes, let's go home," he nodded.

Oscar turned back to Sebastian, ignoring his smirk. Seriously, these people were a freak show, not a family. "If the king wants something from me," he declared coldly, "he is more than welcome to address me in person. He doesn't need to send his errand boy to do his bidding. Give my regards to your mother, we're leaving now."

"You don't have to go with him, Clara," Sebastian addressed his sister.

A sharp retort froze in Oscar's throat when Clara pulled away from him and stepped toward Sebastian. Did she really want to stay here? After everything Oscar had said and done?

Fortunately, her answering tone suggested otherwise. "You're damn right, I don't have to," she spat out, her shock momentarily replaced by anger. "But I want to. I also want you and Mother to leave me alone. For good, this time."

Not waiting for an answer, she turned around and stormed out of the house, not stopping until she was by the carriage. Oscar couldn't help but return Sebastion's earlier smirk before quickly following Clara outside, grabbing the dolls on his way.

Clara diligently avoided glancing back at her former home as they were leaving. As soon as they were off the Redwood property, she curled up to Oscar, only managing to relax a little after he'd put his arm around her.

Oscar swallowed back his questions along with his burning desire to go back and strangle Sophia Redwood. Instead, he pulled Clara closer before tucking some loose curls behind her ear. "You can talk to me," he said after making sure there would be no trace of anger in his voice, "if you want."

Clara absent-mindedly traced along the creases in his palm. It was a strangely enticing feeling, as if sparks were jumping from Oscar's skin to the tips of her fingers. Who knew something so mundane could feel so intimate?

She was quiet for so long Oscar gave up hope of getting an answer before she finally said, "I'm not sure I want to think about it. But I can't seem to stop." An exasperated sigh later, she shifted to look at him. "Would you rather keep believing a pretty lie or know the ugly truth? Even if that truth might be painful?"

Oscar stifled a growl. Perfect. Just fucking perfect. What did Sophia put into Clara's head this time? Could she have known about Alice? Sebastian seemed well-informed about Oscar. For a diplomat with international connections it probably wasn't difficult to dig up dirt.

The sad thing was they wouldn't even have to lie to Clara, especially not when it came to Alice. That was a monumental screwup and Oscar knew it all too well. He should have told Clara himself but damn, it wasn't the type of story you tell to a woman while trying to woo her.

"Clara, I promised I wouldn't lie to you, so…" Oscar hesitated. "Whatever your mother has told you about me… Well, it's probably true but can I tell you my side of the story before you judge me?"

A small wrinkle appeared on Clara's forehead as her eyebrows came together to form a confused frown. "This isn't about you. But now I'd like to know what you are talking about."

"I'll tell you later, I promise." Yes, he had to. No matter how hard or painful it was going to be.

Clara was going to hate him, but he still had to tell her before she found out from someone else, someone who would paint Oscar as a heartless monster. Well, as a worse monster than he had been. Gods, this was so fucked up. Maybe Oscar could get drunk. He surely deserved a drink after this extremely arduous evening.

Avoiding the topic for now, Oscar answered her previous question, "I would always choose the truth, no matter what."

She gave him a coy smile. "Interesting, coming from someone who likes to play with words so much."

"You'd be surprised, but I don't actually lie very often. I usually just take the truth and twist it to suit my needs." Oh, yes, talking about lying was a great way to make Clara trust him. "Lies are dangerous because sooner or later, the truth always comes out. I prefer to face it on my own terms instead of letting others use it against me."

Clara seemed to be contemplating his words before nodding. "I guess you're right. Could I ask you a favor?"

"Anything."

She took in a deep breath as if to calm herself, before continuing, "Could you find out whether my father cheated on my mother with prostitutes? Or if it was just another one of her mind games? Because she sure as hell didn't seem to be lying."

"I can," Oscar started carefully, "but do you really want to know?"

Seriously, what the fuck was wrong with Clara's mother? Even if it was true, why did she have to pull it out now? Badmouthing her dead husband in front of their daughter? What kind of spiteful creature does that?!

Clara heaved a sigh. "Yes, I think so. But could we not talk about it anymore, please? I just want to enjoy being with you one last night before I leave."

Oscar had to tame his rising...excitement. No, Clara wasn't ready for sex, he'd seen that earlier. However, there were countless other possibilities of how they could 'enjoy' being together.

Chapter 33

Clara shoved all intruding thoughts about her father into an imaginary dungeon in her mind. She was leaving tomorrow morning and wanted to spend her remaining time with Oscar, without dwelling on such dark topics.

There was one nagging thought she couldn't let go of, no matter how hard she tried. Knowing she would be gone for so long, Oscar might want to...consummate their marriage tonight. Even the mere thought was making Clara anxious but she'd already decided she would do it for him. Oscar had been nothing but kind and supportive, he deserved to finally get what he desired.

Clara just hoped she wouldn't disappoint him. What if he thought she wasn't good enough? She had no experience and no idea what to expect, aside from her mother's very biased description. Gods, Clara hoped she wasn't going to have a panic attack and start crying.

As they walked through the palace, Oscar's warm hand holding onto Clara's icy one, she pondered over her mother's words about men, deciding they were nonsense. Not all men were the same and Oscar certainly wasn't a monster. He wasn't perfect, but neither was Clara. When she looked at him, he gave her a genuine, honest smile. A monster with a cock? Bullshit.

When their chamber door finally closed behind them, Clara felt relieved. Home.

Oscar gently stroked her cheek. "Would you like to take a bath? You should enjoy the little luxuries while you can. I don't think you'll get to bathe much while out on the dusty road or in some military encampment," he teased her.

Steaming hot water did sound amazing and Clara nodded excitedly. Oscar left to order servants to prepare the bath while Clara examined the dolls they'd brought back from her room. Picking up Ally, Clara gave the doll a quick hug. The feel of Ally's pigtails brushing against her face was familiar and surprisingly soothing. The 'proper' lady in her was appalled that a grown woman, a married one nonetheless, was cuddling with a children's toy, but Clara ignored the pompous snob.

Putting Ally down, Clara looked over at the blonde porcelain doll, a gift from her father. Suddenly, Clara was furious. If what her mother had told her was true, then Clara's whole life had been a lie. The perfect childhood, the perfect family. The perfect father.

In a moment of blind rage, Clara grabbed the doll. She wanted to smash it on the floor, listen to it shatter and watch the pieces fly in all directions. Only the thought of the poor soul having to clean up the mess stopped Clara's hand. Sighing in resignation, she opened one of the low cabinets and stuffed the doll between the empty parchments, quills, and ink vials before slamming the door with a loud bang.

Looking up, Clara noticed Oscar standing by the door, watching her. He didn't comment on Clara's action, offering her a glass of brandy instead. She accepted it, hesitantly.

Clara had never been allowed to drink alcohol before she got married due to technically still being a child. She'd only ever tasted it after finding out about Nicolas missing, and only because she had seen her father drink when he was nervous or upset.

Oscar raised his own glass, smiling. "To being home?"

"Home," Clara nodded. "No place like it." Clara had to fight off the coughing as the liquor burned its way down her throat.

Oscar caressed her cheek. "You are a strong woman, Clara. I admire you."

Admire? That was a word Clara wouldn't imagine someone using in connection to her. Neither was being a 'strong' woman. How the hell was she strong? She cried all the time, being scared or clueless was her daily bread. Where was the strength in that?

"You are, even if you don't see it," Oscar insisted. "How about you go and enjoy that bath? I just need to write something down, then I'll join you afterwards in the bedroom."

Precious oils had been added to the steaming water, making it smell amazing, but Clara was struggling to enjoy it. Too many distracting thoughts whirled through her mind. She tried to focus on the heat permeating her skin, warming her icy hands and feet. Why did fear and despair always make her feel so cold?

Unsated, Clara dried herself before putting on her nightgown and heading into the bedroom. Oscar was just setting a piece of paper down on his nightstand when she entered. "Just give me a minute, I'll be right back," he said, giving her a kiss before disappearing behind the bathroom door. Even though it had been just a brief touching of their lips, Clara's heart sped up.

She curiously glanced over at the piece of paper on his nightstand, briefly considering reading it before rejecting the idea, ashamed that such a thought had even crossed her mind.

Sitting cross-legged in the middle of the large bed, Clara ran her hand over the sheet, trying not to overthink what was about to happen. She was certain Oscar wouldn't hurt her, but other than that? Her mother's voice kept telling Clara how disgusting, painful, and humiliating it was all going to be. Even though Clara truly believed her mother's words were a lie, the voice was hard to ignore.

She was so nervous that she flinched when the bathroom door clicked. Oscar slowly walked over, wearing short breeches and a warm smile. "Clara," he sighed, "I told you..."

"But I'm going away tomorrow," she interrupted him. "And...I know I'm a useless wife but I just don't want you to...to be disappointed or..." Was he going to be with another woman while Clara was away? Was that what men did? Oh, how Clara loathed her mother for planting all these seeds of doubt into her mind.

It would only be fair if Oscar got a chance to satisfy his needs with someone who wasn't a sniveling parody of a wife. But just the thought of it sent a pang through Clara's heart.

Oscar rolled his eyes. "Clara, you are the most amazing wife a man could wish for. I swore to be faithful to you and I intend to keep my promise, if that's what you are worried about. No matter what your mother claims, I am not some wild beast driven only by primal instincts. I might not like you going away and I sure as hell will be worried the whole time, but that doesn't mean I'll seek solace in some other woman's arms."

Ashamed of her thoughts and doubts, Clara's head lowered, mumbling, "I'm sorry. And, you don't have to be worried about me." Why would he even? He wasn't in love with her.

"Of course I will. Just promise me one thing," Oscar appealed, crouching down to capture her gaze.

Captivated by his intensity, Clara nodded. "I will come back to you, Oscar."

"Right." Amusement flashed in Oscar's eyes. "Promise me two things then. Promise you will always stay with Karina, no matter what happens."

Oh, so that was the 'important thing' he wanted from Clara? To protect Oscar's one true love with her life? That hurt. "Don't worry," Clara replied, her voice shaking. "I'll do what I can to keep her safe." Clara wasn't sure what she could actually do. She imagined shooting arrows at human beings would be very different from shooting at targets. Did she have it in her to kill someone?

"What?" Oscar frowned in confusion. "No. That's not what I mean, Clara." He cupped her cheeks, his thumb wiping at a stray tear. "Our foolish king will no doubt march his men straight into the most dangerous areas of the North. But he will do anything to protect Karina. If you stay close to her, that protection will extend to you too. You are the one I swore to keep safe."

His words washed the pain away, warming Clara's heart. Did he mean them? Or was it just sweet lies? He'd said he wouldn't lie to her but maybe he was lying to himself. Hope was dangerous and yet, Clara couldn't help but let a seed take root in her soul. "You be safe," she returned his sentiments "No getting kidnapped or murdered by mysterious crime lords," she whispered, her fingers trying to permanently etch the familiar features of Oscar's face deep into her memory.

Their lips met in a frenzy of need, desperate to enjoy each other while they still could. Oscar must have been uncomfortable in his crouched position because he tried to stand up. Clara pulled him onto the bed instead, wanting to feel his body against her own.

Oscar's mouth was everywhere, his tongue playing with hers, exploring and probing so wildly her breath hitched. Her hands traced the muscles across his shoulders then down his back. Oscar groaned when her arms wrapped around his waist, pulling him closer. He was supporting himself on his forearms but Clara's hold allowed her to feel his weight press down against her body.

She slid one of her hands up to Oscar's hair, pulling it back to reveal his neck. Her lips left his as she started kissing the newly exposed skin. This time, Clara didn't stop at just a couple of fleeting touches, letting passion override her fear with proper, passionate kisses. Clara's moans mixed with Oscar's as she savored his sweet masculine scent.

Oscar shifted, freeing one of his hands to reveal Clara's neck in turn. His kisses were more deliberate, tracing a line down from her ear, sucking and nibbling as he went, leaving her skin burning with desire.

When he got to the crook of Clara's neck, he continued down to the center of her cleavage, stopping right at the edge of her gown. Oscar was panting just as heavily as Clara, his gaze darkened by raw desire. Even though a part of her wanted to go further, Clara still flinched when Oscar ran his hand up her leg, resting it above her thigh.

Oscar blinked the haze out of his eyes before smiling at her. "Don't worry," he whispered, "I know you aren't ready. But..." He hesitated, tilting his head with an inquisitive look. "I thought I might give you something else that would convince you to come back to me and not fall in love with the first handsome, sword-swinging idiot you meet up north." His grip on Clara's thigh tightened. Wow, was he really jealous? "I promise, I won't hurt you," he added, noticing her slight hesitation.

"I know you won't." Her ragged breathing made it hard for Clara to speak. "I don't need any extra reasons to come back to you." Oscar's gaze softened and he was about to pull his hand away. Clara placed her own on top of his to keep it in place before sheepishly adding, "But... I might be a little curious."

Chapter 34

O scar grinned at her. "Curious? Hmm. Curiosity is a dangerous thing."

"I know." Clara shivered, suddenly not as confident as she'd thought. But... His kisses had left her with an unfamiliar ache, a feeling she didn't really understand but knew had to do with Oscar. The fact that his hand was under her nightgown, resting high up on her thigh, should have been terrifying. However, all Clara felt was jittery anticipation and, as she'd told him, curiosity. "Could you...kiss me again?" It felt silly to be asking openly like this but Oscar didn't seem to mind, humming in approval as he lowered his head back to Clara's neck.

His kisses were setting Clara's skin on fire, making her giddy and light-headed. His hand traveled higher, reaching her hip before changing direction and moving closer to her pulsating center. When his fingers ran through the soft hair between her legs and his palm pressed against her most private parts, Clara's breath drew in sharply. Her first instinct was to squeeze her knees together but Oscar's thigh was lodged between them, preventing her from moving.

Pausing his movements, he inquired, "Good or bad?"

"Hmm?" Clara hadn't really thought about what was happening in that way. Now that he'd mentioned it, she realized it actually did feel good. Whatever bad feelings Clara might be having were all in her mind so she pushed them aside. "Good, I think," she replied hesitantly, running her fingers through his hair.

"It only gets better," he grinned. His teeth grazed the skin of her neck, exerting a quiet moan from Clara's lips. "Just trust me and try to relax."

Trusting Oscar was not a problem but relaxing turned out to be quite difficult to execute, especially when his fingers parted the folds of her womanhood and circled around a particularly sensitive spot. It was an intense sensation, filling Clara with such raw desire she instinctively raised her hips to move closer to Oscar's hand. Was this what carnal pleasure felt like? If so, Clara never wanted it to stop.

And stopping, it wasn't. If anything, the feeling was getting stronger, to the point Clara was barely even registering Oscar's lips against her neck. Her entire mind focused on that one little spot between her legs that Oscar kept teasing. His fingers were sliding around it and over it, rubbing and pressing, gradually making her want to moan or worse, scream out loud.

Clara pulled Oscar in tighter, wanting his naked chest brushing against hers through the thin layer of her nightgown. It wasn't enough. She needed more, needed him to do something about this pressure building inside of her that threatened to explode and shatter her mind into millions of tiny pieces.

Raw, intense anger flared through her body when she heard Oscar's chuckle. He was laughing at her. That bastard was mocking her instead of doing something about this searing need throbbing inside of her! The need that he had ignited in order to torment her, no doubt.

Clara fisted his hair and yanked on it to bring his ear closer to her mouth, not caring whether she was hurting him. She was the one in agony. Except it wasn't really painful. It was pleasant, more pleasant than anything she'd ever experienced in her entire life and Clara wanted it to last forever. She also wanted it to peak right now as the building pressure was becoming unbearable.

Torn by her conflicting needs, Clara growled, "Stop laughing at me, you asshole, and do something. I can't..."

Her words were cut short when the pressure finally exploded into pure ecstasy and a scream tore out of her throat. Clara froze as waves of pleasure she'd never thought possible washed over her, occasionally jolting as the wild pulsating crested inside her. Fortunately, she had let go of Oscar's hair somewhere along the way because she'd have certainly hurt him by now. The pulsating eventually ebbed and weakened until it was reduced to a pleasant afterglow. It was still there, only now it seemed manageable.

Oscar wiggled his fingers, stoking the flames. "Breathe, Clara," he teased. Clara knew he was smiling but couldn't pry her eyes open to check.

Breathe? Her brain didn't have the capacity for something so meaningless as breathing right now, but Clara tried. Inhale, exhale. Yes, that was better. Fresh air helped to clear her head, slowly chasing away the haze.

What had just happened? Clara tried to gather the shattered pieces of her mind to form one cohesive memory but it was all a blur. Except for one particular memory which made her gasp in horror. Had she really called Oscar an asshole? Gods, she was so stupid! "I'm sorry," she whispered, praying that the bed would open up and swallow her whole, "I didn't mean to call you that."

"I don't mind in the slightest," Oscar chuckled. Clara finally opened her eyes to be met with a wide, cheeky grin. "You're a feisty little thing. I like that," he winked.

Clara didn't particularly enjoy being teased but for once, she felt like she deserved it. Besides, his teasing tone and cheeky grin proved that Oscar wasn't angry with her. Perhaps that was his point.

Why had Clara called him an asshole, anyway? Her feelings in that moment were blurry, she only remembered feeling a searing need for something, though she hadn't known what for. And the pleasure that came after was...indescribable, beyond her wildest imagination.

Was that it? Had they had sex? She didn't think so. Gods, Clara felt so damn clueless in these matters!

She glanced over at Oscar to confirm he was still wearing his underpants, although it looked like something was trying to pierce through the fabric. Clara had to hold back a giggle at the sight.

He'd only touched her with his fingers, so it probably didn't count as sex. Did it really matter, though? It felt so amazing Clara wanted more. Now she understood why he'd said he wanted to show her something that would make her come back to him. She wasn't sure she wanted to leave now!

Clara had dozens of questions but she clamped her mouth down, embarrassed by her own ignorance. It didn't escape Oscar's attention though. His grin morphed into a kind smile as his hand gently caressed her cheek. "You can ask me anything, Clara," he said. "I promise not to make fun of you."

He seemed sincere enough so Clara decided to take the plunge. "Is that what sex feels like?" It was like the complete opposite of what her mother had described.

"No," Oscar shook his head, "sex feels even better."

Frowning, Clara studied his expression, trying to see if he was lying or making fun of her. He didn't seem to be doing either.

"For me, at least," Oscar continued. "I don't know, maybe it's different for women. But I've always found the close intimacy of the act better than simply...well, having my physical needs taken care of. What you felt is achievable by many means. You can even do it yourself, which I'm quite surprised you hadn't figured out on your own yet."

So much information at once was overwhelming. "You've met the reason why I haven't figured out anything on my own," Clara growled. Yes, even touching her own body had been described as something disgusting. Clara had felt so guilty while trying it never gave her any pleasure. Gods, had she been missing out this whole time?

"Right. Sorry, that makes sense." Oscar smiled softly, "I just wanted to show you what I have to offer, so you won't forget about me when you are gone," he admitted, sounding strangely insecure.

Forget about him? Impossible. "Why are you so worried that I won't come back?"

"Clara," Oscar sighed, his smile turning sad. "I'm well aware that I'm not the best looking man in the country. Or the funniest, or the most courteous. And, I'm very far from one of those knights in shining armor from your books. With both eyes closed, I'd maybe fit into the 'good guy' category but that's about it."

Why was he talking about himself like this? Clara realized this was exactly the way she spoke about herself when anxious and she didn't like it one bit coming from the usually confident Oscar. Perhaps she'd infected Oscar with her insecurities, passed them to him like some sort of a contagious disease. That was something she simply couldn't allow.

"Listen to me," she ordered, pushing Oscar's shoulder until he rolled onto his back before swiftly climbing to sit astride him. "You look amazing. You've been nothing but good to me. And," her index finger pressed forcefully against the center of his chest, "I'm supposed to be the insecure one in this marriage. So stop it."

"Truly feisty," Oscar chuckled, regaining most of his previous confidence.

As Clara shifted her weight to move her knee into a more comfortable position, Oscar's breath hitched sharply. With his head tilted back and his eyes closed, he looked to be in pain. Then Clara suddenly realized that she'd been wriggling directly on his still hard manhood. That couldn't be comfortable for him.

"Oh gods, I'm sorry!" she exclaimed, carefully extracting herself from his lap. "I didn't mean to hurt you."

Oscar grinned mischievously. "Oh, I'm not in pain."

This time, it only took Clara a few seconds to figure out what he meant. Seriously, she was so damn ignorant when it came to sex. Why had no one ever educated her on it? She certainly didn't count her mother's horror stories as education.

Clara sat up and hugged her knees, not sure what to do or say. "Uhh... Should I...?" It should work both ways, shouldn't it? He'd given her pleasure, she should...how did he say it? Take care of his needs? Clara only had a vague idea of what that even meant.

"Clara, this is not a barter or trade. You don't owe me anything." Oscar pulled her into his arms. "Let's just go to sleep. You need to rest while you can." His lips, still smiling, tickled the side of her neck as he hugged her tighter, pulling a blanket over both of them.

"You are wrong," Clara mumbled as she drifted off to sleep, "I owe you everything."

Chapter 35

The morning came too soon. It was still dark when Clara woke up to get ready. Oscar grumbled, clearly not a morning person, but he dutifully got dressed and even carried Clara's bag and bow to the courtyard near the stables where the king's soldiers were already preparing for their departure.

Clara couldn't have looked less like a highborn lady if she'd tried, and in a way, she had. Wearing her favorite worn leather breeches, knee-high lace-up boots and simple white shirt with a sturdy, dark gray jacket to combat the morning chill, Clara was determined to be comfortable for the long journey ahead. Her wild, unruly mane was plaited into a thick red braid that fell over one shoulder. Hopefully, it would prevent the locks from tangling since it looked like the day was going to be windy. Clara also had a thick, hooded cloak sitting ready on the top of her saddlebag, just in case it started raining.

Karina rushed over to greet her. "You came!" It was obvious she had tried to sound excited but the result was spoiled by a long yawn. "Sorry," she mumbled, "I hate getting up before sunrise."

"You chose a perfect place to go, then," Oscar quipped, rolling his eyes. "I'm sure your enemies will stay their attacks until you've had your fair share of sleep." Oscar dropped the friendly tone, "Can I speak with you in private?"

Blatantly ignoring him, Karina turned to Clara. "Your horse is over there," she said, pointing to the brown mare Clara had been riding the day before, "all saddled up and ready to go. I think your husband should go with you and help secure your bags for you," she added, turning to smirk at Oscar.

"Thanks, but I can do it," Clara responded. "You guys talk."

It was only natural that Oscar wanted to say goodbye to the woman he loved, Clara thought. Wasn't it? It hurt, somewhere deep down inside, but Clara hid the pain, focusing instead on properly strapping the bag behind the saddle, then shifting things around to the bags on the sides, making sure the weight was evenly balanced. There was a scabbard ready to store her bow, which made her chuckle. Karina had thought of everything.

Overwhelmed by curiosity, Clara glanced back at Oscar and Karina. They were standing off to one side, exchanging quiet words but it hardly looked like two people in love, or even two friends saying goodbye to each other. No, it looked a lot like they were arguing. As she watched Oscar's scowl grow deeper, Clara wondered what had made him so angry. Was he mad at Karina for putting herself in danger?

"So, you're the one Karina insisted on bringing with us?" Clara turned to see the king staring at her in concern. She quickly curtsied but without the long gown, it didn't really have its normal visual effect. Shaking his head, the king continued, "Clara, are you sure you know what you are getting into?"

Clara tried to look as confident as possible, in spite of feeling incredibly nervous. "Days in the saddle and nights in a tent? Don't worry, my lord, I won't slow you down." Clara had ample experience with both, but not on this scale. However, she was determined not to be a burden, no matter what.

"Hayden?" Karina returned, briefly rising up onto her tiptoes to peck the king's cheek. "Please, be nice."

"Yes Hayden, please be nice," Oscar repeated sternly.

The king shot him a glare before addressing Clara again, "Fine then. Your choice. If you can't keep up, you're going home on your own. And if someone tries to kill y-" He paused mid-word upon seeing Clara's bow strategically placed into the scabbard. "What's that?" he asked incredulously.

Before Clara could even open her mouth to respond, Oscar was already throwing condescending remarks at Hayden. "That, my dear king, is a bow. One would think you'd recognize it-"

Clara squeezed Oscar's hand roughly to stop him. Starting a fight with the king was the last thing she needed right now. "Be nice," she repeated Karina's words. To her surprise, Oscar followed her command, forcing out a dutiful smile. Clara turned to the king once more. "I'm aware of the risks, Your Majesty," she said calmly.

"Do you even know how to use that?" Hayden inquired in a condescending tone.

Oscar was getting ready to say something but Clara didn't need him to. For once, this was something Clara could be one hundred percent certain about, perhaps the only thing in her entire life she knew she was good at. Giving the king her sweetest smile, she calmly replied, "You'd be surprised."

Hayden's eyebrows shot up. Both Karina and Oscar started chuckling quietly at seeing his dumbstruck face. "Oh, shut up, you two," he growled, shaking his head. "Whatever. I need to check if the men are ready." Muttering something about running off to war to escape from women, he stormed off.

"See you, Oscar," Karina waved her hand and went to mount her horse, leaving Clara alone with her husband.

"What were you two talking about?" Clara asked, unsure if she really wanted to know.

Oscar let out a deep sigh. "I was just telling her I'm not happy that she's putting you in danger like this."

Putting Clara in danger? Was Oscar really that worried about her? Now, there was a warming thought. Clara gave him a bright smile but before she could assure him that she was going to be okay, Oscar pulled her into a hug so tight she could barely breathe. "This is for you," he whispered as he reached into his pocket.

Clara recognized the parchment he'd left on his nightstand last night. He'd written something for her? Her excitement was quickly doused by Oscar's sigh. "It's not a love letter or anything like that. Perhaps, that would have been more appropriate. But...I promised to tell you my secrets and this is the darkest one."

Shaking her head, Clara pushed the note away. "You don't have to tell me anything, Oscar."

"Take it," he insisted, placing the parchment into Clara's hand and forcing her fingers to wrap around it. "Do you remember what I told you about the truth yesterday? It always comes out. And this is something I want you to hear from me, not from someone else."

He seemed desperate. Whatever was written on this piece of paper must have been terrible and Clara wasn't sure whether she even wanted to read it. But, she knew she was going to.

"Just..." Oscar hesitated, "don't judge me too harshly, please. We all make mistakes. I'd like to think I've changed since this. Oh, and...could I ask you to keep it all a secret? Nobody knows the whole story. Karina knows some parts, but not everything," he whispered, avoiding Clara's eyes.

Was he really going to tell Clara something not even his lifelong friend and secret love interest knew? That was strangely reassuring. Clara cupped Oscar's cheeks, waiting for his eyes to meet hers before softly saying, "Whatever your secret is, it won't change my mind. I...I will miss you." Clara barely stopped herself from saying something else, something that would be impossible to take back. Something that scared her immensely.

"I'll miss you more," Oscar replied. Their kiss was unhurried and gentle, as if they had all the time in the world and not just a couple of minutes before they were to part ways for a long time.

Horseshoes clicking against the cobblestones nearby made Clara look up and finally pull away from Oscar. It was the queen on her beautiful Seranian mare, a horse that every single soul in the courtyard silently envied. Except for the king, who was riding his own pitch black stallion, looking every inch a mighty warrior. "Ready?" Karina asked.

"No," Clara chuckled before briefly kissing Oscar again. "But more time won't won't make it any better." With Oscar's note safely hidden in the inside pocket of her jacket, Clara pulled herself up into the saddle. She almost cried out at the feeling of Oscar's hand on her thighs as he helped her up.

"Sorry," he grinned, letting her know that he wasn't sorry at all. "I couldn't resist. Stay safe, please?"

Clara gestured at the crowd of heavily armed knights, archers, and soldiers all gathered in the courtyard. "I think I'll be fine," she noted. "You stay safe."

Oscar didn't seem bothered by the possibility of being branded a threat by this mysterious 'player' or being forcibly removed from 'the game'. Clara, on the other hand, worried about it a lot. But this was Oscar's area of expertise, she should probably just trust him. Not that there was anything she could do to stop or protect him.

Oscar had to step back to avoid getting trampled by the dozens of horses suddenly making their way toward the gate. Clara could see his hand as he waved at her, raising her own in return before pulling on the reins of her mare and joining the other riders, searching the crowd for Karina's long braid.

The day was long, longer than a day deserved to be.

It didn't start out bad. The wind had calmed down for the most part. The soft breeze that remained was just enough to bring fresh air from the fields to the road and cool the people and their horses down as the sun began to rise, the summer showing its strength one last time before giving way to fall.

The group set a steady pace that wasn't as challenging as Clara had feared. It wasn't for the benefit of the riders but, more importantly, to protect the horses.

When they stopped for a quick lunch, a couple of pieces of bread with some smoked meat, Clara felt relaxed, like she would after a nice ride through the countryside that she used to love so much. Normally, she'd be looking forward to heading home and soothing her irritated muscles in a hot bath. Getting back up on her horse to ride for a couple more hours didn't seem so appealing anymore.

The king's amused smirk at seeing Clara carefully stretching her arms and legs was enough for her to put on a determined expression and hop back on her mare, pretending her butt wasn't already sore. Fortunately, just as Karina had promised, Hayden didn't make any comment or force Clara to go back home. No doubt he was convinced she'd give up on her own.

The queen didn't seem so excited anymore either, but just like Clara, Karina didn't let any doubts show on her face as she mounted her horse. Not letting the king win proved to be a strong motivation.

The women talked throughout the day, not continuously but on and off as they thought of something interesting to say to each other. Hayden didn't seem to mind his wife spending most of her time with Clara instead of him. He rode in silence, occasionally exchanging a couple of words with the officers.

The men didn't really pay too much attention to the female members of their party. Judging by the quiet remarks Clara had overheard, they were convinced that the queen and her lady in waiting, or whatever they considered Clara to be, were just joining them for the day and would be heading back tomorrow.

When the sun touched the horizon, Clara was almost at the end of her tether, the only thing keeping her in the saddle was her iron resolve. She almost moaned in pleasure when the group finally stopped at a small coaching inn. Clara directed her mare, who'd apparently spent her entire life going by the ridiculous name of Betsie, to rest beside Demon and

Seraphina, the king and queen's steeds. As she dismounted, Clara nearly stumbled to the ground, her poor legs refusing to carry her weight.

Someone pulled at the reins she was still clutching. "Go, rest and eat, both of you," the king commanded. "I'll take care of your horses." For once, the king sounded sympathetic so Clara and Karina gladly accepted his offer.

To Clara's relief, Karina looked just as exhausted as she did. They both groaned as they entered the inn and sat down on the too hard benches near the hearth. The men stayed outside, probably pitching tents and making their dinner. Being a noble lady came with the privilege of being excused from work and being given a bowl of hot stew prepared by someone else. The meat inside looked dubious but Clara devoured it anyway, scraping her spoon on the bottom of the bowl to make sure she'd gotten every last bit.

The tiny room with its uncomfortable straw bed was a luxury Clara hadn't even hoped for. Under normal circumstances, the thought of which tiny creatures could possibly be roaming around the mattress wouldn't let her fall asleep, but this was far from normal circumstances.

She'd barely managed to take off her shoes before exhaustion took over.

Chapter 36

C lara felt so bruised and battered she didn't think she'd be able to get up in the morning. Yet, by the power of sheer will, she had. She also didn't think she'd be able to get in the saddle again or even look at her stupid horse. And yet, she did that as well.

Betsie was probably confused as to why her mistress was giving her such hateful glares. The poor mare had been the one to do all the hard work. The small apple Clara had shamelessly stolen from a tree growing by the roadside appeased the mare enough to allow Clara to put the saddle and her bags back on.

The king loomed nearby, smirking as he listened to the women's painful groans. It was seriously annoying. Both Clara and Karina rolled their eyes at the same time, causing them to burst into fit of giggles, realizing a little too late that laughing hurt as well for some fucked up reason. But going home was not an option for either woman so they mounted their horses.

The discomfort became a constant for the next several hours. Sometimes spiking, sometimes ebbing a little, but it was always there. The upside of shared suffering was that it had brought Clara and Karina closer than any amount of afternoon tea parties or walks through the park ever could.

Just before sundown, the group stopped for the night at a small clearing by the roadside. Clara suppressed a sigh. No inns tonight.

Getting down from her horse proved even more difficult than the previous evening. However, Clara couldn't stay in the saddle forever so, with heavy groaning and a couple of colorful curses, she dismounted. Her wobbly legs nearly gave up on her again so Clara leaned lamely against her mare for support.

"Let me get that for you," a vaguely familiar voice suggested.

Clara turned to see one of the soldiers reaching for her reins. His blue eyes gave away where she had seen him before. Of course. He was the officer she had met at the training grounds a few days back, the Levantian. Clara had never gotten around to asking his girlfriend to be her maid.

Clara's first instinct was to refuse help but her legs were protesting so vigorously she had to go and sit down nearby before they gave out and dropped her where she stood. Defeated, she nodded at the officer.

"Alec, right?" he grinned as he tended to her horse. "I thought you were too pretty for a boy."

Yes, her masterful disguise didn't exactly fool people from up close. "It's Clara. And thank you."

"No problem," he replied, waving his hand in dismissal. "You are tougher than you look. I think our beloved king will lose the bet. By the way, what happened to the queen's previous maid? The blue-eyed one? I'd expected her to come along."

Karina appeared, snapping at the soldier, "The bet? Larkin, what the fuck are you talking about?"

He gave her a bow and a sincere smile. "My lady. Well...the king and a couple of us officers made a bet on how long you two are going to last. I said you would never give up," he added quickly, raising his hands in self-defense under Karina's furious glare.

"Oh, really?" Her voice was ice cold as she pushed the words through her gritted teeth. "How many days did my beloved husband put his money on?"

Larkin grew pale and hesitated. "I...uhh...I think I'll shut up now. My apologies, my lady. I mean, there are no flagpoles around here, but a tree would work just as well. And sweat stings like a bitch in whip welts."

Clara was beyond confused but it looked like Karina knew what the man was referring to. "Oh, don't worry. If anyone is getting whipped tonight, it will be Hayden," she growled. "Where is he?"

"I'd love to see that," Larkin laughed. "He went with the men to bring some water back from a stream down that way," he pointed away from the road, "you can't really miss it."

With a painful groan, Karina forced her legs to move in the indicated direction. "Perfect," she snapped. "Could you please get someone to take care of Seraphina?" She waited until Larkin nodded before turning away. Just before she disappeared between the newly erected tents, she called at him, "Oh, and by the way, she's not my maid. This is Lady Clara Huxley."

"Lady Clara Hu-Oh. OH. Shit." Larkin's eyes found Clara, still sitting on the grass, and he gave her a horrified look. "I...I apologize, my lady, I had no idea. I'm truly sorry if I said anything that offended you today. Or back on the training grounds."

Clara rolled her eyes. "If I recall correctly, you described me as young and pretty, that's hardly offensive. Just forget about it. I look like shit and smell like my horse. I'm not really a lady right now, so please, just call me Clara. Is there any food?"

Larkin was still nervous around her but he picked up their rations before bringing Clara to a group of men sitting around a small fire. More bread and a piece of salted beef. And an apple, what luxury! Clara was beginning to understand why soldiers always grumbled about food in the books she read. It was quite on point.

"Well, look at him. The Levantian is stealing another Orellian girl," one of the men scoffed as they came closer. The words were harsh but Clara could sense it was just friendly banter. "Are you bored of the one you have back in Ebris already?"

"Would you shut your mouth, Kiligan?" Larkin snapped at him. "This is not just a girl, it's Lady Clara Huxley."

The soldiers looked at each other in confusion and Clara raised her hand in a hesitant greeting. "Hi. I...uh...I used to be Clara Redwood, maybe that's more familiar." It felt cowardly to hide behind her maiden name in a vain hope the men might be friendlier toward her but Clara was too tired to deal with hostility or suspicion. It worked like a charm.

"Admiral Redwood's daughter?" asked the man Larkin had called Kiligan. He gawked at Clara before jumping up. "Of course, you are more than welcome here. Would you like to sit down?" He waved to his spot on a large flat stone.

Clara winced over the idea of placing her sore butt on something hard and cold. "Thank you, but I think I'll just stay on the grass. I don't think my backside would be thrilled over being pressed against a stone right now," she winced. Several of the men chuckled over her words, which was her intention, but they quickly stopped under Larkin's angry glare.

Not wanting to be treated like a porcelain doll, Clara quickly stopped him. "It's alright," she nodded at Larkin before turning to his men. "As I told lieutenant Larkin here, I'm hardly a lady right now, so please, don't mind me at all. I'll just lie down here and die for a few minutes, then I'll be on my way to find a place to sleep."

A mouthwatering smell wafted from a small pot hanging above the fire. Whatever was bubbling inside made Clara's stomach rumble but she forced herself to ignore it. Nine men sat around the fire and there would hardly be enough food in the pot for all of them. Clara hadn't come here to steal their food, no matter how good it smelled. She tore at another piece of the dried meat with her teeth, her jaw muscles already sore from chewing on it.

"We will take care of your tent, my lady," Killigan offered. Without waiting for Clara's response, he and two others rushed to her saddlebags and pulled out her tent. It was merely a large square of thick, hopefully waterproof fabric and two sticks meant to hold it up at both ends. Long nails needed to be hammered into the ground along the fabric sides to keep the construction up, creating barely enough space for one person to crawl into.

Sometimes it was good to be a woman among so many men, Clara thought as she watched them pitch the tent for her and roll out her sleeping mat inside.

Larkin chuckled over their eagerness. "Perhaps you Orellians aren't so inhospitable after all," he teased after they returned.

"Lady Clara is one of us, Levantian," a big man with an ugly scar stuck his tongue out at the lieutenant. Clara remembered him from the training grounds as well. It seemed that insulting Larkin based on his country of origin was a regular routine here. Good thing he didn't seem to mind it at all.

"I already told you it's Lieutenant Levantian for you, Blaggar," Larkin smirked. "And if you take those shoes off here, I'll have you whipped."

The other men chimed in. "Yeah, don't you fucking dare!"

"Alright, alright." The scarred man raised his hands up. "I won't. But just because we have a lady present."

Quirking a brow, Clara carefully sniffed her shirt. "The lady smells like a sweaty horse," she snickered. "I doubt it could get worse than that."

"Oh, it could. Trust me on that," Larkin insisted.

Listening to their friendly banter was fun. Larkin introduced the other men and Clara tried her best to remember all their names. She was usually quite good at it but her brain seemed too tired now. "That ugly brute with smelly feet is Blaggar," Larkin continued, "and the brooding archer over there..."

"Is Enzio," Clara finished the sentence. "We've met," she added hesitantly.

His brows formed a wrinkle on his forehead as he looked at her, visibly straining his brain trying to remember. "I'm sorry, my lady, I can't seem to recall our meeting," he said after a while.

"I wasn't a lady then. I was a boy named Alec," Clara admitted, giving him a sheepish grin. The proper lady inside her was appalled. Was she really going to brag in front of these men?

Enzio's eyes narrowed, his frown deepening. Then he noticed the bow resting against her saddlebag. His eyes jumped between her and the weapon a couple of times, widening as comprehension dawned. "Oh no. Please, tell me you're joking." A pained groan escaped him as he threw his head back. "Oh gods. This is so humiliating."

The other soldiers seemed confused. The man sitting next to Enzio elbowed him, giving him an inquisitive look. The archer sighed. "Alec was the boy who almost won the tournament last year."

"No fucking way! You nearly lost to a woman?"

"I did lose to a woman. Didn't I?" He turned to Clara. "You let me win. Now at least, I understand why. Gods, I'm so fucking useless. I guess I'll just retire and start growing potatoes."

Damn, insulting him was not Clara's intention. Showing off was fun but not at the expense of someone else's feelings. "I'm sorry," she rushed to apologize, "I didn't mean to-"

"Nah, leave him to it," Larking interrupted her. "Enzio is our little diva. You just gave his enormous self-confidence a proper beating, which is something we are all very thankful for, by the way. He'll live. And you aren't useless, Enzio. While I wouldn't eat potatoes grown by you since they'd probably taste like shit or be poisonous, you did put meat on our proverbial table tonight. So stop your whining and come eat, I think it's done." He stirred the pot one more time, carefully putting a spoonful of its contents into his mouth before smirking. "Yeah, I don't think it's gonna get any better."

As the men handed their bowls to Larkin to fill each with a small portion of the stew, Clara lay down on the soft grass. The smell of the food was tempting but she didn't want charity and she certainly didn't want to take away from the little these men had managed to rustle up to improve their rations. The dinner she'd been given at the inn last night was no doubt better than what the soldiers had eaten.

"My lady?"

Larkin's voice made her open her eyes. He was standing over her, offering her a small bowl. Clara frowned. "Firstly, I told you to call me Clara. That goes for everyone," she added in a louder voice. "And secondly, there's not enough food even for all of you."

"Don't worry about that, Clara," Larkin grinned. "This is not meant to be a proper dinner. It's more like a dessert, a few spoonfuls of something warm in our stomachs. Plus," he added, his grin growing wider, "I couldn't care less if you eat, since I'm an outsider and everything, but the men were claiming you were one of them. So please, just take it and eat."

Since the others were nodding and smiling at her, Clara hesitantly accepted the bowl, sniffing its contents. It smelled better than anything she'd ever eaten before in her entire life. She couldn't put the spoon into her mouth fast enough, a blissful expression spreading across her face.

The stew contained lots of beans and probably some roots too, Clara couldn't really tell what kind. But, more importantly, there were pieces of meat. A little stringy but still better than the salted beef she'd been chewing on for the past half an hour.

The men ate in silence pierced only by an occasional satisfied groan. "Those were some good rats you brought in this time, Enzio. Not the usual skinny lot," someone complimented.

Clara froze with the piece of meat in her mouth. A rat?! Part of her wanted to spit it out in horror and throw the bowl far away but she was so damned hungry. Did it really matter where the meat had come from?

"We're in a forest, dumbass," the archer chided, "rats are hard to spot here. These were squirrels."

It didn't matter, Clara decided. Food was food. "Aren't squirrels just rats with fluffy tails?" Clara teased, putting another spoonful into her mouth.

"Hey!" Enzio mock glared at her. "You can come with me tomorrow. Let's see if you can hit something other than a target, Lady Alec," he poked his tongue out at Clara, earning a scowl from Larkin.

That sounded interesting. Clara wasn't really sure whether she'd be able to shoot an arrow at a person but hunting animals seemed like a useful skill, especially since the rations on the road were not likely to improve in quality. Her answer was interrupted by a deep voice saying, "There you are."

Clara looked up to see one of the king's bodyguards, his brows raised upon seeing her company. "The queen sent me to see if you needed any help with your tent or anything else, but it looks like you managed on your own," he smiled.

"I had help," Clara admitted. Realizing that Karina was probably looking for her, she blushed. "I should go see her."

An amused headshake stopped her from getting up. "I wouldn't go anywhere near them right now. They tend to be quite loud."

The men laughed but Clara grew nervous. "Are they fighting?" she asked. Karina had seemed angry about the bet the king had made.

"Not that kind of loud," Larkin grinned.

The realization dawned on her. They were having sex. Gods, Clara felt like a clueless child between these, no doubt very experienced, men.

Fortunately, Larkin noticed the discussion was making her uncomfortable and turned to the guard with a friendly smile. "Want to sit with us, Lamar? I'm afraid we are all out of rat stew, but-"

"Squirrel stew!"

"Shut up, Enzio. There's no stew left but I'm sure Blaggar has a bag of nuts stashed away somewhere."

The scarred man glowered. "Keep your filthy hands away from my nuts, Levantian."

The men burst out in laughter and Clara joined them. She might have been clueless when it came to sex but she understood that joke.

Chapter 37

The night was surprisingly cold and the morning even colder. Clara felt that if the temperature dropped any further, she would actually start seeing vapor coming out of her mouth as she breathed. Wasn't it supposed to be summer? Very late summer, yes, but still summer.

With an unhappy groan, she crawled out of her tent onto the wet grass, cursing as the morning dew quickly soaked through her breeches.

Dozens of small fires were burning all around the camp, groups of men standing around them in solemn silence, trying to catch a bit of heat to warm their stiff bodies. Wisps of fog were rolling across the clearing, giving it an eerie look. The sun hadn't come up yet but it wasn't dark anymore, enough light for Clara to locate Larkin's group around the same fireplace as yesterday.

The men were already packed up so as soon as Clara joined them, Larkin put a bowl of hot tea into her hands then went to fold her tent. "Hey, you don't have to..." she tried to stop him.

He waved his hand dismissively. "Save your strength, you're going to need it."

He was probably right. Every muscle in Clara's body, including those she hadn't even known she had, were screaming at her to just crawl back into that stupid tent and sleep through the whole day. Just the thought of getting back up on a horse made her shudder. But she'd already gone this far, she couldn't simply give up now. It had to start getting better at some point.

As she tried to wrap her jacket tighter, a quiet rustle reminded her of the paper Oscar had given her before leaving the palace. With shame, Clara realized she had been so absorbed in her discomfort she had completely forgotten about it. She sat down on the flat stone, as close to the fire as possible, and pulled out the note. In hopes it would smell like Oscar, Clara raised the paper to her nose, smirking immediately. It reeked of her own sweat.

"Clara," Oscar had written.

"You wanted to know my secrets. This is the biggest and darkest one. I probably should have told you earlier but...a person's greatest failure is not something they brag about in front of a girl they are trying to impress. You are my wife and while that fact warms my heart, it also fills me with fear, since my dark secrets affect you now, as well. It's only fair you know about this, even if it means you are going to despise me for the rest of your life."

Carefully sipping the tea from the bowl, Clara frowned at the paper. Oscar had told her that his secret was something bad and the first few lines of this note confirmed it. Should Clara even read on?

Since Larkin had packed all of her things and loaded them onto her horse for her, Clara had plenty of time. She forced herself to read further before her resolve could falter.

"I told you I've had lots of women and that my bad reputation is very much justified. I think since I couldn't have the one I truly desired, I wanted to get through the rest of them as quickly as possible, trying each one to see if maybe she could fill that emptiness inside of me. And when they didn't, I simply tossed them aside like broken toys."

The words were almost too painful to read. Was Clara just the next in line? The only difference was that Oscar couldn't really get rid of her so easily, since they were married.

The men resumed their friendly bickering around the fire but Clara tuned them out, focusing solely on Oscar's letter.

"About a year and a half ago, I met Alice. She was from a small, insignificant noble house. A naive girl not much older than you. She loved to read romantic stories as well, hoping that a beautiful knight in shining armor would come and take her away from her boring life, so they could live happily ever after together. That's when I appeared with my sweet words. It didn't take much to make her fall for me.

"I know I said I don't lie much but I lied to Alice. I promised her things I had no intention of delivering. I told her that I loved her, something I often used to say to make a woman go to bed with me. It meant nothing to me, just words with no real meaning. But, unlike the other women, Alice was naive enough to believe me.

"She fell in love with me. It was that instant, blinding love from her stories. And I used that love to talk her into having sex with me. It wasn't her first time but close to it. The experience convinced her that I was 'the one'. I enjoyed myself with her for a while but when she got too clingy and started planning our future, I ended it."

Clara swallowed around the lump in her throat, closing her eyes to take a break. It was a brutally honest confession and she had a solemn feeling that the worst part was yet to come.

"Normally, that would be the end of it but Alice refused to accept it was over. She kept trying to contact me. No matter how hard I tried to evade her, she kept stalking my every move. I agreed to meet up with her one last time to end it properly, only to find out that as stupid and careless as I was, I'd gotten the girl pregnant."

"Ready to go?"

Clara was so focused on the note that Larkin's voice made her jump. Her thoughts were scrambled. At first, she didn't realize where she was or what she was supposed to be ready for. Noticing Betsie's reins in Larkin's hand snapped her back into reality. "Yes, sorry I was..." she trailed off, not sure what to say. "Thank you so much, Lieutenant."

"Don't mention it," he gave her an earnest smile. "Hey, how come I have to call you Clara and you are still calling me Lieutenant?"

He had a point. Clara folded the paper before putting it back into her pocket. "Oh, right," she grinned at Larkin as she took the reins. "I forgot you prefer Lieutenant Levantian," she teased, wincing from the pain in her thighs as she climbed up into the saddle.

The day felt even longer than the previous ones. The group was crossing vast grassy plains and the warm, gentle breeze had turned into an annoying, chilly wind. It was relentless, exhausting, and impossible to escape. When they finally stopped for a quick lunch, Clara pulled out her cloak and wrapped it around her body before finding herself a spot behind a large rock to hide from the wind.

Chewing on a piece of dried beef, she hastily pulled out Oscar's note, wanting to finally finish reading it. Not knowing how the story ended had been bugging her mind all morning. Did he have a child somewhere back in Levanta? Was that the big dark secret? Or was it something even worse?

Clara tried very hard not to let her thoughts dwell on his description of Alice. The girl was just like Clara – young, naive, the only kind of love she knew was the one from her romantic stories. Then Oscar came around – a handsome, silver-tongued gentleman, who made her fall in love with him.

Alice, of course, not Clara. Because the words Clara had nearly blurted out as she was saying goodbye to Oscar in the courtyard were definitely not 'I love you'. That would be stupid and would only mean more pain and disappointment for her.

Oscar loved Karina. Clara was just someone who life had put into his path. He must have liked her, otherwise he wouldn't be so kind and patient with her. But liking and loving were two very different things. Clara knew that and poor Alice seemed to have learned it the hard way.

"I swear, I'm normally very careful about that. I'm quite certain there aren't any tiny Oscars running around Levanta. But I failed with Alice, another one in the long line of my fuckups. She was so naive to think it would

make me come back to her. I think she even had some baby names in mind, images of our happy family. I...

"Damn, this is hard even to write down. I don't think I'd be able to tell you in person.

"I was an asshole back then. A smug bastard who only took interest in other people's lives when I could use them for my own benefit. I laughed at Alice. Of course, I told her I'd give her money to raise the child. I mean, I'm a bastard but not that kind of bastard. But I made it clear that I'd never go back to her and walked out of the room while she was still crying desperately. I thought she would get over it.

"She didn't. She drank poison that very day."

The tears that had been welling up in Clara's eyes finally overflowed and rolled down her cheeks. Oscar had said he was a scoundrel. Based on this, scoundrel was a wild understatement. A monster with a cock, Clara's mother's words echoed in her ears. He said he'd changed since then, but do people really change that much?

Clara had to force herself to continue reading.

"Just by sheer luck, Alice didn't die. But she did lose the child. My child. No matter the fact I hadn't wanted it or that I didn't love its mother, it was my child and now it's gone. Because of me.

"You can't possibly hate me more than I still hate myself, almost two years later. I don't think the guilt will ever go away. Hell, I hope it doesn't, because it changed me. I know you are probably thinking that people can't change who they are deep down inside, but I did. I don't ever want to hurt anyone in that way ever again, which, as I realize now, is ironic, since my words are probably hurting you as you read them.

"I swear I didn't mean to cause pain to anyone, no matter what people might tell you. I was stupid and selfish but I'm not a cruel man that enjoys watching others suffer. I'd really like to think I'm a better person now. And yes, I still fuck things up occasionally, but I'm really trying.

"The only women I've been with since then were the ones I paid and I always made sure there was no other relationship between us. Then you came along and... I'm terrified I'll do something stupid and hurt you, Clara, and

I don't want that. You are such a kind and amazing soul, a much better wife than a piece of shit like me deserves.

"If you are still reading this and haven't tossed the paper into the fire, then you need to know one thing. I care for you. More than I thought I'd ever care for anyone in my life. And yes, I know what you are asking yourself, I care for you more than I care for Karina. She has never needed my care before and she needs it even less now. I think I'm tired of living in an illusion, waiting for a miracle. It hurts to think about her. It doesn't hurt to think about you at all and I've been thinking about you a lot ever since I met you.

"I don't know if it counts as love. It's so different from anything I've ever felt before that I don't even know how to describe it. But I'd like to see what it grows into, if you are still willing to give me a chance, that is, even after reading about my biggest life failure.

"If you don't want to have anything to do with me anymore, I promise to not hold it against you. I know we are married, but I will do my best to stay out of your way if that is your wish.

"Just please, be safe out there.

"Oscar."

Chapter 38

Clara gaped at the paper, not even bothering to wipe the tears from her cheeks anymore. There were so many conflicting emotions raging through her mind right now she didn't even know which one to pick. How was she supposed to deal with all of this? Gods, it felt as if her head was about to explode. And, to make matters worse, lunch break was over. Clara could already see men climbing back on their horses and knew someone would come looking for her soon. She needed to pull herself together, fast.

For once, she actually chose to focus on her stiff, aching muscles. The pain in her back felt like sharp bee stings all along her spine. Her legs weighed a ton each, refusing to bend, carry her weight, or do something so outrageous as to climb into a saddle again. Her shoulders were in so much agony that even something as mundane as shrugging seemed impossible. Her neck was useless. It could no longer support her heavy head. Being in pain sucked, but Clara had become so used to it over the past few days that she clutched onto it to distract herself from her heartache.

Clara blew her nose and wiped her cheeks, knowing that it wouldn't mask the signs of tears but hoping it would at least help to mitigate the damage. After sniffling one last time she stood up, putting the cloak over her shoulders and pulling the hood over her head. A lot of men had them on now, as the wind didn't seem to be stopping, so it wouldn't draw any extra attention to her.

The note was carefully tucked away in her pocket again and she picked up the food she had barely touched, knowing she was probably going to get hungry later today once the shock wore off. Damn, why had she read it now?

Karina definitely noticed something was amiss with Clara but didn't ask about it, letting the girl ride along in silence. The slow, regular rocking movement of the horse's back was surprisingly soothing, helping to calm Clara's mind enough so she could start dealing with Oscar's message, carefully picking out the elements one by one, not wanting to get overwhelmed again.

He seduced women, telling them sweet lies so they would have sex with him. That was nothing new, he told her that much during their wedding night. Clara wasn't surprised that many had fallen for him, not after having experienced firsthand how charming he could be. Lying to women wasn't exactly a gentlemanly thing to do but Clara could live with that, especially since he didn't seem to be doing it anymore.

But what about Alice? A naive, young girl, not unlike Clara. And Oscar had destroyed her life, hadn't even realized he was doing something wrong until it was too late. It must have been a brutal wake-up call, having someone nearly die due to his own selfishness. He had acted like a bastard back then, not caring about anyone or anything besides himself. But could Clara really blame Oscar for everything that happened? Sure, Alice's broken heart was totally his fault, he'd lied to her and deceived her. But the baby? How could Alice try to kill herself knowing she was with a child?

No matter how desperate the situation, Clara would never do that, especially not over a man. The idea of having a child in the near future wasn't particularly attractive to her, she still felt like a child herself, unready for such responsibility. But if it happened (and despite being clueless in the matters of sex, Clara did know it led to babies being conceived), she would take any measure possible to protect the little thing, even if it meant taking care of it on her own. And Oscar had at least offered to support the child financially, even though he could have easily denied any connection to it.

He clearly blamed himself for it, tortured himself by the thought of being the cause of the death of his own child, and Clara felt sorry for him. If only he was here with her, she would hold him and tell him it wasn't his fault, or at least not to the extent he believed it to be. The image of Clara comforting Oscar for once refused to leave her mind. His head on her lap, her fingers caressing his long hair, her lips kissing his temple... It made her heart ache with longing to be home in his arms.

And that was the answer she needed to the whole situation, wasn't it? The Oscar from this story was not the same man as Clara's Oscar. He claimed he had changed, that he was a better man now, and Clara had no reason not to believe him. He had been kind and compassionate with her even though he was by no means compelled to do so. He never put any pressure on her to have sex with him. Hell, he'd even supported this whole crazy endeavor which had sent Clara away from him for weeks. No, she certainly didn't hate him for a mistake he'd made in the past, no matter how grave that mistake had been.

And as for the rest of his note? Oscar claimed it was not a love letter but... What else could that thing he described be? He cared for Clara more than for Karina.

It was silly and immature but Oscar's admission pushed tears into her eyes every time she remembered the words. Clara understood very well what he meant when saying it was painful to think about Karina. Clara knew because she'd felt the same. It was painful to think of Oscar in that way, knowing she would never have all of him, knowing his heart belonged to someone else.

But what if she could have him? What if she could have him and keep him forever, with all of his flaws and secrets, but also with all his warm smiles and hugs, his never-ending patience and support, his brilliant mind?

His amazing body? His scent, even the memory of which nearly made her cry from desire to be near him again? Would she want that? And why was she even asking herself such stupid questions when she already knew the answer?

"Clara?" Karina's voice interrupted her thoughts. Clara suddenly realized she had been so lost in them she'd slowed down and started falling behind the rest of the group.

"Oh, sorry." Clara nudged Betsie to pick up the pace and soon the women caught up with the soldiers. "I've just been...thinking."

A corner of Karina's mouth curled up. "About something? Or maybe, someone?"

"About a lot of things." Oscar's note was not something Clara wanted to discuss with Karina. Any part of it.

"Sure, sure," Karina smirked. "It's a magnificent view, isn't it?"

Clara had no idea what she was referring to. The view around them had consisted of the same flat grassy expanse for so long Clara had stopped looking around in the vain hope of seeing something interesting. But Karina's head jerked toward the northern horizon so Clara squinted, trying to focus on what could possibly be there.

Her eyes widened when she realized the gray mounds far off in the distance weren't clouds but huge, snow-covered mountains. The road led straight to them, even though it looked like there was no way humans could possibly cross such a gargantuan natural barrier. Maybe the birds that soared in the clear blue sky would be able to reach the other side, but passing over it on poor Betsie's back seemed impossible.

There was a dark strip of what was most likely a thick forest, covering the foot of the mountains. The road clawed its way through it in a brutally straight line. As they got closer, Clara could see where any trees blocking the way had simply been cut down to make space. The stumps and roots of those directly in the way had been dug out and removed completely, the rest were left standing by the side of the road as a silent tree graveyard.

The forest itself was very different from the lush groves Clara was used to. There were almost no deciduous trees. No magnificent oaks or beeches that were so common in the woods around Ebris. Most of the trees surrounding them when they'd finally entered the forest were pines or spruces, dotted by the occasional birch or a poplar. There was a thick layer of lichen growing mainly on the northern side of the tree trunks.

They came upon a large clearing with improvised defenses around the perimeter. It was mostly sharpened logs tied together, pointing toward the treeline, but they did provide the group with a sense of security.

To Clara's surprise, their group headed straight there and the men started dismounting, even though there must have still been several hours of daylight left. It was strange. On the previous days, they'd always kept traveling until just before sunset.

"We are stopping already?" Clara asked, trying not to get her hopes up, just in case this was only another short break and they were supposed to keep going until dark or even overnight.

But Karina nodded, relief clearly written all over her face. "Yes, I think Hayden mentioned something about horses needing a longer rest on the third day. We still have about two days' journey ahead of us."

The extra rest sounded amazing. It was tempting to just lay down and sleep for a few hours, but Clara remembered Enzio's offer to go hunting with him. And even though the archer probably didn't really expect her to come, she was truly curious about it. However, it meant she had to find him before he disappeared off somewhere in the forest.

Luckily, Karina didn't seem to mind Clara spending time with the men from Larkin's group. She was probably relieved she didn't have to babysit the girl and could have more alone time with her husband.

Clara noticed Blaggar's scarred face in the crowd and pulled on Betsie's reins to follow him, knowing the rest of the group wouldn't be far. She was right. While Larkin himself was absent, checking on other soldiers under his command, the rest of the men were gathered in one corner of the campsite. Clara was worried that they wouldn't want her around but their bright smiles upon noticing her convinced her otherwise.

Enzio raised an eyebrow upon seeing her pull her bow out of the scabbard. "I was just joking, my lady, I don't expect you to-"

"It's Clara. And I'd love to come with you, if that's alright?" Perhaps he didn't really want to bring a girl along or was still upset over her bragging about the tournament in front of his friends?

An indifferent shrug was not exactly the excited response Clara was hoping for, but it was better than a straight-out no. "Sure. I'll just take care of my horse then we can go."

Damn, Clara hadn't even realized she should have tended to Betsie first as well. What a spoiled rotten noble-born lady she was, always expecting others to take care of everything for her. She put her bow aside before turning to her mare, gently stroking her neck. "I keep forgetting you are the one doing all the work, having to drag my sorry ass on your back," Clara mumbled into Betsie's ear, scratching the soft brown fur. "How about I take a few bites of this apple and then give the rest to you? I'm hungry too, you know." The mare seemed intrigued by the fruit in Clara's hand, immediately trying to snatch it.

"You can go, guys. If you bring something other than this wretched dried beef for dinner, we will take care of your horses." One of the men, Clara was sure his name began with an N, stepped closer and reached for her reins.

Clara hesitantly handed them over. "Thank you, N...Norman?"

"Nolan." His bright smile made dimples on his cheeks. He was young, much younger than the rest of the group which Clara had so rudely infiltrated. Had she met him a few weeks back, she would have thought him irresistibly cute, blushing and stuttering every time he would look in her direction. Now, she found herself comparing him to Oscar and as a result, Nolan fell short in every respect.

"Right. Sorry, I'll eventually manage to remember that." She gave him a friendly smile before picking up her bow again. After carefully unwrapping the cover, her fingers traced over the ornate handle, lingering on the Redwood and Huxley crests that Oscar had instructed someone to engrave into the wood. A thoughtful gift, so personal. How ironic it came from a man who hadn't even known Clara in person when he was getting it.

Clara settled the quiver over her shoulder. The arrows hadn't exactly fared well being packed and carried on horseback. They were usable but she'd have to make some time to repair the feathers on a few of them that evening. She fished her bracers out of the saddlebags and slid them on, enjoying the familiar feeling of leather brushing against her skin. Fortunately, the bowstring didn't seem to have suffered during transportation and, after a few moments of grunting and struggling against the toughened wood, Clara managed to set it in position.

Finished with her preparations, Clara raised her eyes to see the men were watching her with curiosity and poorly masked amusement. Her first instinct was to run and hide around the nearest corner. Not that there were any corners in a forest clearing.

But why the hell should she be ashamed? This was something at which she knew she was just as good as Enzio. Why should it matter if she had breasts and long hair? Bow in hand, she looked around the group with all the confidence she could possibly muster. One eyebrow raised in silent question, daring them to speak up. Nobody did.

"Ready?" Enzio called from behind her. Clara turned, giving him a firm nod. This should be interesting.

Chapter 39

Enzio kept quiet as they crossed the tree line and walked through the forest together. This was a strangely damp and cold place, very unlike the woods Clara was used to. The ground was covered by a thick layer of brown pine needles fallen from the tall pines and spruces surrounding them, muffling the sound of their footsteps. There didn't seem to be anything living around though. What were they supposed to be hunting?

Clara opened her mouth to ask but Enzio's firm head shake stopped her. Right, if there were any animals nearby, hearing voices would probably make them run away.

Letting out a resigned sigh, Enzio stopped. Turning to Clara, he gently touched her hand to grab her attention. "Listen." The word was barely more than a whisper as he raised his index finger, tapping on his own ear to make sure she understood him.

What was Clara supposed to be listening to? There was nothing. But that was probably not the answer Enzio was looking for. And she had come along to learn something new, so she kept her mouth shut. Taking a deep breath, Clara really tried to hear whatever it was the archer was hearing.

At first, there were no distinguishable sounds. Clara armed herself with patience and closed her eyes. There was a soft humming with a strange, quiet creaking sound accompanying it. Was that the wind gently bending the trees, making them moan over such a small transgression? But there was more.

A quiet beeping somewhere from above, interrupted by a flapping noise, so loud it almost made Clara flinch with surprise. Birds. She hadn't even noticed them before but now she could hear several.

There were many sounds to hear, now that Clara was really listening, like an indistinct scratching or an occasional twig snapping, and more sounds she couldn't even describe. But one thing was for sure. The forest was alive, much more than it had originally seemed to her untrained senses.

Enzio nodded as he noticed the change in her expression. He listened for a few more moments and then reached for an arrow, nocking it without even sparing a glance to his hands. Clara had no idea what he was aiming at, the only animals she could see right now were a couple of birds soaring in the sky high above the trees, too far for them to shoot at. He took a step toward her, standing so close that she could smell the sweat off his shirt. He could probably smell her too.

His hand pointed halfway up one of the taller pine trees, where the first branch met the trunk. Clara squinted at a dark shadow clinging to the bark and suppressed a chuckle. A squirrel.

Enzio smirked before drawing back the string and releasing it in one smooth move. Clara noticed he hadn't used the full draw, probably because he didn't want to pin the poor animal to the tree. The arrow hissed through the air, the squirrel squeaked and fell down.

"A small one, not much of a catch," he grumbled as he headed to pick it up. "But it's better than nothing. I was worried that the others had already chased everything in this part of the forest away."

Naturally, Enzio wasn't the only one heading into the woods to try and catch something to supplement the rations. Clara remembered she had to be careful not to shoot anyone by accident.

"How did you know it was there?" It was baffling, Clara hadn't even noticed the animal until he pointed it out.

Enzio shrugged. "I listen and watch. I'm not really a tracker, I just shoot at what I see. It gets better with experience. May I?" Clara hesitantly placed her bow into his extended hand, her fingers not wanting to part with it. "Hmm, a piece of art," Enzio mused, sounding almost offended that a bow could be so pretty. As he examined it more closely, his expression changed.

Clara barely caught his own bow when he tossed it in her direction; needing both his hands free to try and draw hers. "A few inches shorter and a bit lighter than what I'm used to but it suits your stature better. Beautiful and deadly," he nodded in appreciation, handing it back to Clara, but not before he'd paused to admire the carved crests.

"It was a gift," she rushed with an explanation. She didn't want him to think that just because she was a girl and of noble birth, everything she owned had to be special and pretty. "From my husband."

Enzio's brows shot up in disbelief as he shook his head. "I'm getting too old. Back when I met my wife, I gave her a silken scarf. Then a pair of earrings when I asked for her hand. Giving her a bow was not something that would have ever crossed my mind."

Clara couldn't help but laugh, probably scaring off any prey in the immediate vicinity. "Yeah, I'm a bit weird. But Oscar doesn't seem to mind. So, you have a family?" Enzio looked to be about his early forties, one of the oldest men in their group.

"That I do." He smiled warmly as he was no doubt recalling pleasant memories. "I will be a grandfather by the time I get back home. Come on, let's try and get something meatier than squirrels. If I remember correctly, there should be a large grassy patch behind those birches over there, perhaps we'll be lucky enough to find some rabbits."

Clara let the archer lead the way, surprised to find that he had been here before. But since this wasn't the first time the Ruthian tribes had started attacking people passing through the mountains, it made sense that every soldier would eventually be stationed at one of the outposts lining the road. Just like Clara's brother.

It was hard not to think about Nicolas, especially now as they were getting closer to the destroyed outpost. Was he wandering alone through these woods, injured and scared, hiding from the enemy and unable to get back to his people? It sounded too good to be true. No, most likely his remains were lying under one of these huge trees in the middle of nowhere, mutilated by animals beyond recognition.

Soft thumping made Clara snap out of her gruesome thoughts. Enzio cocked an eyebrow, querying whether she'd heard it too. There indeed were rabbits in the clearing, several of them, munching on the hard grass while carefully looking around, their ears moving constantly as they tried to detect any incoming threats. Clara froze in her tracks, afraid that the slightest sound would startle the tiny beasts.

Enzio reached for an arrow and motioned for her to do the same. His index finger tapped on his chest and then pointed at one of the rabbits on the left. He repeated the same motion, this time pointing at Clara and on a group to the right. The message was clear.

Clara was nervous, not wanting to screw this up. Her hand grabbed the arrow and nocked it by instinct, the movement so familiar to her she didn't need to think about it.

Nodding, Enzio raised five fingers, waiting for a heartbeat before curling one into his palm. Another heartbeat, another finger.

Clara drew the string, aiming at the largest rabbit on the right, smoothly releasing the arrow just as the fifth heartbeat announced the end of the countdown. The frightened animals immediately darted away, making surprisingly long leaps in an effort to get out of the clearing as quickly as possible. Before she even realized what she was doing, Clara was drawing the string again and another arrow flew across the clearing.

As she'd expected, there were two rabbits laying dead on the grass. The first shot had been almost impossible to miss. Both Clara's and Enzio's arrows had gone straight through the chests of the small animals, killing them instantly. Clara shuddered over how easy it had been for her to actually kill something. Yet, this was still far from shooting at a person.

Clara knew that Enzio had also fired and struck twice as she saw him leaning down to collect a second rabbit at the outer edge of the grassy patch. His second shot was as accurate as the first one, unlike Clara's.

Her second rabbit was still alive. She'd only hit him through the stomach, merely pinning him to the ground. The poor little beast desperately tried to get away, its tortured squealing piercing the relative quiet of the forest. "Crap. That was sloppy," Clara cursed at herself, hating herself for causing the poor thing so much pain.

"They zigzag a lot," Enzio noted. "The second arrow is always a lucky shot. You did well."

While it was great to hear such praise, the sounds coming from the poor animal made Clara almost nauseous. "Can't you do something about it?"

"Me?" Enzio raised an eyebrow and pulled out a hunting knife, offering it to Clara. "You shot it, you deal with it. Just slice its throat."

What?!

Clara stared at the blade in his hand, unable to react. Slice its throat? Was he kidding?

"Arrows are clean and easy," Enzio smirked, stepping closer, "but they are your responsibility, even after you fire them. You shot the rabbit, it's going to die. It's up to you whether it will die slowly and in pain, or you end its suffering right now."

Shivers rolled down Clara's spine as she wrapped her fingers around the hilt of the knife. Enzio was right, though. Archery was fun when it was just a game. Out here, it wasn't just an amusement, or a past-time activity. It was a matter of life and death.

Sure, right now it was merely the death of a tiny animal but Clara knew exactly how that arrow had become plunged into its stomach. But, it wasn't just her conscious thought that had made her shoot it, she was also fueled by instinct. She'd seen the rabbit moving and some primal part of her had wanted it dead. So she'd shot it. The responsibility of that decision was hers and so was having to deal with the consequences.

Gripping the knife tighter, she crouched over the frightened animal. "Grab the loose skin on the back of its neck to hold it down. One swift cut will do it," Enzio directed her.

"I'm sorry you are in pain," Clara whispered, running her fingers over soft gray fur, wrapping them around the loose part as Enzio instructed. "Enjoy your rabbit afterlife." The rabbit continued to squirm, ignoring her soothing words. Not that it really mattered, since they were meant to calm Clara, not the animal. She put the blade to its throat and sliced downward, making a large cut across the rabbit's neck which immediately filled with blood.

Enzio nodded in approval as he reached for the knife, making similar cuts on the other rabbits' necks. "Here," he tossed her a piece of string, "tie the back legs, we need to hang them upside down to let all the blood drain out."

It felt a little barbaric to be tying up the feet of a dead animal but Clara trusted that Enzio knew what was necessary. She had never seen an animal carcass this close before, let alone knew how to butcher it properly. All the meat in her life so far had been cooked and neatly served on a plate, not squealing in pain or bleeding profusely over the mossy forest floor.

While they waited for the blood to stop dripping from the rabbits, Enzio and Clara talked. Mostly about archery, reminiscing about the tournament, laughing at the mistakes some of the other contestants had made, exchanging stories. Enzio told her more about his family, surprised that she would be interested in such information. When all of the blood had finally drained from the poor animals' bodies, the archer tied all of the strings together and threw them over his shoulder, carrying them all the way back to camp.

"Well, well, well," a familiar voice interrupted their friendly chatter as soon as they crossed the treeline. "You do realize you two were technically poaching, right?" Hayden's arms were crossed in front of his chest yet there was an amused smirk on his face.

Clara's eyes widened in fear. She never even realized they might have been doing something wrong, but it was true. Unless the woods were part of a private property, they belonged either to the nearest town or village, or to the crown. And only the official gamekeepers were allowed to hunt on crown land. Enzio didn't seem to be worried though, he just rolled his eyes and reached for the animals hanging over his shoulder.

"And I'm not taking a rat as a bribe this time," the king grumbled. Clara could see he'd been mocking them. Most likely.

Enzio's shoulders twitched in a suppressed chuckle. "A rabbit then, Your Majesty?" he smirked and offered one of the animals to the king.

"Nice catch today." Hayden grabbed the rabbit and raised an eyebrow upon noticing the remaining three.

"I had help," Enzio shrugged.

The king sized up Clara, his eyes pausing on the bow in her hand. He shook his head but whatever he was going to say was interrupted by a rider approaching the camp. Hayden's brows furrowed as he walked away to greet him.

"Don't worry, he was just kidding," Enzio soothed, but despite his words, Clara couldn't get rid of her jitters. The king clearly wasn't happy with her being here.

Their small group welcomed them with a loud cheer as they returned. Two of the men immediately started skinning the rabbits along with the poor squirrel, debating on how to cook them best.

There was still plenty of daylight left so Clara decided to use this time to look over her arrows. Some of the feathers needed replacing so she sat down on the ground cross-legged; her hands occupied with the work, listening in to the friendly banter of the men around her and chuckling at their antics from time to time. It was a strangely peaceful moment, as if they were all just going on a long journey and not headed into a war.

"Wow, three rabbits? Nice job," Larkin complimented them as he finally sat down to join the group. Stretching his back, he let out a pained groan.

Apparently, Larkin was in charge of many of the King's soldiers on this mission, not just the small group gathered around the fire as Clara had originally assumed. And while he clearly liked spending time with Blaggar,

Enzio and the others, he had a responsibility to make sure the rest of his men were taken care of and didn't get into any trouble.

Enzio sighed. "There were four, actually, but we had to...pay the tax."

Clara smirked over his choice of words and Larkin laughed, "Ah, so the king stole one."

"Stole?" the king snickered as he approached Larkin from behind, causing Larkin to visibly flinch. Shaking his head, the king stepped closer. "That's such an ugly word. I believe I'm entitled to a fair share of the game your people hunt down in my woods. Plus, I have a starving wife to feed."

"Gods!" Larkin shook his head, rolling his eyes at Hayden. "Are you seriously stalking me? Waiting until I say something against you so you can make fun of me? Or is there something you actually want? Sir?" He wasn't treating the king with much respect but surprisingly, the king didn't seem to mind.

"Yeah, like I have time to personally stalk all of the Levantian assholes in my contingent." The king mimicked Larkin's expression, clearly mocking him. "There's a rider with messages from the capital. Since by some miracle, you are still a high-ranking officer, you need to be there for the meeting."

"Fine," Larkin conceded. There were some pops and cracks as he got up and stretched out his arms. "I'll be there. Sir," he added sarcastically. He and Hayden clearly had an interesting history.

"Is there something wrong?" Clara asked, curious over what was happening.

"No," Nolan answered, giving her another one of his bright, sexy smiles. "It's normal. They send messages back and forth between the capital and wherever the king is currently located to keep him updated. The messenger will sleep here and return to Ebris in the morning."

That caught Clara's attention. An opportunity to send a message to Oscar was too tempting to pass up. Plus, she really ought to find Karina. After all, she was invited here as the queen's friend and companion, not to spend all of her time with a random bunch of soldiers.

Clara packed her arrows away before heading to the area of the campsite where she'd seen the king's guards earlier. "Don't be late for dinner!" Enzio called after her, causing everyone to burst out in laughter.

"Don't worry. Hey, can I bring someone along?"

The men shrugged. "I think there will be more than enough meat tonight, you can bring a friend if you want. No more guys with smelly feet though, we already have one too many."

"I don't think that is going to be a problem," Clara chuckled as she walked away.

Chapter 40

F inding the queen was easy, Clara just headed to where the king's guard were gathered.

Karina was searching through her saddlebags, pulling out some clean clothes. "Clara!" she greeted her excitedly. "I was just about to come and find you. I've been told there's a small lake nearby and even though the water will most likely be cold as hell, I really need to wash myself at least a little. Wanna come? My guards will come along to make sure nobody sees anything inappropriate." Her eye roll made it clear that the guards were more Hayden's idea than her own.

"Sure!" Bathing? Washing the sweat from her body? It sounded too good to be true.

Clara had never felt this dirty in her entire life. Not actually dirty, like when one rolls in the mud, but the awkward combination of her horse's sweat mixed in with her own, and the ever-present dust that made her feel sticky and filthy. After rushing to grab clean clothes from her saddlebags, Clara returned to Karina, telling her all about the hunt as they headed for the lake together.

Saying that the water was cold, was a wild understatement. It was so freezing that it felt like thousands of tiny needles stabbing Clara's skin. But the need to feel clean for at least one night was too great. "Fuck it," Clara growled. After checking that the guards were still facing away, she started to take off her clothes.

Karina watched her with uncertainty, rubbing her hands together. "Oh gods," she sighed, reaching for the lower hem of her own shirt. "This is not going to be nice."

It wasn't. It was painful, agonizing even.

Clara's toes curled inwards as soon as her bare feet touched the water but she forced herself to continue, ignoring her muscles clenching as the water reached to her knees, her naked buttocks, then finally, her waist. She didn't dare go any deeper. Of course, she knew how to swim. But she also knew how easily a person could drown if their muscles cramped in deep water.

While Clara frantically scrubbed her body, trying to focus on the way her skin felt clean rather than how she was slowly turning into an icicle, she heard some splashing and rather inventive cursing behind her.

"F-fucking h-hell." Karina's teeth were chattering wildly. "Whose stupid idea was this?" she laughed, bending down to splash some water on her face, squealing as it dripped down onto her chest as well.

Clara knew damned well whose stupid idea it was but she wasn't going to point it out to the queen. Upon realizing Karina was completely naked, Clara quickly averted her gaze, but not before she noticed a small scar below Karina's left collarbone. It looked almost like a burn mark, but it felt inappropriate to ask about. Just as it felt inappropriate to ask about the fading bruises covering the queen's buttocks.

Clara's concern hadn't escaped Karina's attention though. "Hayden likes it rough," she noted casually as if that explained everything.

It took Clara a moment to process her words. And while it was no doubt incredibly rude to gape at the queen, Clara couldn't help herself. "He hits you? During sex?" That sounded dangerously close to what her mother had been telling her.

"Don't worry, it's completely consensual. It can actually be quite...pleasant," Karina added with a smile.

Pleasant? Clara couldn't imagine how something like that could be pleasant but kept her mouth shut. This was not a topic she was comfortable debating with anyone.

"And I really don't think Oscar's into that," Karina continued, "so you have nothing to be afraid of. He didn't hurt you, did he?"

Oh gods, this was so humiliating. "No," Clara shook her head. "We haven't actually..." Damn, she couldn't even say it. Preferring one torture over another, Clara took a deep breath and submerged herself completely under the freezing water, wetting her greasy hair. It didn't help much. And, it didn't stop the queen from continuing with the conversation either.

"I understand." Karina tried to sound warm but her blue lips and chattering teeth spoiled the effect. "Honestly, I couldn't even imagine meeting a complete stranger and then jumping straight into bed with him. I mean, seriously, what's with these stupid customs? Hey, uhh... Could you please help me wash my hair? I can't put my head under water. It's just...a thing with me."

Clara ignored the growing numbness in her feet and legs and moved behind Karina, who let out a tortured moan as she knelt down until the water reached up to her neck. Using her hands as an improvised bowl, Clara poured the ice-cold water over Karina's hair which, despite losing a part of its usual silky smoothness, still looked better than whatever mess was happening on Clara's head.

When they were both frozen from the inside out, the women headed back to shore. After using a piece of cloth to dry herself, Clara put on her clothes as quickly as possible. Then she jumped up and down like an excitable rabbit in an attempt to warm up her stiff muscles.

"F-fuck, that was stupid." Karina twisted her wet hair to squeeze out the water. "But it was worth it."

Clara had to agree. The feeling of being clean was better than she'd have ever expected. "Totally. Can't your husband wage war somewhere warmer next time?"

"I'll suggest that at the next council meeting," Karina laughed and tilted her head, watching Clara try to get her wild locks under control again. Even wet, the tendrils stuck out inconveniently. "Oscar is a good guy," Karina murmured, a sad smile on her still blue-tinted lips. "I know you don't really want to talk about him but I don't want this to be a wedge between us. I've never thought about him as anything more than a friend and he-"

"It's fine," Clara interrupted her. "Really." And it was. After what Oscar had written in his note to her, Clara didn't see Karina as competition anymore so she could fully embrace the blossoming friendship with this very interesting woman. "Oscar told me everything and I think we'll be able to sort out our issues. If I don't freeze to death right here, that is. Let's go find a fire."

Karina nodded excitedly, wrapping her jacket tighter around her body. "Come with me," she suggested. "Hayden somehow obtained a rabbit, so the dinner will be much better than that rock-hard salty crap they feed us normally."

"Oh, did he?" Clara snorted. "You mean one of the rabbits Enzio and I killed? That he stole from us all while threatening to have us arrested for poaching?"

"What?!" The queen burst into laughter. "He somehow forgot to mention that. I'm sorry, Clara. I'd give you the rabbit back but the guards were so excited I don't have the heart to take it away from them."

Clara waved her hand in dismissal. "Don't worry about it. We brought back three more. And a squirrel," Clara added, grinning over Karina's nauseous expression. "They're not so bad when you're hungry," Clara reassured her. "Why don't you come with me? Your guards can have the whole rabbit for themselves."

"I don't know," Karina sighed, suddenly looking miserable. "I don't think your friends will be too excited to have the queen around. Everyone gets too nervous."

Clara knew exactly what Karina meant. It wasn't easy to relax in the presence of royalty. But this was Karina, the kindest and most down-to-earth noble lady Clara had ever met. She wasn't some shallow, pompous queen who would start yelling and ordering punishments as soon as something didn't go according to her royal standards.

"It will be fine," Clara reassured Karina. "But first, do you happen to have any writing supplies?"

"Nope, but I'm sure Hayden does," Karina replied without asking why Clara needed it. After rummaging through the king's saddlebags, she handed Clara an empty parchment and some writing utensils. Realizing it would take some time to summarize her thoughts, Clara stashed it all in her pocket, nervous about stealing from the king.

Karina reluctantly accompanied Clara back to Larkin's group where the rabbits were already being roasted over a low fire.

"By the gods, girl, have you been swimming?!" Enzio exclaimed, noticing Clara's wet hair. He gave her a disapproving look. "Are you crazy?" he chided. "You're going to catch a cold."

Clara knew Enzio was only grumbling because, as he'd told her before, she reminded him of his daughter. And like all the men from his group, he'd quickly developed protective tendencies toward the young girl.

It felt odd to have strangers care about her wellbeing but it wasn't unpleasant, so Clara just went with it. "Sorry, Dad," she replied in the most sarcastic tone she could manage, rolling her eyes so far up they almost disappeared into her skull. Just as she'd expected, it caused a huge burst of laughter from everyone around the fire, including Enzio.

"I'm sorry," he apologized, probably realizing he was out of line talking to a highborn lady like that. "Come sit by the fire to get warm." He moved to make space for her.

Karina had been hiding behind Clara this whole time, so the men hadn't noticed her yet. Grabbing her freezing hand, Clara pulled Karina forward. "I brought an extra person for dinner," she said. "I hope it's okay."

"Sur-Oh!" Enzio's eyes widened as he recognized the queen. Immediately, he sprung up to his feet, bowing deeply. The rest of the men quickly followed his example.

Karina sighed. "See, I told you it was a bad idea," she mumbled toward Clara then addressed the soldiers. "Stop that, please. I get it. I'm a queen.

But I really don't want any of these formalities. So, unless you are able to treat me like...I don't know, a superior officer? Yes, I think that would be the best...Unless you can treat me like a superior officer and nothing more, I shall leave. I don't want to disturb your meal."

The men blinked in surprise, unsure how to respond. It was Blaggar who spoke first, the skin around his scar flushed red. "You are more than welcome by our fire, hmm...my lady?" he tried a less formal title.

Karina gave them a bright smile. "Thank you."

"You know," Clara chuckled, "the superior officer thing probably wasn't the best idea." They both sat down by the fire, their stiff muscles reveling in the warmth. "I think Larkin is their commander and they insult him all the time."

"That's just because he's a Levantian," Blaggar confessed, rolling his eyes as he repeated his usual argument. A split second later, he froze in absolute terror as he realized he'd just insulted the queen.

"HA!" Larkin's mischievous laugh interrupted the sudden silence. "I knew it! I knew one day you were going to say it at the worst fucking moment possible." Larkin continued laughing as he walked closer and crouched next to a deathly pale Blaggar. "You are so getting executed."

"Oh, shut up, Larkin." Karina glared at him before turning to Blaggar with a much friendlier expression. "It's absolutely fine, I don't get offended easily. Plus, you've been saying it in front of Clara this whole time and she didn't get angry either. Her husband is a Levantian as well, or didn't you know?"

Blaggar gave a frightened look to Clara before hiding his face in his hands. Reaching over, Clara tapped his shoulder to get his attention. "They're spreading like a disease, aren't they?" she whispered loud enough for everyone to hear, earning a soft smack on the back of her head from Karina and another round of chuckles from the men.

Larkin kept teasing Blaggar, trying to convince him that the king was going to punish him with some obscene sounding torture method, but Clara tuned out. Writing in the flickering firelight was difficult and her bent knee didn't offer proper support for the small parchment. To make matters worse, she had trouble finding the right words.

The tantalizing smell of cooked meat interrupted Clara's thoughts, making her look up from the parchment. "What are you writing?" Larkin inquired, offering her a piece of the rabbit.

"What do you think?" she responded in a playful tone. Attempting to hide her words, Clara placed a hand over the paper, no doubt adding a few more ink smudges to the already undecipherable mess. "I'm writing down the rat stew recipe so I can cook it for my husband when we get back home," she teased, grabbing the meat from his hand.

A satisfied groan escaped her as she took a large bite. It was delicious. The knowledge that this was her rabbit, something she'd hunted herself, not just some random anonymous food served on a priceless plate, made the meat taste even better.

The messenger didn't need much convincing to deliver Clara's letter to Oscar since he was headed to the palace anyway. Clara gave him a few coins for good measure and went off to return the writing utensils to the king.

Her hope of sneaking in and out of the king's tent unnoticed died quickly, since Hayden was waiting for her. "You surprised me," he told her. "I took you for a stiff and proper noble lady, plain and boring like the rest of them. I'm glad I was wrong."

Clara was still blushing from his praise as she finally crawled into her tent.

'I care for you.' She repeated Oscar's words over and over in her mind as she drifted off to sleep.

Chapter 41

Oscar was never one to have nightmares but ever since Clara had left, he kept waking up drenched in sweat, unable to catch his breath, his heart pounding wildly. His dreams were haunted by Alice's tear-stained, desperate face and the despicably hurtful words a monster kept telling her. A monster with Oscar's voice.

He thought he'd gotten over the guilt, had dealt with it somehow, but it was worse than before. Because the Alice in his nightmares didn't have the smooth blond hair he remembered, her tortured expression was framed by Clara's red curls instead. Sometimes the dream woman's teary eyes even flashed that beautiful emerald green Oscar had learned to love.

The story had needed to be told, that was indisputable. Clara needed to hear it from him before someone else twisted the truth in a way that made Oscar look like an even worse monster than he already was. But why the hell had he given Clara the letter when she was leaving?! Stupid, stupid, stupid. Now, Oscar had no idea how she'd reacted to it and had no control over what she was going to do because of it. He could only guess which left him torturing himself with the worst possible scenarios.

Did Clara hate him? Was she off crying somewhere alone? Was a young, sympathetic soldier offering comfort? Would she seek solace in the arms of someone else upon realizing what kind of bastard she was married to? Or maybe she would be so disgusted, furious enough to make his confession public?

Writing it down was a risk Oscar hadn't fully considered.

Would Clara show it to Karina? His lifelong friend knew about Alice, she even knew about the suicide attempt. But she had no idea about the child. No one did, except for Alice and a few women in her family. He'd paid them to keep quiet, to protect both himself and Alice, but money couldn't fix everything.

The price for his stupidity was weeks of uncertainty, waiting for Clara to come home. If she even came back. The nightmares were just an added bonus.

He didn't even want to think about the last few sentences at the end of his letter. In a desperate attempt to fix some of the damage, Oscar had expressed some of the many confusing feelings clouding his mind. It was out of character for him and probably futile, since Clara would have stopped reading long before reaching the end.

Sighing, Oscar headed into the bathroom to wash the sweat from his body, not feeling rested at all. All the while, the redheaded rag doll sitting on Clara's pillow kept smiling at him.

Damn, wasn't it easier when women were just entertainment for a couple of nights, not some lifelong commitment?

Oscar rejected the idea. Had he met Clara two years ago, the only thing he could've offered her was fleeting pleasure then the pain from the inevitable rejection. Hopefully, he had grown enough since then to be able to give her more. If she was still willing to accept it.

Since there was nothing he could do about it now, he chose to focus on work. Aside from a meeting he had planned in a rather shady part of Ebris later that day, his schedule was clear, so he put on a plain and simple outfit then headed out for a walk. Some days, the best pieces of information were acquired while sitting in a corner of a dirty, common inn, sipping on a rather disgusting ale, and listening in on the conversations. Sadly, today was not one of those days.

Heading toward the docks, Oscar was less than pleased to see that he was still being followed, and not very inconspicuously, which annoyed him even more. The mysterious player kept sending people to watch Oscar's movements but hadn't tried to contact him yet. However, it looked like that was about to change. Finally.

The two shadows trailing Oscar as he moved through narrow alleyways drew closer, not even bothering to hide anymore.

If they wanted him dead, they would have killed him a long time ago. At least, that's what Oscar kept telling himself as he took a sharp turn into a dead-end lane, calmly waiting for the men following him to appear around the corner. Since greeting his potential kidnappers with an excited smile would have looked odd, Oscar masked it with a stern frown.

The first man stopped at the entrance to the lane and scratched his head, clearly unsure what to do. Definitely not the brains of this operation.

The second man sized Oscar up with a smirk. Masking his excitement became even harder as Oscar recognized the man's watery, gray eyes. This was the man who'd kidnapped Clara.

"You were going in the right direction, Lord Huxley," the man sneered. "We are just here to make sure you safely reach your destination."

So the meeting Oscar was headed to was a set-up. "No ropes or blind-folds? How disappointing," he teased, knowing he was safe for now.

"Just move," the gray-eyed man growled, clearly not appreciating Oscar's humor.

Oscar's adrenaline was pumping from a mixture of excitement and fear. He'd promised Clara he would stay safe and going with these men definitely violated that promise. But nobody was going to be safe unless Oscar figured out what these people were planning and how to stop them.

He didn't risk his neck for Orellia, the kingdom that was now supposed to be his home. He was doing it for Clara, Karina, and even for that asshole Hayden, because despite his mistakes and shortcomings, he was actually a good king.

Oscar was also doing it for the thrill that resonated through every cell in his body right now. The excitement was most likely short-lived, doomed to die down as soon as he made the slightest mistake and they started punching him, but for now, it was fun. Also, it distracted him from his conflicting thoughts on giving Clara the letter. After all, if Oscar did get killed, he wouldn't have to deal with feelings and relationships anymore, would he?

The meeting place was a small warehouse, one of the many that lined the riverbank. Oscar rolled his eyes over the moldy stench and trash scattered over the floor of the dilapidated building. Seriously, couldn't they have met in a nice, clean tavern?

Oscar's newly acquired guards stayed outside, apparently not considering him a threat. They didn't even bother searching him or taking away the dagger hiding in his boot. Not that Oscar would know how to use it. Obviously, he knew to stick the sharp end into someone's body but he was usually so hopeless in combat that considering his skills, the blade would probably end up in himself.

He was alone for now so he found a wall that looked stable enough to lean against and waited. If they were hoping to make him anxious or afraid, they were very wrong. Oscar was actually glad to have this moment to clear his mind.

Oscar pushed away all thoughts about Clara and the wild mix of emotions concerning her. He couldn't afford to be distracted now since a single mistake might prove lethal. For now, he had to go back to being the heartless asshole who'd once made a girl so sad she'd tried to kill herself. No matter how much Oscar hated his former self.

The door creaked and the soft light of a lantern illuminated the room. Crossing his arms in front of his body Oscar took a confident step forward, ready to face the 'player'.

It was him. The man with eyes so dark they looked like the deepest pits of the Underworld. Oscar would bet money on it being the same man who'd given Clara the potion to make the king go insane. His face wasn't covered this time and Oscar noticed a distinct scar running from his left ear to the corner of his mouth, making the man look as if he was perpetually grinning.

"Lord Huxley," he addressed Oscar with a feigned smile before hanging the lantern on one of the pillars supporting the roof construction.

Oscar responded with his own insincere smile. "Yes. The last time I checked, that was still my name. Do you have one? I mean, at least a fake one, for the sake of conversation."

"I have many names," the man replied. The darkness in his eyes was truly unnerving, no wonder Clara had been so frightened. "But you can call me Kan'thar. For the sake of conversation."

Wow, the man had some ego to call himself after the god of justice. Did it mean he truly believed in whatever cause these people were pursuing? It would make things easier. Fanatics were simpler to deal with.

"Sure," Oscar scoffed, "are you going to strike me down with your magical flaming hammer if I tell a lie?" he teased, referring to one of the myths about the god whose name the man had chosen to use.

"I'm sure one of my associates can bring a hammer if it proves necessary," Kan'thar retorted with an indifferent shrug.

A shiver ran down Oscar's spine but he didn't let it show in his expression. Bad choice of words. He should start being more careful. "Well, this building does look like it could use some renovations," he replied, his voice level thanks to years of experience. "One hammer would hardly be enough to fix everything though. We could have met at some nicer location. Somewhere with good food and ale, a warm fire, comfortable chairs? Maybe with some pretty women?"

"Pretty women?" Kan'thar sneered. "Hasn't it only been a couple of days since your young bride left the capital?"

Oscar didn't bat an eye over the mention of Clara. "Every man has needs," he shrugged, forcing a lascivious smirk to his lips. "But I have to say, the quality of the local brothels is abysmal compared to the ones in Vantia." Oscar had visited a few to meet up with his informants. He hadn't told Clara about it. Hopefully, she'd understand, she was a smart woman. Damn, no thinking about her now! he mentally scolded himself. He couldn't afford the distraction.

Turning his attention back to Kan'thar, Oscar grinned sleazily before suggesting, "Perhaps you could give me a recommendation?"

"Lord Huxley," Kan'thar smirked, sounding annoyed. Good. Annoyed means distracted and distracted people make mistakes. "I did not meet with you to make small talk," he said, pausing to gauge Oscar's reaction.

Oscar said nothing, merely raising his brow a little, as if he had only been mildly interested in what Kan'thar wanted with him. His dismissive expression annoyed Kan'thar even further.

Failing to get a response from Oscar, Kan'thar continued in a slightly disgruntled tone, "I invited you here to see if you would be interested in cooperating with us. From what we've heard, you are not a fan of King Hayden."

Seriously, this was going better than Oscar had hoped for. Still, he had to choose his words carefully so as not to seem too eager. "Who told you that? It's a lie. I'm as loyal to our beloved king as any other nobleman living in Orellia," he proclaimed, his words laced with subtle sarcasm.

"Really?" Kan'thar scoffed.

"Yes, really." Oscar tilted his head to the side, sizing up the other man. "Listen, I understand the king wants to test my loyalty, but this is a pretty stupid way to go about it."

"I'm not here to test your loyalty, Lord Huxley. Based on your reputation, your loyalty to anything other than power and money is dubious, to say the least."

What a hurtful thing to say to a person. Oscar smiled as if he'd received a compliment. "And I'm just supposed to take your word for that?"

Kan'thar looked him straight in the eyes, responding without hesitation, "Yes. We are going to rid this country of the Burning Fury once and for all. I believe that is something you desire too, or am I wrong?"

Chapter 42

O scar stared at the man in front of him. It couldn't be so simple, could it? Just say yes and become a part of the conspiracy?

No. No sane person would immediately agree to participate in the Burning Fury's assassination, especially with the offer coming from a questionable source. Oscar had to play hard to get for a little longer.

"You want to kill the king?" he scowled. "And you want my help doing it? You're insane!"

"I never said anything about killing him," Kan'thar retorted, clearly enjoying the sight of Oscar flabbergasted. "I said we were going to get rid of him. Does that sound interesting to you?"

Still carefully maintaining his expression, Oscar let an evil glint peek through his eyes. It wasn't difficult, all he had to do was remember how much he'd hated Hayden for making Karina fall in love with him. "Are you trying to make me say something that would incriminate me?" Oscar pretended to look around cautiously. "Will the King's guard jump out of the shadows to arrest me if I say yes?"

"Aren't you already incriminated just by talking to me after I revealed my plan to you?" Kan'thar smirked, visibly pleased by what he thought he saw. "I understand your worries, Lord Huxley. But we can all benefit from this and what we want from you isn't dangerous at all. We know that the king occasionally consults you about potential threats to the throne."

That was true. "Let me guess, you want me to say everything is peachy?"

"On the contrary." Thinking he was getting through to Oscar, Kan'thar grinned victoriously. What an idiot. "We want you to tell the king there is a very serious threat, and it's coming from the lord chancellor."

So Lord Egmont was their first target. It made sense. The lord chancellor ruled Orellia in Hayden's absence and had the biggest chance of keeping the country stable should something happen to the king.

"That's ridiculous," Oscar objected, "the king trusts Egmont indiscriminately. He would never believe the Chancellor is plotting against him. The amount of fake evidence it would take to convince the king of Egmont's betrayal is..." Oscar shook his head, "unimaginable."

"We'll provide you with enough evidence to plant a seed of doubt into the king's mind. That is all we need."

Because they thought Hayden had drunk the potion and turned into a paranoid madman. A seed of doubt would soon grow by a monstrous proportion.

"Hmm," Oscar mused, pretending to consider the offer. "What's in it for me?" Greed was supposed to be his main motivator, right?

Kan'thar grinned. "The usual. Titles, positions, money. Or was there something else you wanted?"

"Maybe. But, no offense, I won't discuss it with a messenger. I want to talk to whoever is in charge."

Kan'thar was smart and no doubt dangerous, but he didn't strike Oscar as a criminal mastermind capable of organizing such a complex plot. There must have been someone else pulling the strings.

Tilting his head to the side, Kan'thar scrutinized Oscar's expression. "I'm afraid that's not possible," he refused. "The man in charge, as you called him, does not meet in person with anyone. Protecting his identity is too important." A public figure then. Someone close to the king. Living in the palace maybe? Damn, Oscar needed to find out more.

Kan'thar continued, "But I can relay your wishes to him and see if we can reach a compromise."

"Fine," Oscar conceded. "I want the queen." Oscar was supposed to look like an unscrupulous bastard and this was the easiest way to go about it. He let both lust and hatred sound in his voice. "I've wanted her for years. Then that asshole king of yours came and stole her from me. What's worse, she chose him," he spat out, "and she is going to pay for that. I don't give a shit what you do with the fucking Burning Fury but the queen is MINE." Pretending to lose control of his emotions, Oscar drew in a shaky breath as if saying all those lies had exhausted him.

Bringing up Karina's name in this discussion was not something Oscar had planned but it was the easiest way to gain the man's trust. Such a lowly and despicable motive was exactly what was expected from him. Plus, laying claim on Karina in this way would give her extra protection in case something went sideways.

Kan'thar blinked in surprise. "The queen? What about your wife?"

"What about her?" Oscar scoffed. "My wife is an adorable little thing, fun to play with. Plus, she's rich, which is nice, so I'm keeping her. But I will have the queen, whatever it takes. If you can't promise her, there will be no deal. Tell that to that precious little boss of yours." Not wanting to overplay his hand, Oscar turned to leave, curious whether they would let him.

"I will talk to him and let you know our decision," Kan'thar called after Oscar before ordering his men to let him pass.

Oscar maintained a neutral expression, not letting his relief show until he was safely alone in his chambers. Only then did he let his guard down, shuddering in disgust over the words he'd said and how easily they'd came to him. The monster was still inside of him, still part of him, like a dark stain on his stupid soul. One that Oscar could never get rid of. At least now, Oscar could utilize that monster to do something good.

He went over the conversation a couple more times in his head, analyzing the words, pinpointing any mistakes, and putting the pieces together to form a bigger picture. However, he still needed more information in order to identify the person pulling the strings.

Still, all things considered, Oscar felt like he had done a good job. He'd gained their trust and hopefully, he didn't screw himself over by making such an outrageous request. Hayden was not going to be happy about it, Oscar realized with a chuckle, but that was a problem for another day.

A soft knock at the door interrupted his thoughts. It was too early for the response from the mysterious man in charge but what else could it be?

An unknown man in dusty, worn-out riding clothes stood behind the door. "Lord Huxley?" he asked, suppressing a yawn. When Oscar nodded, the man pulled out a letter. "This is for you."

Fear warred with excitement when Oscar noticed the Redwood seal on the smudged parchment. The seal created by Clara's signet ring. With shame, Oscar realized he hadn't given her one with a Huxley crest on it yet. That was something he ought to fix soon, if she still wanted him.

After giving the messenger a few coins for his service, Oscar waved him away. He set the letter down on the table, staring at it indecisively. He definitely needed a drink for this.

He grabbed the first bottle he stumbled upon and, with a drink in hand, sat on the sofa, staring at the paper in front of him. A glass later, Oscar finally gathered the courage to reach for the letter. He caressed the seal, trying to imagine Clara as she'd placed her ring into the wax. Was she crying? Trembling with anger? The answer was written inside but damn, Oscar was too frightened to find out.

When the seal cracked under his trembling fingers, Oscar winced, taking a deep breath in the desperate attempt to calm himself before unfolding the paper. The words were uneven and smudged, it was obvious they weren't written at a proper desk but rather in much more primitive conditions. Still, it was clearly Clara's handwriting.

Bidding himself to stop being a pussy, Oscar forced himself to read the words.

"Oscar. I hope this letter gets to you, I'm not sure the messenger won't tell me to fuck off or if he isn't just going to throw it away somewhere. I'm sorry if it's not legible, I'm writing it while sitting by a fire, holding the paper against my knee, and my hands are still shaking from bathing in a freezing cold lake. Seriously, when I get home, I will take a steaming hot bath every single day."

Oscar chuckled over her words, allowing himself a little hope. She was planning to come back home. Although, that didn't necessarily mean she would come back to him.

"I read your letter and kept thinking about it all day. It provided a good distraction from the constant pain from my sore muscles. Sorry, that was a bad joke.

"I think it's safe to say I was absolutely shocked by what you wrote. I have a lot of things I want to tell you now but there is one that needs to be addressed first. You said you weren't going to lie to me and I believe you broke that promise."

Crap.

Oscar tossed the letter back onto the table. Tears were threatening to fall. It was somewhat surprising, since he never cried. Crying was a waste of energy and a sign of weakness. Plus, it was pointless. Tears couldn't fix the situation. Still, his body wanted to succumb to the urge and break down into a sobbing mess but he forced back the tears, choosing to finish his glass instead before immediately refilling it.

So, he did fuck it up. No surprise there.

It felt a little unfair because he'd tried so hard to be good but his past got in the way. It was always going to get in the way. There was no way he could get rid of it, to separate himself from the man he used to be. Perhaps his life would be easier if he could become that asshole again, but he couldn't. If Oscar went back to being a heartless monster, he wouldn't be able to live with himself anymore.

Clara's letter taunted him. There were still plenty of unread lines but Oscar wasn't sure he could take that much hate and reproach. Unable to resist, Oscar picked it up again, deciding to see the matter through to its inevitably bitter end.

"When you gave me the parchment, you said it wasn't a love letter. And that was a lie. Because what else were those last lines if not a confession of something dangerously resembling love?" Oscar's breath hitched. Did she mean...? *"I'm hardly an expert on the matter. I don't know what love is supposed to feel like or if it even has an exact definition. As I already told you, I like you, a lot. I care for you and I miss you terribly."*

A drop of liquid splashed down onto the paper. Oscar paused in surprise as he realized it was a tear. His tear. So much for not crying. He blinked to prevent more tears from escaping and went back to hungrily devouring Clara's words.

"I've been afraid to tell you, or to even acknowledge it because I knew I could never have you, not fully, not when your heart was somewhere else. Don't get me wrong, I respected it. I understand that your feelings were not something you could have changed even if you wanted to. But that didn't make it any easier for me.

"If what you wrote is true, and I don't have any reason not to trust you, then perhaps we could...I don't know, build something together? Is that the right word? To have an actual relationship?"

Did that pathetic sniffle come from Oscar?

"I know you are worried about how I feel about Alice. It's a heartbreaking, shitty story, full of pain and suffering. Yes, the man from that story was a bastard who would get nothing but an arrow from me. But that's not you, Oscar.

"You are nothing like that man anymore so please, don't be too hard on yourself. What happened to Alice was a mistake from which you've learned your lesson. What happened to her baby... She's the one to blame for that, for doing something so stupid and irresponsible while knowing she was with child. It was not your fault, or at least not only your fault. Please, stop beating yourself up over it."

There was no stopping the tears anymore. Oscar hadn't realized how much he'd needed to hear those words, how hard he'd wanted for someone to forgive him so that he could start forgiving himself. And his miraculously amazing wife had just given him exactly what he needed.

"There is so much more I want to write but I'm exhausted and this paper is too damn small. The people are great, much friendlier than I'd expected. The food rations are abysmal but I did just finish eating a rabbit I killed earlier today and, no kidding, it was the best meal I've ever had."

Wiping his nose with the back of his hand, Oscar chuckled. It sounded like Clara was happy.

"I miss you. I wish I could be there for you because you've been there for me when I needed it and I would really like to do the same. I promise I'll make it up to you when I get back.

"Please stay safe.

"Clara."

Even though it felt silly, Oscar cradled the letter to his chest, a wave of relief forcing his eyes closed. Being accepted like this, with all his flaws and mistakes of the past, was a completely new feeling for him, something so liberating he wanted to burst into song. He needed to write a response to Clara right away.

As he jumped up staggering, his vision blurred by the amount of alcohol he'd drunk, Oscar reconsidered. Composing a letter for Clara could wait until morning when he would be sober.

Chapter 43

E agle Peak outpost was an admirable fortress, especially considering it was built in the middle of the wilderness. The inner part was protected by a solid stone wall and the military encampment sprawling around it was surrounded by a tall wooden palisade. The number of tents couldn't compete with the amount Karina had seen in Hayden's camp back when they'd first met, but the numbers weren't small either.

Hayden didn't waste any time. Once he'd made sure all the men he'd brought along were settled, he took his guards and went off to talk to the neutral tribes, those that had refused to accept his messengers, stating they wouldn't talk to 'just a man'.

Karina suggested she go with him but his furious glare made her clamp her mouth shut. They were in enemy territory now, he'd pointed out. Even staying inside the outpost wasn't entirely safe, let alone wandering around the woods to meet up with potentially hostile locals. She understood that he only wanted to keep her safe but being left behind was still frustrating.

At least Karina had Clara to keep her company. They spent a lot of time talking since there wasn't much else for them to do, unless they wanted to join the soldiers in peeling mountains of potatoes, scrubbing gargantuan pots, chopping piles of wood or other, rather unappealing duties, like digging latrines.

The king returned a few hours later, fuming. When he barged into the room, Clara flinched and got up to leave. Grabbing her hand, Karina made her sit back down. Dealing with a riled-up Burning Fury was an acquired skill, one Clara should start learning.

"The negotiations went badly?" Karina asked carefully, trying to keep her voice as calm as possible.

Hayden walked over and sat down on the bed next to her, his frustration slowly taking over from the anger. "There was no negotiation. I seriously don't get their point. What the fuck do they want?"

"What did they say?"

"The same thing as before, that they wouldn't talk to just a man," Hayden scoffed, his clenched fist hitting the mattress. "Apparently, I'm not good enough for those stupid savages either."

Karina tried to pull him into a hug but he jumped up, pacing the room restlessly. "I need to get through to them somehow," he rambled, "but they simply refused to let me into their territory. If we use force, they'll retaliate and all the tribes that have been neutral so far would become our enemies as well. And we just can't afford that right now. If only I could somehow reach the damn *seftha* and talk to him directly. But there's no chance with so many warriors surrounding him."

The word was unfamiliar to Karina but she assumed it was a title for the Ruthian leader. It was Clara who frowned, asking, "What exactly did they tell you?"

"What?" Hayden looked at her in surprise, as if he had only now noticed her being present in the room. "As I said, that they won't talk to-"

"No," Clara interrupted him, "in their language?"

Hayden raked his hand through his hair. "I don't remember exactly, the interpreter was handling that. Something like '*ka simia poe higar*'?"

"Are you sure they said '*higar*'?"

Hayden's fists clenched again. "Yes, that part I'm very sure of. A man. Assholes! What more important man than me do they want?!" His tirade was cut short by a violent banging at the door.

"SIR!" someone shouted from outside. Hayden leaped to open the door, revealing a winded, gasping soldier. "There's been an attack on a group of merchants just an hour's ride away from here! The general is already gathering men."

"I'll be right there," Hayden responded with a decisive nod before turning back to give Karina a quick kiss.

She wanted nothing more than to pull him close and enjoy his presence for a few more seconds before he disappeared again but knew she had to let him go. "Please, be safe!" she called out after him, not even sure whether he'd heard her as he sprinted out of the door. "Aaand, there he goes again," Karina sighed.

Clara didn't react, looking lost in thought. "It's funny, you know," she said after a minute. "It sounds almost as if... No, it's ridiculous."

"What is it?"

"Well," Clara hesitated, "the thing is, the normal word for a chosen chieftain of multiple tribes fighting together would be *sefth*. *Seftha* is usable as well but...it's more of a feminine version. And yes, *higar* means a man but I think they got the context wrong.

"I believe the Ruthians didn't say 'just a man' because they wanted to talk to someone more important than the king's messengers and diplomats. That word is used to refer to a man as a...guy," she chuckled, struggling to find the right word, "a...male! Yes, I think a male would be the right translation."

Karina's eyes narrowed, the realization slowly dawning on her. "Wait a second. Are you saying that they didn't want to talk to Hayden because he is a man? Because their leader is a woman and she wants to...talk to a woman instead?"

"It would be very unusual," Clara shrugged, "some of the tribes are matriarchal but when more of them work together and elect a *sefth* to lead them, it has always been a man so far. I mean, as far as I know. I haven't exactly studied their history, it's just from stories my father told me."

What Karina had to do now was obvious, just as it was obvious that Hayden was never going to allow it. To add to the general obviousness, he would be furious upon finding out she went to the Ruthians behind his back. It still didn't change the fact that she had to go.

After quickly scribbling down a note with an explanation and a pointless apology, Karina grabbed the warmest cloak she could find. It was late afternoon and no doubt, she was going to arrive wherever these people were hiding after dark.

Clara watched her with growing concern. "Karina? You aren't doing what I think you are doing, right? Listen, I'm not really sure about that translation. I don't actually speak the language, I just know a few words."

"But it makes perfect sense. And I need to go before Hayden returns. You stay here."

"No!" Clara exclaimed. "If you are going to get yourself killed, I'm coming as well."

Karina wished she could bring Clara along but she'd given her word to Oscar to keep his wife safe. No, the only life she was willing to risk was her own, just like when she went to negotiate with Hayden after the battle between Levanta and Orellia. Her only thought was to protect her people. Now she was no longer a princess, but a queen, but the only thing that had changed was that now she had more people to protect.

"You will stay here," Karina snapped at Clara. "That's an order." She hated using her authority in this way but it was necessary. "Try to convince Hayden not to do something stupid when he returns, please." A fool's errand, Karina knew that all too well.

As she closed the door behind herself, Karina realized she had no idea where she was going. The forests stretched for dozens of miles all around. Karina needed to employ some brave souls unafraid of the king's wrath. And she knew just where to find them.

The camp surrounding the outpost was eerily quiet as most of the men left with Hayden to protect the merchant caravan. Followed by a frowning Markos, Karina quickly located Larkin and explained her plan to him.

Naturally, he called her insane. But he didn't refuse to help and gathered a group of men who had been stationed in these mountains before and knew their way around the woods. Clara's archer friend was among them.

With her new escort, Karina hurriedly left the outpost. The guards at the outer gate looked hesitant to let her pass but didn't dare to argue with the queen.

As the sun set, the temperature dropped and Karina was glad for the fur on the inside of her cloak. Gods, this place must have been a freezing hellhole in winter.

They followed the main road north for a few miles before taking a sharp turn onto a barely recognizable path deep into the forest. As she rode, Karina began to realize the flaws in her hastily constructed plan, but it was too late to turn back now. Hayden was going to get mad anyway. The least Karina could do is get something out of it. Or die trying, that was always an option.

The soldiers slowed down as they approached the enemy territory. Karina had no idea how they could possibly know they were near the border. All she could see was trees, trees and more trees, but she trusted them. Seeing their hands anxiously grabbing the hilts of their swords, she tried to soothe them. "Calm down, we don't want to provoke a conflict."

A sharp shout from the bushes ahead made them stay their horses.

"They are telling us to go the fuck away," one of Larkin's men growled. It was the one with the ugly scar over his face. Karina thought his name was Blaggar but wasn't entirely sure. Surprisingly, he was almost fluent in the Ruthian language.

"Tell them we are here to negotiate with their leader," Larkin instructed, his voice strained. Karina guessed that the fear of being killed by the savages paled in comparison to fear of what Hayden was going to do after finding out Larkin helped Karina put herself into this dangerous situation.

Blaggar barked a few words toward and received an angry response.

Karina didn't need to wait for a translation, she recognized a 'fuck off' when she heard one. She dismounted and took a few steps forward, careful not to trip over anything in the growing darkness. Markos and Larkin were quick to join her side, the other men staying slightly behind.

A man with short red hair magically appeared from behind a tree. Fortunately, Karina was controlling herself well enough not to show fear or yelp out in surprise. The Ruthian spat out more words before pointing a spear against Karina's chest. She quickly raised her hand to stop Markos from jumping forward and striking the man down.

"Leave or die," Blaggar translated, his brows furrowing as he looked around, his posture changing as he prepared for a fight.

Karina could hear them too now. The low bushes rustled all around, no doubt they were surrounded. "Tell him the queen is here to talk to the *seftha*, woman to woman," she ordered.

Blaggar hesitated. "Are you sure about this, my lady? Because if their leader is a man, he will take this as a mortal insult and we are as good as dead."

No, Karina wasn't sure about it but it was too late to change her mind. "Just translate it."

As Blaggar talked, the Ruthian spat in front of Karina's feet, raising his spear to attack. Well, it was worth a shot, Karina thought as she mentally prepared herself to run to her horse.

Something hissed through the air and the man flinched as the spear was nearly knocked out of his hand. He stared at the long wooden hilt in disbelief, gawking at the white-feathered arrow sticking out of it. Karina wasn't that surprised. She knew there was only a very small chance Clara would follow the order to stay behind.

Another Ruthian stepped out of the shadows near the first enemy. This one was a woman, and she snapped at the man angrily. They had a short, heated debate after which the man was forced to back off. He snarled at Karina, as if whatever happened was her fault. It probably was.

The woman moved so close Karina could smell her strong, earthy scent. "Just you," she said with such a heavy accent the words were barely understandable.

Karina was too scared to do this on her own. "What about her?" she asked with a heavy heart, motioning Clara to come forward. She'd hoped to protect Clara by making her stay behind with Larkin and the other men, but going into an enemy village alone was just too frightening.

The Ruthian woman sized Clara up with a raised eyebrow. Her eyes stopped on the girl's thick red braid then on the bow in her hands. "Girl yes," she nodded. "Men stay."

"Great. Thank you." Karina lowered her head in respect, waiting until Clara confidently strode past the men and joined her. "Is that how you listen to your queen's orders?" Karina hissed at Clara quietly.

Clara rolled her eyes, clearly trying to hide her fear. "No, actually, this is how I listen to my husband's requests. I promised Oscar I would stay near you no matter what. I doubt that this is what he had in mind but..." she trailed off with a shrug, watching the Ruthian woman turn around and head away. "Are you sure about this?"

"Of course not," Karina sighed. "But I'll go anyway. You guys stay here," she turned to the men, "I'll be back."

Chapter 44

B y the time Clara had figured out what to say to Karina to stop her from leaving, the queen was already gone. It was infuriating. Did Karina actually expect Clara to just stay behind in the safety of the outpost while she ventured alone into the woods, risking her life in the process? Ridiculous.

The guards at the gate tried to stop Clara from going out but her angry snap made them step aside.

It wasn't difficult to follow Karina's group. Clara was sure some of the men had noticed her but nobody alerted the queen to the girl's presence and no one tried to stop her. She watched from afar as Karina tried to talk to the Ruthians, too far to understand the words. The man's actions were pretty self-explanatory though. Clara raised the bow, aiming at his chest, exactly where she knew the heart would be.

From this distance, there was no way she could miss, but she hesitated. Killing a rabbit was one thing. But this man was just defending his home. Yes, he might have a stupid and aggressive way of going about it, but did it really mean he deserved to die? Karina wanted to negotiate and even someone as inexperienced in politics as Clara knew that dead bodies weren't a good ground for diplomacy.

The man's spear twitched toward Karina and Clara instinctively reacted. She shot not to kill but to protect, and the arrow hit its mark exactly, pushing the weapon away from the queen, giving her time to react. A normal person would use the opportunity to run, but of course Karina stayed and talked to the Ruthians. And now she and Clara were on their way to the village. Alone, the only thing to protect them was Clara's bow which she was now clutching so hard her knuckles had turned white.

Constantly looking around, Clara tried to guess how many enemies could she stop before they would reach them, always coming short. Enzio had told her where to aim when the archer didn't want to kill, showed her the points on the neck and shoulders where even the heavily armored knights had weak spots between the plates. Then there was always an option to go for the thighs or knees.

The Ruthians weren't wearing any armor. There were just too many of them. If they decided to attack the women, Clara could get maybe two or three and then... Better not think about it.

Karina didn't seem to be bothered by the fact that they were utterly defenseless and surrounded by potentially hostile barbarians. Confidently striding through the camp, she followed the female leading them, sending pleasant smiles in the direction of everyone who looked at them.

The place looked more like a military camp than an actual village, there were mostly warriors surrounding them, sitting around small fires in front of primitive huts made of large hides and long branches. Both men and women, armed with spears, swords, axes, bows, and various other oddly-shaped weapons, watched on with wary looks on their faces. Not exactly hostile but definitely not friendly.

Their guide stopped in front of a larger building and pointed at Clara's bow. No words were necessary, Clara knew damn well what the Ruthian wanted but still found herself unable to let go of her weapon. Mostly because she was so damn scared, and the thought of being unarmed only made it worse. But a tiny part of her reluctance could be accredited to simply not wanting to let go of Oscar's gift and hand it over to strangers.

"It's fine," Karina told her in a calm voice. The queen was already holding two daggers, one that Clara was certain came from Karina's boot, and the other one... Clara actually had no idea where the queen pulled that one from. Probably a hidden scabbard on her back.

Not really having any other options, Clara gave the bow to the female. "*Rizza*. Careful. Mine," she tapped on her own chest, frowning at the Ruthian. The woman cackled, saying something Clara didn't understand before running her fingers over the ornate handle of the bow. Clara pulled the quiver over her head and removed the small hunting knife, a gift from Enzio, from the scabbard on her belt. She had grown so accustomed to walking around with a weapon she felt almost naked now. Of course, the constant danger she and Karina were in didn't exactly help to make her feel better.

The woman motioned them inside, pulling a pelt hanging over the building entrance to the side so they could pass through the low door. The air inside was smokey, a fire crackling in a large fireplace in the center, illuminating the long room with flickering orange light. There were a couple of indistinct figures sitting on a long bench at the opposite side and Karina marched right toward them.

"*Povah*," the one in the center nodded. It was an elderly woman, maybe in her sixties, still tall and strong but the deep wrinkles around her eyes gave her age away.

Her hair had probably been red when she was younger and even though it had long since turned silvery-white, it was still thick and long, plaited into intricate braids falling down from her shoulders. She wore rich ceremonial jewelry and was holding a spear adorned by several tribal symbols. Which meant it was true, the tribes really had chosen a woman to lead them. Two men and two women were sitting next to her, probably important leaders themselves, that now answered to her.

Clara stepped forward to stand next to Karina and lowered her head. "The *seftha* is saying welcome," she said quietly. The queen seriously hadn't thought this through. Clara barely understood a few basic words of the Ruthian language, there was no way she could act as an interpreter for diplomatic negotiations of this importance.

"Thank you for accepting us, *Seftha*," Karina gave the woman a respectful bow.

Right. Thank you was easy. While Clara strained her brain trying to come up with a solution on how to convey the 'for accepting us' part of the message using her limited vocabulary, the *seftha* smirked. "I'm glad King Hayden finally understood my message." Her accent was barely even noticeable and Clara sighed in relief. It looked like she was off the hook. At least with the translation part. Dying a horrible death tied to one of the poles outside while the entire camp watched on, was still very much on the table.

"I'm Ulaia, the leader of more than forty big and small tribes of the northern mountains," the *seftha* continued. "My people chose me to lead them through these dangerous and trying times in hopes that I could provide them with protection against the reignited hostilities between our nations."

Karina lowered her head again. "I'm very pleased to meet you, *Seftha*. You probably already knew this but I am Karina, the wife of King Hayden, the ruler of Orellia." Clara noticed that she didn't say she was the queen, as if she was almost ashamed to be using the title. Or maybe just didn't want to look like she was flashing it around to impress the Ruthians. Because these people surely weren't going to be amazed by such a thing.

"Yes, we are aware that the king finally found himself a woman," one corner of Ulaia's mouth curled up, "and we were hoping it would help him settle down and stop with the constant warmongering. It seems like you had the opposite effect though, Karina."

What the hell was this woman talking about? It's not like Karina had urged Hayden to go to war. The Ruthians were the ones to attack first! Clara had to bite on the inside of her cheek to keep quiet.

The queen didn't seem to be moved by the subtle insults and disrespect seeping from the *seftha's* words. "It's not like you managed to stop your people from going to war either, Ulaia," the queen poked her softly, earning an amused chuckle. "The king is only defending our citizens, as is his duty. I was under the impression the situation here in the north was stable and that there was some sort of silent non-aggression pact between the Ruthians and King Hayden. He was satisfied with the status quo and had absolutely no intention of changing it until the attacks on the trade caravans and the destruction of our outpost. Even now, he still seeks a peaceful solution."

"That is not what we have been told," one of the women next to the *seftha* said. The sides of her head were shaved clean, leaving only a thick stripe of long dark hair running from her forehead back to her nape. The skin around it was covered in tribal tattoos, giving her a wild look. "That is not what the bastard's first messenger said."

Ulaia glared at her. "*Kazzar!*" Quiet. "There is no need for such insults here."

"I understand the emotions," Karina said, much calmer than Clara would expect. She nodded at the tattooed woman. "May I know what exactly the 'first messenger' told you?"

The addressed woman just snarled and spat into the dirt in front of Karina's feet. The *seftha* shook her head and let out a resigned sigh. "Most of the tribes were repeatedly approached by a man claiming to be the king's official messenger. He said that just like the people of Levanta, the Ruthians are now considered citizens of the Kingdom of Orellia and are under King Hayden's protection." Ulaia paused, observing Karina's reaction. Whatever she found there must have satisfied her because she continued. "And that in exchange for this generous protection, we are to pay rather harsh taxes and tributes to the crown."

"I see." Karina closed her eyes for a moment, probably carefully choosing her next words. "And many tribes believed him."

The *seftha* tilted her head to the side, her eyes narrowed. "Why wouldn't they? He was carrying documents with the official seal of Hayden's diplomatic office. I've seen it with my own eyes, it was the same one as on the documents previously delivered to us from the king after we made peace last time. It was not a fake."

The 'messenger' they spoke of was obviously someone sent by the Cchen-lian but how could he have had official documents from the palace? That made no sense.

"Most tribes became angry, naturally, and chose to go to war. *Sefth* Gishri has always hated the king and now he has an opportunity to strike back, in revenge for all that our people have suffered from the hands of the Burning Fury and his father before.

"Those who were willing to seek a peaceful resolution gathered around me. We do not wish for war and bloodshed. We even tried to take care of some of the wounded soldiers from your destroyed outpost that wandered into our territories. Most of them died, sadly, their injuries were too severe, but there is still one in our healer's tent that has a chance of survival."

A survivor from the Blackwater outpost? Clara had trouble masking her excitement. Perhaps he knew something about Nicolas? She knew it was a desperate hope and that she was likely to be disappointed but still couldn't help herself.

Karina raised an eyebrow, taken aback by the *seftha's* words. "What would you want in return for releasing him?" she asked carefully.

"You can have him once he is strong enough for transport," Ulaia waved her hand dismissively. "As I said, we seek peace. Consider it a token of our good faith, something that your side clearly lacks."

Karina's brows furrowed, but when she opened her mouth to say something, a young Ruthian barged into the room, rushing toward the *seftha* and whispering into her ear. That must have meant trouble.

"It seems that the king of Orellia has brought a significant military force to our border, threatening to 'burn down the whole fucking forest' unless his queen is returned to him immediately," Ulaia smirked. While the others around her looked enraged, the *seftha* still seemed mostly amused, which was probably the only reason Clara and Karina were still alive.

"Shit," the queen hissed, "I thought I would have more time. Ulaia, please, listen to me." She took a step forward, ignoring the guards that pointed their weapons in her direction. Hands raised in a gesture of surrender, Karina continued talking, her voice gaining intensity. "This 'first messenger' was not sent by Hayden. It was a trick meant to instigate hostilities and drag both our people into a long and bloody war again. We want nothing more than to live in peace, just like you."

Karina paused for a moment, rubbing the bridge of her nose, letting out an exasperated sigh. "Please, if you could tell your people to stand down, I will go to the king and sort out this misunderstanding and then return here so we can continue our conversation."

The tattooed woman scoffed and said something, clearly not believing a word the queen said. The others looked indecisive but what they thought didn't really matter, the final decision was the *seftha's*. "Go get your husband under control, Queen Karina. You prevented him from killing your people, do the same for mine now." Ulaia turned to Clara for the first time since the women walked into the room. "You are welcome to stay in the meantime if you wish so, *hari i borren*."

Karina promptly grabbed Clara's hand, pulling the girl behind her back as if she wanted to protect Clara with her own body. "I don't know what that means but she's coming with me."

"It means a child of flames. I think she's referring to my hair," Clara explained quietly, trying to squirm out of Karina's grip. The queen was surprisingly strong. "I am not one of you, *Seftha*," Clara attempted to find a tone that wouldn't sound offensive. "I might have a bit of Ruthian blood coursing through my veins but that does not make me one of your people."

Ulaia stood up and, leaning against the ceremonial spear, walked closer to Clara. "You are a fierce warrior and a fearless woman." A soft smile brightened her wrinkled face. "You are more one of us than one of them. And either way," she turned back to Karina, "the girl would be safe with us. I was merely offering her an opportunity to find out more about her heritage.

"My people will not attack first but they will fight to defend our territory. If you intend to prevent that, you should hurry. Rimea will guide you back. I really hope that when we meet again, it will not be on the battlefield."

Even at her age, Ulaia would fight to the last breath to protect her people. And she would be a formidable enemy. Age or gender didn't matter when it came to the fighting skills of the Ruthians.

"Thank you." Karina bowed before letting go of Clara's hand, turning to leave the building.

Clara didn't move. Damn, was she really going to do this? The logical part of her brain was telling her that staying here was suicide. Who would be the first to die if the fighting started? Certainly not the lone defenseless girl conveniently located right in the middle of the enemy's camp. But something kept telling her to stay. An instinct, maybe intuition? The name didn't really matter. What mattered was the strong feeling that she would regret leaving this place right now.

Almost at the door, Karina finally realized she wasn't being followed. "Clara? We need to hurry."

"I'll stay here." Clara was surprised how confident her words sounded. "I'll be fine," she quickly continued, silencing Karina's protests. "You go. Better yet, you run. You are the only one who can stop Hayden from doing something stupid."

Karina's eyes jumped between Clara and Ulaia a couple of times, indecision clearly written on her face. She knew she had to hurry to stop the bloodshed but clearly didn't want to leave Clara behind. Fortunately, her sense of duty won out. "I'll be right back. If anything happens to her-"

"She will be safe," the *seftha* interrupted her. "Go."

Giving them one last look, Karina sprinted out of the room, leaving Clara completely alone, surrounded by very unfriendly barbarians.

Noticing her nervousness, Ulaia smiled, gesturing to an empty space on the bench by the fire. "Come, child, sit with me."

"Actually," Clara hesitated, not wanting to insult the woman, "could I please see the wounded soldier first? I would like to speak to him."

The *seftha* smirked. "I'm not sure you will be able to speak to him, he has been unconscious most of the time, but you can see him if that is your wish." She used the spear as a walking cane again, heading outside. "Come then, my lost child."

While Clara didn't exactly appreciate being called a child, she didn't protest and followed the old woman out of the building and through the village. The healer's tent was a large hut on the edge of the village, surrounded by the pleasant smell of herbs. It took a few seconds for Clara's eyes to adjust to the darkness inside but when they did...

She gasped at the pale figure lying on the bed. "Nicolas?!"

Chapter 45

D amn, what was Clara thinking? Karina muttered, quietly cursing as she rushed through the forest, trying to avoid bushes and low-hanging branches while jumping over treacherous protruding roots and random chunks of wood lying on the ground. Choosing to stay behind? Sure, the *seftha* seemed determined to keep the peace, but not at all costs. If the fighting started, Clara would be the first to die. And it would be Karina's fault because she'd dragged her into this stupid wilderness and let her come to that stupid village.

The wounded soldier, that must have been Clara's reason to stay. A desperate attempt to find out something about her missing brother. Karina could understand that, even though she disagreed. But Clara's safety was the least of her problems now. A furious Hayden, that's what she should be worrying about.

There were angry voices coming from up ahead and Karina picked up the pace, sprinting straight through the bushes, barely even flinching when a thorny twig scratched her cheek. "STOP!" she cried out upon seeing

Hayden and a couple of his knights with their swords drawn, exchanging angry glares and shouts with several Ruthians.

Rimea, the woman who'd been showing Karina the way, barked a couple of orders and the Ruthians reluctantly took a step back. The Orellians didn't.

"Stand down!" Karina shouted. It was hard to sound authoritative while panting.

The knights didn't move but Hayden angrily marched toward her. He was beyond furious, his face twisted by a seething rage so intense she barely even recognized him. Karina had never seen her husband like this before and instinctively took a step back as he approached. Hayden didn't seem to care, roughly grabbing her arm and forcing her to move back toward the waiting soldiers.

Karina shuddered upon noticing Larkin and his men kneeling on the ground, tied up. The lieutenant had a black eye and a split lip. Crap. This was all her fault. She'd seriously underestimated the king's reaction.

"Hayden, stop!"

It was as if he didn't even hear her, lost in his rage so deeply he was barely paying any attention to the outside world. She tried to struggle but it only made him tighten his grip to the point Karina was certain she would have bruises tomorrow.

She needed to snap him out of it, and fast, before he did something he would later regret. There was a way to snap him out of it but Karina hated herself for even thinking about using it. But there didn't seem to be any other choice. Leaning closer, she hissed right into his ear, "Let me go, you fucking MONSTER!"

Hayden flinched at the word, finally letting go of her arm. Karina thought it would make him back off slightly but it seemed to have only made him angrier, as if such a thing was even possible.

"Shut the fuck up!" he snarled at her, literally showing all of his teeth and letting out a guttural growl like a wild beast. The knights stepped away, not wanting to be near him in this state.

Karina didn't have that option. Trying to take another step back, she stumbled over a root.

Hayden grabbed her arms again, pulling her so close to his face she felt his quickened breath on her cheeks. "You..." He paused, maybe because he didn't want to insult her, or maybe he couldn't find a word that would insult her enough.

Knowing that the only thing she could do was to stay absolutely calm, Karina looked deep into his eyes, forcing out a warm smile. It certainly wasn't an easy task. "Hayden," she said quietly, "I'm here. I'm fine. I was never in danger."

Somehow, she managed not to flinch when he raised one hand to her face, even though she wasn't entirely sure he wasn't going to slap her. But he just placed his palm onto her cheek, running his thumb over her skin. When he raised it to show it to her, there was blood smeared over it.

"Yes, that happened when I was running through these damned woods to stop you from starting a war. I'm sorry. I know you are doing all of this because you were scared for me but I promise, I'm safe." Karina spoke slowly, as if she were speaking to a frightened animal, because her husband was barely more than one right now. The problem with that was that the terrified man in front of her, who was struggling to control himself at the moment, had unlimited power over the lives of many people. And the ability to start wars.

Hayden didn't speak. Karina felt his body trembling as she raised her own hands and cupped his face. "Hayden, I know you are in there somewhere, fighting this. Please, come back to me so we can talk. Like normal people."

He closed his eyes and lowered his head for a moment. "You want to talk like normal people?" His voice sounded surprisingly calm, albeit so cold it made Karina shudder. "What the fuck were you thinking?"

"I'm sorry I didn't talk it through with you but I knew you would never let me go."

"You are damn right I wouldn't! You don't know shit about these people or this situation! What were you hoping to achieve by putting yourself in danger like this?"

Now, that was insulting. Did he really consider her so useless that he allowed her to come with him just to make her happy? To take a trip across the kingdom so she would feel included, as long as she didn't bother him too much? So he could have a quick fuck on the road?

Even though Karina really tried her best to stay calm, her next words came out as an angry snap. "*I* was achieving something that you hadn't! I was just talking to the *seftha* when you barged into their territory, threatening to slaughter innocent people!"

"You were what?!" The surprise overshadowed his rage for a few moments.

Unable to contain her smugness, Karina smirked at him. "You heard me. She didn't want to talk to you because you are a man, and, like all men, you are apparently incapable of using your brain. Always thinking with your dick instead! Were you seriously going to start a war with the last of the neutral tribes in these fucking mountains just because you were worried about me? That's stupid and reckless."

"She?" Hayden shook his head in disbelief. Then returning to his anger, he continued, "I would burn this entire forest to the ground and kill every living thing inside it to protect you. So you better remember that before you try to run off like that again!"

Karina's eyes narrowed and she shook his hands off, stepping away from him. "I'm not your fucking slave, my dear king." Her words were way out of line, but she was so pissed off she couldn't stop herself anymore. "You were the one to tell me I can do whatever the fuck I want to. So, I'm going back to continue the negotiations, because I was actually learning some very interesting information before you barged in and nearly fucked it all up. And as long as you and your soldiers don't do something stupid, I'll be perfectly safe, so there is no need for burning down forests or slaughtering people."

"Like hell you are!" Hayden stared at her in outrage, reaching to grab her arm again.

Karina pushed him away. "Don't touch me," she hissed. That seemed to have done the trick, Hayden recoiled as if she'd struck him, uncertainty flashing through his eyes. "And don't you fucking *dare* to touch them!" Karina pointed at Larkin and the others that had accompanied her to the woods.

"That is none of your concern." Hayden's features hardened again. "They disobeyed their orders and will be punished accordingly."

"No, they won't." Karina couldn't possibly let the blame for this fall on someone else. "Look, I apologize for not talking this through with you before going away. That was a mistake." A big one, as Karina realized now. Hayden trusted her and she betrayed him. "But if someone is to be punished for it, it is going to be me. These men were merely following my command, so if you were planning to have someone whipped for disobeying orders, you are going to have to start with me."

Hayden's eyebrows rose up and he ran his hand through his hair when Karina moved to stand between him and the men, crossing her arms in front of her chest. "Don't play with me, woman," he said quietly, a distinct threat underlining his words. "You think I won't do that?"

"Haven't we been in this situation before?" Karina scoffed, trying hard not to let her fear show. "I know you will. Just like you should know that I won't back down."

Hayden smirked, a hint of amusement creeping into his expression as he was no doubt recalling their very first meeting. "A whip is very different. You wouldn't want that."

"Of course I don't want that, I'm not insane." The image of the whip in Hayden's hand and of Larkin's bloodied back refused to leave her mind. Karina doubted she would last that long. "But I made a mistake and I refuse to let other people pay for it."

His expression was serious when he moved closer to her, speaking quietly, only for her ears. "Karina, when we are out here and at war, I'm the one who makes the decisions and gives the orders. Just me. I need to know about everything that is happening, because I am ultimately responsible for everyone under my command. No matter how smart you think your ideas are, you cannot just run off and act on them without talking to me first. I thought we were supposed to deal with our problems together."

That hurt. A lot. Those were her own words, her own definition of marriage they often joked about. And she was the one to break it. She lowered her head in shame. "I'm sorry," she murmured, all traces of anger having disappeared from her voice.

His palm on her cheek forced Karina to look up. Hayden's expression was warmer than she would have expected, there was even a hint of kindness hidden beneath his scowl. "Good," he said, letting go of her face, his fingers slowly trailing along her chin before he lowered his hand again. "Release them," he nodded at one of his knights. "The queen is responsible and she will be the one punished for this."

"What?! You can't-"

"Shut up, Larkin." Karina interrupted the lieutenant before he could say something that would get him in trouble. This was her fault, she deserved to be punished, she kept telling herself while listening to the men behind her shuffle up to their feet. Everyone was clearly nervous about what the king was going to do.

Hayden looked around with a raised eyebrow. "Relax, I'm not going to have my own wife flogged, for fuck's sake," he rolled his eyes and Karina let out a shaky breath, unable to hide her relief. "No matter how much she deserves it." There was a smirk on his face when he turned to her but it was mischievous, not a mean one. "I'll devise some punishment for you later. Now, you are going to tell me exactly what the *seftha* has said to you about this whole mess. And, by the way, where the hell is Clara? Wasn't she with you?"

"Oh, you are not going to like this," Karina hesitated. Perhaps it was going to come to the whip after all.

Chapter 46

C lara stood frozen in place, afraid that if she moved even a little, it would all turn out to be an illusion. That her desperate, tortured mind was only playing tricks on her. But even as she continued to blink, the male figure was still lying in bed and his face still belonged to her brother.

Sure, he was deathly pale, with beads of sweat lining his forehead. His dark brown hair was longer than Clara remembered and he had a scruffy beard instead of being clean-shaven. But none of it changed the fact that this was Nicolas.

"Nicolas?" she whispered again, taking a hesitant step forward. Nothing happened. Nicolas' feverish body didn't vanish into thin air. He didn't turn into someone else.

Suppressing a sniffle, Clara quickly crossed the remaining distance, landing on her knees next to the bed. Her fingers carefully touched the man's shoulder, she needed to make sure he was real. How was this even possible? Out of all the people from that destroyed outpost, what were the odds of Clara finding him here, in this village, where she wasn't even supposed to be? It seemed that her instincts had worked after all.

There was a small bowl of water with a washcloth set beside it so Clara picked up the cloth, gently wiping the sweat from her brother's forehead. She had given up all hope of seeing him alive again, or even of finding out what had really happened to him before this moment. The odds were very much stacked against her on that, a fact she had been painfully aware of, especially after entering these woods and seeing the enormous amount of area they covered.

And yet, here he was. Both her brothers were alive after she was sure they were dead. Maybe the gods were trying to repay her for all the disasters they'd put her through?

"You know him?" *Seftha's* quiet voice interrupted Clara's thoughts. The old woman slowly walked across the room, lowering herself into a chair with a slight groan.

A couple of tears rolled down Clara's face but she quickly wiped them away with the back of her hand. "He's my brother," she answered in a whisper. Composing herself, Clara noticed the ropes wrapped around Nicolas' wrists, chest, and legs, tying him to the bed, reminding her just where she was.

These people weren't her friends. Most of them were hostile toward the Orellians already and, especially if Karina failed, would quickly turn into enemies. Clara couldn't even defend herself right now, let alone get her unconscious brother out of here.

"Ah, that makes sense," Ulaia chuckled. "He's just as feisty as you are. We had to restrain him because every time he regained consciousness, he either attacked the people taking care of him or tried to escape, tearing open his stitches in the process."

An angry scoff sounded from behind a pelt that covered a low door leading to another part of the hut. "*Pashir.* More Orellians. Great."

Clara didn't know what the word meant exactly but the way the man entering the room said it, it was obviously an insult. He was young, not much older than Clara, and his short, bright red hair stuck awkwardly out the sides, looking like he used a knife to cut it himself. Oddly attractive, even though his eyes held nothing but contempt right now.

"This is his sister, Kadri," the *seftha* spoke in the common tongue for which Clara was grateful.

The Ruthian scoffed again, raising an eyebrow in Clara's direction. "Great," he repeated. "You can take care of this asshole then. I'm done being spat and cursed at." His accent was heavy but the message was clear.

"I'm sorry," Clara said quietly, feeling like should apologize on her brother's behalf. "Nicolas has always been...a bit rough." Yes, she had experienced it firsthand many times. Clara's relationship with her brother was far from ideal, they fought and argued more often than not, but he was still her brother and she loved him. "Of course I'll take care of him, if I'm allowed to stay." Unless there was a war, which went without saying.

Not without a little fear, Clara wondered what would happen if Hayden did attack Ulaia's people. The *seftha* seemed fairly friendly, determined to keep the peace. But not at all costs, as she had told Karina. If the Orellians attacked, the neutral tribes would fight back. And Clara?

Would they let her go? It wasn't like she had diplomatic immunity, these people probably didn't care about such matters anyway. Would they slit her throat right away? Or threaten to kill or torture her unless the king pulled his soldiers away? It was better not to think about it. Clara decided to focus on Nicolas and trust Karina to solve the bigger problems.

"As I said, you are welcome to stay for as long as you want, child," Ulaia smiled and turned to the young healer. "And you, Kadri, stop grumbling. You chose this path and it is your duty to help everyone."

Kadri pulled up the sleeve of his loose shirt, revealing a bandaged forearm. "The bastard bit me! Like a fucking dog! Weren't you supposed to be the more civilized ones?" He spat the words out before storming off.

"Men," Ulaia chuckled. "Always fighting, always angry. They would sooner see the world burn and perish than stop and think. If you manage to convince your brother we mean him no harm, his recovery would be much faster and Kadri's job much easier."

Were all men really like that? Clara thought about it. Hayden, sure, that was a prime example of what the *seftha* said. Nicolas as well. But Clara couldn't stop herself from thinking about Oscar, who seemed to be quite the opposite. Always thinking, never fighting. Never angry. Well, almost never angry. "Not all men are the same," she objected. If there was one thing she had learned since her wedding, it was this.

Ulaia laughed in response. "If you've found one that is different, hold on to him for your dear life, my child."

"I intend to." Feeling her cheeks turning red, Clara diverted the conversation back to her brother. "What happened to him?"

"Someone slashed his stomach and left him for dead." Kadri returned, holding a pile of clean linens. He still sounded annoyed, but there was a reluctant admiration in his voice as well. "But this asshole simply refuses to die. Our people found him stumbling through the forest, holding his own fucking innards in his hands. I stitched him up the best I could but I didn't actually expect him to live. The bastard didn't get the message though. He just won't give up. But he's been in this fever state for days and if I can't get him to drink more water, his body will decide to lose the fight for him and shut down."

Clara blinked in surprise, staring at her brother. The Nicolas she remembered was an annoying mean boy that teased her mercilessly, constantly belittled her, even hurt her from time to time when their arguments got physical. This man in front of her was a battle-hardened veteran, a tough and loyal soldier worthy of admiration, which was a word she would have never thought to use in connection to her brother.

As Kadri pulled the thin blanket from Nicolas' body, Clara shuddered at the sight of the stained bandages covering his entire abdomen. Her stomach twisted as the healer began carefully removing them, slowly revealing the huge cut across Nicolas' stomach, held together by dozens of tiny, neat stitches. How could anyone have survived that?

And yet, Nicolas was here, his breathing shallow, with the occasional painful groan as Kadri gently washed the wound. "I told you...to keep your hands off me...you filthy barbarian." His voice was weak but his fists clenched and he struggled against the ropes. Even though she knew they were there for his own protection, it still made Clara feel uneasy.

"You didn't seem to be complaining when I was shoving your entrails back inside your precious Orellian body and sewing your skin together so they wouldn't fall back out." Kadri rolled his eyes and turned to the *seftha*. "You see what I have to put up with?"

Nicolas growled quietly. "I was...unconscious. Couldn't...protest. I didn't need your help."

Despite the horribly precarious situation they were in, Clara had to laugh. This was so typical of Nicolas it brought back dozens of memories from her childhood. How he fell down from a tree, refusing anyone's assistance despite his entire leg being covered in blood. How his arrows kept missing the target and yet he kept chasing his little sister away when she wanted to give him advice. "Of course you didn't," she chuckled. "You never needed anybody's help."

"Huh?" Squinting in the dim light, Nicolas frowned at her before diverting his gaze back to the healer. "What the fuck did you give me? Mushrooms? Or that stupid lichen?" He tried to spit but his mouth was too dry. "I already told you I don't know anything. And even if I did, a bunch of dumb tricks wouldn't make me tell you anyway."

He clearly thought the Ruthians had drugged him to get information. "As if I would waste the good stuff on an Orellian," Kadri rolled his eyes, holding a bowl of water to Nicolas' lips, putting one hand at the man's nape to help him lift his head. "Drink, idiot."

"Fuck off," Nicolas muttered, flinching his head and nearly knocking the bowl out of Kadri's hand.

Clara sighed and reached for the water. "Will you refuse me as well, brother?"

"Well," he scoffed, "you aren't real, so-OUCH!" He yelped out when Clara's sharp fingernails pinched his earlobe, using his favorite pain-inflicting method against him for once.

"I'm very real, Nicolas. And this is nothing but water." Under his careful watch, she sipped from the bowl, putting it back to his mouth. The look of absolute confusion twisted his features but his lips did part and he took a couple of slow, long gulps.

His brows furrowed as he closed his eyes for a moment. "Am I dead? I mean, it wouldn't be very surprising. But fuck, I thought at least the pain would stop."

"No, Nicolas, you aren't dead, you-"

"You can thank me later, asshole," Kadri interrupted Clara, smirking at her brother before his eyes went back down to Nicolas' abdomen. The healer was putting a layer of a thick dark mixture over the stitches before covering them with clean bandages again.

Clara nodded. "Yes, you should definitely thank this man for saving your life."

"Clara, I have absolutely no idea why you are here, but you don't know anything about this situation." Nicolas' tone was dismissive and condescending, just like Clara remembered. "These people are our enemies, they attacked us and killed everyone at the outpost. You should just get out of here, find our soldiers, and wait there. This is no place for a girl. Especially not one like you."

Seriously, her brother hadn't changed a bit. Clara had to laugh again. "Why not? I still shoot better than you."

"This is not a joke, Clara!" Nicolas let out a quiet moan when the healer put pressure on the wound. It was probably intentional and Clara could hardly blame Kadri for doing it.

"Men," Ulaia chuckled. Whatever she was going to say next was interrupted by a young Ruthian boy approaching her hesitantly and whispered a few words into her ear. The *seftha's* face brightened. "Perfect! Bring her here, my bones are too old to keep walking back and forth all the time."

The boy sprinted out and soon returned, followed by Karina. Clara noticed a scratch on her cheek but she seemed otherwise unharmed, which meant the current crisis was averted. Clara felt as if a boulder had just been rolled off her chest at the sight of Karina entering the tent. She jumped up to hug the queen, suddenly overwhelmed by emotions. Nicolas was alive, and there would be no war between the Orellians and Ulaia's tribes, which meant Clara was going to live as well, and they would both make it out of here and return home. To Oscar.

"Sorry," she mumbled after realizing that she was probably acting too familiar with the queen.

Karina waved her hand dismissively. "Hug me all you want. Nobody does it anymore. Not since I became the queen, it's kind of sad."

"The what?" Clara didn't think her brother could look or sound more surprised but, apparently, she was wrong.

"Karina, this is my brother, Nicolas. Nicolas, this is our new queen," she introduced them quickly, enjoying the sight of Nicolas' dumbstruck face.

Eyes widened, the man on the bed turned to Kadri. "Are you sure you didn't give me any drugs?" The healer just chuckled and shook his head. Nicolas turned back to Karina and immediately tried to sit up but the ropes were still holding him down. "I...I apologize, Your Majesty, I would greet you properly, but...it appears I've been tied up."

"Yes, it also appears that you have a huge hole in your stomach, so perhaps it is better if you remain in bed for now. I'm very pleased to meet you," she gave him a warm smile and turned to Clara. This time it was the queen who pulled her into a tight embrace. "I'm so happy for you, Clara. Oh, *Seftha*," Karina flinched upon noticing Ulaia quietly sitting in the corner, "my apologies, I didn't see you there."

"Don't worry about me," Ulaia replied calmly. "I might be old but I'm not hours away from my death. I can wait a few moments for you two to share the good news."

"How did it go with Hayden?" Clara asked carefully, knowing that the king was most likely furious that Karina had run off like that. Damn, Clara was probably in trouble too.

The queen rolled her eyes. "Great. I might get flogged later but, other than that, everything went smoothly. Well, as smoothly as dealing with the Burning Fury can go."

Flogged? Seriously? That didn't sound like something to joke about.

"I'm really grateful for your patience, *Seftha*," Karina continued, bowing her head in Ulaia's direction. "The king respects your wish to talk to a woman and I'm authorized to make a deal with your people that would ensure peace. He would be honored if you would be willing to talk to him as well, though. Those were his exact words," she added quickly, "in case you were wondering."

"Very well." Ulaia stood up with a quiet groan. "Damn these old bones. You have done a good job taming that king of yours, Karina. I shall speak with him. I assume your companion wishes to stay here?"

Clara didn't even realize the *seftha* was talking about her at first, but when both Karina and Ulaia looked at her, she quickly nodded. "Yes, please. Could I have my weapons back?" Realizing that it probably sounded quite rude, she quickly continued, "I know I won't need them but the bow was a gift and I would really hate it if something happened to it."

Fortunately, Ulaia didn't seem to be offended by the request, probably because it was common for the Ruthians to carry their weapons with them at all times. "Sure, Rimea will bring them back to you. Just make sure your brother doesn't bite anyone again," she smirked, leaving the hut.

"How the hell am I supposed to do that?" Clara muttered, trying to resist the urge to giggle happily.

Chapter 47

As usual, Nicolas had a way of bringing Clara down almost effortlessly. "Untie me, Clara, we are getting out of here. You have no idea what you've gotten yourself into. This is war, not a game or some fantastic tale."

"No," she growled at him, getting up from the bed. She was seriously done with the ungrateful bastards that called themselves her family. "I'm not a little girl you can insult and boss around without consequences anymore, Nicolas. So, show me some fucking respect or keep your mouth shut. Because if you keep talking to me like this, I'll walk out of here and leave you in the care of Kadri, who, unless you haven't noticed, doesn't like you very much."

Nicolas seemed taken aback by her words. "I must be hallucinating from the fever because it sounded like my little sister was talking back to me." His next condescending remark was cut off by the Ruthian female, Rimea, entering the hut with Clara's weapons.

"*Rizza*," she grinned while handing them to Clara. "I take care. Pretty thing," she tapped on the bow. "You good?"

"You bet," Clara replied, mirroring Rimea's expression.

Rimea chuckled. "See morning. Now sleep. Come me?"

It took a few seconds for Clara to realize Rimea was offering her a place to sleep. It must have been almost midnight and as all the fear and excitement were slowly leaving her body, Clara was becoming more and more tired. But it was not like she'd leave Nicolas alone, no matter what she told him. "Thank you, but I will stay here."

"If want," Rimea shrugged indifferently before leaving.

There was a flicker of relief flashing through Nicolas' expression but he hid it quickly. Still, Clara knew he was glad she was staying with him. And that he would never admit it. "Are you going to untie me?" he growled.

"Are you going to stay in bed?" Clara retorted, giving him a doubtful look. She didn't want to keep him tied up out of some sick desire to see him defenseless or out of revenge, but after seeing the wound on his stomach, it was clear that he shouldn't try to move for a couple of days.

Nicolas' eyes narrowed but he grumbled in defeat. "Do I have a choice?"

"No, you do not have a choice, brother." Clara waved the tip of her bow in front of his face. "Don't try anything."

Putting her weapons aside, she bent down to loosen the rope on one of her brother's wrists, then the other one. As soon his hand was free, Nicolas immediately raised it to his head, furiously scratching his scalp. "Daaamn. I needed that." His voice was weaker again and he seemed to be struggling to keep his eyes open. "Since when are you friendly with the queen?"

Since I tried to poison the king, Clara wanted to say, but stopped herself in time. "Since I married her best friend." That was a safer answer.

"Oh, right, you're married already. You know, I wanted to surprise you by coming to the wedding, had all my things packed, and then...it all turned to shit here." The sudden wave of bad memories made him wince.

Clara finished untying the ropes and looked up into his face in surprise. "You wanted to come to my wedding?"

"Of course," Nicolas rolled his eyes. "You are my sister. Of course I wanted to be there, especially after Dad... It must have been hard to go through all that with just Mother."

No kidding. But somehow Clara doubted having her brothers around would have been much of an improvement. "It's fine," she shrugged the unpleasant thoughts away and stood up to get more water from the pitcher standing on a low trunk. The room wasn't exactly well furnished.

"So, this husband of yours, is he good to you?" Nicolas gladly accepted the cup from her hands. As he raised his upper body a little to drink from it, a painful groan slipped through his lips. "Crap," he growled, falling back to bed with his eyes closed, his face contorted in agony. "Isn't he some sort of politician?" He had to pause to catch his breath, pearls of sweat beading on his forehead again. "What is he doing on a war campaign?"

Of course, Nicolas thought Clara would only be here to accompany her husband. "Stay down and rest," she ordered in the most authoritative voice she could muster. Luckily, her brother had no strength to argue with her. "Yes, he is good to me. Yes, he is a politician. And no, he isn't here. He stayed back home in the palace," she answered his questions. "And yes, he knows I'm here. He even encouraged me to go." The last thing Clara wanted was for people to think that she ran away from Oscar.

"Madman," Nicolas breathed out, his eyes closed already.

Clara slid a washcloth over his forehead again, enjoying the simple act of taking care of him. It was something he would never allow her to do if he were fully conscious. "Sleep, brother," she whispered, knowing he couldn't hear her anymore.

A rustle from outside caught her attention and she quietly got up, peeking out from beneath the pelt covering the door to see Rimea standing there grinning. The woman handed Clara a rolled up sleeping mat and a thick blanket then left without a word. Had the *seftha* ordered her to do this or was it just courtesy of the suddenly almost friendly Ruthian? It hardly mattered, but Clara hoped it was the latter.

Grateful, Clara put the mat on the floor next to her brother's bed and laid down, stretching and wriggling to get comfortable. She'd barely managed to pull the blanket over herself before falling into a deep sleep.

Rays of sunlight were beginning to shine through the tiny window into the room. Clara woke up, groggily wiping her eyes and trying to figure out where she was and what was happening. "You snore," her brother's voice sounded from somewhere above her head.

"I do not." Did she? She had no idea. Oscar never complained but he was a gentleman so he probably wouldn't have told her. Making a mental note to ask him when she returned home, Clara pulled herself up slowly. Nicolas had stayed in bed, which was good. Whether it was because he was too weak to move or because he'd followed her orders didn't really matter.

Kadri entered the room, scowling at them. "Good, you are up. Feed him. I'm not treating you if the fucker bites you." He set a small bowl of soup down on the nightstand before promptly leaving the room.

"Oh, come on!" Nicolas defended himself. "It was instinctual. I woke up to discover I was tied down and there were hands trying to pry my mouth open. I just...reacted. His bedside manners suck, by the way," he noted in Clara's direction.

"Not an apology!" a voice called from the other room.

Letting out an exasperated sigh, Nicolas shouted back, "Sorry, asshole!"

Clara couldn't help but chuckle as she reached for the soup. It was just a clear broth but it smelled so amazing her own stomach rumbled. She hadn't packed any food along when rushing after Karina yesterday.

There weren't any extra pillows around so Clara rolled up her sleeping mat and propped it behind Nicolas' back, putting a spoonful of soup up to his mouth. "Eat."

"I can feed myself," he growled. His shaky hand reached out for the spoon but he was so slow Clara easily moved it out of his range, putting it into her own mouth instead. It was delicious, hot and strong, and Clara groaned in satisfaction.

"Open your mouth or I'll eat it all myself." To make sure he took her threat seriously, she ate another spoonful.

"Fine!" Nicolas crossed his arms in front of his chest, looking like a moody teenager. "Your bedside manners suck too," he grumbled but let her feed him, quickly devouring the whole bowl. No surprise, since he probably hadn't eaten in days. But it also meant nothing was left for Clara. Damn, was she really such a horrible person that she'd considered stealing soup from her gravely injured brother just because she hadn't had breakfast?

More light spilled into the room as someone pulled back the pelt covering the entrance. Clara turned to see Rimea, just as the Ruthian asked, "Eat? Shoot?"

Clara could finally get a better look at the woman in the daylight. Her hair wasn't brown, as Clara had thought originally, but red. A much darker shade than Clara's and also much less curly and wild, but still red. It was long and plaited into dozens of thin braids that were then gathered into a ponytail at Rimea's nape. Probably in her mid-twenties, the Ruthian was tall and very muscular. Clearly a warrior.

"Some food would be great, thank you," Clara answered, grabbing her weapons before glancing back at Nicolas. "You stay in bed."

His brows came together to form an angry scowl. "Hey, I'm not letting you go anywhere with these savages! What do you think you are do-"

"Stay. In. Bed." Clara used a clearly threatening tone in her voice, poking Nicolas' chest with the tip of her bow. "Or I'll have them tie you up again. I'm sure they would enjoy that very much." With those words said, she walked out of the hut, grinning over Rimea's excited nodding. "My brothers are serious assholes," she sighed, following the Ruthian woman over to a large tent in the center of the village. "Do you have any?"

At first, Clara thought Rimea was going to ignore her question because she didn't respond, leaning over a large pot of stew instead. Only after each of the women was holding a full bowl of broth and a large piece of odd looking bread, Rimea said, "*Tarra.*"

"Four brothers?! Wow, that must have been hell when you were kids."

The Ruthian shook her head and grinned. "No. Fear Rimea."

Clara laughed. Of course, it made sense that local girls probably didn't allow their brothers to bully them. And Clara was not going to do that either, not anymore.

It was almost noon when Clara returned to Nicolas, only to find him sleeping soundly. She'd spent all morning with Rimea, first shooting at targets behind the village and then, when the woman was satisfied with Clara's skills, walking through the forest.

They didn't talk much and not just because of their limited vocabulary in each other's languages. There didn't seem to be any words necessary, not even when Rimea was showing Clara how to move around the woods quietly, or which berries were edible, or how to set traps for catching rabbits. It was so refreshingly different from everything Clara knew, she excitedly absorbed all of the information, craving even more.

After helping her brother eat lunch and wash himself, Clara went out with her new friend again. Nicolas still grumbled over Clara not listening to his orders or his well-intended advice, but she simply chose to ignore him. Whenever he got really annoying, she left the room not wanting to fight with him.

Two days passed in the same manner; Clara was surprised by how comfortable she was beginning to feel amongst these strangers. On the third afternoon, realizing she ought to find out what was going on with the negotiations, the war and other important things, she packed her weapons and asked Rimea to guide her back to the open road. From there, Clara hoped to find her way back to the outpost. Fortunately, Karina had arranged for Clara's horse to be brought to the Ruthian village so she wouldn't have to take the whole journey on foot.

Rimea brought her own horse, a small but sturdy white mare with black speckles, and both women left the village together. Clara was nervous when traveling out in the open like this, unprotected. Even though the *seftha's* tribes had made peace with the Orellians, there were lots of Ruthians who were still their enemies, especially the tribes gathered around *Seftb* Gishri. Hopefully, Hayden and Karina were going to resolve that conflict without any more blood spilled or lives lost.

Only when the palisade surrounding the outpost was in sight did Rimea turn her horse around to go back home. Clara offered to find a place for her to stay but the Ruthian refused. "Walls," she shook her head, pointing at the stone wall guarding the inner part of the outpost. "No sleep in walls."

"As you wish," Clara shrugged, slightly relieved that Rimea didn't want to come with her because she had no idea whether the guards at the gate would actually allow a Ruthian to enter. "I'll be back tomorrow. *Se maelle!*" Clara waved at the surprising new friend she'd made.

Stay safe.

Chapter 48

The guards looked surprised to see Clara but they let her through without complaint. She headed to the main building to find Karina but the sight of Larkin's bruised face caught her eye. The men greeted her excitedly. "Our lost lady returns!" Enzio exclaimed. "We thought you had joined the barbarians for good."

"Hey, I was just taking care of my brother." Great, the last thing Clara wanted was for them to think she was a traitor. But it seemed they were just teasing her.

"Yes, we heard you found him," Enzio gave her a warm smile as Larkin softly patted her back. "We're really happy for you. He sounds like a tough guy."

No kidding. "He is. Where's the queen?"

The men exchanged nervous glances and Clara remembered how Karina joked about getting flogged. Hayden wouldn't really do that, would he? Seeing her pale face, the lieutenant quickly answered, "Don't worry, she's fine. She's in the kitchen, over there."

The kitchen? "Thanks, I'll go see her. What happened to you?" Larkin's eye was swollen shut and half of his face was purple. The split lip made it difficult to talk.

"What do you think?" he rolled his healthy eye. "The Burning Fury happened. I actually got off easy. He was ready to stab me on the spot." There was a grin on Larkin's face but Clara could tell that this time he wasn't joking. Not all stories about the king were made up. He was a dangerous man. Deadly, even.

The kitchen was a long spacious tent illuminated by a couple of lanterns hanging from the roof. Tables were lined up around the sides, knives, cutting boards, pans, pots, and various utensils laid out on them, all ready for the morning. It was empty, save for Karina sitting on a low stool in the middle, next to a large pile of potatoes.

With unrecognizable smudges and dirt in her hair, face, clothes and arms, she barely looked like a queen now, more like a lowly kitchen wench. Clara immediately felt sorry for her. "Are you alright?" she asked carefully.

"Clara!" Despite looking absolutely exhausted, there was a bright smile on the queen's grimy face. "I wanted to send an escort for you tomorrow to make sure you traveled back safely, since there are still lots of enemies in the forests around here. I'd hug you but you don't want to be covered in the filth I just scraped out of the pots after dinner." Karina let out a sad chuckle, wiping the sweat off her forehead with her forearm, adding more smears onto her pale skin. "How is your brother?"

"Uhh. He's well." Clara wasn't exactly sure how to act in this situation. "Why are you slaving away in the kitchen?"

The queen put down the knife and a potato she had been peeling, stretching her arms out and arching her back with a loud groan. "Damn, my back is killing me. But it's better than yesterday. And it beats being flogged. I think."

"It most certainly does." Larkin's bruised face appeared in the tent entrance. "You should really pick up the pace if you want to sleep at all tonight, though," he smirked.

Karina snorted. "If you have come to mock me, I'm pretty sure I can still order someone to kick your ass out of here."

"Do you want me to shoot him?" With a mischievous grin, Clara reached for an arrow.

"Nah," Karina sighed and picked up the knife again. "He already has a black eye because of me. I deserve this."

Clara wasn't so certain about that but she wasn't going to argue with the queen. Setting the bow aside, she pulled out the knife Enzio had given her and picked one of the potatoes. How hard could it be? She pursed her lips while rolling the round thing in her hand, trying to determine where to start.

Larkin watched them, shaking his head in disbelief. "Gods, women! How do you not know how to peel potatoes?"

"That's not exactly the type of skill noble ladies are taught," Karina rolled her eyes, tossing the finished potato into a pot with water.

"Yeah, dancing and reciting poetry will do a shit load of good for you out here," he retorted sarcastically. "You are doing it wrong. This way there's not even half of the potato left when you are done 'peeling it'."

Karina frowned at him. "I don't really give a damn."

"You will give a damn tomorrow when there's only half the rations ready for the men. And you." Sighing, he pulled out his own knife, sitting cross-legged on the ground next to Karina. "Let me show you how it's done."

It certainly looked easy when he was doing it. Clara tried to repeat his movements, ending up nearly cutting herself. "What about the Ruthians? Have you made any progress with the other tribes?"

"Ulaia promised to contact *Sefth* Gishri on our behalf," Karina answered, not raising her eyes from her work, "and hopefully we can meet with him and some other tribe leaders and try to solve this matter peacefully. These constant skirmishes are not good for anyone."

"That's true," Larkin growled, finishing at least three potatoes by the time Clara was done with hers. "We've already lost a number of men that had been assigned to the merchant caravan escorts. Plus, a lot of others are injured."

Karina nodded. "You should go see Lamar, he doesn't seem to be taking to bed rest well."

"What happened?" Clara remembered the captain of the king's guards as a friendly man and Karina and Larkin seemed to have a close relationship with him.

"He got an arrow through his thigh. Nothing serious but he has to stay off his feet for a couple of days, at least. Needless to say, he is not happy about it."

Men. "Try tying him to the bed, it worked with my brother," Clara chuckled, hissing in sudden pain. Damn, where did all the blood come from?

"Gods, you two are useless," Larkin let out an exasperated huff. "Good thing you don't have to cook for your husbands since they'd probably starve to death. You," he pointed his blade in Clara's direction, "put that down before you cut your finger off. I was under the impression that archers needed those. And you," scooting closer to Karina, he grabbed her hand, twisting it into a different angle, "don't cut it against your wrist unless you want to bleed out. Damn, it's like babysitting toddlers."

Clara was going to ask him what he could possibly know about kids since he didn't have any but shut her mouth after someone loudly cleared their throat at the tent entrance. "Larkin?" The king's voice was cold and there was a distinct threat underlining it. "Did I not make myself clear about what would happen to you if you touched my wife again?"

The lieutenant's face lost all color as he quickly let go of Karina's hand. "Great," she moaned. "More audience. Just what I need. Why don't you all get out of here and let me suffer in peace?"

"I just came to see whether you were coming to bed soon," Hayden smirked, his tone getting much lighter, almost playful. "But, judging by the size of that pile, it doesn't seem like it."

He barely evaded a potato flying in his direction. "You can shoot this one, Clara," the queen hissed. "Let's see how he dodges an arrow."

"Yes, please do that," Larkin chimed in.

This was not something Clara was comfortable joking about but the others didn't seem to mind. "So disrespectful," Hayden sighed, shaking his head in faux indignation. Pulling out his own blade, he sat down beside Karina and reached into the pile.

"You don't have to help me." Karina tried to stop him.

The king's hands were just as fast as Larkin's. Apparently, waving a sword around was not the only thing soldiers were taught to do. "I know. But the men wouldn't be happy if they had to starve tomorrow because the queen has no clue how to peel potatoes." He stuck his tongue out in Karina's direction and Clara had to force herself not to gape at him. This was not something she would expect from the Burning Fury.

They all worked in comfortable silence for a few minutes, even Clara finally figured out how to peel without running the knife over her own skin. "Well, look at that," the king commented on her efforts teasingly, "maybe one day you will be able to cook for your husband after all. Speaking of," he wiped his hands onto his shirt then reached into his pocket, "have you two seriously been using the royal messengers to send love letters to each other?"

Clara couldn't help but blush at seeing an envelope in his fingers. "Maybe?" she replied hesitantly, not sure if she was in trouble or not.

"Unbelievable." The king shook his head but didn't stop her when she reached for the letter. "What has the world come to," he grumbled quietly. "My wife is being groped by my soldiers, my messengers double as postmen for a couple of annoying newlyweds and I'm sitting on the ground peeling potatoes so I won't have to starve tomorrow." Karina burst out in laughter, even Larkin and Clara had difficulty holding back chuckles. "And my subjects are making fun of me. Some king I am."

"The best king." Karina gave him a warm smile and leaned over for a kiss.

Larkin shook his head. "Get a room, you two."

"Shut up." Despite the harsh words, Hayden still sounded like he was just teasing the lieutenant. The king's eyes narrowed as he looked down at Larkin's hands. "What the hell are you doing? By the gods, is that how they teach you to peel potatoes in Levanta? No wonder you lost the war! OUCH!" Apparently, it was more difficult to dodge objects thrown from such a short distance.

Clara was exhausted when she finally managed to reach the tiny room she was occupying in the central building of the outpost. But there was no way she would be able to fall asleep before reading the letter from Oscar.

She hesitated before breaking the seal on the fancy envelope. It was nothing like the scrunched up smudged piece of parchment she'd written her words on. Perhaps she had been too open and forward in her letter? Had she scared him away? Oscar clearly wasn't used to being in a serious relationship and Clara... Well, Clara wasn't used to being in any kind of relationship. Some couple, they were.

The wax made a surprisingly loud snapping sound when she finally broke it, opening the envelope and pulling out the large parchment. There was a smaller piece of paper too, folded and sealed by a few drops of wax. *Read the letter first*, the note scribbled on the top of it said, so Clara set it aside for now, curious over what might be inside.

"My dear, beautiful wife. I hope you are safe and well. I have just enjoyed a long, steaming hot bath and a several-course breakfast after spending my night in our large, comfortable bed." Clara grinned, knowing Oscar was deliberately teasing her. *"It's rather cold and empty without you. Luckily, there is a smiling redhead named Ally that's been keeping me company. She's not as funny or as warm as you, though."* He really was sleeping with her doll, how sweet.

"I have to say I was left speechless by your letter, which doesn't happen very often to me. I still don't understand what I did to deserve such a perfect wife but I promise I will try my best not to disappoint you. I never thought anyone could forgive me if they knew the entire truth because I wasn't even able to forgive myself. But what you wrote was... I don't have words to describe it. Thank you from the bottom of my heart and soul.

"The days are long without you here. I have too much spare time. I'd wanted to spend it getting to know you better but now I just walk around the palace like a ghost, trying to find something to occupy my time. I have had

some success with the person I told you about earlier but it's best not discussed on paper where anyone could read it.

"I know I promised to stay safe, and I'm really trying to keep that promise, but sometimes I have to take risks to make sure everyone is safe. I hope you can forgive me for that. Knowing you and Karina, you two are probably doing the exact same thing, making Hayden mad, aren't you?"

Clara chuckled. Yes, he truly knew them well.

"Please, just make sure you come back home in one piece. I mean, if you are missing an arm or a leg, I can live with that, as long as you keep that pretty face of yours. And your boobs, of course. Damn, that was a stupid joke, sorry.

"If I had more time before the messenger leaves, I would rewrite the letter, but now I'm forced to leave it in. You are free to slap me when you get home. If you still have hands. Crap, I'm doing it again. Sorry, I'm just nervous about you and this whole war business.

"I haven't forgotten about the things you asked me to do before you left. Well, I have, but I have remembered them again, so that counts as not forgetting, I hope?

"The woman, Mina, seems perfect. She's never been in any trouble at the palace, no scandals (if you don't count the social suicide she committed by dating a Levantian). She is even known to dislike gossiping, which is a fairly rare trait for a maid. I haven't talked to her, I will leave that to you, but if you want to employ her, I have absolutely no problem with it."

Even though she'd seen Larkin every day, Clara had almost forgotten about wanting to ask his girlfriend to be her maid. The whole idea of having a maid seemed so absurd in these conditions. Clara hadn't bathed in days, and even then it had been in a freezing lake, there was dirt under her fingernails, her clothes were covered in smudges and torn in several places, and there was a rather unpleasant odor following her wherever she went. Not to mention the mess that was happening on her head.

Having a maid was something her mind was unable to comprehend right now. She would have to leave it for later, when she gets back to civilization.

"As for your other question… I did find the truth about your father. It's written on the small piece of paper that is inside the envelope. I will leave it up to you whether you want to read it or not."

Clara nervously glanced at the small sealed note on her nightstand. It was bad, obviously. If Oscar hadn't found anything, he would have just told her straight away. Now she had a choice between living in a fragile illusion, where her dad was perfect, or potentially shattering it all by learning the truth, staining every happy childhood memory in the process. She already knew what she was going to pick, no matter how sad it made her feel.

"I miss you. There are moments I hate myself for letting you go, promising myself that once you get back I really will chain you to the bedroom wall and never let you out of my sight again (another stupid joke, please ignore that).

"From what you wrote in your letter, it actually sounds like you are enjoying yourself, even though it must be a rather unpleasant and uncomfortable experience. If that's true, I'm happy for you. If not, well… At least you will be more motivated to come home, I hope?

"I try very hard not to think about all those 'friendly people' around you. I never thought of myself as the jealous type but I guess I was wrong. If any one of them lays a finger on you, I'll get on a horse and ride north to deal with him myself, because there is no way some stupid sword-swinging sweaty soldier is stealing my amazing wife.

"Right, sorry about that outburst. Damn, I should have written this last night, that way I would have time to rewrite it and have a chance to leave out all the dumb remarks. Please, don't be mad at me.

"I almost wrote I love you, which would be silly since it turned out I have absolutely no idea what that word even means. I miss you. I want to hold you in my arms, to feel your warm, smooth skin under my fingers, to kiss you. To make you happy, and to support and protect you."

Clara sniffled, a couple of tears trailing her cheeks. What was this if not saying I love you? Oscar was not using those exact words but the message seemed clear.

"I know it sounds stupid when you are the one who left to go to war while I'm sitting around here doing nothing, surrounded by luxury. I can't protect

you from physical threats but I promise I will protect you from everything else once you get back. And everyone else, even if it includes those weird people that call themselves your family.

"Your mother came looking for you here, by the way. I wish you could have seen her dumbstruck face when she realized you did actually leave the palace. On a horseback. With your bow. Dressed as a man, with a regiment of soldiers. I made sure to paint the whole picture for her. Her face went from pale to red a couple of times. I know this probably isn't the way a proper gentleman should talk about his mother-in-law, but what the hell. I'm a scoundrel, not a gentleman, right?"

A bit of both. The corner of Clara's mouth curled up imagining Sophia Redwood's expression when Oscar had told her all of that. That must have been a sight to behold.

"I have to finish writing now if I want to catch the messenger before he leaves. I miss you. I know I've written it a couple of times already but I'll write it again. Just please, please be safe. I don't want to lose you.

Oscar."

Clara curled up in bed, wrapping the blanket tightly around her chest. Reading about her father's sins could wait. Oscar's loving words were something Clara wanted to hear over and over in her head while falling asleep.

Chapter 49

A couple of Larkin's men accompanied Clara back into the village the next morning. The Ruthians weren't exactly thrilled to see them arrive but didn't protest, letting the soldiers pitch tents in a clearing behind the healer's hut. Hayden insisted that they stay there to protect Clara since the hostile tribes still refused to negotiate with the Orellians and there was constant threat of an attack.

Clara didn't mind at all, since it meant she got to spend time with all of her new friends. She even managed to convince Rimea to bring Enzio along on their walks through the woods, and even though the two of them barely spoke a word to each other, the silence between them was surprisingly comfortable. Karina promised to come to visit Clara after her punishment in the kitchen was over.

Once Nicolas stopped fighting Kadri and started drinking and eating properly, his injury began healing at a satisfactory rate. A few days after Clara had returned to the village, he even managed to stand up and take a couple steps on his own. If it weren't for the constant threat of war looming in the back of her head and missing having Oscar around, Clara would be happy.

One afternoon, when Nicolas was taking a nap, Clara sat down on her sleeping mat and pulled out the small note from Oscar's letter. She didn't want to avoid it any longer. The truth was better, no matter how hard it was going to be.

"As much as it pains me to say this, your mother was telling the truth. Admiral Redwood was known to have lots of women and to be a frequent visitor of brothels in Ebris and other cities he traveled to.

"I know you don't want to hear this right now, but this doesn't change anything about your childhood. He might have been a shitty husband but that does not automatically make him a bad father and it doesn't change anything about his relationship with you. Please, try to keep that in mind. I wish I could hug you. And I will, as soon as you get back."

Even though Clara had already known what the note was going to say, it still hurt. Pulling her knees closer to her chest and hugging them, she tried to cry as quietly as possible, not wanting to wake up her brother. Despite the fact that the only thing she wanted to do now was to scream and curse.

How could he do that? How could he treat his wife like that, a woman that he married out of love, as he'd always claimed? That was not the kind man she'd known her whole life. And she couldn't even ask him, confront him about all this shit, since he had to go and get himself killed by some stupid pirates. She sniffed sharply, rustling through her things to find something to wipe her nose with.

"What's wrong?" Clara's head jerked up to see Nicolas' troubled face. Her brother was lying on his side, in a position that was probably quite painful for him just so he could look at her.

Did she want to talk about it? This was her brother, it concerned him as well, but with all the differences between them... "Did you know?" she asked quietly. "About dad's other women?"

"Damn." Nicolas let out an exasperated sigh and rolled onto his back again. "No," he answered after a moment of silence. "Not until I joined the military. The men kept making comments about whores and me and our dad. I didn't understand at first, but... It was not a well-kept secret. Who was the 'kind' soul that felt you just needed to know about it?"

Clara scoffed. "Mother. I didn't believe her.I thought it was just another one of her manipulations, so I had Oscar look into it. And he confirmed it was true."

"Well, crap, couldn't he have lied to you to spare you from all of this? What a dick."

"Hey!" Leaning over to punch her brother's shoulder, Clara scowled at him. "Don't talk about him like that. He would never lie to me. And I was the one who wanted to know the truth. I'm sick of lies and deceptions and our mother's games. I'm not a little girl anymore."

His mouth curled up into an amused smirk. "You will always be a little girl to me." Before Clara could protest, Nicolas lifted his index finger to stop her. "And this time, I mean it in a good way." Letting out a pained groan, he shuffled to the side of the bed before tapping on an empty spot next to him. "Come on, little sister. I might not be your handsome and amazing husband but I can hug you just as well."

Clara carefully scrutinized his expression for a moment, trying to figure out whether he was making fun of her but, surprisingly, he seemed sincere, so she slowly lowered herself onto the bed. Putting her head on his shoulder she cuddled up to Nicolas, carefully avoiding his injured stomach. It was comforting having someone's arms wrapped around her again, even if it wasn't Oscar. "I need to wash your shirt tomorrow, you smell horrible," she mumbled.

"Well, I've been tied to this bed for days, so excuse me for not smelling like roses." Despite not being able to see his face, Clara was quite certain he was rolling his eyes. "By the way, sister, you stink almost as bad as I do. Some lady you are."

There was no arguing that. "I was never very good at being a lady. I think I'm way better at being...whatever it is I am right now." What was she even? It felt strange to not fit into any common category. Strange, but freeing. She could be whatever she wanted to be.

The comfortable silence between them was interrupted by a soft rumble from Clara's stomach. "Hungry?" Nicolas chuckled, flinching in pain as any kind of laughter still put too much strain on the stitched muscles across his stomach.

"Starving, actually. I shot a deer today and Rimea and Enzio forced me to butcher it myself. It's fucking disgusting. But I bet the meat will be awesome. I'll go get us some, it should be ready by now." Clara reluctantly squirmed out of his arms, knowing that she probably wasn't going to get another opportunity to get close to him again like this.

After leaving the hut, she bumped into a familiar figure. "Karina!" Clara exclaimed excitedly upon recognizing the queen. "You are out of the kitchen!"

"Yes, finally." Karina shuddered. "I don't want to see another fucking potato in my entire life."

Clara unsuccessfully tried to hold back a giggle. "How about a piece of a roasted deer? I was just going to get some for me and Nicolas."

"A piece of good meat is something I never refuse. Lead the way!"

Engaged in friendly conversation, they walked over to the large fireplace where the animal was being spit roasted, obtained a few large slices of the meat and several pieces of flat bread which had been baked on hot stones around the fire, then lazily headed back to the healer's hut. Sadly, there didn't seem to be any progress in the peace talks with *Sefth* Gishri's tribes. It was hard to talk to someone who strictly refused to communicate with the Orellians.

Upon seeing Karina, Nicolas stood up, grunting and gritting his teeth, having to lean against the wall to hold himself upright. "My lady, I couldn't greet you properly last time. Please, allow me to remedy that."

"Sure, if you can promise me that your intestines will stay on the inside of your stomach," Karina smirked, teasing him lightly.

Despite fighting the urge, Nicolas chuckled, then groaned in pain. But he did manage a respectful bow before collapsing back onto the bed, wiping his suddenly sweaty forehead.

"You are one tough guy," Karina smiled before glancing at Clara. "It seems to run in your family. Oh, here's your dinner."

The juicy meat wrapped in flat bread smelled absolutely delicious and Nicolas gratefully took it from Karina's hands. "Thank you, my lady. Hmm, I never thought I would be served dinner by a queen," he joked, sounding nervous.

"If you were at the Eagle Peak outpost, you could eat potatoes peeled by the queen." Clara couldn't help but poke Karina. "That's not something you get every day either."

Karina's eyes narrowed. "Don't even say that P-word in front of me!" she hissed. "By the way, you also disobeyed a direct order, my dear friend. You are lucky I'm such a merciful ruler."

That was true, Karina did specifically order Clara to stay in the outpost. "Oh, thank you, Your Gracious Majesty," Clara rolled her eyes. "It's not like you actually expected me to follow that order."

"No," Karina took a large bite of the meat, chewing on it as she spoke, "mot wea-ry. Bwut," she swallowed the food and cleared her throat, "I did promise Oscar I wouldn't put you in any danger. He's not going to be happy."

"Don't worry," Clara waved her hand, "he'll get over it. I think he totally expected us to get into trouble." At least it seemed that way from what he'd written in his letter.

Karina sat with them until she finished her meal and then went off to talk to the *seftha*, promising she would stop by in the morning. Since Rimea insisted they would go hunting for some birds that were best spotted before sunrise, Clara went to bed early, wriggling around on her sleeping mat until she found a somewhat comfortable sleeping position.

It felt as if she hadn't even fallen asleep when a sound woke her. It was a horn of some sort. A high-pitched, screeching noise that sent chills deep into her bones. Nicolas moaned in his sleep, rolling to his side and curling up. "No...please," Clara heard him whimper. She called his name, shaking his shoulder to wake him, when the horn sounded again, closer to the village this time.

Crying out desperately, Nicolas jerked awake as he roughly grabbed onto her wrist, his other hand ready to strike. "Hey, it's me." Clara tried to keep her voice calm but couldn't help but shiver in fear. What was happening?

"Shit," he growled and sat up, his eyes jumping around the room in confusion. "Clara? You need to get out of here."

He was probably still disoriented from the nightmare he was having. "It's fine, it's just..." She had no idea how to continue because she had no clue what was going on.

"No! They're coming, you need to run!"

A soft light filled the room as Kadri peeked in, holding a candle. "You both need to run. Now. Clara, go tell your soldiers to grab whatever they can and move to the western path out of the village. I'll help your brother."

"What's happening?" It felt like she still wasn't fully awake. Perhaps this was all just a strange, terrifying dream? She bent down to pick up her bow and other weapons, the familiar weight of the wooden handle in her hand helping her to calm down a little.

"They've come for the queen, no doubt." Kadri's voice was solemn. "And they will kill every Orellian they come across. Gishri's men," he added in explanation upon noticing her confusion. "The *seftha* went to talk to them and our men will hold them off for a while if necessary, but you all need to run. NOW!"

His sharp command finally broke Clara out of her stupor. She darted outside, quickly explaining the situation to the soldiers and leading them to the western path. They all looked relieved upon seeing Rimea standing there with Karina, who was still wiping the sleep out of her eyes. Kadri soon joined them, half carrying Nicolas. One of the Orellians quickly rushed in to help him.

Clara's brother was biting his lower lip, sweat beading on his forehead already, but there was a determined look on his face. "You need to leave me here," he said in between quick, shallow breaths. "I will just slow you down."

"No fucking way," Clara scowled at him.

Karina nodded. "Yes, that's not happening. So, where are we going?" A couple of Ruthians joined them and the group hastily left the village, entering the dark, cold forest.

"For starters, as far away from them as we can," Kadri answered, breathing heavily from having to support Nicolas' weight on his shoulders. "And then...there's a place where we can hide and even fight them off for a while until your people come and save us."

Wishful thinking. How could anyone find them in these huge woods? Except for their enemies, of course, they knew the land too well.

Chapter 50

K adri's desperate plan wasn't completely stupid and they had no other choice but to make it work. Clara tried to remind herself of that repeatedly because stumbling through pitch-black woods with the thought of being hunted down by their enemies was beyond frightening. They walked as fast as they could for what felt like hours before finally stopping for a short break.

Nicolas was barely conscious by this point, his clothes drenched in a layer of sweat that quickly began to cool in the cold night air as soon as they stopped moving, making his teeth rattle. Clara placed her own cloak over his shoulders, trying to ignore the chilly breeze that immediately started to bite into her own skin. "How far are we?"

"Not far enough," Rimea shook her head, handing a thin blanket to Clara.

"Just go...without me." Nicolas was hugging his knees, forehead rested against them, his voice weak, interrupted frequently by strained gasps. "Give me...a knife...and go."

Kadri gave him a disapproving look. "I didn't spend all of my time patching you up and taking care of you just to leave you here to die."

"Listen, asshole." Lips rolled back into a snarl, Nicolas raised his head to face the healer. "I'm not letting...my sister and my...queen die...because of me."

Rimea interrupted their argument by jumping up and shushing them loudly. The entire group grew silent instantly, all gazes fixed on the Ruthian female.

She listened to the sounds of the night forest for a few moments before shaking her head with a grim expression. "Gishri," she spat out. "We go. All go." The way she grabbed Nicolas' arm and pulled him up was rough but it didn't give Clara's brother any chance to protest. Blaggar moved to Nicolas' other side and they threw his arms over their shoulders, ready to carry him.

"Go, we'll be right behind you," the scarred soldier mumbled, nodding at the healer to take the lead.

Every twig snapping, every owl hooting, every single sound around them made Clara flinch. Any of it could mean enemies sneaking up on them, ready to jump out of the shadows and attack. They took turns in carrying Nicolas and Clara winced at seeing fresh blood starting to soak through his bandages again.

Kadri swore they were close to wherever they were headed but it felt like an eternity before they finally arrived at the edge of the forest. Spread out in front of them was a huge clearing, ending at what looked like a sudden cliff drop. The first traces of the morning light revealed a structure built on the edge of the cliff, a tower of some sort, overlooking the large valley with the forest surrounding it on 3 sides.

"Are you insane?" Karina paused to catch her breath, glaring at Kadri. "This is not a hiding place. If we go there, we will trap ourselves with no way out!"

He opened his mouth to answer but Rimea interrupted him. "They behind now. Tower supplies. Defend wall. Or die in forest. RUN!" Her last word was nearly inaudible, interrupted by the loud screeching of the horn, sounding so close Clara's eyes bulged out in terror. The group sprinted across the clearing, Kadri and Blaggar staying behind to help Nicolas who couldn't move his legs anymore.

Even running, Clara could see that the tower and the wall surrounding it had seen better days. The whole thing was probably built by the Orellians decades ago and had been neglected ever since. As she reached the thin gap in the fortifications, the only access point to the tower, Clara turned around, her heart nearly skipped a beat. Several figures were leaving the treeline, quickly closing in on Nicolas and the two men with him.

There was no way she was going to lose her brother, not now. Not if she could help it. Her grip on the bow handle tightened and she reached for an arrow, aiming at the closest enemy. It was too far for a precise skillshot but even as she released the string she knew the arrow would find its mark. The man fell, almost immediately followed by another one.

Clara glanced to her side to see Enzio standing next to her, bow in hand, grabbing another arrow. "Bigger than rabbits," he smirked, and not even a heartbeat later another enemy cried out and stopped moving. "Aim for the stomach if you can."

Her hands moved almost on their own, just like when Clara was shooting at a target. It didn't matter that these were real human beings and not bundles of straw. They'd just spent an entire night trying to hunt Clara and her friends down and slaughter them. She didn't give a damn about taking their lives.

The Ruthians with them disappeared into the tower and reappeared carrying bows and quivers filled with arrows, ready to join Clara and Enzio. The archer stopped them. There was no need to waste ammunition, since Blaggar, Kadri, and Nicolas were almost at the tower and the enemies had given up the chase, retreating to the safety of the treeline.

Clara swallowed roughly, seeing her own exhaustion and fear mimicked on the faces around her. They were safe, for now. But there was nowhere to go. They could shoot at anyone who dared to come closer, at least until they ran out of arrows.

Fortunately, the tower seemed to be well supplied with all kinds of weapons, materials, and food to last them for weeks. But the enemy was not going to give them weeks, that was obvious. Gishri's men would suffer serious casualties before getting to the crumbling walls. But once there, they would crush the defenders by sheer numbers alone.

The group occupying the tower was pitifully small. Eight Orellian soldiers, plus Nicolas, but he was hardly in any condition to fight. There were also six Ruthian warriors, Kadri, Rimea, Clara and Karina. Nineteen people against gods know how many men Gishri brought along for the hunt. The odds definitely weren't in their favor.

The horn kept calling the hunters in, letting them know the prey was discovered and huddled into a corner. As the sun was slowly rising above the horizon, Clara could see dozens of figures moving between the campfires burning along the treeline. Too many to count. Too many to kill.

"Attack night." Rimea was balancing on top of the crumbling fortification, frowning at the men at the other side of the clearing. "Sleep now. Sun down, fight. Rimea watch." She tapped on her chest and sat down, her feet dangling down from the broken battlement.

"We'll take turns," Enzio nodded at her before turning to the rest. "Make a fire and some food. Get as much rest as you can."

Clara noticed Karina disappeared in the tower but instead of following the queen, her green eyes searched the small place between the walls and the edge of the cliff for her brother's figure. Her heart faltered when she discovered Nicolas sitting curled up in a corner, hugging his knees, a pained expression on his face. Clara rushed toward him, reaching him at the same time Kadri did. The healer tried to touch Nicolas' arm but got shoved aside.

"You should have...left me." Nicolas' voice was so weak they could barely understand his words. "Now we all...die because...I slowed you down."

"Nobody is going to die," Karina answered, having finished the tower inspection and joined them. "Hayden will be here soon, we can hold them off until he arrives." There didn't seem to be a shadow of doubt in the queen's voice or expression, she spoke with such certainty Clara had to admire her.

Pulling a small vial out of his satchel, Kadri nodded. "Right. And we all need to rest now. Drink this." He tried to hand it over to Nicolas when the horn sounded again from the woods, more than one this time, in a horrible cacophony that made Clara shiver.

Nicolas let out a tortured moan, tightly closing his eyes, his hands flying up to cover his ears. Clara hesitated, not sure whether he would push her away as well, but seeing him suffer like that was heartbreaking, so she crouched down next to him. At first, she just put her hand on his shoulder, surprised by how much he was trembling. When he didn't protest, she wrapped her arms around his chest as tightly as she could.

He stiffened and, for a second, it looked like he was going to pull away, but then Clara heard a quiet sniffle and felt his body leaning against hers. "That sound, it's... It just brings it all back," he said in a quiet, shaky voice. "They could have killed us...back at the outpost, all of us. We thought...lucky us, we managed to escape. Escape..." Cackling, he wiped the tears from his face with the back of his hand, smearing dirt all over his cheeks.

"They hunted us. For fun. One by one... And when they caught someone...the screams...gods...you could hear them from miles away. Escape..." he repeated, shaking his head, "there was no escape. I thought you were one of them," Nicolas smirked at Kadri. "You complain I bit you? If I'd had more strength...I'd have ripped your fucking arm off."

Clara hid her face in Nicolas' hair so nobody would see the look of absolute terror in her eyes. To go through something so horrible and still stay sane and strong, keep fighting despite all the odds...she had never admired anyone more than her brother at that very moment. Seething rage bubbled in her chest, slowly replacing the fear and desperation. They were going to pay for this. For all of it.

"*Pashir.*" Kadri spat on the ground, looking disgusted. "Apology accepted then, asshole. I admit I could have been more forthcoming. It's just that you are such an annoying prick, something makes me want to punch you every time I see your ugly face." The mischievous grin on his face let everyone know he was merely joking.

Despite battling between being terrified and angry, Clara found herself chuckling. "Now you know how I've felt my entire life."

"Bastards." Nicolas' shoulders twitched as he let out something between a sob and a laugh. "Both of you." He didn't pull away from Clara though, so it was probably just a tease.

"You really need to expand your vocabulary," Kadri rolled his eyes. "You've been calling me the same four or five names for days now. Lie down, I need to check your stitches." Nicolas grumbled but obeyed, sliding out of Clara's arms and onto the soft grass.

The healer carefully removed the stained bandage, nodding with a quiet satisfied grunt. "Good, it's nothing serious. You're one tough son of a bitch. Uh, I mean..." he hesitated, realizing he insulted Clara as well. "Sorry, I'm sure your mother is a kind and proper lady."

It took a lot of Clara's self-control not to start laughing out loud. "Nope. Bitch fits better." Had Sophia always been so bitter and hateful or did it only start after her husband constantly cheated on her and humiliated her? This was probably not something Clara should be thinking about right now.

After Nicolas drank the potion and fell into an uneasy sleep, Clara finally had time to properly look around the place of their last stand.

The walls protected a small patch of grass from the side toward the forest, with a thin gap in the middle where a gate would be if this place wasn't just a crumbling pile of weathered-down stones but an actual fortress. The other side was technically unprotected but Clara didn't think Gishri's men would manage to scale the cliff that dropped down just a few steps away from her feet. The tower stood at the edge of the cliff, old and battered, leaning dangerously to the side as if it was too tired to stay up straight anymore.

It was definitely not an imposing fortress. But was it defendable with the small number of people they had? Clara had absolutely no idea. The closest to any fight she had ever been was witnessing a brawl at the royal tournament and even that looked scary enough for her. Spotting movement on the upper level of the tower, she headed inside, admiring the bundles of arrows, racks of weapons and crates of supplies for a moment before walking up the stairs.

Parts of the staircase had long since crumbled to dust, forcing her to jump over large gaps and climb over piles of debris. Enzio was looking out of a small window, brows furrowed in concentration. "How's your brother?" He didn't need to turn around to know it was her.

"He'll live." That came out more ironic than Clara had intended since it looked like they were all going to die anyway. She walked over to the second window. It was a perfect spot. She could see the entire area between the walls and the tower while having a good angle to shoot at the enemy inside the fortifications without the risk of injuring allies.

"We'll start on the walls and kill as many of them as we can. But when they get too close, you and I retreat here." Enzio finally turned to her, his face deadly serious. Even though his words weren't posed as a question, he expected an answer so Clara nodded.

She didn't like the idea of running from a battle and hiding in safety while others were fighting, but she would be useless down there. From here, she could at least do some damage. "It would be nice if you managed to convince the queen to join us," Enzio added. "It's the safest place for her."

Yeah, that was definitely not happening. "I can try." But no doubt fail. Clara couldn't imagine Karina agreeing to hide away while other people bled and died to protect her. Maybe if Hayden were here to order it she'd obey. But then again, if the king was here, they wouldn't be in this mess in the first place.

Kadri claimed that Ulaia had sent several messengers to the Orellian outpost to let Hayden know what was happening. But who was to say whether any of them made it out of the forest swarming with Gishri's hunters?

Clara leaned forward to catch a glimpse of Karina, who was relentlessly moving amongst the resting men, talking to them, smiling, and encouraging them. So calm and confident that it even soothed Clara's soul a little, despite her still feeling like a scared little girl.

"Why did you tell me to aim for the stomach?" That question had been bugging her ever since they'd arrived here. "Wouldn't targeting the heart be smarter? If you put an arrow through someone's stomach, they won't die." Or at least not right away.

"That's the point." With a sigh, Enzio ran his hand through his hair. "Damn, I never thought I would be explaining this sick shit to a girl. Gods help me, you are so young and innocent, you should be sitting on a garden swing reading a book, not learning about dirty battle tricks from an old prick like me." Shaking his head, he looked out of the window again and went silent.

So now she was just a girl again? To hell with this. "Stop that, old man," Clara scowled at him. "If I'm to choose between dying young and innocent and growing old, sinful and corrupted, I'll take the latter without a second's hesitation. The fact that I have a pussy doesn't make me a worse archer. It just means that while you will have a quick death, I will suffer for hours."

Damn, how she regretted not having had sex with Oscar while she'd had the chance. How fucking ironic it would be if her precious virginity was taken from her by a bunch of bloodthirsty savages. "So please, stop whining and start talking. I want to know every dirty trick in the book, anything that is going to give us a better chance at surviving."

Enzio gaped at her, lost for words for a moment, before nodding slowly. "Is the rest of your family this feisty and stubborn?" He grinned. "Alright. Imagine you and your very good friends are attacking, running toward your enemy. One of your comrades suddenly falls down, an arrow in his chest, dead on the spot. What do you do?"

"I...I don't know, I guess I get sad and...angry?" Clara tried to imagine it happening to the man in front of her and, to her own surprise, the prevalent emotion wasn't grief but a burning rage.

"Exactly," he said slowly as if that explained everything, even though Clara still had no idea where he was headed. "You get furious, even more determined to slaughter your enemies and win the fight. But if that same friend gets an arrow to the gut instead and he's lying there on the ground, screaming in pain, begging you to help him? Will you continue attacking or will you stay behind and try to do something for him, breaking the formation, weakening the resolve of everyone around you?"

Clara's stomach turned over the image her mind readily provided. "That's..." Sick? Wrong? Evil...? Necessary? She remembered how Nicolas trembled in her arms from the mere memory of being chased by those people. Fuck them. "I'll keep that in mind." The stomach was easier to hit than the heart anyway.

Enzio looked like he regretted ever opening his mouth to say anything. But it was not like he had much of a choice. The problem with dying a noble death was that you were too dead to enjoy your moral superiority. "When they are outside the wall, we need to slow them down. But once they are inside, shoot to kill. Even a mortally wounded enemy squirming on the ground under your feet can be dangerous."

Yes, anyone could be dangerous when chased into a corner with no way out. Clara was beginning to feel the effect of that on herself, finding something hard and solid deep inside her gut that definitely wasn't there before. Something that refused to cower in fear. Something that longed for a fight, for revenge. Something that craved blood.

Chapter 51

C lara really did try to get some sleep but it was impossible. In the end, she just cuddled up to Nicolas, taking advantage of the fact that he was drugged and couldn't protest. He began to stir when the sun touched the western horizon. Clara got up to fetch them some food.

Their last meal was nothing fancy, a stew made of whatever supplies the Ruthians had in the tower and pieces of flat bread baked on hot stones. Still, it was better than dying hungry. Clara couldn't shake the dark thoughts away anymore.

Nobody came to save them. The king either didn't know what was happening or was held up on the way and wasn't going to make it here in time. There was going to be a battle. And, judging by the number of people moving along the treeline across the clearing, they were going to lose.

But not without putting up one hell of a fight. All around Clara, men and women were finishing their meals and preparing for the battle ahead, checking their gear and weapons and stretching out their stiff muscles.

Enzio, Kadri, and Karina were standing at the opening between the walls, the only access point to the courtyard, engaged in a serious debate.

Clara noticed that the archer pointed at the queen and to the top of the tower but Karina just shook her head. The same answer Clara had gotten when suggesting the queen stayed hidden away in safety.

"I'm sorry I've been such a dick to you, Clara." After sleeping through the day, Nicolas looked much better. He'd found himself a sword and a shield from the tower supplies and seemed almost eager to fight.

Last confessions before they all died? "It's alright. I always thought we were too different to have a closer relationship. But-"

"It's quite the opposite, isn't it?" He smirked, shaking his head. "We are the same, that's why we've always fought and competed."

That wasn't exactly true. Nicolas was the one who fought and competed, Clara just wanted to be treated as his equal. "All I wanted was a little bit of respect." Why the hell were there tears welling up in her eyes? She lowered her head so her brother wouldn't notice and tried to blink them away.

"Clara." Nicolas' voice was surprisingly gentle and his hand on her chin forced her to look up at him. "You think I didn't notice you killed four men this morning to save my sorry ass? I respect you. I admit it's too little too late now since we're... I'm just trying to apologize for the way I've treated you. If by some miracle we both make it out of here, I promise to do better."

He extended his hand toward her and when Clara reached to shake it, he grabbed her forearm instead, pulling her into a tight embrace and patting her shoulder. The warriors around them were saying goodbye to each other in a similar manner.

"Thank you. By the way," a corner of Clara's mouth curled up, "the shattered greenhouse, five years ago? That was me. Sorry I framed you," she chuckled, squirming out of his hug when his eyes narrowed.

"You?! Damn, I always thought it was Sebastian. And of course, nobody believed it wasn't me," he snarled. "I was grounded for weeks, you little rascal!" It looked like he was about to reach for Clara but stopped after glancing behind her, bowing his head in respect.

"Can I get a hug too?" Karina appeared next to them, nodding at Nicolas and giving Clara a warm smile.

Clara didn't need to be asked twice and threw her arms around the queen. "You should really hide somewhere, Karina."

"Don't worry. I'll be in the back with Kadri, helping him with people who get injured. But what kind of a queen would I be if I hid somewhere while you all fought to protect me?"

"A normal one?" Clara rolled her eyes.

Chuckles erupted from Karina's throat. "Exactly! It's like you don't know me at all. You know, I kind of envy you two. I've always wanted a sibling."

"You haven't missed out on anything, my lady," Nicolas shook his head. "They are nothing but trouble."

Kadri moved toward them, handing Nicolas a small water pouch. "They are getting ready. One gulp, no more," he raised a finger.

Nicolas' brows furrowed in confusion for a moment before realization hit him. "Wait. Really?" he asked incredulously. Clara had no idea what they were talking about but it was obvious it wasn't water in the pouch.

"Really," Kadri nodded, sighing. "Jokes aside, in your condition it's very likely to kill you. But I think you are the type of guy who would prefer to die fighting. It will block out the pain. Among other things."

Karina raised an eyebrow, leaning forward to sniff the liquid, her face twisting in disgust. "What is it?"

"Nothing for queens," Kadri smirked. "Or archers for that matter," he added quickly before Clara could even open her mouth. "You need your hands steady." Under the healer's careful watch, Nicolas took a large gulp, immediately reaching for water to wash the taste down. "Don't let it get into your head too much," Kadri told him. "It makes things a bit blurry but don't forget who's fighting on your side. If you kill one of my people, I'll rip those guts of yours out myself."

Clara watched as Nicolas' pupils widened slightly and a vicious smirk twisted his mouth. "Wow," he clenched his fists, "this is some serious shit. No wonder you savages fight like madmen."

Kadri just rolled his eyes and moved to the Orellian soldiers to offer them the drug as well. Most accepted. There was no need to hold back now.

Rimea's sharp cry pierced the air, interrupting quiet conversations. It felt as if Clara's heart had momentarily stopped before resuming beating again, thumping in her chest as if it was trying to jump out and run away. She realized she'd still been hoping that someone would come, someone would save them at the very last moment. That hope was gone.

Gishri's men started moving, dozens of them, coming from the west. Clara had to squint against the last rays of the setting sun, making it difficult to aim, which was no doubt their intention. She shuffled her feet to find a stable position atop the crumbling wall. Enzio was standing on her left, Rimea on her right, several more Ruthians and Orellians spread across the whole length of their pitiful fortifications. Anyone who knew how to shoot an arrow was holding a bow, ready to reap death through the enemy lines.

Clara glanced back down at Nicolas and Karina, standing next to a small group of soldiers near the entrance to the inner courtyard. Nicolas looked like he had completely forgotten about his injury; sword in one hand, shield in the other, he was balancing on his tiptoes, seemingly eager to charge at the enemy. Karina had a large dagger in a scabbard attached to her waist and Clara was certain that it wasn't the queen's only weapon.

"Shall we?" Enzio smirked at her, reaching for an arrow. "Keep track of your count, girl. The winner buys the loser a bottle."

Clara's fingers caressed the Huxley crest on her bow. She'd promised to come back to Oscar and she sure as hell wasn't going to break that promise. "Hope you have enough money, old man. My tastes are rather refined."

Gishri's men were moving slowly, certain they were still out of range. And they weren't wrong, the distance was still too large for a regular archer. But for two of Orellia's finest? It was just about right.

Clara nocked the arrow, pulled the string back to her cheekbone, and aimed at an ugly large brute, heavily tattooed, with what looked like a necklace made out of human ears hanging down from his neck. Disgusting. The arrow hissed and a heartbeat later, the man was on his knees, screaming as he stared at the feathered piece of wood sticking out of his abdomen.

The Ruthians around him exchanged nervous glances, clearly not sure what had happened. They were supposed to be out of range, right? Not the sharpest tools in the shed, Clara thought as Enzio's arrow hit another one. Only then they realized they were very much in range and started running, leaving their dying comrades behind.

It was hard to miss with the crowd advancing toward them. Clara counted eighteen before the first of the enemy reached the wall, although one was debatable because she and Enzio hit him at the same time. "Let's go!" he shouted at her, jumping down from the wall.

Clara wanted to protest, she could keep shooting from her current position just fine, but as more and more men poured onto the courtyard, she realized she would be in danger of getting surrounded and taken out. The tower provided better protection.

Desperately trying to ignore the sounds of weapons clashing against each other and the grunts and screams of pain, as well as the sight of blood splattered all around, Clara sprinted across the yard and entered the structure, jumping over obstacles as she made her way up.

Enzio was already there, briefly nodding at her before resuming shooting, releasing one arrow after another. "Ever shot a fire arrow?" he asked, his gaze fixed on the battle below.

"I have, actually." Clara joined him, her arrow piercing the neck of a man who was just about to slash Nicolas' back. Every tiny bit of self-control she managed to pull together was used to holding the fear at bay, locked away in a corner of her mind.

It was hopeless. No matter how many they killed, more kept coming. Several of the defenders were already gravely wounded, if not dead.

No, Clara couldn't afford to think about that. Nock an arrow, pull the string, aim, release. Repeat. That was the only thing allowed into her mind right now.

She caught a glimpse of Karina's long braid whirling through the air as the queen tried to run away from two Ruthians. Clara shot one and Nicolas took care of the other one, separating the head from the body in one smooth strike.

"Clara!" She realized Enzio had been talking to her and she'd completely tuned him out. "The piles of hay over there!" He pointed to the gap in the wall through which the new enemies kept coming. "Set them on fire, now!"

Right. There was a brazier next to her and several arrows ready with pieces of cloth dipped into oil wrapped around the ends of the shafts. Clara grabbed one, smirking at the memory of burning down a small tool shed in the Redwood mansion gardens. She wasn't going to get scolded this time.

The flaming arrow hissed through the air and the hay caught fire almost immediately, no doubt soaked in oil as well. There were pieces of wood and blankets and whatever other flammables the defenders could find in the tower, all laid out across the gap between the walls, and when Clara set the hay ablaze, the flames quickly spread, sealing the entrance off. At least, for a while.

The people in the courtyard, with Clara's and Enzio's help, quickly killed off the remaining enemies and got a moment of reprieve before Gishri's men started to climb over the walls. Their large figures emerging above the stone battlements were easy targets. If only there weren't so many of them.

As the fighting continued, Enzio suddenly jerked his head back, listening carefully for a few moments. "Shit. Stay here. That's a fucking order!" he shouted at Clara before rushing down the stairs. There were screams and sounds of fighting coming from inside the tower and Clara's first instinct was to run and help the archer. But she stayed put as he'd ordered, her hands full with trying to keep the queen, Nicolas, Kadri, and Rimea alive.

There weren't many of the defenders besides those four left standing anymore. Clara noticed Blaggar's scarred face in a pile of bodies. He seemed to be alive but just barely. There was nothing Clara could do to help him.

An imposing figure jumped down from the wall, a large man, nearly naked, tattoos covering every inch of his skin including the face. His hair was long, falling down his back in a thick braid. He shoved his own men aside, making his way toward the small group protecting the queen. The enemy Ruthians quickly got out of his way, giving him quick, respectful bows. There was little doubt about this man's identity. *Sefth* Gishri had arrived to claim his victory.

Clara reached for an arrow, prepared to rid the world of this asshole once and for all, but a strong, callused arm grabbed her shoulder, yanking her away from the window. She found herself staring into the ugly face of a man with several teeth missing. Before she could think what to do, he slapped her so hard her head banged against the stone floor, leaving her utterly disoriented, her vision spinning.

Another Ruthian appeared at the top of the staircase. They were here, which meant Enzio was dead, her shaken brain surmised. She snarled, suddenly overwhelmed by anger. It was all for nothing, all their efforts, all the fighting, all the deaths. They were all going to suffer and die here, in a crumbling tower at the edge of the world.

Judging by the sleazy looks on the faces of the two men towering above her, Clara's suffering was going to start right away. Her fingers desperately scoured the floor for her bow but one of the Ruthians kicked it away. A sudden wave of desperation washed over Clara as she heard it rattle down the stairs. One man crouched down next to her, licking his lips, mumbling something Clara was glad she didn't understand.

As he reached for her shirt she tried to push him away but he was almost twice her size, the bulging muscles on his arms and shoulders almost breaking through his tight leather jacket. Clara had to fight the urge to retch as his foul breath entered her nostrils.

No! Panic threatened to take over but she reached for anger instead, letting it fill her heart until all she could feel was a burning rage. Enzio was dead. Blaggar and most of the others that had fought with her were probably dead too. Nicolas? Karina? Kadri and Rimea? If they weren't dead already they soon would be. Maybe even wishing for it now if they were being tortured like Nicolas' friends from the outpost.

No, there was absolutely no way she was going to let this ugly brute rape her while her friends were in dire need of help. Clara let out a whimper as he tore her shirt open and chuckled over the sight of her undergarments, the other one chiming in with what was no doubt a nasty remark.

Biting on her lip, Clara closed her eyes, trying to ignore his hands groping at her chest, quickly going through her options. There weren't many, really. Just one that could work. It had to work.

She kept struggling as he tore her bra, revealing her breasts. His dirty palms on her skin felt disgusting but she needed to wait until he was closer, especially since the other one was moving toward her as well. Just a few inches closer. She sniffled when he finally lowered his head to suck on her nipple, her stomach twisting and churning from the thought of his rotting teeth touching her skin. At least it put him into the perfect position.

Now or never.

The knife Enzio had given her was still in the scabbard attached to her belt. Clara clutched the handle tightly, pulling it out and running the sharp edge of the blade across the man's throat. Just like a fucking rabbit, she thought with satisfaction when hot blood sprayed all over her naked chest. The Ruthian gurgled, nearly collapsing right onto her. Clara pushed the body toward the second man, struggling onto her feet as he stared at her in disbelief.

She couldn't possibly fight him, not from up close. With that thought in mind, Clara bolted toward the door, not really sure what her plan was, only that she needed to get away as fast as possible.

The barbarian was faster, jumping over his friend's twitching body to grab Clara's hair, yanking her back into the room. The knife still in her hand, she slashed at him but he easily grabbed her wrist, twisting it so brutally she couldn't hold on to the blade.

Kicking his nuts was a last-resort option and Clara didn't really expect it to succeed. To her surprise, her knee found precisely the right spot as the man howled, letting go of her hair. Clara quickly bent down to pick up her blade and plunged it into the man's stomach, exerting another scream from him. Before she could stab him again he reached for her and she barely jumped away.

Run! She fought against the urge to stay. Her bloodlust wanted revenge, wanted to feel that bastard's blood run through her fingers, to shove the knife right into his heart and listen to his last ragged breath. But there was no time.

She was almost on the staircase when a sharp, piercing pain erupted from her thigh. Her leg gave out on her causing Clara to stumble, suddenly falling instead of running, rolling down the stairs. Her hands and legs took the brunt of the damage as she struggled to grab onto anything in a desperate attempt to slow down her fall.

The stairs were incomplete. Clara only remembered that fact when her body rolled over an edge and she experienced a second of freefall before landing hard on a pile of rubble on the ground level. Something in her chest cracked and it was suddenly painful to breathe. Searing pain in her ribcage joined with a similar pain in her leg, blurring her vision with tears and forcing her to bite down hard on her lip so as not to start screaming.

She managed to lift her head, horrified to find a long, gaping cut in her thigh. That asshole upstairs must have thrown a knife at her. A wave of fresh blood gushed out of the wound with every one of Clara's heartbeats. That couldn't be good.

Blood...blood was supposed to be on the inside of the body right?

Her mind was a bit foggy. Stop, stop, stop. Stop the bleeding. But with what?

She chuckled, remembering the pile of bandages Kadri had prepared outside. She could walk there and get them.

Except she couldn't walk. Well, if she could, she wouldn't need the bandages, no? Nope. That won't do.

Her nipples hardened in the cold night air and Clara realized she was half naked. Her shirt was torn and...wait, that was something, no? A piece of cloth was...a bandage? Right!

Smart girl, she congratulated herself, chuckling again, feeling more and more lightheaded.

The surge of pain coming from her ribs as she sat up to take the rest of her shirt off was unimaginable but it brought some clarity, making Clara come back to her senses, at least for now. Enough for her to tie the cloth tightly around her leg, causing another wave of agony to nearly drown her.

The bleeding seemed to have stopped. Or perhaps there just wasn't any more blood left inside. What did she know?

She was so tired. And cold. Maybe she should take a little nap? Just close her eyes for a few moments, rest, and then she could go...where was she supposed to be going?

Her fingers aimlessly scoured the floor until they came across something hard and familiar. A bow. Her bow. From Oscar.

Oscar!

She'd promised she would come back to him. No sleeping.

Grabbing the bow tighter, she looked around. Arrows. A bow needed arrows, it would be useless otherwise. Fortunately, the tower was more than well stocked with them.

Cursing and sniffling, Clara pulled herself up, standing on her healthy leg, trying to ignore the urge to cough violently, knowing it would only cause the pain in her chest to spike.

Leaning against the wall, she slowly hobbled toward the door, grabbing an arrow on the way. One had to do it. With the darkness creeping into her vision, Clara doubted she would have a chance to shoot more anyway. She peeked into the courtyard that was filled with enemies now, everyone standing quietly, watching two people in the middle.

Clara recognized Karina, covered in blood, on her knees, bruised face raised defiantly to look at the tattooed man towering above her. A bad man. Clara's tired brain insisted on that. An important bad man.

Good thing her hands knew what to do even when her brain was indisposed, nocking the arrow and raising the bow. It was a bad angle, lots of people in the way, and Karina was too close to the target. But it wasn't like Clara had another option. Plus, she hadn't missed in years.

Her ribcage protested violently when she pulled the string back but Clara ignored it, trying to focus on aiming through the darkness that had almost taken over her vision. As she sent the arrow on its way Clara smiled, knowing it was a good shot. It was always a good shot.

She really deserved to rest now and her body didn't really give her any choice, slowly sliding down the door frame. Every time she blinked, the darkness swallowed more of her vision until she could no longer see anything. She barely felt the touch of the rough stone on her skin. If only she weren't so damn cold, it was uncomfortable.

Just before the darkness swallowed her completely, Clara registered a strange distant noise. Like...a horn maybe? But not a screeching one like the hunters had used. No, this one sounded clear and strong, strangely familiar.

The darkness didn't care though. It covered Clara like a thick, warm blanket, wiping all the thoughts from her head.

Chapter 52

Karina had to fight hard to maintain her calm and composed demeanor throughout the day. She'd smiled, joked, and comforted, assuring everyone that they were not going to die, that everything was going to be alright. She was surprised how easily people bought that lie. Because that's what it was, a big fat lie. But her people needed hope and it was the least Karina could give them considering that she was completely useless otherwise. And that all of this was her fault.

Hayden hadn't wanted her to go. Too dangerous, he'd said. She'd smiled and kissed him and gone anyway. And now everyone was going to die because of her stupid recklessness.

The woods had been safe for Clara, her brother, even for the Orellian soldiers staying with Ulaia's people. Gishri had stopped with his attacks to strengthen that feeling of safety, to lure the queen into a trap.

Of course they'd gone after her, knowing she'd left the protection of the outpost. Because she was the Burning Fury's greatest weakness. Once again, his enemies were hunting her to get to Hayden. And of course, she had made it so easy for them, going out almost alone, in the naive belief that she'd be safe, that there was a peaceful resolution to this conflict.

It was her fault that Clara, Kadri, and all of the other people that had come along to protect her were now trapped inside this stupid crumbling fortification with no way out, sentenced to fight in a hopeless battle until the bitter bloody end.

Regret filled her like a ball of searing hot pain. How could she even look them in the eyes? They all looked up to her, she was supposed to be their fucking queen, the one who protected her people, kept them safe. And hadn't she done a marvelous job at that!

Everybody prepared for the battle, picking up weapons from the large selection stored in the tower, trying them out, sharpening them. Kadri prepared bandages and other medical supplies to be ready whenever necessary, but he also had a spear and a strangely curved blade in his hands. Even Clara looked so confident with her bow, making sure there were plenty of arrows at all of the possible shooting locations, debating over angles and distances with Enzio.

And Karina? Karina smiled and patted people on their backs, feeling like the most useless piece of shit in the entire universe. Yes, she had a dagger, more than one actually, but she couldn't possibly hold her own in a fight. Someone was going to have to stay with her the entire time, trying to protect not only their own life but hers as well. She was a liability, a dead weight the others were forced to drag along.

Only Ulaia's words had stopped her from walking across the clearing and surrendering herself to Gishri in exchange for her people's lives. The *seftha* had warned her that he would hunt down the rest of the Orellians anyway, even if she handed herself over. At least the Ruthians would survive, though. Gishri didn't tend to kill his own people, not even the ones from different tribes, not unless they raised arms against him.

When the attack started, Karina stayed in the courtyard with those who couldn't wield a bow, admiring Clara's smooth and confident movements as the girl released one arrow after another.

Clara wasn't supposed to be here. The others were soldiers, warriors, them being here and taking part in the battle was somewhat justifiable. But Clara had only come here because Karina had invited her in a selfish desire to not be the only woman around, to have someone to connect with. Well, now they could connect by dying together, how's that for strengthening a friendship?

She could hear the screams even before the first enemies poured through the opening of the walls and quickly started to flood the courtyard. Ruthians and Orellians armed with long spears charged against the enemy, trying to take them out from as safe a distance as possible.

The archers on the walls dropped their bows and jumped down, grabbing spears and blades and joining the fray. Enzio sprinted toward the tower and Clara followed behind, weaving her way between the fighting groups. She should be safe. For now.

A couple of enemies slipped past the defenders and charged toward Karina. Kadri and Nicolas made quick work of them.

If Karina hadn't seen the huge wound on Clara's brother's stomach, she wouldn't have even guessed he had been injured. He moved with ease, eagerly waving the sword as if it weighed nothing, taking Gishri's men down one by one, a look of fierce satisfaction on his bloodied face. From what he'd told them, Karina assumed he was enjoying the opportunity to get vengeance for his friends. Those poor souls hunted through the woods and tortured brutally. Maybe even for all the suffering he had gone through.

The arrows kept coming from the top of the tower, often saving the defenders from the direst situations, precisely striking down enemy after enemy. Despite the incredible guilt Karina felt for dragging Clara here, the queen was glad to have her around now. Especially when two attackers caught sight of Karina and sprinted after her.

The queen turned around to seek a safer position since she was obviously being targeted by the enemy. When she looked back, the men were lying dead on the ground, a white-feathered arrow sticking out of the neck of one of them. The other one's head was slowly rolling away from its body, Nicolas standing above with a bloodied sword and a vicious grin.

Karina swallowed roughly, trying to ignore the blood squirting out of the lifeless torso's neck. Now was not the time to be squeamish.

One of the Orellians fell down, trying to crawl away from the main fight, and Karina quickly shook off the fear and stupor and rushed over to help him.

Kadri joined her and together they dragged the man to relative safety before rolling him on his back. Horror and utter disgust made Karina freeze as she stared at a huge cut across the man's abdomen. The foul stench of the contents of his shredded insides quickly filled the air, making her stomach twist and turn.

The healer shook his head, grabbed his weapon, and got up, returning to help the fighters. Leaving Karina alone with the dying man.

He was young, so damn young, almost a boy. Probably no older than Clara. His devilishly handsome face was now contorted in agony and fear. "M-my l-lady." He recognized her, looking at her with such fear it pushed tears into her eyes. "I-I'm sorry. I f-failed you. I-I don't w-want to die," he sniffled. And died.

Karina gaped at the body with no idea what to do or say, her mind totally blank. Not only did she not have a chance to help him, she didn't even have time to comfort him, to at least lie to him by saying everything was going to be alright, that he was definitely not going to die here in this stupid battle at the end of the world. That he was going back home, to hug his mother, find a nice girl, and have a bunch of kids.

What the fuck was she good for?!

Trying to stand up, Karina doubled over, no longer able to control her stomach. The remains of her dinner stained the ground near the dead soldier. She coughed and retched violently even when there was nothing left to bring up anymore, tears freely rolling down her face.

She barely even noticed the fire in the opening was now lit and the sounds of the battle died down for a few moments before enemies started to scale the walls. All Karina wanted to do was to curl up in a corner and cry, let out all the wailing and desperate sobs that were piled up deep inside of her. But she was the fucking queen and had no such luxury. She had no choice but to get up and do something, to fight. Why the hell should others die for her when she wouldn't even lift a finger in her own defense?

Her hand found the hilt of the long dagger at her waist. She knew how to use a knife, it wasn't overly complicated. Hilt in hand, blade toward the enemy. She had taken a life before. Lamar said the next one would be easier. Well, she certainly wasn't going to grieve over these fucking barbarians.

Kadri's water pouch was on a table in the back and Karina grabbed it with newly-found determination, taking a big gulp from its contents.

It felt like liquid ice pouring down her throat, freezing her insides, making her eyes nearly pop out of their sockets. Everything slowed down, certain sounds became more distinct, the rest faded into the background. Her vision somehow got blurry yet sharper all at the same time. Those things she focused on were crystal clear, the rest were smudged and strangely monotone.

Karina looked around the courtyard, almost overwhelmed by the number of heightened sensations pumped into her brain. She caught a glimpse of Nicolas' broad shoulders in the crowd.

Clara's brother was fighting two enemies at once. Blocking out one strike with his already battered shield he turned around to face the other Ruthian, completely oblivious to a third one moving in behind his back.

Without even realizing what she was doing, Karina grabbed her blade and raced toward the enemy trying to flank Nicolas. It was almost too easy. The man's attention was focused on the Orellian, he didn't notice her stalking closer until she plunged the dagger deep into his back. The blade went in easily, creaking as it slid along the rib.

Karina didn't really think it through. She had no idea what would happen when the man turned around to attack her. But it didn't matter. Her brain switched into a more primitive mode now, awakening an ancient fight-or-flight instinct embedded deep in every human mind. And there was nowhere to run. All that was left to do was fight, to stab and cut, scratch and tear, kick and bite.

A hand landed on her shoulder and she swirled around in a smooth movement, the dagger ready in her hand...nearly stabbing Nicolas. Huh? Wasn't he fighting two men just a second ago?

Karina looked down at her hands to find out she was completely covered in blood. The dead man on the ground in front of her had his back covered by wounds and cuts. Apparently, she had been mindlessly stabbing him over and over.

"Wild ride, huh?" Nicolas grinned, unphased by the fact that his queen had almost killed him in whatever wild rage she was possessed by. Damn, was this how Hayden felt when he lost control?

There was no time to ponder over the subject as more enemies charged at them. Nicolas shoved one aside, attacking the other with his sword. But the third one passed around him and went straight for Karina.

The first jab of the spear in her direction was easy to avoid. Karina felt somewhat faster than the thin, short man fighting against her. She wasn't sure what to do next, though.

Logic commanded her to get out of his range but the range of a spear turned out to be fucking huge, especially compared to the length of the blade in her hand. The primal part of her brain made her growl and grab the wooden shaft. She pulled on it with all the strength she could gather.

The sudden movement caught her enemy by surprise and he stumbled forward, right into her waiting blade that hungrily slit the flesh of his neck.

As the hot red blood gushed out of the wound, staining her already drenched clothes, Karina tilted her head back and let out an inarticulate roar. She had never felt more alive than at this very moment. But as blissful as her victory felt, there was no time to spare. Allies faltered and fell. More and more enemies flooded the courtyard.

For the first time that day, Karina actually felt excitement. The blood-thirsty beast that had awakened inside of her rejoiced over the thought of more blood to be spilled.

But no matter how many they killed, more kept coming. The enemy was pushing the survivors back toward the edge of the cliff, step by step, strike by strike. The arrows stopped coming from the tower. Karina knew it meant something bad but her raging mind refused to think about it at that moment.

Suddenly, the enemies stopped, taking a few steps back. There were still weapons in their hands, keeping the defenders cornered, but they didn't attack anymore. Karina used the moment of reprieve to wipe the blood off her hands as the hilt of her blade was getting dangerously slippery.

What was happening? The logical part of her mind fought for control and won, making Karina snap out of the wild rage, allowing her to think clearly again. For the most part, at least.

A large man weaved his way through the crowd. He was tall and muscular, almost every inch of his skin covered by tattoos. The others bowed in respect, stepping out of his way. He impatiently shoved the slower ones aside, stopping in front of the pitifully small group of defenders that were still left standing.

Nicolas, Kadri, Rimea, and the last remaining Orellian soldier moved in front of Karina, determined to protect her with their own bodies.

The man scoffed, his eyes finding Karina's. "You wished to speak with me, queen?" he asked, giving her an evil smirk.

Gishri. Karina took a deep breath to clear her mind, trying to figure out a way out of this. "I did." She stepped forward, making her way between her defenders to stand against the *sefth*. "I'd really hoped it would be under different circumstances though. Not standing over piles of dead bodies of your own people." Oh, awesome. Very fucking diplomatic. Leading negotiations while high on some badass berserker drug was definitely not a good idea.

Rage flashed through his eyes and he stepped forward, ignoring the weapons aimed against him. "There are quite a few bodies of your people in these piles as well. And before the sun comes up, we will add a few more," he smirked before shouting a quick order.

The enemies swarmed them all at once. There was no escape, no chance to win.

Karina slashed against one man who easily avoided her blade. Before she even finished the movement, two more were grabbing her arms, twisting her wrist so she had to drop the dagger. A fist landed on her chin and as she fell down, a foot in a leather boot kicked her stomach, making her gasp for air. She barely even realized they'd dragged her out in front of Gishri, pushing her to kneel at his feet.

"Yes," he chuckled, "that is much better. Do you want to show me what else you can do with that foul mouth of yours?"

Karina spat out some blood, fighting to stay upright as the world swirled around her. "Fuck you."

"Oh, I will, don't worry," Gishri laughed. "Since your dear husband killed my wife, I think it's only fitting that I kill you in return. Eventually. After we've had some fun."

Was that why he was going after her so hard? Revenge? If he truly hated Hayden that much, there could never be any peace, not while this man remained alive.

Karina was going to die, that much was obvious. But maybe she could take Gishri with her? So Hayden would have an easier path toward making peace with the remaining Ruthians. Provided he didn't slaughter every single one of them in revenge, of course.

She still had a hidden blade, they hadn't tied her up. She had a chance to pull it off. The only thing she needed was a distraction. Something, anything, to take Gishri's eyes off her for a second so she could grab the dagger out and plunge it right into his heart before he could react.

Desperate, she looked around, hoping for a miracle. Her friends were on their knees as well, tied up and guarded. Nicolas had collapsed, struggling to stay conscious as the drug was wearing off and the pain from his injuries, both old and new, was flooding his mind once again. There was no help coming from that front.

Chapter 53

Karina didn't really believe in gods but she sent a quick prayer in their direction. What harm could it do? All she needed was a tiny bit of luck, the slightest noise or movement that would force Gishri's attention away, even for a split second.

Whether it was in response to her silent prayers or just sheer luck, a miracle came. An arrow whizzed through the cold night air, passing right by Gishri's head. It didn't hit him, at least not more than a nick, but he yelped in pain and surprise as there was suddenly blood running down his earlobe.

Karina didn't look where the arrow had come from or what damage it had done to Gishri's ear. It didn't matter. Her mind had planned the movement precisely while she'd been praying and now her hands followed the instructions to the letter, grabbing the blade and shoving it straight into Gishri's heart as she rose up on her knees. She didn't miss.

Gishri stumbled and Karina jumped up, pulling the blade out and plunging it back in, wanting to make sure this asshole never drew another breath. The look of bemusement remained in his expression even when his body slid down to the ground.

The blood frenzy threatened to engulf her again but Karina fought against it. There were still dozens of enemies around who could start attacking any second. But, hopefully, there was a way to deter them from doing that.

Bending down to Gishri's body, Karina grabbed his long braid and pulled on it, revealing his tattooed neck. What she was about to do was horrible and disgusting but she didn't allow her mind to ponder over it and quickly ran the blade over the exposed skin. The spine was surprisingly hard to cut through but, with some twisting and tearing, Karina managed to separate the *sefth's* head from his body. She let out a feral scream as she straightened up, holding the severed head out in front of her.

The Ruthians gathered around just gaped at her, not sure what to do. It would only take one of them to resume the attack, the others would quickly join in. But so far, nobody moved.

Keeping the rage in her expression, Karina walked over to the closest enemy, waving the head in his face. "This fucking battle is over!" She glanced back at Kadri, flinching her chin toward the other Ruthians. He looked shocked but nodded and translated her words.

"We won!" It sounded stupid. They were surrounded by countless enemies, defenseless, and Karina was standing there, proclaiming that they had just won the fight? But the attackers didn't move, their eyes jumping between Karina's furious face and the head of their dead leader she lifted up in the air. "If you want to live, get the fuck out of here! NOW!"

An absolutely empty threat but still, a few of the men hesitated, glancing back toward the treeline. The one directly in front of Karina didn't though. He took a step forward and raised his spear against her, opening his mouth. She never found out what he was going to say since a horn sounded in the distance. An Orellian horn. Help had finally arrived.

The man's resolve faltered and Karina knew she needed to take advantage of that. She shoved his spear aside and moved so close to the man that their faces were just inches away from each other. "I said," she growled, "get the fuck out of here!" There was still blood dripping down from the severed head she was holding and it stained the man's shirt when Karina pushed against his chest. "LEAVE!"

The horn sounded again, closer this time, and a few of the enemy Ruthians in the back turned around and sprinted away. As if a small stone had set off an avalanche, more and more Ruthians chose to flee, panicking when the Orellian cavalry appeared at the edge of the forest. The horses galloped toward the tower, mounted knights striking down anyone in their path.

Karina found herself unable to move, her heart beating frantically as the courtyard filled with armed men once more. Panic took over when one of them got down from a large black horse and ran toward her, bloodied sword in hand.

There were always more coming, always, no matter what she did. But she was not going down without a fight.

Lips curled back into a snarl, she took a step back to find more solid footing and raised her blade against the man. It was ridiculously small compared to his sword. The man stopped, watching her cautiously, saying her name. His voice and face were familiar but it was almost impossible to think over the haze of rage and fear clouding her mind.

Panting heavily, she gripped the handle of her dagger even tighter. Her fingers clutched the hair on Gishri's head tighter as she tried to find something solid to hold on to.

The man smiled at her and slowly put his sword down, showing her empty hands. "It's alright." His tone was calm and the sound of his voice was soothing. "It's me, Karina. You are safe now."

She knew him, didn't she?

He took a couple of steps toward her, a loving smile on his handsome face.

Yes, she knew him. She loved him, she didn't want to fight him. But it seemed impossible to let go of the dagger.

"I won't hurt you," he whispered, slowly approaching her as if she were a cornered wild animal. She really did feel like one at that moment. "You know that. I promised I would never hurt you." His hand reached for hers and he gently plied the blade from her stiff fingers. "There, that's better."

He glanced at the head in her other hand but Karina scowled and pulled it back protectively. She wasn't entirely sure why, but she'd fought hard to get this thing and it was very important for some reason. "Mine," a quiet growl escaped her lips.

"Don't worry," the man chuckled, "I won't take your head away. I already have your heart." His mouth twisted into a very familiar smirk.

"H-" Karina had to clear her throat as it refused to let any words through. "Hayden?" she asked quietly, the haze surrounding her slowly subsiding.

Tears filled his eyes as he nodded. "Yes, it's me." He pulled her into a tight embrace. Karina stiffened at first but quickly recognized the shape and feel of her husband's body, his unmistakable scent, the sound of his heartbeat. Yes, this was where she belonged, in his arms. Was the nightmare really over? She found herself unable to calm down.

"Gods, woman," he shook his head, chuckling and sniffling at the same time. "How much of that bloody concoction did you drink?"

At first, Karina had no idea what he was talking about. What did she drink? But then it dawned on her. The drugs. She was still on whatever Kadri had given the warriors before the battle, that's why her brain felt so scrambled. "I...I don't know." That particular memory was a bit blurry. "It was necessary." Something important lingered at the back of her mind but she couldn't grasp it.

"Yes." Hayden's smile disappeared, his face twisted by incredible guilt. "I'm sorry, Karina, I-"

Karina looked around, seeing the knights helping the wounded men, Kadri running between them and giving sharp instructions. There were so many bodies on the blood-soaked ground. Stabbed, cut down, with feathered arrows sticking out of them. Arrows. "CLARA!" Mercilessly shutting Hayden out and squirming out of his arms, Karina darted toward the tower. The arrow that distracted Gishri had come from that direction.

"Shit," Hayden growled and pushed Karina aside, leaning down to pick up the lifeless body covered in blood. "She's still breathing," he shouted as he brought her outside, right next to Kadri's improvised infirmary. The Ruthian healer and one of the Orellians had their hands full with bandaging and stitching up the survivors but Kadri sprinted over when Hayden yelled at them.

Clara was naked from waist up for some reason, her chest covered in huge bruises and a layer of dried blood. But what was worse, there was a large, deep cut on her thigh that started bleeding when Kadri removed the improvised bandage. Clara was already so pale, she must have lost a tremendous amount of blood.

"I need more light!" The healer muttered quiet curses as he cut Clara's pants open to get better access to her injury. Several soldiers rushed in with torches, planting them in a circle around her body. With her being almost completely naked now and the amount of blood around, it almost looked as if they were about to sacrifice a virgin to summon a demon.

Karina couldn't bear to watch anymore. As the effects of the drug were fading and her mind was becoming clearer, the amount of guilt she felt was crushing her soul.

She stumbled off, curling in a tight corner at the foot of the tower, finally letting all the tears fall in short, desperate sobs. Somebody put a warm cloak over her shoulders but she barely even noticed. Hayden came over a few moments after that, sitting down next to her, holding on as she sobbed uncontrollably. Whispering soothing words, caressing her dirty hair.

People came and left while he held her but Karina didn't understand a word they were saying. She was so damn tired.

"Clara will live," Hayden said when her tears finally died down. Karina just shivered helplessly in his arms. "She's lost a lot of blood but she's strong, she will get through it. She and that brother of hers are like a couple of damned immortals, simply refusing to die."

Nicolas was still alive? That man really was indestructible. "H-how many?" Karina sniffled. How many lives were on her conscience now?

Hayden sighed. "Honestly, given the numbers you were facing, it's a miracle any of you survived at all." Karina looked up at him, her brows forming an angry scowl. That was not an answer.

"Kadri, Rimea, and one Ruthian male are the only ones that survived from their group. From our people... You, Nicolas, Clara, Kiligan. Blaggar might live but he'll probably lose a leg. Oh, and Enzio, they found him unconscious at the bottom of the tower with a couple of broken bones and a huge lump on his head."

Nine. Which meant ten people died because of her stupidity. Hayden noticed the tears welling up in her eyes again. "This was not your fault, Karina. You cannot blame this on yourself. Those men were soldiers, they followed orders. My orders. And my orders were to protect you at all costs."

Perhaps he was right. But not in everything. Clara wasn't a soldier, she was Karina's responsibility. And it nearly got her killed. "How do you do it? You lead men into battles, knowing many of them won't make it back." With the number of war campaigns he'd commanded, Hayden must have had hundreds, if not thousands of Claras on his conscience.

"It sucks," he scoffed. "I try to avoid as many battles as I can, always trying to find a peaceful resolution. That way I know that when we do fight, I did everything I could to prevent it. Soldiers die, that's an occupational hazard. They all chose to be here." With a long sigh, he ran his hand through his hair. "Most generals like to keep their distance. It's easier to send people to their deaths when you don't know their names or how many kids they've got."

"You don't do that."

Hayden nodded, pulling her back into a hug. "No. I don't. That's why it sucks. I was so scared," he whispered into her hair. "The second I saw Ulaia's messenger, exhausted and bleeding... I was certain all I would find here would be your mutilated corpse." His body was trembling just as badly as hers. "But you always find a way to surprise me." He shook his head in disbelief. "Seriously, the last thing I expected was to see you winning a hopeless battle, the enemies fleeing at the mere sight of you."

It was obvious he was teasing her to distract her from her dark thoughts. "They fled because they heard you coming. I think they were just scared of the Burning Fury."

"Right," Hayden snorted. Karina couldn't see his face but she would bet money he was rolling his eyes as he continued, "It had absolutely nothing to do with you waving the severed head of their leader in the air and yelling at them to fuck off?"

Gods. "Did that really happen? Damn, those drugs really are something." She couldn't hold back a chuckle anymore. "Did you really kill Gishri's wife?"

"Wife?" Hayden sounded surprised. "Is that why he was so set against me? I don't know, it's possible."

"You don't remember killing someone's wife?" Like, really?

Hayden pulled away slightly so he could look into her face. "It's not what you think. I didn't sneak into a peaceful village under the cover of night to murder innocent women. I did kill Ruthian females, yes, but it was always in battle. It's entirely possible one of them was Gishri's wife but how the hell was I supposed to know that? People don't usually introduce themselves when they ambush you in the woods."

"I'm not blaming you, Hayden." Hearing the pain in his words, Karina gave him a warm smile. "It was just something he said. That's how I knew he had to die. Because there could never be any peace while he was around."

Hayden's mouth curled up in a grin. "I really have been a bad influence on you. Stabbing people and cutting their heads off sounds more like my kind of diplomacy than yours." He leaned down to kiss her. "You are such a strong woman. I love you."

"I love you too. But I didn't feel strong, I was frightened the whole time. Well, except for when the drug took over, that was...wild," she smirked upon remembering Nicolas' words.

"I bet," Hayden laughed. "I actually contemplated trying it but after seeing the effects on my calm and peaceful wife, I'm glad I never did. I'd probably just slaughter everyone around me. And it's completely normal to be afraid. Even I get scared when I see the enemy advancing against our lines. Not giving in to that fear is what makes you strong. And you are the strongest person I've ever met."

Karina tried to protest but was silenced by a kiss.

Chapter 54

O scar stared at the package that appeared in front of his door, trying to decide whether he was excited that everything was going well or worried about things getting serious.

WE ACCEPT, the small note on the top said. It seemed that whoever was running this show against Hayden had decided to grant Oscar his wish and promised him the queen. He wasn't exactly sure how to feel about that. Karina was going to hate it, that was certain. Hayden was most likely going to punch him.

Only after the door of his study was safely closed behind him, Oscar unwrapped the soft cloth around the package, revealing a pile of parchments. Even a brief look at the few on the top confirmed his suspicions. It was the forged evidence against the lord chancellor. Oscar was supposed to present these to Hayden as real in order to undermine his trust in Lord Egmont.

The evidence was good. More than good, actually. Most of it looked so real Oscar would never guess it was fake. Some of it must have been true, there was no way they were able to fabricate so many realistic lies about one of the most prominent noblemen in Orellia. As Oscar's fingers lazily flipped through the pages, he was getting more and more annoyed. So much dirt.

When he got to a part where Egmont had supposedly kidnapped and mutilated his opponent's children, Oscar tossed the papers aside in disgust. That shit could wait for another day, Hayden wasn't supposed to be back for weeks anyway. Sadly, neither was Clara.

Oscar pulled out her latest letter instead, reading it again. Despite all odds, she'd managed to find her brother. Who would have thought? Oscar would have bet everything that the man was dead. Not that he would have said that in front of Clara, he wasn't stupid, but he never truly believed there was a chance that Nicolas was still alive.

Clara somewhat reluctantly described how she and Karina had ended up in the Ruthian village all alone. Oscar had a little chuckle over that. Of course, he'd expected Karina to do something crazy. And it was becoming quite obvious that once Clara got over her timidness, she was going to be just as wild and uncontrollable as the queen.

At least Oscar didn't have to feel bad about breaking his promise over staying safe, since his young wife was doing the same. He just had to trust her to know what she was doing. Which was damn hard when she was so far away.

There was another knock at the door of his chambers. Look at that, wasn't he a popular man today? This time, it was one of the palace messengers, carrying a brief note. Oscar quickly skimmed the letter, amusement evident on his face. Yes, this should take his mind off all the filth and politics. He grabbed his cloak and headed out of the palace.

A boy was standing at the corner on the outskirts of Ebris. They were surrounded by small, simple houses with well-kept tiny gardens in the front and slightly larger yards in the back. A poorer part of the town, but people still seemed to be taking good care of their properties here. The blacksmith's house was at the far end of the street, the workshop standing back slightly from other buildings because of the increased fire hazard.

Oscar glanced in that direction before addressing the boy, "How long?"

"She's been in labor for several hours. I don't think it's going well." The boy shrugged as if he didn't really care. He couldn't have been more than twelve years old but life on the street had already made him hard. "They don't have money for a proper doctor."

Of course they didn't. Oscar pulled out a pouch with coins and handed it to the boy. "Get one and make sure he gets here fast." Seeing the greedy look in his eyes, Oscar bent forward and grabbed the boy's shirt. "Payment AFTER the job, you little shit," he hissed, a distinct threat underlining his reminder.

The boy gave him a fearful look and nodded vigorously before sprinting off. Oscar knew he could trust the kid because he had a mutually profitable deal with the leader of his gang.

The gang was mostly made up of orphans, good-for-nothing children who survived as thieves and petty criminals. Not the worst of Ebris' underground but one that suited Oscar best. He paid them well and they were eager to do whatever he needed – spying on people, sneaking into buildings, stealing or copying documents. Having a bunch of little helpers available at all times was extremely handy.

Oscar didn't have to wait long. He was leisurely leaning against a tree by the side of the road, eating an apple, when a small carriage arrived in front of the blacksmith's house and a tall man got out, grabbing a large bag before knocking on the door. There was a short conversation with someone inside but they let the man in and Oscar nodded in satisfaction.

"Good." He heard the boy return and turned toward him. "This is for your boss," a small pouch changed hands, "and this one is for you, just between the two of us." A silver coin in Oscar's hand reflected the sunlight. The boy reached for it hesitantly.

Oscar knew the kids had to take all they earned to the gang leader who would divvy out the profits as they saw fit. If the boy was caught withholding money, Oscar would probably never see him again. Which would be a shame, since he kind of liked this one. "I won't tell if you don't," he winked at the kid in an attempt to reassure him.

"You'll get me in trouble," the boy mumbled but the coin did disappear into his pocket. "By the way, do you still want to know about the barrels?" Oscar nodded, his brows furrowing. There had been some suspicious deliveries to several warehouses all over the city, barrels with unknown contents. The papers concerning them were fake, really good, high-quality falsifications. "Well," the boy shrugged, "there's just this weird dust inside."

Oscar raised an eyebrow. "Are you expecting me to pay you for such a lie? Why would anyone go to so much trouble to smuggle dust?"

"But it was! I saw it with my own eyes!" The boy seemed desperate to convince Oscar he wasn't lying. "We even emptied one of the barrels completely to see if there was anything hiding on the inside, but there was nothing. Just the dust. See for yourself." He pushed a pouch into Oscar's hand. It really did feel like there was nothing more than dust inside.

Another fucking mystery, exactly what Oscar needed. "Just stay here and let me know when the baby is born. I'll be at the Rotten Apple." One of the few decent inns in this part of the city.

After finishing his ale and a reasonable dinner, Oscar opened the pouch and poured some of its contents into his palm. Curious. There truly was nothing but a bit of dust, tiny dark grains with no distinct smell. Why would anyone ship dozens of barrels of this into the city? What could it possibly be used for? He made a small pile on the table and poked it with his finger as if it would yield and give him all the answers he sought. Nothing happened, naturally. It was just dust.

The boy waved at him from the inn entrance and Oscar got up, tossing a few coins on the table and nodding in the direction of the plump, smiling innkeeper. The man bowed and thanked the kind lord for the visit while one of the servant girls cleaned up Oscar's table. Nervous as she was, she knocked over one of the candles.

A sudden loud noise thundered through the room accompanied by a flash of light. The girl squealed, cradling her arm to her chest. Oscar noticed a large burn mark on her skin and a sizable charred spot on the table where the pile of dust had been. One of the coins from the table was now embedded deep inside a wooden beam supporting the roof. Oscar drew in a sharp breath but quickly regained his composure, using the chaos that ensued to leave the inn unnoticed.

"What was it, milord?" The boy's eyes were bulging in fear along with a bit of that innocent, childish curiosity.

Fucked if I know, Oscar thought. "Trouble, no doubt." He needed more time to think.

The doctor was just leaving the blacksmith's house, an elderly woman reverently kissing his hand goodbye and repeatedly giving him deep and grateful bows. Oscar waited until the carriage turned the corner and then slowly walked to the door, curious as to whether they would even let him in. Common folk weren't usually thrilled when noble lords started sticking their uptight noses into their business.

The same woman who had just been giving her goodbyes to the doctor opened the door to Oscar's knock, gaping at him, clearly not knowing what to say. He wasn't even wearing anything fancy. "Hello." He tried to sound as friendly as he possibly could, putting on one of his best and brightest smiles. "Does Melara live here? Enzio's daughter?"

"Uh-wh-...yes, I-I..." The woman stuttered, her face turning red. Perhaps Oscar went a bit overboard with the smile, she seemed to be completely smitten despite being at least twenty years older than him.

"I heard she just had a baby. I'm here to congratulate the parents and make sure everything is alright."

A young man appeared in the doorframe, gently pushing the older woman aside, sizing Oscar up with suspicion. "Why would a noble lord such as yourself care about my wife and our child?"

Great, the last thing Oscar needed now was to be suspected of being the father of random children around the city. This misunderstanding needed to be cleared as quickly as possible. "I'm not here to cause any trouble. My wife is good friends with Enzio and she mentioned that he was expecting a grandchild any day. I thought I would stop by and see how you are doing and if there's anything you need."

"Wow, I didn't know my father-in-law had such noble friends," the man grinned, becoming a lot friendlier. "If you would come with me, my lord."

Oscar followed him around the house toward the smithy. The fire was out in the forge but it still radiated heat and the smell of smoke lingered in the air. The man reached up onto a shelf and pulled out a bottle and two cups that were hidden behind some tools. "I have a son," he grinned happily, looking like he still couldn't believe such a thing had happened.

"Congratulations." Oscar returned the smile, trying to ignore the sudden sting of pain piercing through his heart. Would Alice have given birth to a boy, little baby Oscar? How was he supposed to not torture himself with these thoughts?

The blacksmith poured the liquid from the bottle into the cups and handed one to Oscar with an apologetic smile. "It's probably not what you are used to, my lord. I'm Helman, by the way."

"Oscar." It tasted better than expected. Nothing fancy or refined, of course, but he'd had much worse. Still, it brought tears to their eyes.

After coughing for a moment, the man bit his lip nervously and sighed. "You paid for the doctor, didn't you, Lord Oscar? I...I'm glad, I think Melara would have died if he hadn't come but...I'm not sure how I'll be able to pay you back."

"Don't mention it," Oscar waved his hand. Something near the forge caught his attention and he carefully reached for it. "And it's just Oscar. I don't really like to flash my title around wherever I go," he murmured, eyes fixated on the strange object, his fingers playing with it, turning it here and back. It looked like a handful of nails joined together, the sharp ends sticking out to the sides, forming a pointy ball of sorts, not more than a few inches in diameter. "What is this?"

Helman shrugged. "I honestly have no idea. But there's this weird guy that pays quite well for these, so I make as many as I can."

When one of Oscar's fingers slid over one of the pointy edges, he winced in pain, watching the small droplet of blood roll down. Haven't there been enough mysteries lately? First, there's a strange exploding dust and now these sharp things with no obvious purpose?

Oscar somehow felt those two things were connected but didn't know how yet. There was no point in pondering over it though, a subconscious part of his brain was already working to solve the problem and it was going to let him know once there was an answer available. "Can I take one?"

"Take a dozen," Helman chuckled nervously. "You saved my wife's life, I can never make it up to you. Here, wrap it into this so it doesn't make a hole in your pocket." The blacksmith pulled out a piece of thick leather and handed it to Oscar. "Do you want to see my son?"

Being the youngest sibling and not having any children of his own, Oscar had never even seen a baby this small before. It was all red and wrinkled and incredibly ugly but Helman and the exhausted woman lying in bed were looking at it as if it were the most beautiful thing in the world. It looked so tiny and fragile, swaddled in a blanket, squinting in the dim light. Oscar was absolutely terrified when Helman picked up the bundle and placed it into his arms.

Surprisingly, the child didn't cry even though a stranger was holding it. The boy just fussed a little before yawning in the most adorable way imaginable, then peacefully closing his eyes. Oscar never considered himself a family man, babies were something to avoid, not cherish. But seeing the tiny creature fall asleep in his arms made him think that one day he might want to reconsider that attitude. Not right away though, he wanted Clara all to himself for a while yet.

He still felt a little mushy on the inside when he finally returned to the palace, certainly not in the mood to deal with secret conspiracy filth or any of the other weird mysteries that probably weren't even important. There was yet another letter waiting for him in his chamber. Oscar excitedly rushed to open it, hoping it would be from Clara. His heart sank when he noticed Karina's seal on the envelope. There were only a few reasons why she would be the one writing to him instead of Clara. And none of them were good.

His eyes quickly skimmed the words, his heart sinking further.

Fuck! He should have never let her go. He tossed the parchment aside and sprinted to the closet in the bedroom, quickly packing some clothes.

His paralyzing fear for Clara's life competed with a new searing bitterness and anger he felt toward Karina right now, both feelings trying to take control of his mind. Oscar ignored them both, focusing on the task at hand. Which was getting to his wife as quickly as possible.

Chapter 55

Everything was darkness. Everything was pain. And cold. Horrible, teeth-chattering cold surrounded her, no matter how warm the air might actually be.

Sometimes, there was a vaguely familiar voice in the darkness, a female voice whispering soothing words. Clara was sure that *before*, she'd known what those words had meant but *now*, they made no sense.

At other times, when the darkness became still, she had a feeling there were terrible creatures everywhere, preparing to chase her, tear her clothes, touch her. Hurt her.

Sometimes, the darkness was just an empty void and there was nothing. That was actually scarier than being hunted by the monsters.

Clara fought hard to stay away from that darkness, trying to focus on any sounds she could hear, along with any other sensations that didn't cause pain or fear. She was desperately trying to find her body, a bag of bones and muscles burning in agonizing pain. Wouldn't that soothing nothingness be better?

No.

She needed to keep trying, to keep fighting. Because whoever that woman talking to her was, it wasn't her voice Clara needed to hear.

When she finally did find her body, the pain was overwhelming. But giving up was not an option. Nothing in her body seemed to be listening to her. Her eyes wouldn't open, her mouth wouldn't make a sound, not even her stupid fingers would move.

Clara waited. Time was strangely non-existent in this place, it might have been minutes, it might have been hours. It might have even been days? But eventually, her fingers twitched, curling and straightening, as if searching for something.

Her hand was empty and that was not a good thing. There was supposed to be something in it, something important she was supposed to be holding. Clara tried to tell that to the voices that surrounded her, there were more of them now, but her own voice was still missing. But it seemed that they understood her anyway because the next thing she knew, her fingers touched the smooth surface of a very familiar shape. She grabbed it with all her strength, holding on to it like a lifeline.

From that point, it was easy. Whenever the darkness or the monsters came lurking, Clara gripped the object in her hand tighter. It was the one fixed point she could anchor herself to when the void surrounded her sore body.

Finally, after an unidentifiable measure of time, her eyelids obeyed her commands and slid open just a little. The room was dimly-lit, the orange flickering light coming from somewhere on her right suggested a candle. The ceiling looked somewhat familiar. She'd definitely been in this place before.

There was a steady yet regular noise coming from beside her and, using all the strength she could muster, Clara managed to turn her head to see what it was. She grinned, albeit stiffly, at seeing the woman asleep in a chair in what must have been a very uncomfortable position. The queen was going to be very sore in the morning.

The memories of what had happened were steadily coming back to Clara, perhaps at a greater rate than she would have preferred. The battle, the fighting, arrow after arrow. It was ironic. She was worried she'd never be able to shoot a person and now there were how many? Forty? Fifty dead people on her conscience? She'd lost track at the end.

Karina seemed unharmed, which was odd. Clara clearly remembered the bad guys winning, the queen on her knees, covered in blood, surrounded by enemies. That was before everything went black. What could have possibly happened to turn that situation around? Clara pondered over it, closing her eyes for a moment.

When she woke up again, the room was filled with sunlight and somebody was touching her. There were fingers between her legs, all the way up on her inner thigh, and whatever that person was doing to her was sending waves of sharp pain throughout her body.

Clara instinctively tightened the grip on the bow handle in her hand, testing out the muscles all over her arm. It seemed like they were willing to obey her commands.

In one quick motion, she jerked her arm up and over her body, swinging the bow over the place where she guessed the stranger touching her would be. A short cry of pain told her she didn't miss. But now what?

"*PASHIR*!" A familiar voice shouted. "I'm seriously done treating this fucking family! Why the hell did you give her a weapon?"

A chuckle sounded from the door. "She looked like she needed it. Clara?" Karina's voice was closer now and Clara felt a soft hand touching her shoulder. "It's alright, you are safe. Kadri was just checking on your stitches."

Clara tried to say something but her throat and mouth were so dry it came out as a hoarse groan. Strong hands gently lifted her head and a cup with water touched her lips. "Just take it slow." Kadri still sounded a little irritated and Clara couldn't exactly blame him.

"S-sorry," she managed to whisper after taking a few small sips.

Squinting in the daylight, Clara managed to open her eyes enough to see Karina rolling her eyes. "He's absolutely fine."

"I'm bleeding!"

"Suck it up, it's just a scratch," Karina snapped at him before turning back to Clara. "You have nothing to be sorry for." Her voice was shaky as if she was barely holding back tears.

Kadri scoffed. "Right, I'm supposed to be glad she didn't bite me too, right?"

Bite him? That reminded her... "Nicolas?"

"He's alive." Kadri shook his head in disbelief. "Seriously, are you sure you two are even human? You're both fucking immortal, simply refusing to die."

Clara ignored his quiet grumbling, closing her eyes as a wave of relief washed over her. Her brother was alive. Somehow. "How...long?"

"The battle was eight days ago," Karina sighed.

Eight days? Did she seriously just say eight days? Clara knew she'd lost track of time but she never would have guessed it was for that long. How was she still alive after such a long time? Don't you need to drink and eat?

Now that she thought about it, she did feel very thirsty and even a bit hungry. "We were beginning to worry you wouldn't wake up at all, you lost so much blood..." A couple of tears rolled down Karina's cheeks and she sniffled. "I'm so sorry, Clara. It's all my fault, I got you into this situation, you nearly died because of me, I-"

"S-stop," Clara interrupted her. "I chose to...be here. I don't want to hear...any more apologies. Tell me what happened. How did we survive?"

Karina sniffled again but told Clara everything about the battle, Gishri's death, and Hayden's timely arrival. The last part made Clara roll her eyes internally. Like seriously, couldn't he have arrived an hour earlier? So many lives could have been spared. Still, it was a miracle that anyone survived at all. Including Clara.

She was forced to stay in bed for the next few days but at least they gave her proper food. At first, it was just a bowl of soup, Karina stayed by her side and carefully spoon-fed her. Even though it was just a clear broth, it was the best food Clara had ever eaten.

Four days after Clara had woken up, Kadri finally took the stitches out of her leg. It was definitely not an experience she would want to relive again.

Clara insisted on going to see her brother and the others who'd survived the battle. Seeing that there was no way to convince her to stay still for any longer, Karina summoned one of the men standing guard in front of the door. It was Larkin, eyeing Clara with great respect, as he scooped her into his arms and carried her over to the infirmary before gently setting her down on an empty bed.

Nicolas was awake, looking much better than Clara felt, which was unfair. Wasn't he the one who had a huge hole in his stomach while she'd only got a cut on her leg?

"Clara!" He winced upon getting up but moved closer to carefully hug her. "I'm so glad to see you. I'm so sorry. I should have been there protecting you but-"

Why did everyone keep apologizing to her? "You kept the queen alive, that's more important. She was the one who saved all of us in the end." Kadri told her in vivid colors how Karina scared the enemies off by waving the severed head of their leader in front of their faces. Clara wished she'd been conscious to see that.

"Yeah, but you are my sister. And you saved my sorry ass several times during the battle, I remember that well." His eyebrows rose up in astonishment as he recalled the memories. "Those arrows flying from above just when I needed help... You and Enzio were like our fucking guardian angels. Remind me to never get on your bad side," he smirked.

"You'd better not," Clara chuckled, relieved to see him well and in such a good mood.

Enzio was grumpy but it was probably because since both his legs were broken, he couldn't move at all. Tears fell from Clara's eyes upon seeing him alive. "I can't believe you survived, old man," she sniffled, trying to mask her emotions with a grin.

"Clara," he gave her a sad smile, "I'm so sorry, I tried to keep them away from you but-"

Gods, him too? "Stop. Seriously, I don't need apologies. You do owe me that bottle though."

"Oh, really?" The archer squinted at her with suspicion. "How can you be so sure?"

"I shot Gishri." A smug smile twisted Clara's lips. "That has to count like a hundred points."

"No way! Plus, you missed."

"Oh no, I didn't!" Clara was fairly certain about that. "Karina said he was bleeding."

Enzio rolled his eyes. "You scratched his ear, that doesn't count as a hit."

"Well, excuse me for not having the most accurate aim while bleeding like a slaughtered pig!" Even though it made her ribcage hurt like hell, Clara chuckled. "I didn't see you crawling over to shoot him yourself," she teased before sitting down on his bed, carefully lying down next to him.

He hesitated only for a moment before putting his arm around her shoulders. "I'm glad you are alive, girl," he whispered. "I don't think I could live with myself if I had to add you to my conscience."

The way he acted with her gave Clara an intense feeling of safety. He was so protective, not like a man trying to impress a woman he loves but rather as a parent trying to protect his child. A child that he was proud of. "I was so sure you were dead," she sniffled. "But you were right about one thing. It did make me angry enough to kill those two bastards. I just wasn't fast enough."

"Clara," he sighed, shaking his head, "you aren't a soldier. Nobody expected you to fight off two armed men and survive. You surprised us all. You, and the queen. I mean, the men sneered at you two for being around before but now... You know what the men call her?" he whispered. "The Blood Queen." A soft chuckle escaped him. "Not very original, I know. But they respect her now. You as well."

Oh, Karina was going to hate that, Clara was quite certain. But perhaps it was going to help her with being respected around the palace and at Hayden's council meetings.

Clara was still so tired and soon she realized she was slowly dozing off, cuddled up to Enzio. "Sorry," she mumbled, "you must be in pain." Broken bones probably hurt like hell.

"Nah. The combination of our medicine and whatever that Ruthian healer gave me is quite something. It makes me sleepy but..." he yawned, "the pain is manageable."

"Unbelievable." An amused voice sounded from the door. Clara's eyes widened upon recognizing it and she jerked up into a seated position, wincing when her injured ribs protested against such sudden movements. "I ride across the country day and night to see my gravely injured wife, only to find her in another man's bed."

It couldn't be. "Oscar?" Clara gaped at the man standing just a few feet away from her. Was she hallucinating? Or perhaps Kadri had given her drugs as well? But the man didn't look like an apparition. He was really here, having come all the way from Ebris to see her.

With absolute horror, Clara realized that her husband just found her cuddled up to another man which usually only had one explanation. "Oscar, I-" she started, jumping out of the bed, completely forgetting about her injured leg which refused to carry her weight. As she was stumbling to the ground, Oscar leaped forward and caught her, carefully pulling her up into his arms. "I...I swear it's not what it looks like, I-"

"It's alright, Clara." The smile on his face was genuine. "I was just joking, sorry about that." He set her down on an empty bed, sitting next to her, nervously touching her hand. "You look better than I expected based on Karina's letter."

Karina had somehow forgotten to mention that she'd written to him. Clearly, she'd managed to convince him Clara was near death.

"You should have seen her a few days ago," Enzio noted quietly. "She was unconscious for a whole week. I've seen corpses that had more color than she did." How did he know? He smirked at her inquisitive look. "I bribed a few of the men to carry me over to your room for a few minutes. I needed to be sure you were still alive. And I do apologize, my lord," he turned to Oscar, looking somewhat startled, "I swear I did not touch your wife in any...inappropriate manner."

Fortunately, Oscar just waved his hand, his smile never faltering. "I know. You are Enzio, right? I'm glad she's had such good friends around here." Clara gratefully pressed on his hand. Touching him was just as perfect as she remembered, if not better. The corners of Oscar's mouth rose even higher. "By the way, congratulations. You have a grandson."

Enzio stared at him in shock and another soldier lying on a bed at the other side of the room cheered loudly. "Look at that! You are officially an old man!" he laughed. "Have you seen the child, my lord? I bet he is as ugly as this old twat."

"Hey!" Oscar playfully frowned in his direction. "Don't talk like that about my godson!"

Clara and Enzio spoke at the same time. "Your what?"

"Your son-in-law seems to like me," Oscar shrugged. "And your daughter didn't protest. Now, if you will excuse me, I haven't seen my wife in a month." With a nervous smile, he turned back to Clara, leaning down to carefully scoop her up into his arms.

Still too shocked to protest, Clara winced in pain when his hand pressed against her sore rib cage. "It's alright," she said quickly, seeing him open his mouth to apologize. "The ribs weren't even broken, just cracked. I'll be fine." The truth was it hurt like hell but she didn't want him to put her down, afraid that if he stopped touching her, he would vanish into thin air, proving that she was just hallucinating him being here.

"Gods," Oscar shook his head, carrying her out of the infirmary. "You do know I was just joking about you missing arms and legs? Now, where is this room of yours?"

Chapter 56

O scar set Clara down on her own bed before lying down next to her, propped up on one elbow so he could watch her face.

What should she say? Clara hadn't even thought about it yet, believing she would have enough time to figure it out on their way back to the capital. But he was here now, smiling at her, his hand caressing her face and hair.

He looked a little different to how she remembered. There were dark shadows below his eyes and a short beard had sprouted on his chin, which absolutely fascinated her, probably because she had only seen him clean shaven before. Her hand rose up to touch his face, sliding her fingers over the rough bristles.

"I know," he smiled, "I look like shit. I did not actually ride day and night but it felt quite close to it. Still, it took me a week to get here, and I feel so damn sore I'd rather die than go near a damned horse again. How you managed to get here in just five days is beyond me."

"You look amazing," Clara whispered, not sure what to do with all the happiness that started spreading in her chest. Her heart wanted to start laughing out loud but her bruised body strongly disagreed. "Maybe a bit more...hmm...dangerous? But still amazing." She took a deep breath, enjoying that scent she had missed so much.

Oscar quirked an eyebrow. "Dangerous? I better shave and get cleaned up then. One dangerous person per marriage is more than enough." His fingers hovered over her cheek. He was being gentle, as if terrified that the slightest touch would somehow hurt her. "From what I've heard, I really need to be careful about making you angry." Giving her a lopsided smile, he bent his head down to briefly peck her forehead. "I'm so proud of you."

Proud of her? That was certainly not the reaction Clara had been expecting. But he didn't seem angry with her for nearly getting herself killed. Clara opened her mouth to ask about it but closed it again without saying anything. Dissecting her emotions and the complicated relationship between them was not what she wanted to be doing right now.

Bringing her hand to his nape, she gently pulled him closer until his lips were touching hers. She hadn't realized how desperate she was to kiss him again, to taste his lips, to feel his body close to hers. Oscar didn't exactly fight her but he pulled away for a second, his fingers brushing Clara's hair away from her neck. "I don't want to cause you pain," he whispered.

"Kissing...is fine," Clara answered between gasps of air. Her chest still hurt when she breathed but she was somewhat used to it by now. And with her injured leg, there was no way they could take it any further anyway. That would probably be agonizing. But even just the feeling of his lips on her skin was spectacular.

Oscar carefully supported his weight with his hands and knees to avoid putting pressure on her bruised rib cage. The muscles of his arms trembled from the exertion. Clara realized he must have been exhausted after the long ride but it didn't stop him from hungrily attacking her mouth and her neck with countless kisses.

Her fingers untied the string holding back his hair and the dark tresses fell toward her face, tickling softly, making her chuckle. She brushed Oscar's hair to the side but groaned in pain trying to lift her head high enough to kiss his neck. Getting a deep cut, losing a ton of blood, and falling down a flight of stairs weren't exactly the greatest prerequisites for a passionate make out session.

Neither of them heard the door open. "I hope you are hun-Oh!" Karina yelped upon noticing a man on top of Clara and the way they were kissing each other. "Shit! I-Damn, I...I thought you and Oscar... Sorry, I'll go." She stopped babbling and darted toward the door.

"She and Oscar what?" Oscar asked, carefully rolling away from Clara and sitting up to look at Karina, giving her an amused smirk.

The queen froze in her tracks upon hearing the familiar voice. "Oscar?" Her brows furrowed when she looked at him, clearly not believing her own eyes. "What are you doing here?"

"What does it look like I'm doing? I'm kissing my wife." Clara still had problems catching her breath, her ribs protesting against the short gasps she was making, so she just let out a quiet 'mhm' sound and waved at Karina, causing Oscar to chuckle. "What are you doing here?" he asked.

"I...uh..." Karina seemed to be way more taken aback by Oscar's presence here than Clara. "Food. I brought food." She pointed at a bowl of stew and a few pieces of bread. "I...will bring you something as well." Why was she in such a hurry to leave the room?

Oscar's features hardened. "I think I'll manage to do that myself. But you and I clearly need to have a very serious conversation about what it means to keep someone safe." His voice was so cold Clara barely even recognized it. Was he angry with Karina for putting Clara in danger?

"Right," Karina nodded, looking like she was barely holding back tears, and quickly slipped out of the room before Oscar could say anything more.

"Please, don't do that," Clara pulled on her husband's hand to get his attention. "None of this was her fault. No," she added decisively upon seeing him open his mouth to protest, "it wasn't. Karina is already torturing herself over all the men that died in that stupid battle and I will not let you make it even worse." And he could. Oscar had known Karina all her life, he would know just what to say to hurt her. Clara simply couldn't allow that, no matter how weird and inappropriate it felt to give an order to her husband. "You will not be mean to her about this, Oscar."

He blinked in surprise, watching her with his head tilted to the side. Damn, had she gone too far? The old Clara would have never said something like that. What if he was going to hate her now? "Feisty and dangerous," he smirked, his expression softening as he looked at her. "I really need to be careful around you now."

His tone didn't exactly give away what he was thinking. Clara swallowed roughly, not sure whether she should start apologizing or not. The old Clara would have already apologized by now. But, to hell with it, she hadn't done anything wrong.

"I'm sorry, I didn't mean to be so stern," she went for a compromise. "It's just... Karina is not in a good place. She needs support, not reproach. I chose to be here, knowing the risks. So please, don't hold whatever happened to me against her."

Oscar let out an exasperated sigh but there were hints of mischief playing in his eyes. "I knew your self-confidence was just hiding somewhere deep inside of here," he gently tapped the center of her chest, "and only needed support to come out." Falling down on the bed next to Clara, he pretended to look disappointed. "Does that mean I'm going to be one of those poor henpecked husbands now and you will boss me around all the time?"

Clara couldn't help herself but burst into laughter over the idea, even though it hurt like hell. "Yep," she tried to sound serious but it was damn hard, "and every time you try to disobey me, I will put an arrow in your butt." Her finger poked the side of his thigh to indicate the exact spot, making him chuckle.

How was this so easy? A month ago, Clara would be horrified to even think about those words, she would never let them leave her mouth. Was it the near-death experience that had convinced her there were very few things in life that truly mattered and that she should stop worrying about everything so much?

Or perhaps those few letters they'd exchanged. All of those hard truths and sweet words that finally convinced her she could fully trust him? Plus, he'd come for her, clearly worried about her and even rode across half the country just to see her. What more proof of his love did she need?

"Oscar?" she whispered, groaning in pain as she tried to roll on her side to see his face. "I think I am in love with you." Her confession was followed by silence and she couldn't keep looking into his eyes, suddenly afraid of what she would see in them.

Oscar's finger traced the outline of her cheek down under her chin, softly pushing against it until she looked back up at him. His smile was so warm it made Clara's heart swell. "That is very good to hear," he replied quietly, "because I'm fairly certain I love you too." How could just a few simple words make her heart flutter so hard it threatened to jump out of her chest?

The kiss he gave her was slow and reverent, there was no desperate need in it this time, just an honest declaration of love. When Clara grimaced in pain, Oscar pulled away, letting her roll onto her back to find a more comfortable position. "I really wish I could take that pain away for you," he sighed, caressing her face.

"It's not so bad," Clara tried to shrug nonchalantly and winced again. "It only hurts when I move. Or breathe. It's not like I need to do either of those things," she grinned, attempting to lighten his mood.

It seemed to work. Chuckling, Oscar got up and reached for the food Karina had brought in earlier. "You really are unbelievable." He helped her eat the whole bowl, visibly satisfied with her appetite. "How about you get some rest?" he asked, noticing her yawn a couple of times.

Clara had really tried to hide it but she was exhausted. Ever since waking up earlier in the week, she'd needed so much sleep it was ridiculous. Hadn't she just spent over a week doing nothing but lying in bed unconscious? She should have been well-rested and not require a nap every hour or two. "I'm afraid that if I close my eyes and then open them again, this will all be just a dream," she confessed, feeling silly.

"I promise to be here when you wake up," Oscar gave her a warm smile and kissed her forehead. "I'll just go talk to Karina. Nicely, don't worry," he added upon seeing her eyes narrow, "then I'll get some food and crawl right back into bed. I'm exhausted too."

He glanced back at her before walking out of the door. "I better not find another man in this bed when I return," he grinned and left before Clara could say anything in her defense. Even though she was quite certain he was just teasing her, she still should stop cuddling up to strangers from now on.

Chapter 57

C lara woke up feeling warm, which wasn't something she was used to feeling during the past month. Usually, no matter how many layers of clothes and blankets she piled on herself, she would still end up with freezing cold feet. But now she had a personal heater in her bed again and her whole world was warm and cozy.

Said heater was still asleep, occasionally wriggling to find a better position, in constant danger of falling out of the narrow bed which clearly wasn't designed to be shared by two people. It would be better if he cuddled up closer to Clara and held her but he was probably too scared of reigniting the pain from her injuries. She watched him sleep, listening to his steady breathing, still unable to believe he was really here. That he loved her.

Her own husband had admitted he was in love with her. Probably not a great accomplishment for normal people but for a couple that met the way they did and had been through so many obstacles, it was a miracle.

It was such a shame her body was so sore that all they could do in bed was sleep next to each other. Clara was way past being afraid of finally having sex with Oscar. Now she was curious about it. But beaten as she was, there was no way she would enjoy it. Even the idea of her muscles convulsing if she managed to reach the peak made her wince.

However, Oscar was not injured. And, judging by how he'd started to stir restlessly, he was not going to sleep much longer anyway. Karina had given Clara some pointers, certainly more accurate and useful information than Sophia Redwood would ever offer. The question was, whether Clara was brave enough to follow through on the instructions. She had faced down an entire army of barbarians and survived, pleasuring her own husband shouldn't be such an issue, should it?

She rolled on her side, putting a pillow under her chest to make it a little less painful. Her hand snuck under the blanket, slowly sliding up Oscar's thigh until she reached his cock. To her surprise, it was already half erect, and Clara wondered whether it was normal or if he was dreaming about something that had caused it to rise. Maybe he was dreaming about some of the countless women he had been with before? No, she didn't want to think about that now.

Gently stroking his manhood through the breeches, Clara carefully watched Oscar's face. He didn't wake up but there was a smile curling his lips as he moaned quietly. Feeling his cock getting harder, Clara tried to sneak her hand under his pants, but the moment she touched his skin, he jerked awake and roughly grabbed her wrist.

He frowned, looking around in confusion that melted when his eyes found her face. "Uh...Clara?"

"Oscar?" she grinned, wriggling her hand out of his grip and sliding her fingers over the skin on his abdomen.

His breath was ragged and he tilted his head back, letting out a quiet groan. "What are you doing?" he asked and Clara hesitated. Was she doing it wrong? Or maybe he didn't want her anymore? She was gone for a month, that was a long time for him to spend alone.

"Do you want me to s-"

"No," he replied before she could even finish the question, a blissful smile taking over his expression. "I most certainly don't want you to stop. I just meant...you don't have to do this if you don't want to."

Of course she didn't have to do it. "I know. I want to."

"Gods." When she finally touched his cock, hesitantly running her fingers along the shaft, he inhaled sharply. "Am I still asleep?" His brows furrowed and he blinked a couple of times. "Because this does seem like a dream."

Clara pinched his thigh, chuckling when he yelped in pain. "You aren't asleep." She gripped his shaft as tightly as she dared, which wasn't very much, and started slowly moving up and down, enjoying the almost tortured look on his face. "I'm not really sure..." Oscar's hand covered hers, made her fingers squeeze him harder, and guided her to move along the whole length before letting go of her again. Yes, those were instructions Clara could work with.

Still surprised by how hot his manhood felt compared to the rest of his body, Clara kept moving her hand up and down, captivated by the way Oscar was biting on his lower lip to stop himself from moaning. When she started to move faster he couldn't contain it anymore, tilting his head back with a loud groan. Clara leaned forward to kiss the exposed skin on his neck, occasionally using her teeth to gently nibble.

She was almost surprised when he suddenly froze and arched his back, his cock in her hand pulsating. Hot, sticky wetness covered her hand and soaked the front of his breeches.

Oops. Clara hadn't thought that part through. But this was a military encampment, surely there would be some spare pants for him to borrow. She chased the strange thoughts away, focusing on his ragged breathing and ecstatic expression.

Oscar's eyes were shut tight as he tried to regain control. Once his body relaxed and his eyes were opened, he raised a hand to caress Clara's cheek. "Alright," he breathed out, gazing at her, "if I had known that you would greet me like this, I would have come here a long time ago."

"I don't think I would have. Not before." The old Clara would have probably been too scared to even think about touching Oscar like this. Which was ridiculous, considering how simple it was and how much he'd enjoyed it. And Clara wanted to see him happy.

"So, this is the new version of you? Born in battle, blood and pain?" Oscar sounded like he was teasing her but there was a hint of sadness behind his words. Clara suddenly felt an echo of her previous worries and insecurities. What if he didn't like her anymore? Wouldn't a perpetually frightened girl who obeyed his every command make for a better wife?

Oscar noticed the sudden change in her expression, his thumb sliding over her cheek. "Don't do that. I love this new Clara as much as I loved the old one, if not more. It's still you. You haven't changed that much, you know?"

Clara's brows formed a small wrinkle as they furrowed. Haven't changed? She felt like a completely different person now.

"This strength has always been inside of you," Oscar explained. "I could see it from that very first night we spent together and I hoped that if I gave you the opportunity, you would see it as well." A sad chuckle escaped him. "I mean, this," he waved over the bandage on her leg, "is certainly not what I'd had in mind, but I'm happy for you. I just hope you still want me because I haven't changed. I think I've already used up my share of life-changing epiphanies."

"You were already perfect to begin with," Clara objected, blushing. She wasn't used to giving or receiving such compliments. "You are the reason I fought against the darkness. When they brought me here, there was nothing around me, I was lost. That," she pointed to her bow placed on a trunk in the corner of the room, "helped me find a way out. Even back in that battle, I..." Her memories were all scrambled, especially after she'd been stabbed and fell down the stairs, but she did remember one thing. "I kept fighting because I'd promised to come back to you."

There were tears in Oscar's eyes. Clara could see them clearly, no matter how much he tried to blink them away. His mouth opened but his words were cut off by the door opening and a voice shouting, "You better not be having sex right now! Because I'm seriously not stitching that leg of yours again!"

"By the gods," Oscar gritted his teeth, pulling the blanket closer to him to cover his stained pants, "does nobody in this fucking place know how to knock?"

Clara failed to hold back a chuckle. "It wasn't exactly necessary until you got here. Don't worry, Kadri," she turned to the frowning healer, "I'm on bedrest, just like you ordered. My husband just came here to support me."

"Husband," Kadri snickered, rolling his eyes. "He should have locked you up at home. You and that brother of yours are nothing but trouble."

Oscar laughed as well. "If only it was that simple. Is the king back yet?"

"No idea, I'm not his babysitter," the healer snapped at him. "Move, husband, I need to check her leg."

Oscar hesitated, no doubt remembering the stain on his breeches, and Clara rushed in to rescue him. It was her fault anyway. "Could you please give us a few minutes first, Kadri?" She gave him her best and brightest smile. "I promise next time I'm unconscious, I won't try to kill you."

"Next time you or your damned brother are unconscious, I won't come anywhere near you until you are tied to the fucking bed. I'll stop by this afternoon. Try not to die in the meantime." Grumbling words Clara didn't understand, the healer left the room and closed the door behind him.

"Lovely friends you have here," Oscar said, both his eyebrows high up on his forehead. Despite his serious tone, Clara could tell he was having trouble holding back a laugh and when she giggled quietly, he was quick to join her.

Chapter 58

A few hours later they were sitting up on the bed, both dressed properly this time. Oscar was leaning against the headboard with Clara carefully cuddled up to him, her head resting against his shoulder. It was the most comfortable she had been in weeks. They had spent the time talking about what had happened while they were away from each other, catching up on the small, unimportant things that didn't make it into any of the letters that they'd exchanged using Hayden's couriers.

A quiet knock at the door made them look at each other and chuckle again. "They learn fast," Oscar whispered into Clara's ear before calling out for whoever it was to come in.

Karina peeked in nervously, clearly not wanting to interrupt another heated moment, satisfied upon seeing them in a decent position. The king followed her into the room, closing the door behind them.

"Hayden," Oscar bowed his head in respect, "I didn't know you were back, I would have come to talk to you."

Waving his hand dismissively, Hayden lowered himself into one of the chairs, pulling Karina onto his lap. "I just got back. I have to say I'm surprised to see you here."

"Why?" Oscar replied defensively. "Wouldn't you have come to see your wife if she'd been gravely injured and nearly died?"

The king frowned but nodded. "You had a job to do. But yes, I would have and I understand. You can stay here and head back with us. I've made peace with the remaining Ruthian tribes, so there's nothing keeping us here anymore."

"They all agreed?" Clara asked, surprised it went so fast.

"Yes. With Gishri dead, there was nobody to lead them and *Seftha* Ulaia has been very helpful in negotiating peace. Plus," he smirked at Karina, "they were all frightened that the Blood Queen was going to sneak into their villages and cut their heads off for some mysterious head collection she is apparently making."

Karina groaned, hiding her face in her hands. "Seriously, who keeps spreading these bullshit rumors? Unbelievable, you behead one man and it sticks with you for the rest of your life?"

"Welcome to my world," Hayden laughed and Clara joined him.

Even Oscar's shoulders twitched as he barely suppressed a laugh. "Lovely. The Burning Fury and the Blood Queen. It's great that we have such an amazing royal couple to rule over our wonderful country. And, just so you know, my dear king, I've actually made great progress with the job you've given me." He looked around the room and shrugged before continuing. "I've been meaning to come and talk to you since it wasn't something I could trust a messenger with, but I guess we can discuss it now. Our beautiful and intelligent wives know all about it anyway."

Hayden nodded. Clara was glad that Oscar wanted her to be included, having to remind herself that even though they had averted the danger from the Ruthian tribes for now, a much greater enemy still lurked in the shadows. The great empire of Cchen-Lian.

"Well," Oscar started, "the people who gave Clara the potion have approached me, clearly convinced that since I hate you so much, I will be happy to help them take you down. I agreed, naturally." Oscar grinned smugly.

The king rolled his eyes. "Ah, so you've been betraying me ever since I left the city, wonderful. What did they offer you that I couldn't?" Even though it sounded like he was just joking, Clara couldn't help but shudder. It was never a good thing when the king started throwing words like treason around.

"The usual," Oscar shrugged but his voice was a little strained. "Money, power, titles. Oh, and I asked for Karina and they agreed."

"Excuse me?!" Karina cried out. "You did what?!"

Clara felt Oscar wriggle nervously as he glanced at Hayden, fully expecting the king to go furious. To be honest, Clara herself was taken aback by her husband's words too, trying really hard not to let the feeling of betrayal overwhelm her. There must have been some logical reason for it, right? He said he loved her. He couldn't exactly expect to have them both.

Hayden scoffed and shook his head. "You truly are one sleazy bastard. A normal person would never even think of that. But," he sighed, caressing Karina's hair, "I get where you were headed with it and even though it's disgusting, it was a smart move."

"What the fuck are you two talking about?" Karina jumped up, clenching her fists, striding toward the bed. "I'm not some item to be bartered!"

"Relax," Oscar soothed, gently stroking Clara's arm upon noticing her sudden stiffness. "Honestly, I was expecting Hayden to be the one to punch me and you to be the reasonable one who was going to understand why I did it, not the other way around," he smirked. "I said it because they expected me to be a sleazy bastard, as our beloved king so accurately described. And also, because it will hopefully mean they are going to keep you alive in case something goes horribly wrong. You know, since you are my reward for helping them, and I wouldn't exactly appreciate them delivering a dead body to me instead of a living queen."

It probably made sense but it didn't mean Clara liked it. However, since there wasn't anything she could do against it, she decided to trust that

Oscar knew what he was doing. Especially since the king seemed to be all right with such a plan.

"And it worked," Oscar continued with a satisfied smile, "they trust me. I still haven't been able to find out who is behind it all but I now possess a huge pile of evidence proving the lord chancellor has been betraying you for years."

Hayden's eyes darkened. "That's bullshit," he growled, "Egmont would never betray me."

"He didn't," Oscar replied. "They gave the 'proof' to me and I'm supposed to convince you to get rid of him. Or at least 'plant the seed of doubt into your mind'. When you get back to the palace, someone will probably approach you and will try to set you against Egmont even further. By the way, you should have started exhibiting the signs of your madness by now. How come you haven't done anything crazy yet? Or...crazier than usual."

It was quiet for a moment. Hayden smirked and ran his fingers through his hair. "Like what?" He suddenly sounded hostile, maybe even a little desperate. "Should I start executing my men for the slightest transgressions? They would never respect me again. I don't want them to follow me only because they are frightened of me. That's the quickest way to mass desertions at the slightest sign of trouble.

"Or should I have had Karina flogged when she'd disobeyed my orders? I mean, I can't say that I haven't actually considered it but...I just can't do this." There definitely was desperation in his voice now and Clara felt inappropriate to be listening to his quiet confession. "I thought I could do it, that I didn't care, but...I don't want people to see me as an even bigger monster than they already do. I'm sorry. I know it was a good plan, but I just can't go through with it."

Clara pressed on Oscar's hand to make him think twice about what he was going to say. The king was obviously emotional now, vulnerable even. No doubt, he would not respond well to whatever snappy or demeaning remark Oscar might say.

Fortunately, Karina quickly walked over to her husband, gently caressing his cheek and kissing him. "It's alright. This is why I disagreed with it from the start, knowing how you hate all that Burning Fury bullshit. We can come up with another plan."

"Hmm." Oscar sounded a little frustrated but he managed to control himself. "Let's set that aside for now. Before we return to Ebris, we can come up with some ideas that wouldn't be so...drastic." Clara was glad he didn't push it, even though it was technically his plan.

"We might have another problem, though," Oscar continued. "I'm not exactly sure what it is yet, but there is something big going on in the city. And if my instincts are correct, and they usually are, a lot of people are going to get hurt."

Clara shivered, knowing he wouldn't say it if there was a chance he could be wrong. "Does it have something to do with the unknown player?" she asked.

"I think so," Oscar nodded in response. "I think it's all connected. There have been large shipments of barrels into Ebris during the last few weeks. The papers were fake, very good and very expensive fakes, which got my attention. I have had my people check what's inside, thinking it might be weapons or something like that. But, to my surprise, the barrels were filled with dust."

Karina raised an eyebrow. "That sounds like important information. Thank you for sharing that with us, Lord Huxley."

Hayden didn't respond but his face actually lost some color. "Dust?" His voice didn't sound sarcastic like Karina's. No, he sounded worried and that scared Clara more than anything.

"You know what it is?" Oscar frowned at the king who just shook his head and motioned him to continue talking. "You do know something! But fine, I'll go first. This dust explodes when set on fire."

"Explodes?" Clara had a hard time believing such a thing was even possible.

"Yes, explodes. Bright light, loud bang. A general destruction of everything in the immediate vicinity. Care to chime in, Hayden?"

For the longest time, it seemed like the king wasn't going to answer. When he finally did speak, his voice was solemn. "I'd hoped it was a lie.

It was supposed to be some sort of new invention, originally made for breaking rocks while building roads or mining or something like that. But, of course, the possibilities of using it in warfare were endless.

"At least that's what the spies reported, they never managed to bring a sample back home to study it. It was supposedly created by the alchemists on the western continent. In Cchen-Lian. They called it the black powder."

"It's not exactly black." Oscar reached for his jacket and pulled a small pouch out of it, tossing it over to the king.

Clara had to suppress a yelp. If it was so damn dangerous, why the hell was he just throwing it around?

"Relax, it seems quite stable unless it comes into contact with fire," he comforted her and Karina, who had the same startled look as Clara. "The thing is, the explosion itself wouldn't kill many people. It would probably do some damage to buildings if used well, but not many casualties. Not on its own at least."

"You think they want to kill people with it? Why would they do that?" Hayden didn't sound entirely convinced.

Surprisingly, it was Karina who answered. "Because they aren't going to invade us. They can't." Both men and Clara looked at her in disbelief. Wasn't that the main premise the whole time? That Hayden goes crazy and the armies of the empire use it to easily invade and take over Orellia. Karina sighed. "Look, this is still speculation but...you remember my research?"

"Yes, that mess in your parlor is very hard to forget," Hayden grinned, briefly kissing her to let her know it was just a joke.

"That mess," she playfully poked his shoulder, "were notes I took from accounting books of various companies operating in Xi-huan. Not only is it the capital of the empire and the biggest city in the world, but it's also the busiest port in the world. Twenty-five percent of trade worldwide goes through one place. Or at least, it used to."

Clara took comfort from seeing that Oscar and Hayden looked just as confused as she felt. "What does trade have to do with invasion?" Perhaps it was a stupid question but it made no sense to her.

"Everything. Trade means money. You can't have a functioning economy without trade and you can't have a massive army without a functioning economy. Or at least, not for long. Every time I asked anyone, I always got the same answer.

"'They have a bigger army, they would win a war.' But has anyone actually checked whether that was true anymore? Because their economy is crumbling. I bet there's a lot of friction between the individual kingdoms within the empire, I mean, the shipments of wood dropped to less than ten percent and-"

"Wood?" Hayden interrupted her. "I'm sorry, I don't see how information about shipments of wood coming from a few old accounting books is relevant to our situation."

Karina jumped off his lap, standing up so she could get a better look at him and Oscar and Clara. "I know it sounds stupid. But you have to look at the background. The main supplier of wood for the entire empire is the small kingdom of Ix-ino. It's like...their tribute to the empire, Emperor Odi takes a huge part of their yearly production and sells it, using that money to fuel the economy. But the sales have dropped drastically, which means-"

"They stopped paying their tribute?" Clara raised an eyebrow, amazed at how Karina could have figured something like that from some numbers in accounting books.

"Exactly! This is just one dumb example. There's a lot more, all pointing to one thing. Odi is losing his grip, the empire is becoming unstable. Still a worthy opponent, but not nearly as dangerous as we think. That's why they bothered with all the years of whispering into people's ears, setting them against Hayden, making sure he was too busy to notice their problems, instead of simply attacking Orellia straight away," Karina finished, nervously awaiting Hayden's reaction.

He stared at her, unable to say a word. "I... You found all that out from accounting books?" He sounded absolutely astonished.

"It's just a theory," Karina blushed under his intense stare, "but I do believe there is some merit to it. How do you think Levanta was so rich when we were so tiny? Vantia is a huge trading hub. And it wasn't your huge army camped at our borders that convinced the people that the threat of invasion was real. It was when the merchants rushed to empty their warehouses and move their trade elsewhere, not wanting to get caught up by all the plundering and destruction you were planning to do. The profits dropped. Numbers don't lie, Hayden."

"I did not actually plan to burn Levanta down. It was just useful to make people think I did," he noted before turning back to Oscar. "If they aren't planning an invasion, then what exactly are they trying to do?"

"I have no idea." It seemed to bug Oscar greatly. Not the fact that their country and their lives were in danger, but the fact that there was something he didn't know and was forced to admit it. "I would say they will try to use the 'insane' king to destabilize the country, use the exploding powder to create some sort of threat that you will be unable to deal with, which will both undermine your authority with your people and drive you even crazier.

"I will try to get closer to them and find out exactly what they are planning and who is behind it. But I need you to work with me on this. Can you send Egmont on a forced vacation or something? That would help me to gain their trust."

Hayden frowned. "So you are asking me to put the fate of the entire kingdom solely in your hands? To trust you indiscriminately, even though I can't really be sure you aren't lying to me right now?"

"I'm not lying to you, Hayden," Oscar replied calmly, looking the king straight into the eyes. "And I will not betray you. I've made my choice," he smiled at Clara before turning back to Hayden, "and I'm ready to live by that decision. Now, do I need to get on my fucking knee in front of you to swear fealty or will you just take my word for it?"

It was quiet as they stared at each other before the king sighed and shook his head. "As much as I'd enjoy seeing you on your knees, I think I'll just take your word for it and hope for the best. Damn, I should have just had you executed, that way I wouldn't have to deal with you at all now."

"Aww, don't say that," Oscar chuckled. "You'd miss me."

Chapter 59

T he journey back to the capital took more than three weeks and to Clara, it felt like an eternity. Despite her leg getting better every day, there was still no way she could spend a day in a saddle, which meant she ended up on one of the wagons transporting the wounded soldiers. Hanging around with Nicolas and Enzio was fun but knowing that she could have been spending all that time alone with Oscar instead was frustrating.

Most days, he rode beside the wagon, joining in on their conversations. Apparently, his charms didn't just work on women. The men quickly started to like having him around as well. Clara wasn't really surprised. Her husband was so funny and easy to talk to that it basically made him irresistible.

As a result, she now had to listen to Nicolas retelling stories from their childhood, making Clara look like a whiny little girl that constantly followed her big brothers everywhere and annoyed the hell out of them. Clara wondered whose side Nicolas was going to pick when they all got back home and Sebastian started feeding him all the hateful talk about Oscar.

At least she got to spend the evenings and nights just with Oscar, in a proper large tent this time.

The atmosphere around the fires was different from their journey north. Despite the king achieving peace without any more great losses, most of the groups had people missing or at least injured. It was most visible on the group of men Clara had spent so much time with. More than half of the men were missing from around that particular fire.

Enzio still couldn't stand on his broken legs.

Blaggar had lost a foot and the wound wasn't healing well. He was in the infirmary under the constant watch of the army doctors, lying in bed in feverish unconsciousness. It was unclear whether he was even going to survive.

Nolan, the dangerously handsome boy who'd kept giving Clara the brightest smiles, had died inside the tower walls along with several others.

Other men had died or been wounded in smaller skirmishes on patrols or when escorting trade caravans through the mountain passes.

It was a victory. But, even victories came at a cost.

The group gathered by the fire one afternoon. Oscar spread a sleeping mat out on the soft grass and sat down on it, letting Clara lean against him as if they were on a picnic, not in the middle of a military encampment. Nicolas and a few others were sitting around, watching low crackling flames lick at a few pieces of dry wood. Even Enzio managed to convince someone to carry him out of the infirmary to get some fresh air.

Larkin joined the group, no trace of happiness in his glum face. "Blaggar's dead," he announced dryly. He unscrewed the bottle in his hand and took a large gulp before passing it over to the man closest to him.

"Fuck," Enzio muttered. "The bastard gave up. He told me he didn't want to live as a cripple." He reached for the bottle and raised it up. "Asshole has probably annoyed everyone in hell already." A sad chuckle escaped him.

Stunned, Clara stared into the flames. When somebody passed the bottle to her, she drank, barely even noticing the burning sensation in her mouth and throat.

How did they do it? Making friends only to lose them, over and over again? Soon there would be another war, other lives lost. How did they keep going? To allow themselves to get close to someone, knowing that person could die the next month, week, day?

She got up, wincing in pain as she strained the injured leg, but knowing it would support her weight. Short walks were fine, even recommended by the doctors. The army medics certainly weren't as fun to be around as Kadri, but he stayed back with his tribe, just like Rimea. Clara missed them already.

Oscar gave her an inquisitive look when she was leaving and Clara tried to put a smile on her lips, not wanting him to worry. She just needed some space. Ironic, since they were camped at a huge forest clearing. More than enough space around.

After grabbing her bow and arrows, she slowly walked toward the treeline, trying to ignore the pain coming from her thigh. It was no longer the sharp, stinging kind of pain but rather a constant dull throbbing which she could sometimes forget. Occasionally, the men she walked by nodded at her or bowed their heads in respect toward her. It felt really strange.

The forest was quiet, a welcome change from the ever-present noises that a big commotion of people inevitably brought. Clara leaned against a huge oak tree, listening to the quiet sounds around her for a moment before smirking. "Too much noise for a rabbit, too small for a deer. I guess I'll just shoot you and then go see what you were," she joked quietly.

"That would be a shame," Oscar replied playfully, peeking from behind a tree. "Although, I'd probably deserve it. I should know better than to try and sneak up on a hunter."

"Right as always. I wasn't really hunting though. I just..." She sighed, not really sure what to say.

He caressed her cheek. "Needed to be alone? I understand. I'll go, I just wanted to make sure you were alright."

"You don't have to go, I-" A quiet thumping noise interrupted her thoughts and one corner of her mouth curled up as she reached for an arrow. Oscar frowned but wisely stayed silent and motionless, only his eyes darting around as he tried to see what it was she was about to shoot.

Clara didn't waste time explaining. She shifted her weight to be able to aim in the right direction and patiently waited until a couple of rabbits hopped out from beneath low bushes. While the first arrow was flying toward its target, Clara was already reaching for a second one, aiming at one of the rabbits that darted away. She waited for a second, wanting to make it a clean shot. And it was. Right through the tiny creature's chest.

Oscar watched her with a raised eyebrow as she slowly moved toward the dead animals, her injured leg not appreciating her walking over roots and branches on the forest floor. Just as Enzio and Rimea had taught her, she cut the rabbits' necks, attached a string to their back legs, and left them hanging head down from a low branch.

"Brutal." Oscar didn't even try to mask his amused grin.

Clara was worried that maybe he would find it disgusting but her fears melted away when he stepped closer and cupped her cheeks, tilting her head back so he could kiss her. It was a passionate kiss and Clara's body reacted. She arched her back to get closer to him, wrapping her hands around his neck to make sure he couldn't pull away.

She hissed in pain, trying to stand up on her tiptoes so Oscar let go of her to take off his jacket, spreading it out on the ground, and gently lowering Clara down onto it.

"I don't know why," he growled while kissing her neck, "but you look so fucking hot when you are killing things. How weird am I?" he chuckled. His hand slipped under Clara's shirt and she gasped at feeling him sliding his fingers over the wide strip of cloth she used as an improvised bra.

His question made her chuckle. "I don't know," she whispered, releasing Oscar's hair from the band and grabbing it to make him tilt his head to the side. "I think you are just the right amount of weird." Her teeth attacked the exposed skin on his neck as if she wanted to bite him and drink his blood like some mythical creature of the night.

Oscar groaned in pleasure and grabbed her boob, cupping it in his palm, his thumb sliding back and forth over her nipple. Such a simple movement and it almost made Clara lose her mind as it kept sending waves of pleasure throughout her body, especially to her core.

Damn that stupid leg of hers! Even now she felt the pain building up and knew that if they took it further, it would only get worse. Fortunately, her husband seemed to realize that and pulled his hand back, going back to just kissing and nibbling on her neck.

"Sorry," she mumbled in apology, "the stupid leg-"

A kiss interrupted her words. "Don't worry about it." Oscar's breath was ragged and she could feel his erection through the layers of clothes between them but he didn't sound frustrated or disappointed. "You deserve better for your first time anyway." With a sigh, he pulled away from her, rolling onto his back. "But I do have to say, this is definitely new for me," he grinned.

"Kissing a woman and not having sex with her?" Clara gave him a doubtful look. With the amount of experience he had, it was surprising that anything was still new for him.

"No, Clara," he rolled his eyes. "That actually happens quite a lot. But making out with a girl on a wet forest floor? A few feet away from blood dripping down from the carcasses of some poor animals said girl just killed? That's definitely something new. It's so...savage."

It sounded like he was barely suppressing a laugh, making Clara scowl at him. "Are you making fun of me?" she growled, climbing on top of him. "You better not play with me, my dear husband. I know how to kill and butcher a deer. And deers are bigger than politicians." It was impossible to maintain a serious tone, especially when seeing Oscar pretend to be scared.

"HELP!" he called out quietly, unable to hold back a chuckle anymore. "My incredibly hot wife is threatening to butcher me!"

Clara snarled playfully, leaning forward to bite his neck. "There's no help coming."

Her leg was already protesting and she still had to make it back to the camp, so she reluctantly got up and dusted her clothes. "By the way," she glanced back at Oscar, "When we get home, I'm going to spend a lot of time with Friska to learn about all the embarrassing stories from your childhood, since you now know everything about mine." Nicolas had made sure of it.

"Damn, I knew bringing her here would backfire on me at some point," Oscar smirked. "You know," his hand gently slid down her arm, "my brothers would probably be excited to embarrass me as well, if you...would like to meet them?" he asked shyly as if expecting her to refuse. "Once the situation here is more stable, of course, and I hopefully don't have to be a part of the conspiracy to take down the king," he laughed.

Clara smiled warmly at Oscar. "I'd love that." Truth be told, she was a little nervous about meeting his family, but it could hardly be worse than him meeting hers.

Oscar grabbed the dead rabbits, carefully holding them so that the remaining drops of blood wouldn't stain his clothes. "Let me carry the spoils to the camp so I at least look like I'm good for something in this wilderness."

Wilderness? Clara rolled her eyes. "We are like five miles away from a large town. And about fifty from Ebris. Carry them, but don't let the king see. We are technically poaching," she added, nodding seriously to see if it would scare him.

"Ah, so you are a criminal now as well?" he grinned. "What a bad influence I've had on you."

He didn't seem to be worried about getting arrested for it, which was a little disappointing. But then again, the king had already forgiven him for what technically was high treason. Minor poaching charges were inconsequential compared to that.

A criminal and a murderer, Clara should have added, thinking about all the lives she had taken during the battle. She probably should have been ashamed of it, regretted it, been haunted by guilt. The truth was, that the only thing she regretted was that she hadn't killed more of them before they'd managed to hurt her friends.

Did it make her a despicable person? Probably. Did it bother her? Just a little. She hadn't talked to Oscar about these feelings but somehow she knew he would understand, support her even. This pragmatic way of thinking was most likely something she had picked up from him anyway.

Chapter 60

O scar couldn't wait to get back home so he could finally have Clara all to himself again instead of sharing her with her brother and the other soldiers. They seemed to be quite reasonable people, for common sword-swinging idiots, but that didn't mean he would rather spend time with them than with his wife. Fortunately, it seemed that Clara felt the same way.

He loved her newfound confidence. It was much easier to be relaxed around the 'new Clara', as she called herself. Oscar didn't have to be constantly afraid of accidentally saying or doing something that would turn her into that trembling, timid little girl again. He was a little worried that 'new Clara' would realize she could do so much better than Oscar and find someone else, but she didn't. She loved him.

Several women had told him that before but it had always made his skin crawl. 'I love you' meant he'd gone too far with his bullshit talk and the relationship was getting too serious. It meant it was time to move on.

When Clara said it, he felt nothing but relief and immense happiness that she still wanted him. Yes, there would be problems to face when they returned to the palace but, for once, Oscar had decided to be optimistic. Clara was going to stay with him, as long as he didn't screw something up very badly. And he was determined to avoid that at all costs.

He had several conversations with Hayden on the way back to the capital, debating options on how to maintain the ruse with the insanity potion. It surprised Oscar to see just how much the king cared about how his people viewed him, especially the soldiers. Oscar would have never guessed that the Burning Fury was in fact a fairly normal guy.

Finally, they passed through the gates of Ebris and were greeted by crowds of people. The common folk celebrated the return of the soldiers along with their heroic King Hayden, who'd led Orellia to victory yet again. Oscar barely stopped himself from rolling his eyes. Yes, some war the king had won.

The only battle that was fought and won was fought by Karina, Clara, her brother, and the brave men and women who'd fought alongside them at the tower. His Majesty hadn't really played a big part in it.

Clara was no longer confined to the back of a wagon, so was riding Betsie alongside Oscar. After weeks on the road, her leg was mostly healed, her only signs of injury coming from the occasional wince. She was wearing her comfortable riding clothes, the tip of her bow and a quiver full of arrows peeking out from behind her shoulder. It appeared that her time in hiding was over.

She had asked Oscar whether he minded, ready to change into something more appropriate at the slightest sign of displeasure from him. Oscar had merely grinned and openly encouraged her. He couldn't wait to see her mother's reaction.

Sophia Redwood's face lost all color when she saw her daughter's attire but as soon as she spotted Nicolas in the crowd of the inner palace courtyard, Clara seemed to be forgotten entirely.

Oscar quickly dismounted and went to help Clara down from her horse, knowing that jumping from such a height would be quite painful for her. She gripped his hand tightly, clearly unhappy to be in the same part of the country as her mother again, but dutifully walked over to greet her mother and Sebastian, who were taking turns hugging Nicolas.

"Clara." Sebastian turned to her, raising an eyebrow at her choice of outfit and the bow, but had just enough decency not to comment on it. "We were worried about you. The king let us know you were injured." Yeah, Oscar scoffed mentally, but neither of them had rushed north to make sure she was alright. Oscar barely maintained his polite demeanor when Redwood continued, "I'm sorry you were hurt but you should have listened to us and stayed at home."

Clara opened her mouth to say something, but Nicolas beat her to it. "Then I'd be dead, big brother." He patted Clara's shoulder and gave her a respectful nod. "And lots of other people as well. Including the queen. So save your stupid advice for someone who cares."

"Nicolas!" Sophia reprimanded him. "Manners! Come on, let's go home, you need to rest." She turned around, sizing her daughter up one last time. "Clara." Apparently, a polite acknowledgement was all Clara was going to get before being ignored again. It was probably for the best but it still made Oscar feel sorry for his wife. And furious with this horrible creature that called herself his mother-in-law.

Nicolas sighed but didn't protest when Sebastian helped him to their carriage, waving Clara goodbye. Sophia didn't spare another glance in their direction.

"Well," Clara scoffed, "that went better than expected."

"Better? How could it have gone any worse?" Oscar scoffed. It was sad that Clara was so used to being treated like shit by her own family that she didn't think anything was wrong with such a 'warm' welcome.

She smiled and turned to kiss him. "She didn't yell at me, or slap me."

Slap her? Oscar felt his fists clenching. He was normally a nonviolent person, especially toward women, but he could very well imagine punching that hideous creature's face.

Clara noticed Oscar's hackles had risen so gently stroked his arm. "Forget about them. Let's go home."

Home. Their home. They opened the chamber door to find Friska waiting for them with tears in her eyes. She immediately rushed in to hug Clara. Oscar was glad his wife didn't mind the old maid's straightforwardness, something other ladies would probably consider inappropriate behavior. Clara truly was a better wife than he deserved.

Lowering herself into a chair, Clara sighed in relief. As she rubbed the muscles along her injured thigh, Oscar realized she was still in pain which dampened his excitement over finally being home, since it most likely meant no sex tonight. He'd made it crystal clear that they wouldn't do anything until she felt well enough to actually enjoy it.

Friska was just leaving the room when she turned around, reaching into her pocket. "I was cleaning up the parlor and found this under the table, Lord Oscar. I wasn't sure exactly what it was or where you wanted to put it?"

Oscar frowned at the pointy object Enzio's son-in-law had given him. It looked like his vacation was over. Back to solving mysteries. "Just leave it here, thank you."

Clara reached for it, rolling it in her fingers with curiosity. "What is it?"

"I have no idea. Several blacksmiths throughout the city have been paid to make these things. Light, small and sharp, were the instructions. I feel like it's important but..." He wasn't very comfortable admitting there was something he didn't know.

Finger tapping on one of the sharp points, Clara seemed lost in thought so Oscar didn't interrupt her. She was clever. Perhaps she would figure this mystery out for him, Oscar thought. How embarrassing would that be? Then again, since they were married, all their properties were supposed to be combined, which included intellectual property too, right? By that definition, his wife's ideas belonged to him as well. Satisfied with his newly devised loophole to protect his pride, he waited to see what Clara would come up with.

"This reminds me of something... It's probably nothing," she shrugged dismissively but Oscar nodded at her to continue, which she eventually did. "Enzio told me about the time they tested some special arrowheads.

Nasty things, with sharp points and edges. Absolutely brutal when they came in contact with the human body, tearing the tissue to shreds. Most archers refused to use them."

Cold tendrils of fear slid across Oscar's insides. His brain picked out one particular memory to play back – the coin he had left on the table before the powder had exploded. That small piece of metal had ended up wedged so deep into the wooden beam that the innkeeper was probably going to have trouble taking it out.

What if it wasn't a coin, but this sharp object? Or maybe dozens of them? In a whole barrel of the powder? Crap. As if Oscar wasn't already worried. Now he was even more motivated to stop those assholes from whatever they were planning.

Clara was watching him, worry clearly written all over her face, but Oscar shook his head. "Tomorrow," he said quietly. "Conspiracies can wait until tomorrow. Right now, I want to enjoy one last evening of vacation with my beautiful wife." Seeing her smile and nod, Oscar reached for his glass of wine on the table, raising it in her direction. "To heroes." And a hero she was, even though she would never admit to it.

Clara smirked as she raised her own glass for a toast. "To scoundrels."

Oscar grinned, a sudden wave of affection overtaking him. He sipped the wine, his eyes focused on Clara. "I love you." It still felt strange saying those three words and actually meaning them. "Would you like to take a bath? I'd imagine after a month of freezing lakes and dirty buckets, you would appreciate a little luxury."

"Only if you join me," she replied coyly.

His 'new Clara' was so unlike the frightened little girl he'd first met. The girl who'd have a panic attack whenever he tried to kiss her neck. How could Oscar refuse such an offer? Or, more importantly, why would he want to refuse such an offer?

Clara entered the bathroom first, with the promise to call Oscar when she was undressed and settled in the water. Despite having let him touch her body pretty much anywhere he'd wanted, Oscar had yet to actually see Clara naked.

Whether it was because she was still too shy, or because she didn't want him to see the many bruises and scars that had no doubt turned her skin into an interesting tapestry of hues and colors, Oscar didn't know. But he wasn't about to pressure her. Flowers needed time and support to fully blossom. And Clara was the most beautiful flower of them all.

He was waiting for the telltale sounds of splashing to know he could safely enter when Clara surprised him by calling his name. Oscar's breath hitched upon peeking inside to find Clara standing beside the steaming bathtub, facing away from him, completely naked. His dick immediately stiffened, becoming so painfully hard he felt like a fucking teenager again, nothing more than a pile of raging hormones.

The dimly flickering lanterns prevented Oscar from seeing Clara's face clearly as she turned around to greet him, but it seemed she was blushing. "I..." she hesitated, biting on her lower lip. Oscar stifled a groan. So damn hot. "Could you please help me get in?"

Right, of course she couldn't exactly climb the small stairs into the bath or lift her leg over the edge when she still had trouble even walking. Oscar should have thought of that. At least she'd asked for help. "Sure." He tried to keep the lustful hunger from his voice, failing miserably.

Clara shifted her weight nervously when he approached but smiled as he gently scooped her up into his arms. Oscar did his best to look into her eyes but it was impossible. The way her smooth, warm skin felt under his palms easily overpowered both his will and concentration.

As he raised Clara over the edge of the bath and slowly lowered her into the steaming hot water, he noticed that the hair on her head wasn't the only hair that was red. Jackpot.

"Why are you smiling like that?" Clara asked. She must have seen his victorious grin and was now eyeing him with suspicion, one eyebrow raised.

Way to keep a neutral expression, Oscar! he scolded himself mentally. "You are just so beautiful." That always worked.

Clara blushed even harder, wrapping her arms around her chest and diving chin-deep under water. "At least the bruises are gone now," she sighed.

So she really had been trying to hide how badly injured she'd been during the battle from him. As if Oscar cared. Maybe she was worried that he would never let her go anywhere again if he saw her all bruised and battered?

"I wouldn't have cared about them anyway," he replied, pulling his shirt over his head. "I'm just glad you are feeling better." Clara watched on with curiosity but when Oscar reached for his pants, she looked away, grinding her lip between her teeth. So damned innocent.

He tried not to make a splash as he climbed into the bath, keeping a safe distance from Clara, a little unsure of what she wanted from him. His painfully erect dick demanded action but, at least for now, the urge was under control.

Once Oscar was settled, Clara seemed to relax. She lay back with her eyes closed, her head resting against the edge of the bath and a contented smile on her face. Noticing Clara's hands were rubbing her thigh around the spot where she'd been stabbed, Oscar had an idea. A small window of opportunity for him. "Want me to massage that for you?"

She smiled and nodded, watching anxiously as he moved closer.

Her skin felt even smoother with the fragrant oils added to the water and Oscar couldn't resist running his fingers all the way from her foot to her knee and over her thigh. Clara drew in a deep breath but didn't protest.

Oscar quickly reached the area around her scar and gently ran his thumbs over it. It was coarse and wide, spanning from her inner thigh almost to her hip. Dozens of smaller marks were crossing it in regular intervals, Oscar guessed that those were probably from the stitches that had held the wound together.

His breath shuddered and this time it was not from arousal. He'd known Clara was seriously injured but he'd had no idea it was this bad. The wound was too close to her femoral artery. It was a miracle she hadn't bled out completely.

She saw his hesitation and of course, got the wrong impression from it. "Sorry," her voice was so quiet Oscar had barely even heard her. She sounded ashamed. "I know it's ugly."

She tried to pull away but Oscar held on tight, reaching out with his free hand to grab her by the nape. He leaned in for a kiss. "I don't care about the scar," he whispered. "I was just thinking how close I had been to losing you." Clara sighed and opened her mouth, no doubt to apologize again, and Oscar used that moment to slide in his tongue, effectively silencing her. Clara joined in with the kiss but still managed a slight protest by splashing water at him.

"Is that how you lead all of your political negotiations too?" she smirked when he finally paused to catch a breath. "Whenever someone says something you don't like, do you just shove your tongue in their mouth?" Giggling over the idea, she leaned back against the bath while Oscar returned to gently massaging the aching muscles in her thigh.

Oscar couldn't help but join her in laughing. "You have some very interesting ideas." His hands rubbed her entire leg from her thigh down to her ankle then pulled her foot out of the water to playfully bite her toe before moving to the other leg. "I'm not sure about the feasibility of such methods though."

When he was finished with her legs, Oscar pulled on Clara's hand, turning her around so he could reach her back. "I know for sure, at least two or three noble lords would be thrilled to have a handsome young man like me stick his tongue into their mouths." Clara groaned as he ran his thumbs from her spine to just under her shoulder blades. Oscar added more pressure to his movements in response. "But the rest of them probably wouldn't be very happy."

Oscar continued to massage every inch of Clara's shoulders and back, but when his hands finally reached her buttocks, it took all of his considerable mental strength to stop himself from lifting Clara up and fucking her right here, right now. It would be so easy. Just grab her hips, move in a little closer then lift her up until he was rubbing the tip of his rock-hard dick against the soft folds between her legs...

Crap. He didn't even realize his fingers were holding onto Clara's hips now, buried so deep it must have been painful for her. He forced himself to let go and quickly moved to the far end of the tub, causing a huge wave of water to splash over the rim, making a mess on the floor. He pitied the poor soul that would have to clean that up.

Damn it. He didn't need a steaming hot bath with his steaming hot wife. He needed a bucket of freezing cold water dumped over his head.

Amused by his sudden retreat and flushed demeanor, Clara watched as Oscar tried to regain control of himself, her mouth tilted up in a knowing smirk. So much for his famous self-control. "Sorry," he mumbled, fairly certain his face was glowing from embarrassment. Gods, perhaps he should just drown himself.

She crossed the distance between them slowly, careful not to spill any more water onto the floor, and her hand gently caressed his cheek. "Let's go to bed."

Chapter 61

While Oscar's embarrassment was somewhat entertaining, Clara had never seen him blush this hard before, she needed her confident cocky husband to come back now so she did her best to comfort him. She wasn't surprised that Oscar was struggling for control after waiting such a long time for her to be ready, especially when he was touching and caressing her naked body. Clara really didn't want to torment him any longer.

No, the way Oscar looked at her, the way he wanted her, was making Clara feel beautiful and desirable. And aroused. She wanted him just as much as he wanted her.

She dared to look this time when Oscar climbed out of the bath, her eyes sliding down his slender body, stopping to examine his fully erect penis. Clara had touched it a couple of times before. Not just that time in the outpost but also later, on the road home when it was just the two of them in their small tent, cuddled up to each other, but she'd never actually got a good look at it. It didn't seem that big compared to the rest of his body but still, the idea of it fitting inside of her was a bit worrying.

Oscar tried, unsuccessfully, to wrap a towel around his hips. Clara giggled at how his penis always seemed to get in the way, sticking out in front awkwardly. She hid the lower half of her face behind the rim of the bath, hoping he wouldn't notice her laughing at him but of course, he did.

"That's not very nice of you, my dear wife," he growled playfully, coming closer to help her out, handing her a towel.

Facing her back to Oscar, Clara was just finishing drying her body when strong arms wrapped around her. Oscar scooped her up off the floor and started carrying her over to the bedroom. "I can't have you slip on this water and break a leg now, can I?" he grinned.

"No, I think I've had enough injuries to last me a lifetime," she breathed out, running her palm through the soft hair on his chest.

"Yes, that you have." He sat her down on the bed and turned to retrieve her nightgown, but Clara grabbed his hand and pulled him back to her. "Clara," her name rolled off his tongue as a tortured sigh, "I don't think I can control myself if we keep going much longer. You are hurt. I don't want to cause you any more pain."

"You won't." After the hot bath and the massage, Clara could barely even feel the wound on her leg. Yes, she was most likely going to pay for this tomorrow, but for tonight, she desperately wanted to be with Oscar as a husband and wife should be. She lay back, pulling him down with her. "I'm fine, I promise," she said upon seeing hesitancy in his eyes. Clara removed her towel, whispering, "I want this. I want you."

Oscar's cock stiffened so hard it was threatening to burst out of his own towel. He stopped resisting his primal urges and lay down on the sheet beside her, carefully removing the towel while capturing her mouth with his. Clara felt intoxicated. Everything around her disappeared, her only focus was Oscar's hand sliding over her body. He took a moment to cup each of her breasts and play with her nipples, making Clara whimper.

She'd had no idea that something like this could feel so...good? No. Good was too lame a word for the intensity she was experiencing right now. Exquisite? Too fancy. Great? Amazing? So fucking hot it felt like a fire had ignited somewhere deep inside her core?

His lips traveled up and down the length of her neck, kissing, nibbling, and occasionally using his teeth to graze and gently bite her skin. He moved his mouth over one breast and when his tongue circled her nipple, Clara couldn't help but moan from the intense pleasure.

Oscar leaned down slowly, sucking her nipple into his mouth. Clara's mind briefly flashed to the Ruthian in that damned tower, violating her. She quickly chased the terrifying memory away. This was a completely different situation. This was not that vile man in the tower, this was her loving husband. The man she loved deeply, passionately. She wasn't afraid of him. No, all she felt now was searing desire pulsing within her.

Oscar supported his weight on one elbow as his free hand moved between her legs, his fingers stroking her most sensitive places. Clara moaned again and arched her back to get closer to his hand. The pressure was building inside of her until the point it was about to explode. She knew what was coming, knew the exquisite pleasure Oscar would release deep inside of her. She didn't want it like this, though.

"Please," she whimpered, tugging on his shoulders, trying to move Oscar between her legs. He looked at her, his face contorted and his lips slightly parted as he practically panted with raw desire, but there was still a hint of hesitancy in his eyes.

Clara pulled on his arm again, wrapping her healthy leg around the back of his thigh and forcing him to roll on top of her. "I really want this."

Oscar nodded in understanding, clearly needing to hear her words because the moment she'd said it, his hesitation vanished. He vigorously went back to kissing her neck and within moments she felt something hot and smooth press against her opening.

Clara wrapped her arms around Oscar's shoulders, wanting to feel him even closer. She gasped in surprise as he pushed himself completely inside of her in one slow but firm movement, freezing in position with his cock fully seated, waiting for her reaction.

It hurt a little, but not as much as she'd imagined it would. It was both pleasant and uncomfortable at the same time, which seemed impossible, but that was how she truly felt. More importantly, his cock was putting pressure right where she felt that dull throbbing inside, touching it directly, driving her crazy with an intense need she didn't even know existed.

Clara's fingernails were digging into the skin on Oscar's back. She tried to ease her grip, only ending up tightening it again when he slowly began moving in and out of her. Her mind was blank, a different kind of blank than when she'd nearly bled out, but the effect was similar.

She couldn't think, couldn't focus. Couldn't register anything but those parts of her body that were burning with desire. A searing desire that only grew stronger as Oscar continued to move. When the intensity finally reached its almighty limit, Clara screamed out, her back arching and her legs tightening around Oscar's torso involuntarily as if her body wanted to keep him inside her forever.

Oscar held Clara until her body finally calmed down, staying perfectly still. Only then did he pull out and finish himself with a few quick strokes of his hand, groaning as his seed spilled out onto the sheet next to her. Clara didn't understand why he'd pulled out at first, but then she remembered his letter. He was being very careful to not make little Oscars.

And while it was disappointing to not feel him finish inside of her, it was probably for the best. Their lives were complicated enough without babies being thrown into the mix.

She shuffled to the side, pulling the stained sheet out from beneath herself so they could cuddle in a clean bed. Clara felt...she wasn't even sure how to describe how she felt now. Satisfied, tired, happy. Strangely complete. As if this was an important part of her that had been missing until now. She was secure and safe in Oscar's arms and not a single thing worried her right now.

"Thank you," she mumbled quietly, "for waiting for so long."

He kissed the top of her head and hugged her tighter. "I don't think either of us would have enjoyed this on our wedding night."

No. At least Clara definitely wouldn't have. Her memories from that night were still wrapped in such a thick layer of fear and desperation it made her shudder.

"Exactly," Oscar nodded in response to her shudder. "Believe it or not, I don't find sex with a frightened, crying girl very satisfying. Confident, beautiful women are much better."

"You'd better go find one then," she teased him, reaching for a blanket to cover them both. Falling asleep with his scent filling her nostrils was still her favorite part of the day.

Wearing a gown felt almost alien to her now. So was not carrying a bow around, but it just seemed inappropriate in the palace hallways. Clara refused to give up the knife though, attaching the scabbard to her calf so she could easily reach it even with the ridiculously long skirt on.

Larkin's girlfriend Mina, Clara's new maid, was nervously running a brush through her mistress' wild mane, apologizing profusely every time the brush caught on the tangled strands, making Clara wince.

Mina had agreed to Clara's offer of employment immediately, grateful for such an opportunity. Less work and better pay? Who in their right mind would say no to that? But she was so frightened of screwing it up she made Clara anxious as well.

It wasn't like Clara really needed a maid. She'd lived in tents and military encampments for the past month, surely she could manage surrounded by the luxuries of the royal palace on her own. But she really liked the woman and decided to give her a chance.

Oscar was already out and about in the city, leaving Clara to deal with the home duties. Friska peeked into the bedroom with a pile of fresh linens in her gnarly hands, smiling brightly at the women inside. "Don't you both look lovely today ladies."

Mina's cheeks turned red but she put down the brush and rushed to help the old woman with her chores. "Are those for the bed?" she asked, taking the linens out of Friska's hands and setting them aside. "I'll take care of it once I'm done with Lady Clara's hair. Unless you need me to do something else, my lady?" she added quickly, sounding nervous again.

"I don't think so," Clara shrugged. Planning to spend most of the day with Karina, she didn't exactly need a maid standing behind her the entire time. "I hope you two can work together here?" Only now did she realize that there wasn't much work to do in the few chambers Clara and Oscar occupied. "Friska is in charge, she will tell you what to do," Clara turned to Mina, who nodded and gave the old maid a bright smile, apparently loving her already. Who wouldn't? Friska was simply adorable.

"If you find yourself with nothing to do, just take a break, it's not a crime. And please, if you could manage to just call me Clara in private, both of you, that would be great. I'm not a lady. Just ask Larkin next time you see him. He's seen me at my worst. Covered in dirt, smelling like a horse, eating a squirrel. Not very ladylike, is it?" Despite fighting the urge, Mina giggled. Friska just sighed and shook her head, but thankfully didn't comment.

People avoided Clara these days. She heard quiet whispers behind her back when walking around the palace but nobody outwardly mocked her or made any condescending remarks. It felt more like they were afraid of her. She wasn't sure whether it was due to her friendship with the queen or because of the many rumors concerning the battle at the tower that were spreading throughout the palace like wildfire, amplified by people's creativity several times over already.

Karina just rolled her eyes when Clara complained about it. "Try being the Blood Queen. This morning, one of the maids was so damned nervous around me that her hands were shaking. When she inevitably dropped a glass of water, she cried so hard it took me an hour to calm her down. Apparently, she was convinced I was going to grab a cutlery knife and saw her head off for her 'horrible transgression'. Even now, she's still frightened of me."

Despite the irony in her words, Clara could see it was really bothering Karina. The queen was used to people loving her, not being scared of her.

"Just give it time," Clara patted her friend's shoulder sympathetically, "I think it will get better. Look on the bright side, at least nobody will dare to sneer at you during Hayden's council meetings now."

They sat down in Karina's parlor, neatly organized again, with no trace of the previous mess from her 'research'. "True. It's a bit tense there now anyway, with Hayden pretending to be crazy and Egmont gone."

"Wait, he really got rid of the lord chancellor?" Clara couldn't believe it. The evidence against him was all fake.

Karina nodded solemnly. "Not for real. He's just taking a vacation. Hayden told him everything and Egmont agreed that it was necessary to maintain Oscar's cover."

Karina's maid, Laina, brought in their tea and Clara couldn't help but notice some tension between them, the otherwise friendly smile on the queen's face dropped slightly whenever the girl was around. Laina opened her mouth to say something but Karina shook her head vigorously, interrupting her. "I said no. It's crazy, Laina. I will not let you risk your life like that."

"As you wish, Your Majesty," the maid gritted her teeth and left the room.

Clara raised an eyebrow, not really sure whether she wanted to know what was going on. Karina sighed, "Don't even ask." Good. There were already way too many secrets Clara was involved in.

"This situation seriously sucks," Karina added while moving toward a dressing room filled with various beautiful gowns. "What would be the proper attire for the Blood Queen to attend a public execution?"

"You're going?" The only way Clara was going to the main square today would be if she were dragged there kicking and screaming. She had seen enough death to last her a lifetime.

"As if I have a choice," Karina growled, pulling out a bright red dress with black lining. "Might as well just go with the flow, right?"

Clara helped her undress and put the gown on. "At least you will look great," she tried to comfort the queen.

"Oh, yes. It's important to look lovely while watching people beg for their lives and die. I mean, I know those men are the worst of the worst criminals, but still..."

It had been Oscar's idea, actually, which made Clara feel guilty. An opportunity for Hayden to do something totally out of character, rash and brutal without actually making people hate him. Who cared that a couple of rapists and murderers were going to die in front of a cheering crowd?

The king preferred to punish with imprisonment only, locked up in the dungeons below the palace instead of taking their lives. It came in handy since now there was a large supply of people ready to be executed, a subtle hint that the old king was slowly slipping away, being replaced by a new one. A more ruthless and bloodthirsty one. Some might say, insane.

"Do you want me to come with you?" Clara sincerely hoped that Karina would refuse. She really didn't want to be there but knew she should at least offer to support her friend.

To her relief, the queen waved her hand dismissively. "No, there's no need. Go get some rest, it looks like your leg still hurts."

Clara blushed, not really wanting to tell Karina why her leg was feeling more sore than usual this morning. A little too much exercise last night. "I think I will. Are you sure you will be alright?"

"I'm sure I will hate every single second of it. But I'll manage, and so will Hayden. I think he hates this even more than I do." Yes, Oscar mentioned that the king wasn't particularly fond of the plan. But it was the lesser evil and, eventually, he'd reluctantly agreed.

After finishing buttoning up Karina's gown, Clara pulled her into a tight embrace. "You are a great queen," she told her quietly. "This horrible situation will be over soon. Oscar will make sure of it."

"I know. He and Hayden are the smartest and most determined men I've ever met. I'm just worried that once this is all over, we will all be too changed and so jaded by the many 'lesser evils', it's not going to be us anymore."

Clara had no idea what to say to that, Karina's words echoed in her mind long after she had left the queen's chambers. She was already changed, a different person to who she had been before this whole mess started. Was that a bad thing?

Chapter 62

Oscar had to admit that Egmont was a surprisingly reasonable man. Who would have guessed that the Burning Fury had so many normal people around him? The lord chancellor didn't have a problem trusting Oscar, claiming that if the king trusted Lord Huxley, then he would as well.

That was new. People were usually quite wary around Oscar. But, then again, no king had ever vouched for him before.

With his face a picture of pure disgust as he read through the falsified evidence of his supposed betrayal, Egmont agreed to step aside momentarily so that Oscar could get closer to the conspirators. Furthermore, Egmont offered Oscar the use of some of his own assets around the city, giving him the contact details of trustworthy people.

All three of them sat in their secret meeting for a long time, trying to figure out what to do with the mysterious barrels of black powder. Hayden, naturally, was hell-bent on storming the warehouses where it was stored and destroying all of it.

Under normal circumstances, it would make sense. But doing so would only alert the conspirators, making them disappear into the wind or possibly even move up their timetable with whatever they were planning. Plus, several shipments of the powder were already missing from the warehouses. Oscar couldn't be sure there weren't more deliveries that he had no idea about, which meant even if all the barrels they knew of were destroyed, there could still be plenty more left in hiding. It would be wiser, unfortunately, to leave the barrels untouched, keeping the enemy unaware they were onto them.

It had been almost a week since they'd returned to Ebris. Hayden and Karina had just finished personally overseeing yet another round of executions, a spectacle that they both hated immensely. Oscar was heading out for the afternoon when he overheard shouting in one of the hallways and curiously moved closer, only to find Hayden and his guard, Captain Lamar, yelling at each other surrounded by a small crowd of nervous onlookers.

"...disgusting! You're not you anymore!" The captain sounded desperate.

Hayden's eyes narrowed and he leaned closer to snarl right into the man's face. "Mind your attitude, Captain."

"Or what?!" Lamar scoffed. "You're gonna have me whipped? Again? What the fuck are you doing?!"

"Oh, I can do much worse than that." The king's voice was quiet, but the raw threat in his voice made Oscar shudder. Several people around them decided it would be safer to disappear immediately.

The captain shook his head in disbelief. "Yes, I've seen that. I can't do this anymore, Your Majesty." He spat Hayden's title out like an insult. "Whatever sick and twisted game you're playing here, I will not be a part of it!"

Hayden winced as if he'd been slapped but quickly regained his composure. "Get the fuck out of here then, you good-for-nothing asshole!" he shouted at Lamar who swallowed roughly, blinking to chase tears out of his eyes. "You saved my life a couple of times," the king continued, "so you get to keep yours. But I don't ever want to see you around here again!"

Oscar was mostly certain it was a set up. Make-believe to further convince the people Hayden was losing his mind. One Hayden apparently hadn't bothered telling him about. But the pain evident in both Lamar and Hayden's faces looked so real that Oscar felt sorry for both of them.

He looked around at the faces in the crowd. The king had wisely picked a busy location to play out this charade, so even with the deserters, there were still quite a few people standing and watching their exchange in horror. There were maids, servants, soldiers and guards, along with a few of the less important lords and ladies. The whole palace was going to know about this argument by evening. The whole city by the following morning.

One particular face was sticking out in the crowd. Oscar couldn't figure out why at first, Sebastian Redwood seemed just as afraid and surprised as everyone else around him. But then it happened. Just the slightest twitching at the corner of his mouth. The asshole was trying to conceal a satisfied smirk, quite unsuccessfully in Oscar's mind.

Oscar could come up with only two reasons why Clara's brother would be happy about Hayden kicking out Lamar. Afterall, it was quite possible that Sebastian simply hated the captain and was glad to see him scolded. Or...

"FINE!" Lamar shouted at the king. "I hope your new 'friends'," he sneered in Oscar's direction, "will keep you safe. Although, I imagine it will be quite the opposite."

"That's enough!" Hayden's voice boomed down the hallway, onlookers flinching, some of them rushing away. "GUARDS! Get this bastard out of my sight and make sure he leaves the city by nightfall."

A couple of men hesitantly approached the captain, clearly uncomfortable with the whole situation. "No need," Lamar replied indignantly. "I will find my own way out. See you never, asshole."

Hayden's fist moved so fast that Oscar barely saw it, hitting Lamar square on the jaw. The captain stumbled back before landing on his hands and knees on the floor. Slowly rising back to his feet, the captain intentionally spat blood from his split lip at the king's feet.

"Leave," the king growled as if he was barely restraining himself, "before I change my mind about letting you live." He looked around as if only now noticing the gathered crowd. "And what the fuck are you all staring at?!" he bellowed. Instantly, the people dispersed, frightened that the king's wrath would turn on them now.

Oscar followed them, since hanging around the king when he was in this mood would look suspicious. After reaching what he thought to be considered a safe distance, he stood by a window overlooking a part of the gardens, wondering if he should steal another rose for Clara. She'd seemed to like it last time.

"Our hero," Sebastian scoffed somewhere behind his back. "Rushing north to rescue my little sister when it was your fault she'd gone and got hurt in the first place." How the fuck was that Oscar's fault? Oscar bristled and opened his mouth to answer but Sebastian continued, "You never should have let her go. I guess we should all be glad she made it out alive.

"Sending a naive girl off to war with an army of men, what exactly did you expect would happen? I don't care if you prefer your women to be whores, sending Clara out to be used by Hayden's men and whatever random savages they came across is despicable. The next time you let her do something stupid like that, I'll fucking kill you with my bare hands."

It took Oscar a moment to realize what the bastard was actually suggesting he'd done to Clara and after that, he had to use all of his self-restraint not to punch him. Seriously? Was he really suggesting Oscar had sent Clara north to...what? Get fucked by other men? It didn't even make any sense!

"You can't even get one woman under control," Sebastian smirked, "I have no idea how you plan to manage with two."

He left before Oscar could think of anything clever to say. The real meaning behind Sebastian's words struck him an instant later.

He sat down on a bench under the window, covering his face with his hands.

No. No way.

This could not be happening. Not now, when he and Clara were finally so happy together. Happiness that was bound to end the moment Oscar even suggested that Sebastian Fucking Redwood was the man behind the entire conspiracy against Hayden. But how else would he know about Oscar demanding Karina as a reward? Because that was the only meaning behind his words Oscar could come up with.

No, Oscar needed to be sure before going anywhere near his wife. Which meant facing a very pissed off Hayden. The day was getting better and better.

As expected, the king was in his study. Opening the door to Oscar, Hayden furiously glared at him, a half empty glass in his hand. By the looks of it, it wasn't his first. "What do you want?" he snapped, running his hand through his hair frustratedly.

"Uh, I..." Coming here right now was clearly a bad idea but it was not like Oscar could back out now. "Hayden, are you sure you should be drinking at the moment?" he asked carefully, remembering the king's words about not being around him when he was drunk.

Hayden seemed to be contemplating between throwing the glass at Oscar's face or downing it in one big gulp. Fortunately, he still had enough control of his wits to think of a third option. Shoulders slumped, Hayden sighed in defeat, offering the drink to Oscar. "You're probably right. Take it, you look like you need it more than me. Why are you here?"

Oscar grabbed the drink, thinking it couldn't do any harm and sipped from it, savoring the taste of whatever drink was inside. "Are you sure nobody can overhear us in here?" The walls had ears, Oscar knew this all too well. He often paid for information obtained by secretly listening in to people who thought they were safe behind a closed door.

Hayden raised his eyebrow but shrugged and got up, motioning Oscar to follow him. They passed through another door and down a short hallway, ending in the king's bedroom. Hayden shut the door behind them and pointed to the door. "Soundproof. Now, what do you want, Oscar?"

Oscar temporarily forgot why he was here, staring at the wall behind the bed. "Isn't it like...treason to have that on display?" he asked, pointing at the Levantian flag proudly hanging on the wall next to an Orellian one.

"Why?" Hayden smirked. "Do you have one as well? I honestly don't care, as long as there's an Orellian one too. I didn't exactly go around to every Levantian household, confiscating them. That would only cause trouble. I got this one from Larkin's camp. I wanted to make Karina feel more...welcome around here."

Gods, she must have loved it. Oscar had to admit that it was a brilliant move, still surprised that the Burning Fury was much smarter than the rumors made him sound. "Right," he tucked a loose strand of hair behind his ear, trying to focus on why he'd actually come to see the king. How to start? "Hayden, have you spoken to Sebastian Redwood since our return?"

"Sebastian?" The king raised an eyebrow, clearly having no idea why Oscar was asking about Clara's brother. "Yes, a couple times. Why?"

"About?"

"Oscar..." Sighing, Hayden rolled his eyes. "I have other-"

"Just humor me, please."

Something in Oscar's face must have convinced Hayden that it was a serious question. "I don't know, a lot of things. What happened around here while I was north, some fresh gossip from around the city and the palace, just normal talks."

"Did he by any chance mention Egmont?" Perhaps Oscar was just imagining it.

The way Hayden's eyes brightened upon hearing the lord chancellor's name quickly doused any hopes. "Yes, several times actually. I thought it was weird. He always seemed to like Egmont, or at least...tolerate him, but now he sounded quite hostile toward him. Wait a second, you don't actually think...? That's ridiculous!"

If only. Oscar didn't respond, just took another gulp from the glass. Hayden sized him up incredulously. "Sebastian Redwood is one of my most loyal people. To even suggest that he's the one behind this conspiracy is..." he trailed off, shaking his head. "I thought I was supposed to be the crazy one around here."

"I'm not saying he's the one behind it. But he must be involved in it somehow. Hayden, he knew about me asking for Karina as a reward. If I'm not counting you, Karina, and Clara, the only other person who knew about it was the guy who gave Clara the potion."

"The guy who kidnapped Sebastian!" Hayden tried to sound firm but there was a slight hesitation in his voice. "Beat him, then threatened to have him killed."

"That could have been staged easily. Look," Oscar looked the king straight in the eyes, "if you tell me that you are one hundred percent certain he is still loyal to you I will never mention it again."

Gods, how he wished that Hayden would just say the words. But the king's mouth opened and shut again and he let out a resigned sigh. "I can't. It's true that what he'd said was weird, not just about Egmont but other people as well, like General Warren. Not you, surprisingly. Even though he hates you, he made you sound quite trustworthy."

"Because I'm part of his fucking plan." Gods. How the hell was Oscar supposed to tell Clara?

Hayden seemed to be thinking the same thing. "Are you going to tell her?"

"Yes." There was no debating it. Oscar didn't want to lie to Clara again and repeat their fight over not telling her about Nicolas. Even though it meant she was probably going to hate him for accusing her brother of something so outrageous. "Can you play along for now? Not let Redwood know that we know?" This was important. If Hayden couldn't control himself around Sebastian, everything might be in danger.

The king nodded solemnly. "Don't worry. I'll be the most convincingly insane king ever. You just make sure to find out what these assholes are actually planning and how to stop them once and for all."

"That's the plan. Hey, Hayden?" Leaving the room, Oscar glanced back at the king. "It was staged, right? The fight with Lamar?"

A bitter smirk twisted Hayden's face. "Yes. He has a mission. But...it doesn't make it suck any less."

From what Oscar knew, Hayden and his captain had been friends since childhood. It must have been painful for the king to publicly insult and threaten Lamar, then have him kicked out of the palace like some common criminal. "I'm sorry you had to do that," Oscar comforted, the words sounding surprisingly sincere. He raised his index finger, waggling it in Hayden's direction. "No more drinking." Who knows what other horrible things would happen if he did.

Clara was in bed taking a nap while Oscar sat in a comfortable chair, watching the curve of her body rise and fall as she breathed. She had the tiniest hint of a smile on her face and a few loose tresses of wild hair that had escaped from her braid were resting on her rosy cheeks.

How could he do this to her? Now, when they were finally happy together, he was going to barge into Clara's new-found peace and shatter it all once again? Hadn't she been through enough already? Fuck the gods and their twisted sense of humor!

Oscar covered his face with his hands, elbows resting on his knees, desperately praying for a miracle to happen. When a warm hand softly touched his shoulder he looked up in surprise. Clara was standing over him, a smile on her face. He was so lost in his own misery he hadn't even noticed her get up and walk over to him.

"What's wrong?" she asked, sitting down on his lap and resting her head against his shoulder.

Oscar wrapped his arms around Clara, perhaps for the last time before she inevitably became furious with him. "I wish I didn't have to tell you."

"That bad?" She looked up at him, grinning playfully, but her expression quickly morphed into seriousness when he didn't return it. "Alright, it's bad. What happened?"

There was no easy way to say this so Oscar just decided to be straightforward. "I think that Sebastian is involved in the conspiracy against Hayden."

Clara stared at him for a few seconds before chuckling. "Seriously, Oscar, that's not funny." When he didn't react, she did exactly what he was afraid of – slipped from his lap and stood up facing him, arms crossed in front of her chest. "Look, I know you two don't like each other and I can empathize with you on that, he can be a real dick. But this is a serious accusation. You could get him into real trouble spreading rumors about him. You are essentially accusing him of high treason!"

Yes, that he was. "Clara, I would never dare to say this out loud if I wasn't convinced it was true. Even Hayden seems to agree. There are things Sebastian has told him that are just too specific to be a coincidence. Your brother is setting the king against Egmont and other important people *and* he knew about Karina being my reward for cooperating with them."

"That's ridiculous!" Clara's face was pale but she decided to hold on to her anger rather than think about it rationally. Oscar could hardly blame her for it. If this were a member of his own family, he would be the same, if not worse. "Why are you doing this to me?" she sniffled, rogue tears rolling down her cheeks. "I thought..."

This was just heartbreaking. Oscar crossed the distance between them to wrap his arms around her. Her body was stiff but she didn't try to pull away from him. "I swear, I don't want to hurt you," he whispered, "but I promised I wouldn't lie to you or keep secrets from you." Two needs that were clashing in a very painful contradiction right now.

"You really believe my brother is the one behind all of this?"

Oscar shuddered at the hard edge to her voice. "I'm not sure he's the one in charge." Although it looked like it. "But I do believe he's involved with them."

Clara placed her hands on his chest and pushed against him, forcing him to let go of her. It was almost impossible to maintain his composure. Oscar bit down on the inside of his cheek to stop from apologizing or begging her to forgive him. He knew that wouldn't help him.

"Could you...give me a moment, please?" Neither Clara's voice nor her expression gave any hint of what she was thinking but the simple fact that she didn't want to be around him sent a very clear message.

"Of course." Only years of practice at faking it, allowed him to speak in a relatively calm voice. "I'll be in the study. Clara, I...I love you and-" He stopped talking when Clara turned away from him, walking out onto the balcony. Great.

Oscar wiped back the tears that fell onto his cheeks using the back of his hand. He left the bedroom, wondering if the sharp pain in his chest could be dulled by liquor. Perhaps he should go back to Hayden's so they could get drunk together? Getting beaten up by the Burning Fury seemed like an apt punishment for breaking his wife's heart.

Chapter 63

C lara felt like she couldn't breathe as she stepped out onto the balcony, desperately trying to chase away the darkness that crept into the corners of her vision. She found some relief as she leaned against the railing, focusing on slow, deep inhales and exhales, letting the cold biting air rush into her lungs and caress her skin. It was late afternoon and the sun was already hovering over the western horizon, a mild breeze playing with a couple of brown leaves that had fallen from the trees into the gardens.

The summer was long gone and Clara soon regretted not grabbing a cloak or blanket before stepping out of the bedroom. But she'd had to leave. She couldn't have stayed any longer, witnessing the pain written so clearly on Oscar's face. The pain that had finally convinced her that he was being deadly serious about Sebastian. And as much as she wanted to believe it was all nonsense, she couldn't simply dismiss Oscar's claim, no matter how ridiculous it sounded.

It took a few minutes for Clara to calm down enough to start thinking rationally. By then, goosebumps covered her arms and her teeth were tempted to start chattering. She dared to glance back into the bedroom, discovering that Oscar had stayed true to his word and had left her alone, so she grabbed the blanket off the bed and wrapped it around her shoulders before returning back outside. The fresh air was helping to clear her head.

Oscar's tortured expression haunted her mind but she pushed it aside for now. Yes, she regretted hurting him like that but it was hard to focus when he was around. And she needed that now more than ever.

Oscar wasn't one to throw unfounded accusations around. He would have never said anything unless there was a strong possibility it was true. But...Sebastian? Seriously?

The horrified look he'd given Clara when his kidnappers had removed his blindfold was deeply engraved into her memory. She'd kept replaying it in her mind while trying to decide whether to put the poison into Hayden's drink.

If what Oscar said was true, then the kidnapping had been a trick? A trick on her? Her own brother was trying to coerce her into poisoning the king? How the hell was she supposed to believe that?

It was true that Sebastian had never been the most heartfelt person. He definitely took after their mother in that sense. But that didn't necessarily make him evil. Or did it?

Despite being his sister, Clara had to admit that she barely knew Sebastian. He was six years older than her and she had still been a child when he'd started working in Hayden's diplomatic service, which often took him away for weeks or months at a time, so she hadn't exactly spent much time with him. Still, despite him being a condescending jerk, he'd always treated her better than Nicolas had.

Everybody knew that the Redwood family was loyal to the king and that included Sebastian. But even if he wasn't, even if he was willing to betray his king and country, would he really betray his own sister like that?

That was what baffled Clara the most. Screw the country, that was more of an abstract concept anyway. The king was not very likable nor particularly worthy of loyalty either, especially before he'd met Karina. But Clara was Sebastian's family! And he'd used her?!

She realized she wasn't even considering the option of him being innocent anymore, fully trusting Oscar's judgment. Which made her quite the hypocrite, choosing a foreigner over her family as well. But to hell with them, they'd started it.

She had always been a well behaved, loyal daughter and sister, yet received nothing but reproach and contempt in return. And why the hell was she standing here alone, thinking about her horrible family, when the one person who truly loved her was gods know where, heartbroken, convinced she was mad at him or worse, hated him?

Swiftly turning around, Clara marched back into the bedroom. Worry clouded her mind as she crossed the parlor to peek into Oscar's study. Would he even be there? She shouldn't have been so stern with him. Perhaps he'd decided that she wasn't worth all the trouble? Or that she was a traitor like her brother?

Much to her relief, Oscar was sitting at his desk, elbows resting on the smooth wooden surface, face covered by his hands. It was painful to see him like this so Clara quickly moved over to him, softly caressing his hair, tucking a few loose strands behind his ear.

He took a deep breath in before looking up as if expecting her to cast a life sentence judgment on him. Putting on the warmest smile she could manage considering this shitty situation, Clara cupped his cheeks and leaned down for a kiss. Oscar blinked in surprise, it was obviously not the reaction he was expecting.

"I believe you," Clara whispered, closing her eyes and resting her forehead against his. What was it Oscar had said when he'd sworn his fealty to Hayden? 'I've made my choice and I'm ready to live by that decision'? It seemed Clara had made hers now too.

Oscar swallowed roughly. A tear ran down from the corner of his eye but he wore a hopeful expression. "You do? Clara, I'm-"

"Don't apologize, please. None of this is your fault. It's all on my fucked up family. I should be the one apologizing. I've brought you nothing but trouble ever since we married."

"Nothing but trouble?" he grinned cheekily as he placed his hand on Clara's cheek, his thumb gently stroking her skin. "I can think of lots of things you've brought me other than trouble. Like love and happiness."

How the hell did she deserve such a sweet man? Clara sat down on Oscar's lap, relieved when his arms wrapped around her, cradling her like a baby. Yes, this was where she belonged. The entire Redwood clan could go fuck themselves.

"What happens now?" Was Sebastian going to be executed in the main square?

"Nothing."

Really? Clara leaned back to look at Oscar incredulously.

He just gave her a sad smile in return. "We still don't know what they are planning and if we make a move against your brother, it might just force them to move the plan forward. I need to get closer to them somehow, I just have no idea how at this point. Sebastian tolerates me because I'm useful, but he hates my guts, and I don't think he will ever fully trust me."

Yes, from what Clara saw, it was very unlikely that Oscar would ever get close enough to Sebastian to make him spill his secrets. But...she was still his sister, wasn't she? A naive, stupid little girl that nobody would suspect of having ulterior motives if she decided to spend some time with her beloved brother. Perhaps she could try to pry some answers out of Sebastian, or even snoop through his things in the mansion? Wow, what a truly despicable being she had become. Oscar really was a bad influence on her, Clara smirked at that thought.

"Clara?" he asked her cautiously, giving her an inquisitive look as he'd no doubt noticed the change in her expression. "What are you thinking?"

"I have a better chance of getting closer to him than you do."

Oscar frowned. "I don't like what you are suggesting. It's dangerous."

"He's my brother, Oscar. He would never harm me." Or would he? Clara wasn't entirely sure about that anymore "I could...I don't know, spend some time around him? He probably wouldn't tell me anything intentionally but he does consider me naive and stupid, he might let slip some information without even realizing it."

Pulling her closer, Oscar shook his head. "Clara, I don't mean to disrespect you, but I don't think you fully realize what you would have to do, or how risky it would be. For you, for me, for everyone. You'd have to go against your own family. Lie to them. You'd have to go back to the family home. I don't want to put you in such a position."

Go back home. Even the thought of returning to the mansion made Clara shudder but it didn't change her mind. "Are you going to forbid me from going?"

"Of course not," he sighed, kissing the top of her head. "I just don't want to see you hurt again."

Normally, she would appreciate him being so kind and considerate, but now was not the right time for that. "From what I understand, a lot of people are going to get hurt if we don't stop them, right? If I were one of your 'friends' and you were sending me to spy on Sebastian, what would you say to make sure I succeeded?" Clara had no idea how to play these games but Oscar had plenty of experience in this area.

"You are not one of my 'friends', you are my wife and the love of my life," he grumbled, avoiding her question.

Gods, this was Enzio all over again. "Oscar, I'm glad you want to protect me but I need to know what to do. So spill it. Now." She pressed her index finger into his chest.

"Help!" he chuckled, "I'm being oppressed! Alright." He inhaled and exhaled slowly, switching into a more serious tone. "I think you can figure out the basics on your own, that under no circumstances can you let your guard down around Sebastian or your mother. Or Nicolas, for that matter. We can't be sure he isn't involved in this as well. You can't afford to be suspected of having ulterior motives for visiting the mansion either. You need a proper, major reason that nobody thinks to question." Clara wasn't sure she liked where he was headed but nodded and waited for him to continue. "You will have to leave me."

What did he just say? Clara blinked a couple of times. "Excuse me?"

"Not for real, hopefully? But it's the easiest way to get you back home." Oscar's voice sounded calm but Clara could see the pain in his face as he spoke. "Your brother literally told me to get you under control earlier today." Clara rolled her eyes. Yes, that sounded exactly like the type of bullshit Sebastian would say. Oscar paused, his fingers playing with the few locks of Clara's hair that Mina had intentionally left out of the complicated hairstyle she'd created on Clara's head.

"If you really wanted to do this, and I'm strongly against it," Oscar's brows furrowed, "you would need to pack a few things and sneak out of here, returning to the mansion. You would tell your family that I've been mean to you, yelled at you, and threatened to have you locked up somewhere until you start acting like a proper lady." Clara shuddered over the words. Her mother was going to love that. "I'm sure Sebastian would gladly provide you with shelter just to piss me off."

Was this how things worked in Oscar's world? Lies and deception? "But... If I do pretend," she stressed the word out, "only pretend to leave you, won't other people find out about it as well? Won't they see you as a mean husband who chased his wife away?"

"That's what you are worried about?" Oscar shook his head and laughed. It was a strained, nervous laugh, but a laugh nonetheless. "Clara, as long as you know that it's not real, I don't care what other people think about me. It's just... I love who you are now and I would hate to see your family force you back into being that perpetually frightened little girl."

Yes, it was obvious she would have to pull out the old Clara from the dungeons of her mind and let her be in control. She'd have to be that timid girl, scared of her own shadow, never speaking up for herself.

But this time it was going to be different. This time, the new Clara would be there as well, constantly reminding her that it was all just for show, a ruse to uncover a conspiracy and save Orellia.

This time there would be a man who loves her, waiting for her to come back to him. That, she could live with.

Chapter 64

O scar didn't want her to go but he also didn't want to force her to stay. Clara couldn't watch his internal struggle any longer, quickly shifting to sit astride his lap, pulling the skirt of her gown up to her thighs.

Their kiss was passionate, desperate. Oscar wrapped his arms around Clara so tightly she could barely breathe. "Don't go, please," he begged, his hand gripping the back of her neck to prevent her from pulling away as he continued kissing. Not that she wanted to. "I don't want to be away from you again, I just got you back."

Of course she didn't want to leave Oscar, and she most certainly didn't want to return to her mother's clutches for any reason. But if Oscar's theory was right and the conspirators were really planning to use the black powder barrels in combination with the sharp little objects the blacksmiths around the city were making, then dozens if not hundreds of people could die. Clara couldn't just sit around doing nothing when there was a chance to prevent it.

"Let's just..." she paused their kiss to breathe, "talk about it in the morning."

Oscar let out an indistinct 'mhm', too busy kissing down her neck. They'd had sex many times over the past week yet Clara still couldn't get enough. Why had she ever thought sex would be something horrible and disgusting? Something to be afraid of? Gods, she was so stupid!

Her fingers trailed down Oscar's chest then reached for the hem of his shirt, pulling it over his head. Clara loved feeling his warm skin under her fingers, playing with the soft curls of hair on his chest. And elsewhere.

Clara felt Oscar's lips twist into a grin against her neck before he suddenly lifted her up then set her down on his desk. He was standing between her legs, drawing the bottom of her gown aside, his hands sliding up the length of her bare thighs.

When Oscar's fingers reached their destination, gently rubbing her sensitive spots through the thin fabric of her undergarments, Clara drew in a sharp breath. How was it that such a simple touch made her lose her mind every time?

Clara's fingers slid down his chest again. This time she used her nails, applying just the right amount of pressure to leave thin red marks without actually breaking the skin, exerting a quiet growl from Oscar.

She struggled with the ties to his breeches, all the while stroking his rock hard cock through the fabric. Clara gasped as Oscar roughly grabbed onto her underpants and simply tore them apart, giving his fingers direct access to her core. He slid them inside, grinning over how wet she already was. "Seems like you're ready for me, wife."

"I'm always ready for you, idiot," Clara snapped through her gritted teeth. The stupid knot just wouldn't loosen and her trembling fingers were only making it worse. "If you could just-"

Oscar grabbed a sharp letter opener from the desk and pressed the handle into her palm. "Just be careful," he quipped nervously, freezing when she put the blade closer to his crotch.

There were a couple of smartass retorts ready on her tongue but Clara decided to swallow them. The searing desire she felt didn't leave space for stupid jokes. All she wanted was to feel Oscar inside of her, now. She cut the string and tossed the blade aside, eagerly freeing Oscar's cock from his tight pants prison, stroking the length of it with her hands.

Oscar groaned and tilted his head back as Clara continued to stroke him for a few seconds before the pressure became too intense. Grabbing her hips and positioning her at the edge of the table, Oscar lined up his cock and thrust in deep. His movements were rougher than usual, desperate. Possessive.

He'd entered her in one quick stroke, so deep and with such force it had almost hurt. Almost. Clara exhaled sharply and Oscar froze immediately, trying to calm down. "Sorry," he mumbled, his lips gently touching hers.

"It's fine." And it was, the position just took a moment to get used to. "Go on. I love you."

Clara's words had him growling again. He rested one arm around her waist to keep her steady and the other around her shoulders, pulling her into his chest.

Clara instinctively wrapped her legs around Oscar's waist as he started to move again, moaning in pleasure as he pulled back slowly only to thrust in forcefully again. The intensity of each thrust soon had Clara reaching her peak and tumbling over. Wave after wave of pulsating pleasure ran through her body, her legs and arms hugging him even tighter, as if she never wanted to let go.

Oscar waited until she calmed down before pulling out and collapsing into the chair behind him, his hand reaching for his throbbing cock. Clara jumped down from the table, careful of her injured leg, and slid to her knees in front of Oscar. Looking up into his lust filled eyes, she pushed his hand away and reached for his erection herself, sliding her hands up and down, enjoying his tortured expression.

Not giving herself a second's thought, Clara leaned forward and parted her lips, licking the swollen tip of his penis with her tongue.

Moaning, Oscar tilted his head back. "Oh, gods, Clara, I..." he groaned, his knuckles turning white as he gripped the armrests of the chair.

He liked it. Who would have thought? It seemed Clara owed Karina a bottle.

She wet her lips before lowering her mouth over the engorged head, taking as much of Oscar's cock into her mouth as she could. When it became uncomfortable to the point of near gagging, she pulled her mouth back, her tongue circling the tip before lowering her head again. Continuing in a measured rhythm, she relished in the beautifully uncontrolled sounds coming from Oscar's mouth, as if he couldn't stop himself from moaning in pleasure anymore.

When his cock started pulsing, Clara hesitated. But she'd gone into this with her eyes wide open, she knew what came next. With that thought, she firmly secured her lips around his shaft, sucking as she tickled the tip with her tongue. Oscar went from frantic thrusting to frozen in place as his hot seed filled her mouth.

It certainly wasn't something she'd want to taste every day, but it wasn't as bad as it had originally sounded. Tolerable would be the best word, especially after she looked up to see Oscar's thoroughly blissful expression.

Eyes closed, Oscar was panting so heavily Clara could almost hear his heart trying to escape his chest. She placed her hand over it and, sure enough, could feel it pounding fiercely against her palm. Oscar shook his head. "Alright, now I'm seriously not letting you go anywhere," he chuckled quietly.

"We will talk about it in the morning. Let's have a bath."

He looked down at her with a cheeky grin. "Hmm, how long do you think you can hold your breath?"

"Idiot," Clara chuckled and gently slapped his thigh as she stood up.

Climbing under the covers after a long hot bath together, Clara was just as exhausted as Oscar but didn't let herself fall asleep. She listened carefully until Oscar's breathing became deep and regular, a sure fire sign that he was asleep. Then, she snuck out of bed and tiptoed out of the bedroom. She had made up her mind to return to the mansion but knew that Oscar would be able to talk her out of it if she gave him the chance. That was why she had to leave now, even though it was breaking her heart.

Mina was waiting for Clara in the parlor. She helped Clara to quickly change into a simple dress, then threw a thick, warm cloak over her shoulders. "The carriage is waiting for us at the eastern gate," Mina confirmed.

Clara nodded, sending one final look of longing toward the bedroom door, wanting nothing more than to forget all about her self imposed mission. Clara ached to climb back into bed, wrap herself around her husband, and forget all about stupid conspiracies and secrets. But this was a mess her family had made and she needed to fix it.

Mina followed behind in silence, carrying a small bag Clara had packed with some of her clothes. Not many clothes, just what she could hastily pack without being noticed. Clara's bow remained in their chambers, she didn't want to risk her mother destroying it. Only when the women had entered the carriage and it had started moving through the palace gates, did Clara let out a sigh, relieved and yet miserable at the same time.

"Remember," she told Mina, trying to keep her voice steady, "you never saw Oscar and me happy. He was always mean and nasty to me, ignoring me on good days, yelling at me on bad. Right?" The maid nodded, looking down at her hands. "We had a fight this evening, you don't know what it was about, but I came to you straight after so you could help me arrange my escape."

Mina nodded again, her fingers playing with the fabric of her skirt.

"Mina?" Clara gently touched her hand. "You really don't have to come with me, I don't want to force you to lie for me. I wish I could tell you what this is all about, but I can't."

"Is it for the king or against him?" Mina asked, nervously clenching her fists, no doubt uncomfortable asking her mistress such a direct and insulting question. "I'm sorry, my lady, it's just that Larkin told me a lot about your husband and...I really want to help you, I just don't want to betray my country."

Yes, given Oscar's reputation, Mina's concerns were absolutely justifiable. "I swear Oscar is working for the king and the king trusts him." At least, it seemed that way, especially after the conversation they'd had at the Eagle Peak outpost. "This is all part of a bigger plan, but I can't-"

"Alright," the maid interrupted her, a reluctant smile starting to form. "I truly don't need to know any state secrets, that's way above my pay grade. I trust you. And honestly, Lord Huxley is nowhere near as devious as Larkin made him sound," she chuckled, then her eyes bulged in fear when she realized exactly what she'd just said. "I-I'm so sorry, I didn't-"

Clara pressed on her hand to calm her down. "It's perfectly alright, I'm quite used to people not liking Oscar based on his reputation. You don't have to be afraid to speak your mind around me. At least, when we are alone. When we get to the mansion..." Clara sighed. How was it that the thought of returning home to her family felt even worse than the idea that her brother was planning to slaughter dozens of innocent people? "It'll be like I'm a different person there. My mother..." She should probably warn Mina about staying away from Sophia Redwood as much as possible.

"I know, my lady," Mina admitted sheepishly, giving Clara a nervous smile. "Most of the maids in the palace know your mother well. When you two were staying there together, we drew straws to determine who would have to serve you on that day."

Clearly, she expected to be reprimanded but Clara just laughed. Of course, everyone was afraid of the menace that was Sophia Redwood. "I wondered why none of the women ever smiled at me. I don't remember seeing you, though?" Perhaps Clara had been a little too distracted to carefully observe the people around her, especially after her announced engagement.

"Well, let's just say that I always had a long straw up my sleeve," Mina grinned.

The cheerful laughter of both women resonated throughout the carriage. They continued to chat happily between themselves for a little while, but when Clara peeked out of the window to check their progress, her heart sank. They were closing in on the Redwood mansion way too fast for her liking. As much as she hated the old Clara, she needed to revert to her now.

It was only for a few days, just until she got closer to Sebastian and found out what he was planning. Then she could return to Oscar and never look back. If Oscar still wanted her, that is. The sharp stab of guilt pierced her heart harder than expected.

Would he even want her back? She'd promised they would talk in the morning and then had snuck away under the cover of night, like a thief. A liar. A traitor.

Was Oscar going to be angry when he woke up and found out she'd run away? He clearly hadn't wanted her to go, he was just too polite to make it a strict order. That's why Clara had left like that. She knew he would have eventually managed to talk her out of it and she didn't want to fight with him. Would she have a home or a husband to return to once this was all over?

Oh, look at that. All the doubts and insecurities were back!

The old Clara had crawled out of her hidey hole and was already spreading the poison around. Just in time too, as the carriage had already passed through the gates of the Redwood family mansion. As far as Clara was concerned, it might as well have been the gates of hell.

Chapter 65

M ina had sent a messenger on to Sebastian before she and Clara had left the palace so he was already waiting by the door when they arrived, a small lantern in his hand casting demonic shadows across his face. He gave Clara the "I-told-you-so" look but embraced her in a hug when she ran toward him with tears in her eyes. She'd found it wasn't very difficult to force them out.

"Can I stay here please?" Clara sniffled, loathing herself for saying the words. "Please, Sebastian, I know he's my husband but I just can't take it anymore, don't make me go back."

"Clara," he patted her head, his tone surprisingly warm, "of course you can stay here as long as you want. This is your home. Come inside, it's cold out here." With his arm around her shoulders, he led her through the main hallway and into the large parlor.

Clara hoped she could just go to bed but it looked like the torture had only just begun. "So, you've returned." Sophia was dressed in her nightgown, a thick, long robe wrapped around her body. Without the ton of powder she normally wore, her face looked odd, almost as if she were a normal mother greeting her daughter. Sadly, the contemptuous sneer she also wore, spoiled the effect.

"Yes, Mama," Clara whimpered, keeping her head down, not sure if she could actually conceal the raw hatred in her eyes during her next words. "You were right."

"Of course I was," Sophia scoffed, "parents usually are. That's why it is always wise to listen to me." It still felt ironic that Clara was being scolded for marrying Oscar even though it was her mother's decision.

"Come here, girl," Sophia commanded. Clara obediently shuffled over and let Sophia give her a cold, insincere hug. "Fine. Get some sleep now. We'll talk in the morning. Odeine!" An elderly woman in an apron appeared in the doorway, bowing deeply in Sophia's direction. "Show the new maid around. You will assume your duties in the morning," Sophia glared at Mina, raising her index finger, "and if I find out you are slacking off, you'll be out of here in a heartbeat and I will make sure nobody will ever employ you again."

"Yes, my lady." Mina didn't seem phased by Sophia's threats or open hostility. She replied in a calm voice and respectfully lowered her head, following Odeine out of the parlor.

Clara's mother smirked and shook her head. "I'm not sure I like having her around. Those palace maids think too highly of themselves."

"Mama, please, she helped me get away. I like having her around." Clara didn't need to try hard to sound desperate, the idea of being stuck in this house of horrors alone was terrifying.

"Yes, yes, I'm willing to try her out. I do have to say, I like what she has done with this mess on your head. I thought that hair of yours was going to be the death of me."

Oscar loved her hair! Clara had to force herself from yelling at her mother. It was true. Even that very first night, on their horrible wedding night, Clara clearly remembered how he had carefully removed the pins holding her hair in place and ran his hands through her wild curls, telling her how beautiful she was. She hadn't been ready to accept it back then, too much fear and doubt clouding her mind, but he'd meant it and had kept repeating it whenever he had the chance.

But that was not something she could tell Sophia now. "I know Mama, that's why I picked her."

"A pretty stupid reason for selecting your staff, girl," Sophia rolled her eyes over her daughter's naivety. "Go to bed. I expect you to look presentable in the morning. We will be having Lord Perkins and his wife over for lunch."

Clara made a perfect curtsy, lowering her head to hide an eye roll. "Yes, Mama."

Mina came to Clara's chamber first thing in the morning, gently touching her shoulder and calling her name. "I'm sorry to wake you, my lady, but I thought you would want to be ready before your mother comes in?"

"Right. Sure." Wiping the sleepiness out of her eyes, Clara slipped out of bed, looking around in mild confusion. Where was she? It felt as if she had just fallen asleep before the maid came. The bed had felt so cold and empty without Oscar in it and Clara had desperately longed for his presence, his warmth, his hug. She'd tried to hold off the tears for as long as she could last night but ended up crying herself to sleep anyway.

The large mirror above the vanity confirmed she looked just as bad as she felt. Red, puffy eyes with dark shadows underneath them, a bright red nose and one big tangled mess on top of her head. Her mother was going to be furious.

"It's alright, my lady," Mina traced Clara's gaze to the mirror, "we'll fix that right away."

Good thing at least one of them knew how to use powder and eyeliner and the many other creepy potions hidden in her dressing table that Clara had never touched before. Now she was grateful as Mina put it all on her face, making her look 'presentable', as her mother had demanded. She'd be fine as long as she didn't start crying, which seemed like an impossible task for the day.

The maid was almost finished meticulously braiding Clara's hair into a sort of crown pattern around her head. Her dexterous fingers managed to somehow hold more locks of hair at once than Clara would ever think possible.

Sophia barged into the room, not even bothering to knock. "Get up, Clara! We-" She paused, surprised that Clara wasn't in bed anymore, her frown deepening further when she realized her daughter was already dressed and almost ready to start the day. There was nothing to scold her for.

"Good morning, Mama," Clara replied, struggling to sound sincere. "Do you need help with organizing lunch?" Lord Perkins was a grumpy old man and his wife was a pretentious bitch but Clara somehow succeeded in sounding excited over them coming for lunch. To gossip, no doubt.

Sophia blinked a couple of times, her mouth opening and closing. "Well, of course," she finally found her voice again. "Make sure those stupid maids don't mess up the flowers again. Lady Perkins loves begonias, not petunias! Seriously, how hard is it to get it right?" Her index finger was pointing at Mina again. "And you. You'd better be ready to help out in the kitchen or whatever else Odeine will need you for, is that clear?" she snapped at the maid.

"Of course, my lady." Mina couldn't exactly make a proper curtsy since her hands were full of Clara's curls but she did bow a little in Sophia's direction. "I have already spoken with her and plan to help her right after I'm done with Lady Clara's hair."

"Get a move on then!" Sophia shouted angrily and stormed out of the room.

Yes, it was good to be home. "Sorry about her," Clara whispered, shooting an apologetic look to her maid.

"Don't worry about me, my lady," Mina smiled genuinely, "my first employer before I came to work in the palace was even worse. Do you know Lord Umber? Everybody pitied him when he was beaten up but he really deserved it." Clara stopped herself from nodding, not wanting to disrupt the complicated hairdo Mina was doing, and hummed in agreement instead. He definitely did deserve it. "I just hope you can do whatever it is you came here for so we can go back to the palace," Mina added with a sigh.

"You and I both," Clara replied quietly. She certainly didn't want to spend any more time here than necessary.

The guests arrived right on time and Clara was quietly standing behind her mother when Sophia excitedly greeted them. Lord Perkins ignored Clara and rushed inside to have a drink while his wife gave her a look full of pity, patting her shoulder. "Poor girl," she said to Sophia when they headed inside, not really caring whether Clara heard her or not. "I've heard only the worst things about that husband of hers."

Clara plastered a humble smile on her face and kept her mouth shut, not sure what might come out if she opened it.

The lunch was painfully slow. Sebastian was doing gods-know-what somewhere in the city and Nicolas had been summoned to General Warren and other high-ranking officers to give an official statement about what really happened at Blackwater outpost and the aftermath that followed its destruction.

Which left just Clara and her mother to entertain the guests. Well, mostly her mother. Clara stayed mostly silent, wishing she could make herself invisible. Fortunately, the guests ignored her most of the time.

Only after they'd had dessert (Clara's stomach protested, not used to consuming such an absurd amount of food) and the company had moved into the parlor, did Lady Perkins turn to her. "I'm so sorry, my dear girl. I don't know what our beloved king was thinking, marrying you off to that man." She tutted and shook her head, her husband chiming in.

"Yes, those Levantians," he scoffed. "To think that the king had so many Orellian ladies to choose from and he still picked a foreign princess..."

Clara fought to keep both her eyebrows in their normal positions. Wasn't it high treason to speak about their queen in such a way?

Sophia nodded, taking a sip from a priceless cut glass. "Exactly, our own daughters weren't good enough for him."

Gods, couldn't she just let it go already? Despite getting to know Hayden better recently and realizing he's not as evil as he'd first appeared, Clara still couldn't imagine being married to him.

"The stories I've heard about the queen and Lord Huxley..." Sophia made a dramatic pause. "I shouldn't even tell you." From her tone it was obvious Sophia wanted them to ask her about it.

Lady Perkins didn't disappoint. "Do tell Sophia, please. I think we all deserve to know the truth about our queen, don't we?"

Nodding solemnly, Clara's mother lowered her voice. "From what I've heard, she is very interested in occult sciences and even...black magic," she whispered.

Clara snorted, quickly masking it with a cough. Fucking hell. This was ridiculous.

"Right, Clara?" Sophia turned to her, silently commanding Clara to support her story. "Tell Lady Perkins what happened up north. Where she dragged my poor daughter," she was facing her guests again, a single tear being forced into the corner of her eye, "against her will, and nearly sacrificed her life to the dark gods!"

Clara didn't know whether to be angry or start laughing. But she needed to play her part. Hopefully, Karina would forgive her.

"I don't remember much from that night," she mumbled, "since I lost a lot of blood." Lady Perkins inhaled sharply when hearing the word blood, covering her mouth with her hands. She looked so frightened Clara actually started to enjoy this farce. "But I do remember seeing her surrounded by enemies, covered completely in blood. She was talking to their leader. I couldn't understand them, but I did hear her laugh as she shoved a blade into his heart and cut his head off, raising it up to show it to his people. It was such a demonic sound, I'll never forget it."

Lady Perkins looked close to fainting and her husband awkwardly put an arm around her shoulders.

This was fun. Perhaps Clara should tell them Karina drank Gishri's blood or ate his brains or something. People already believed similar shit about the king, it would only make her look like an appropriate match as queen for the Burning Fury.

Sophia seemed satisfied with Clara's words. Of course, now everyone would want to visit the Redwood mansion, to hear the horror stories from the poor girl who'd barely survived the queen's bloody rampage. No doubt that was Sophia's plan all along. A way to get some social significance and become popular. By parading Clara in front of her guests like some freak in a circus. Perfect.

"If you will excuse me," Clara stood up, curtsying toward the guests, "I'm very tired, I barely slept last night. My husband..." she trailed off and sniffled for effect, not really sure what she would even say. "I just...need to rest for a bit. I'm truly sorry."

"Of course, of course, my dear," Lady Perkins nodded before Sophia could even open her mouth. "You are safe here, at home with your mother. I'm sure young Sebastian will protect you from that monster and I will personally plead with King Hayden to have that horrible marriage of yours annulled."

Wow, such concern. "Thank you," Clara mumbled and rushed out of the room, having to cover her mouth with her hands to prevent a burst of laughter from escaping. The idea of Lady Perkins commanding Hayden to cancel Clara's marriage was just too amusing. Gods, she needed to get out of this place or she was definitely going to go crazy.

Fortunately, she was now in the perfect position to do something that would, under normal circumstances, be problematic. Her mother was busy with the guests, her brothers away, most of the staff cleaning up after lunch or performing other duties. Clara wasn't going to get a better opportunity to look into Sebastian's room than right now.

The door wasn't locked so Clara entered, quietly closing it behind her. Why would it be locked? This was his home after all, a place where nobody would suspect him of anything malicious. But Clara had come here to spy on him, hadn't she?

Suppressing a surprising amount of guilt, she looked around the room. The bed was neatly made, no maid would dare to do it sloppily in a household run by Sophia Redwood. There were some parchments on his desk, most of them correspondence with Hayden and other diplomats. At least, that's how it seemed from her quick inspection. Nothing suspicious.

The drawers were locked and Clara quickly looked around to see if she could find the key, but of course, it wasn't that simple. Had he taken it with him? No, instinct was telling Clara that it was hidden somewhere in this room, somewhere in plain sight.

The great Sebastian Redwood was untouchable here, adored by his parents, respected by his siblings, feared by the staff. He wouldn't bother carrying a key around with him, it probably wouldn't even cross his mind that somebody would dare to try and get into his desk.

Clara scanned the room again, her gaze inadvertently drawn to one of the walls. Where Clara had dolls, Sebastian had shelves full of weapons. He wasn't exactly a great fighter, a huge majority of these were never used in any form of combat. But they did have symbolic value.

A lot of the weapons were gifts from their father, just like Clara's dolls. But there were others. Daggers covered in precious stones, beautifully carved curved blades, a spear adorned with what looked like pieces of human bones. Gifts he'd acquired from various foreign dignitaries in his years of service as a diplomat.

But the most important weapon, the one he always showed off to anyone who dared to venture into his room, was a rather simple sword. The only thing that made it special was a crest of the Orellian royal house engraved on the scabbard. Hayden's crest. This was the sword Sebastian had received from the king himself upon being named the youngest diplomat in the entire history of the Orellian diplomatic service. The best day of his life, as he'd often claimed.

It sure as hell hadn't stopped him from plotting against the king. Clara smirked at the irony of finding the key hanging from the hilt on a short string. How totally fucking typical of her arrogant brother.

She grabbed it and rushed back to the desk. Her trembling fingers took three tries to unlock the central drawer, eagerly pulling it out to see what was inside. At first glance, there was nothing of interest, just more documents. Very official looking, but nothing looked wrong with them. Also, there were some pouches with what she presumed were coins.

Clara reached into the very back of the drawer, trying to scoop out anything hiding there. She yelped in pain, recoiling her hand to stare at the drop of blood coming from her finger in surprise. Her second attempt was more cautious, leaning down to see what was inside first before using a letter opener to slide it closer.

Her suspicion was confirmed when the thing that cut her finger turned out to be the same type of sharp pointy object that Oscar had gotten from Enzio's son-in-law. Dozens of which were supposedly being added to the black powder barrels in order to maximize the carnage.

Oscar was right.

Until now, Clara had kept up hope, no matter how small, that it was all a huge misunderstanding. That it wasn't her brother trying to take down the king or hurt innocent people. That Sebastian hadn't pretended to be kidnapped only to coerce Clara into poisoning Hayden. That asshole!

She had half a mind to just put an arrow through him. But she had to think rationally now. The only important thing right now was to find out exactly what they were planning to do with the barrels. She could always kill the bastard later.

Unfortunately, the rest of the contents of his drawers didn't provide any clue as to where or when they intended to strike. Clara was running out of time. Someone could come in here any second and there really wasn't a good explanation for what she was doing. Still, something else caught her attention so she took her time to pull it out and carefully unwrap it from several layers of cloth. A seal. The official seal of the head of Hayden's diplomatic service. Sebastian shouldn't have that.

Seftha Ulaia's words popped into Clara's mind. The fake messengers had official documents with this seal. So Sebastian was involved in that as well? Stirring up unrest among the Ruthians, pitting them against Hayden? What an idiot! Nicolas was almost killed because of that! The selfish prick! Clara growled while wrapping the seal back up and carefully placing everything back into the drawers.

She managed to lock them again and place the key back into its original position without being disturbed, praying to all the gods that the hallway would be empty as she creaked the door open and slid out. Her prayers went unanswered.

"What exactly are you doing?" a familiar voice sounded behind her and she quickly turned around to face her brother.

Chapter 66

"Nicolas?" At least it wasn't Sebastian but still, it couldn't have looked good.

Clara had no idea what to say, Nicolas had caught her completely off guard. She remembered Oscar's words about not telling him anything, that they didn't know whether he was involved in the conspiracy as well. But he'd nearly died during the Ruthian attack, why the hell would he be supporting Sebastian in that?

"I-I..." she stuttered, unable to come up with a plausible explanation.

Her brother gave her an inquisitive look, head tilted to the side. "Sebastian isn't back yet, why were you in his room? And why are you even here? The last time I saw you, you were super happy with that husband of yours and now I hear that you ran away from him?"

Damn, Clara had completely forgotten about him spending so much time with her and Oscar the whole way back from the north. He clearly wasn't buying the story.

"Nicolas, please." Clara looked him straight in the eyes, trying to sound as serious as she possibly could. "Please, trust me. Just walk away and pretend you haven't seen me here. Please."

He pouted. "How do you always manage to get yourself into such trouble?" Oh, Nicolas, you have no idea. "Fine. I won't say a word."

Clara must have looked surprised that he actually agreed, because he grinned and added, "Don't look at me like that, sister. You saved my life, I owe you. Whatever it is you are doing, you better finish it fast though. Mama is looking for you." Damn, Clara was so lucky it was Nicolas and not Sophia finding her exiting Sebastian's room.

"Oh," her brother turned to her one more time, "I guess this means that I don't have to punch Oscar in the face for mistreating you?" Clara shook her head vigorously and Nicolas chuckled. "Good. I kind of liked him."

Clara quickly went downstairs to find her mother, worried that Sophia would be angry over her daughter saying such bullshit lies in front of their guests. But it seemed to be quite the opposite. Sophia was pleased by Clara's performance and was already planning on inviting other important people over, wanting to use up her daughter's horrible experience with the Blood Queen as much as possible. Amazing.

Later that afternoon, Clara overheard a heated debate from the lower parlor. Sophia and Sebastian were arguing about something, yelling at each other. The staff wisely cleared the area and Clara had a chance to catch the end of their exchange, standing quietly just outside the door.

"... said no!" Sebastian sounded frustrated but firm.

"What do you mean no?" Sophia hissed. "I'm still your mother, young man, you don't get to order me around like this!"

Wow, it was a rare sight for Sebastian to get scolded for something. He had always been the perfect child, especially in their mother's eyes. "Mother," he replied coldly, "need I to remind you that I am the head of this family now? When I give an order, I expect all family members to follow it. And that includes you."

It was quiet for a few moments. Clara could picture her mother's dumb-struck face. Hearing such words from her favorite child must have hurt.

"But…" she tried to protest quietly, already sounding defeated, "it's the biggest event of the year! I can't just stay here, that would look-"

"I don't care what it would look like," Sebastian interrupted her harshly. "You are staying home. Good thing Clara is here as well, at least I won't have to chase her around the palace. Three days from now, neither of you will leave the mansion. Nicolas will keep an eye on you."

A cold fear spread through Clara's chest as if a piece of ice was resting inside her stomach. He wanted to keep them at home on that day at all costs. It seemed he was even ready to drag Clara away from the palace by force just to make sure she would be in the mansion. It wasn't hard to guess why.

They planned to attack in three days. But why? What was happening on that day? What was so important that Sophia was having such a big fight with her son?

Clara didn't really take an active part in palace social life, especially after returning from the north. Everything seemed so boring and unimportant. But there was something, wasn't there? Clara remembered Karina mentioning a festival to celebrate Hayden's victories over the past year.

The cold spread faster through her body, gripping her heart and not allowing her to breathe. The festival was for the entire city. Hundreds, maybe thousands of people were going to gather in the town squares to enjoy free food and drinks, music, and other entertainment. The nobles were invited to a great ball, that'd be where Clara's mother wanted to go. Everyone important was going to be there.

Clara leaned against the wall for balance, sudden darkness clouding her vision.

So many people. It couldn't be. It just couldn't be Sebastian's plan!

He was her brother, not a bloodthirsty monster planning to murder and hurt innocent people. He might hate the king, that was understandable, the Burning Fury wasn't exactly a loveable person. But common Orellian citizens? Innocent men? Women? Children?! Did she not know her brother at all?

Clara had to pull her shit together and fast, since the debate in the parlor had ended. Either her mother or Sebastian were soon going to leave the room to find Clara just outside the door, pale as a ghost with tears in her eyes. Sure, they thought her to be emotionally unbalanced so it probably wouldn't come off as a surprise to find her crying on the floor but right now, she couldn't afford even the slightest hint of suspicion. Not with what was at stake.

But what could she possibly do? Sebastian would never let her get close enough to him to share such a secret. As far as she could tell, there weren't any detailed descriptions of where and when his people planned to attack in his room. He'd probably hidden them somewhere else. And there was no way Clara could follow him around unnoticed. If only Oscar was here, he would know what to do.

But he wasn't. She was on her own and she needed to figure out how to stop her brother from becoming a mass murderer. How to save countless lives while the fate of the entire kingdom hangs by a thread. No pressure, right?

The night was long and Clara didn't sleep a wink. Tossing and turning, she kept trying to come up with a plan. Then finally, she did.

It was desperate, stupid, and, worst of all, it depended entirely on her. If she failed, people were going to die. Sebastian was going to get away. Oscar would be in danger. Hayden's authority would be severely undermined. But it was workable, and it was the best plan she could come up with.

Now she needed to pass a message on to Oscar and hope he would trust her enough to go through with his part of the plan, because she needed Hayden's guards on board to initiate the whole thing. There was one sure fire way to send a message from here, but it meant Clara would be left alone in the Redwood mansion without any support, emotional or physical. Unless she counted Nicolas, but her brother was officially still on duty so he'd be spending most of his time in the barracks again.

As she thought about it, she realized that her decision was already made. She was willing to do whatever it takes to stop Sebastian. Spending two days alone with her mother was not such a huge price to pay.

Clara quickly wrote down everything she'd found out along with her theory about the attack on the festival, and outlined exactly what she needed for her plan to work. There was no way for Oscar to contact her in return, or to let her know whether he and the king agreed to go ahead with it or not. Clara just had to trust that it would all work out.

Mina agreed to do her part without hesitation, carefully hiding the piece of parchment in the inner pocket of her gown. The kind woman was eager and willing to do anything to help Clara, the only thing she didn't like was leaving her mistress alone in the mansion. But it was necessary.

Clara's heart pounded wildly as they stood in the hallway, ready to play out their carefully prepared scene, just waiting for Clara's mother to be within earshot.

Sensing Clara's nerves, Mina leaned closer and briefly hugged her. "It's going to be alright, my lady. Say and do what we agreed upon. I will make sure your husband gets the letter without any suspicion falling on you," she whispered before quickly stepping back at the distinctive sound of Sophia's heels clicking on the stairs.

There was a glass of dark red wine sitting on a small table next to them. Mina grabbed the glass and poured its contents over the front of Clara's gown. It was one of her better gowns, a very beautiful and expensive piece. It was actually one of Clara's favorites, and her mother knew it very well.

Clara yelped out as a few cold drops splashed on the skin on her neck as well. "What are you doing?!"

"I-I'm sorry, my lady, I was just-" The maid nervously stuttered an apology.

"I don't care!" Clara interrupted her harshly. Catching a glimpse of Sophia entering the corridor, she shoved Mina into a wall. Clara forced tears into her eyes then let them fall and roll down her cheeks. "This..." she sniffled, trying to sound hurt and angry, "this was one of my best gowns, you sloppy wench! And now it's ruined!"

Mina cowered in fear, her face losing all color when she noticed Clara's mother quickly coming closer. "P-perhaps some cold water and powdered soap. I c-could-"

"What the fuck did you do, you incompetent bitch?!" Sophia only needed a second to assess the situation, then she grabbed the maid's hair and yanked on it so hard Mina stumbled to the ground.

Clara ignored the intense feeling of guilt rising at Mina's treatment and sniffled again. "She destroyed my favorite gown!" Turning to the poor maid on the floor, Clara's voice became a spiteful hiss. "You're fired! Get out of here, go back to the palace, or crawl back to that asshole that calls himself my husband. I don't ever want to see you again!"

Mina started to pick herself off the ground but Sophia leaped at her. Before Clara could do anything to stop it, her mother slapped the maid across the face so hard Mina's head almost hit the hardwood floor again. The woman stayed down, sobbing, protecting her head with her arms.

"I will make sure you pay for this," Sophia growled and pointed at Clara's ruined gown. "Even if you have to slave your ass off for the rest of your life. Now get the fuck out of here!"

Crap, this was not part of the plan. Clara's heart was breaking as she listened to Mina's quiet sobs and watched the big red mark blossom across her cheek. She desperately wanted to rush over to the maid and comfort her, but she couldn't.

Mina seemed to understand how Clara was feeling, she even winked briefly in Clara's direction when Sophia turned away from her. They were seriously going to have to raise this woman's salary.

People were looking at Oscar with even greater contempt now, just as he'd expected. He wasn't just a Levantian with a dubious reputation anymore. Now, he was also the horrible husband whose wife had run away from him. Like he cared what those pretentious assholes thought. All he wanted was for Clara to be safe and come back to him so he could hug her, protect her, and love her. He missed her so much it caused him physical pain, as if a giant fist had gripped his heart and squeezed it.

There was no way for him to contact her or pass on a message, not without endangering her cover. He'd briefly considered using her brother as a messenger, Nicolas had been hanging around the palace and training grounds a lot, but it wasn't safe. There was no way of knowing whether he was involved in this mess or not.

Oscar had to wait and hope that Clara would find a way to contact him. He also had to trust that she would stay safe and not take any risks. Although, knowing his wife and considering what had happened up north, the last part was quite unlikely.

He was a little disappointed that she'd snuck out like a thief in the middle of the night, but it was understandable. She was probably worried he would talk her out of it. Which he totally would have. It was dangerous, not to mention it required spending days with her horrible mother. But his young wife was just as stubborn and determined as the queen. He couldn't help but smirk over that thought.

The world was filled with timid, obedient girls, and Oscar just had to be attracted to the two wildest and most uncontrollable ones. Well, just one now. Karina barely even crossed his mind these days.

Walking through one of the palace courtyards, Oscar heard footsteps quickly closing in on him from behind. Turning around, his gaze fell on one of Hayden's officers, the blue-eyed one, Clara's friend. Larkin, that was his name. The one who'd apparently come close to killing the king during the royal wedding celebrations. He did not seem happy.

"Huxley!" Larkin growled as he stepped closer to Oscar, his features contorted in anger. "What the fuck did you do to Clara?!"

A couple of people stopped to watch the drama unfold, curious whether the unpopular Lord was going to take a punch to the face. "I don't think that's any of your business, Lieutenant," Oscar replied, trying to sound as calm as he could. This was the downside of the plan – all Clara's friends were going to hate him for presumably hurting her and chasing her away.

"Oh, it's very much my business." Larkin's fists clenched and Oscar gulped. This was certainly not a good situation. The crowd watching their exchange were unlikely to rush in and help Oscar if the lieutenant decided to beat him up, and Oscar could hardly fight off a professional soldier.

Larkin leaned even closer, their noses were almost touching now, and he gripped Oscar's jacket. "Stay away from her, you piece of shit. She deserves better."

Oscar's first instinct was to shove the man away but he waited, feeling Larkin slip something into the inner pocket of Oscar's jacket. "You are forgetting yourself, Lieutenant," he snarled when Larkin was done, shaking his hands off. "I don't think the king would be too thrilled upon hearing about one of his soldiers attacking a noble lord."

"I don't see any noble lords around here," Larkin scoffed and spat on the ground in front of Oscar's feet. "Stay away from her unless you want to find yourself with a couple of broken bones." He turned abruptly and left before Oscar could react. It probably wasn't hard for the lieutenant to fake such hatred and anger toward Oscar. Being a Levantian, he knew all about Huxley's bad reputation.

Oscar glared at the audience they had picked up, most of them disappointed there wasn't going to be an actual fight, straightened his jacket, and rushed back to his quarters. Only when he was safely inside did he reach for the paper Larkin had passed to him, hoping it was a message from Clara and not another threat from her pissed-off friends.

His heart fluttered over seeing her tidy handwriting but his excitement quickly dissipated as he read the letter. Of course they were planning to strike during the festival, how had he not seen that coming? It was so fucking obvious. If their goal was to kill as many people as possible, what better opportunity was there than the crowded streets of Ebris during the celebrations? Damn, Oscar should have let Larkin punch him, perhaps it would restart his brain.

The worst thing about Clara's letter was that she had actually come up with a good plan. So good that Oscar couldn't think of any adjustments that would improve it, or more importantly, keep his wife out of danger. Because it was going to be her life on the line the whole time.

If her brother had even the faintest suspicion that she was lying to him, he wouldn't hesitate to get rid of her, Oscar was certain of that. And, as much as he admired Clara, she didn't exactly strike him as a skilled liar. But, perhaps he was wrong about that.

He didn't have another choice anyway. The plan was solid. It was their one chance to stop the conspirators and save everyone. Oscar's job now was to convince Hayden to put the fate of his kingdom in the hands of a seventeen-year-old girl. Piece of cake.

The last two days in the Redwood mansion had felt like an eternity to Clara. She was both her mother's prisoner and a puppet to entertain her guests, forced to endure it without a single moment of complaint. Being seen as a good girl was the only thing that stood a chance of getting her out of the house on festival day, which was a vital part of her plan.

Since Sophia had been denied the opportunity to attend the ball that the royal couple were hosting at the palace, she'd decided to throw a small party of her own. She'd spent most of the morning overseeing the staff and making sure everything was ready for a large number of guests, hoping at least some of her friends would take pity on her and come.

Clara seriously doubted anyone would miss an opportunity to attend such a prestigious event by choosing to spend this evening with Sophia Redwood instead, but she dared not mention it in front of her mother.

Sebastian was headed out right after lunch, disappointing their mother even further by saying he wouldn't be back until the following day.

Clara rushed to Sebastian as he was leaving, giving him her best smile. "Wait for me!" Before Sebastian could protest, she pulled him aside and whispered, "I have a surprise for Mama to make her a bit happier tonight. I just need to quickly swing by the central square to pick it up. Yes, yes, I know, we aren't supposed to be out tonight, and I promise I won't be, I'll head straight back. Can you give me a ride to the city?" She fluttered her eyelashes, playing the naive little girl her brother considered her to be.

"Clara..." he sighed, obviously preparing to say no.

"Pretty please, big brother." Puppy dog eyes weren't a thing Clara used often so she had no idea if she'd pulled it off, but Sebastian's resolve faltered. "Please, it's just a small gift for her, to make her a little more...tolerable. You know she will be a menace tonight. Thanks to you! So you owe me. Please, please?"

Sebastian rolled his eyes. "Fine. But you head back home straight after, understand?"

Clara let out a cheerful giggle, jumping up and down excitedly. Damn, was she overplaying it a little? "Yes, yes, of course. Thank you!" Rising up to her tiptoes she gave her brother a quick peck on the cheek and rushed to his waiting carriage before he could change his mind.

The ride into town went by in silence. Sebastian kept fidgeting in his seat, occasionally straightening out his clothes or running his hand through his hair. He was clearly nervous. Sure, Clara would be nervous too if she was about murder dozens, if not hundreds, of innocent people.

She was also nervous, but for an entirely different reason. Had Oscar agreed to her plan? Had he managed to convince Hayden to go along with it? Would she be able to handle her part without messing up? To successfully lie and deceive her brother? Gods, she hoped so.

The road to the main square was already blocked by the festival preparations. Tables and benches were placed along the walls and a small platform for the musicians and entertainers stood in the middle of the square. Barrels containing drinks and crates of food were being brought in by an endless stream of wagons.

Unable to continue in their carriage, Clara and her brother got out and walked slowly toward a small jewelry shop where Clara had supposedly ordered a new necklace for Sophia. Clara's nervousness grew with every step they took.

Now, she prayed silently. Please Oscar, just trust me.

Her prayer was answered. A couple of soldiers marched through the street, people moving out of their way to let them through. Sebastian stepped aside to let them pass, but the moment the commander spotted his face, the group headed straight toward Clara and her brother.

"Lord Redwood?" The soldier in charge was young but looked and sounded serious. Sebastian nodded in response. "I'm afraid you are going to have to come with us, my lord. You are under arrest."

Chapter 67

Sebastian's life was great. Everything was working out perfectly, almost too perfectly.

He'd always strived to be the best at everything he did and surprisingly, it took little to no effort to actually achieve it. He was the best in his classes, the best in the diplomatic academy. The best assistant to one of the king's most trusted diplomats.

And, when his master had fallen ill in the middle of important negotiations with barbaric kingdoms on the eastern continent, a young Sebastian had assumed his role, effortlessly pushing forth a peace treaty that Hayden had desperately wanted.

Upon his return, the king had named him a fully fledged diplomat, the youngest in the history of Orellia. The two men had even became friends, or at least, close acquaintances. At the start, Sebastian had admired Hayden – being crowned king at the young age of fifteen was not a thing to be envied, and ever since then, the king had been doing his best to ensure the safety of his subjects.

It was not until Sebastian had visited Cchen-Lian, the greatest and mightiest empire in the world, and met with the exalted Emperor Odi, that he realized that Orellia was nothing. That Hayden was nothing but a savage, no better than those primitive tribes Sebastian had dealt with in the east. Nothing could compare to the beauty and the strength of the empire.

Orellia deserved better. How could the people ever be happy under the yoke of such a primitive? The madman that called himself the Burning Fury? Ridiculous! No, Sebastian didn't need much convincing to see the truth. Orellia should be part of the grand empire, under the rule of the illustrious Emperor Odi.

Odi's people hadn't exactly told him their entire plan but he was smart enough to read between the lines. They stirred trouble, pitting other countries against Hayden, and Sebastian was in an excellent position to help them. Sabotaging his own negotiations would be too obvious but he could provide them with other things. Like forged documents bearing the fake seal he'd created by carefully copying the official one, sculpting it to such perfection the result was indistinguishable from the original.

The fact that Nicolas had almost died thanks to those documents was unfortunate, but this was war. Collateral damage was expected. It was the same with the innocent citizens that were going to die during the festival. A necessary evil. A sacrifice needed to finally undermine Hayden's position enough that people themselves would want to see him gone and would welcome Odi's army as liberators, not fight them as invaders.

Just like with Clara. His little sister proved to be a surprisingly useful asset. It was so easy to manipulate her into putting the potion into Hayden's drink. Yes, there were some sacrifices on Sebastian's side as well, getting beaten up by Kan'thar and his thugs certainly wasn't a pleasant experience, but it was worth it.

The potion hadn't worked as well as Odi's people had told Sebastian it would. He'd certainly expected Hayden to be way more out of control by this point, but he'd managed to get rid of the lord chancellor, which was the main target. Huxley's whispers had probably helped as well.

Damn, how Sebastian hated working with that snake! All he wanted was to see that Levantian bastard suffer and die, not promise him rewards for cooperation. Sebastian couldn't believe that Huxley had actually asked for the queen. The audacity! While he was married to Clara? Sure, Sebastian didn't particularly care much about her well-being and happiness, but she was still his sister, and with their father gone, her honor was his to defend.

Alas, Huxley had proven to be useful, so he got to live. For now. He even got to dream about his little harem or whatever the sick fuck was planning to do with two women. Sebastian didn't care. All the promises were empty anyway, he had no intention of delivering on them. Once Huxley's cooperation was no longer needed, Sebastian was going to personally beat the shit out of that parody of a man before watching him draw his last breath.

The plan was now in full motion. By the time he arrived at the main square, dragging that annoying little sister of his along, the barrels filled with the powder and sharp projectiles were already planted in various locations throughout the city. They were hidden beneath podiums and disguised between barrels of mead and ale. One pile was even placed at the bottom of a huge ceremonial bonfire that would be lit at sundown. That one was going to be one hell of a bang, Sebastian thought with a smirk.

Of course, he knew he could get caught. Despite being extra careful, the further the plan went along, the bigger the chance of discovery. Many people were involved in the plan at this point. Granted, most of them had no idea what was really going on, and the explosions were conveniently going to kill them as well. But any one of them could have talked and raised suspicion.

Yes, Sebastian was well aware he was in constant danger of being arrested. Yet, when it finally did happen, it still took him by surprise.

He stared at the four soldiers in front of him, his heart beating frantically as he tried to figure out what to do. "This must be some mistake," he declared, clearing his throat in an attempt to put authority into his voice. He was a nobleman, a friend to the king, not a fucking lowlife the guards could just pick up off the street. "Get out of my way," he snarled and tried to shove the officer away.

The man didn't move.

"What's going on?"

Great, just what Sebastian needed, his little sister's sniveling. Although, perhaps she could distract the soldiers while he escaped?

Clara's eyes jumped between Sebastian and the soldiers, she looked like a frightened child. "Arrested? What for?"

The officer's features hardened. "Step aside, my lady. This man is under arrest for high treason and conspiring against the king."

So they did know. This wasn't just a random mixup or a prank from Sebastian's colleagues.

Clara covered her mouth with her hands, staring at him in disbelief. If he planned to use her, he needed to do it fast. "Clara, please, this is complete nonsense. You don't honestly believe that I'd betray King Hayden?"

Her brows furrowed and she slowly shook her head. So gullible, Sebastian thought. What had Huxley said about her? 'Adorable little thing'. Guess he was right about something.

"Whoever these men are, they certainly weren't sent by the king. They are probably just common thugs dressed as soldiers trying to kidnap people right from the street!" He raised his voice so more passersby around them stopped moving, watching their exchange with curiosity.

"Sir," the officer looked around nervously, "I can assure you we have been sent by the king. You need to come with u-" He tried to put a hand on Sebastian's shoulder, holding heavy shackles in his other hand, but Clara screamed out and shoved him away.

"Don't touch him!" She stood between the soldiers and Sebastian, hands on her hips, looking as dangerous as their mother did when she was angry. "My brother is a respected diplomat and a personal friend of the king! He's not a traitor! You are going to let him go!"

The soldiers had clearly had enough. The officer rolled his eyes then, shaking his head, pushed Clara aside. It was clear he expected her to move out of his way so her attack caught him by surprise.

Sebastian was a little taken aback himself. However, he couldn't help smirking as he watched his little sister shove her knee between the man's legs and slap him so hard he staggered back. "Come on!" she screamed out and grabbed Sebastian's hand, dragging him away.

It was probably a smart move since he could see another group of guards coming around the corner. The soldiers wasted a few precious seconds to help their commander up which the now fugitives used to gain a head start. But it was clear it wouldn't be enough. Or at least, it seemed that way to Sebastian until Clara took a sharp turn toward one of the stalls lining the street, picking something from the shelf and turning against their pursuers.

She didn't hesitate for one second, drawing the bow she'd just stolen and sending an arrow toward the closest soldier. The man let out a tortured scream and stumbled to the ground, the others quickly stopped and took cover.

"Grab that!" Clara shouted, pointing at a quiver full of arrows, pulling a second one over her head. The merchant tried to protest but raised his hands in surrender when she glared at him, wisely deciding that throwing himself on the ground would be safer right now.

Look at that. His little sister could be useful after all, who would have thought? Sebastian tried to wrap his head around what the hell was happening as they raced through the streets, Clara sending arrow after arrow against the men in pursuit until they managed to shake them off in the narrow alleyways of the Lower City.

Sebastian watched Clara stumble a couple of times, her leg probably not being fully healed yet, but since she had proven to be useful, he caught her and helped her up.

"This way," he nudged her shoulder softly, directing her toward the docks. It was time that he took control of the situation again. He led her to one of the warehouses and banged on the door.

It was fairly dark inside, the large empty space lit only by a couple of lanterns. Sebastian couldn't hide his satisfied grin. This warehouse hadn't been empty yesterday. No, yesterday it had been filled with the powder barrels that had now been distributed to their intended destinations. A few of which had been secretly delivered into other hideouts. Sebastian intended to use them to cover his tracks once everything was done. And, hopefully, to get rid of Kan'thar and his goons. That idiot was seriously getting on his nerves.

As their eyes adjusted to the darkness, Clara cried out and raised the stolen bow again.

"No." Sebastian roughly grabbed her arm and forced her to lower it back down. "They are with me."

"B-but..." She seemed absolutely horrified and he could hardly blame her. Facing the men who'd kidnapped her and forced her to poison the king was probably not a pleasant experience. "T-they...didn't they...?"

Sebastian noticed Kan'thar step forward with a smirk, opening his mouth to say something, but he angrily waved him away. Clara was already frightened enough, these assholes didn't need to add to it. Not that her feelings really mattered to him, but taking care of a sobbing child in the midst of a mental breakdown was certainly not what he needed to be doing right now.

"S-Sebastian? What's going on?" Clara was leaning against the wall, her breathing fast and shallow, looking like she was barely holding back the tears. "I-Those soldiers, they...I..." Her eyes widened as she looked at the bow in her hand and she dropped it on the ground. "Oh, gods! I-I shot them! Soldiers! The king's soldiers!"

She was hyperventilating and seemed close to passing out. And while Sebastian wouldn't really mind it since it would shut her up for a few minutes, he kept reminding himself that this was not just a nameless pawn in the game. This was his little sister who'd just saved his ass back there.

"Clara." He grabbed her arms and waited until she looked at him. "You did nothing wrong. Everything is going to be alright, I promise. Do you trust me?" He certainly wasn't going to waste time and energy explaining everything to her. But it looked like his big brother authority was enough, since Clara bit on her lip and nodded hesitantly. "Good," he gently patted her shoulder, "just wait here and don't worry about a thing. You are completely safe here for now."

After she seemed to have calmed down enough to not burst into tears, Sebastian left her standing in the corner and moved to the men patiently waiting on the other side of the warehouse. "Somebody talked," he growled, glaring at them. "I was almost arrested right on the street!"

"All of my men are accounted for," Kan'thar shrugged. "Everything is running smoothly, the soldiers don't seem to know about the barrels or anything about our plan. There was only one outside person involved," he suggested.

One outside person, until Sebastian had dragged Clara along to his secret hideout. But the girl was harmless, she barely knew what was happening or where she was. Her husband, on the other hand... Fucking Huxley! Had he betrayed them? Sebastian might have slipped a word or two in front of him in anger that could have pointed Oscar in his direction, but the man was supposed to be working with the conspirators to get rid of Hayden. How long had that snake been playing them?!

"Get him." The words came out as a barely audible snarl. "He has outlived his usefulness anyway. Alive! I want that asshole for myself!" A surprised gasp from behind him indicated that Clara had overheard their conversation. "Sorry, sister," Sebastian smirked, unable to contain himself anymore, "looks like you are about to become a widow."

Fear flashed through her eyes but it disappeared quickly, replaced by iron determination. "Good," she nodded. "Let me know what I can do to help."

Help? She actually wanted to help him? Even without knowing what was happening? Wow, she really was stupid. Too bad he didn't have any use for her right now.

"Just stay here, don't leave this warehouse. I will send someone to pick you up once it is safe. Hey, you!" Sebastian yelled at one of Kan'thar's men, the one that didn't look as stupid as the others. "Stay here with my sister and keep her safe. Don't you fucking dare lay a finger on her! Oh, and while you're at it, get rid of those papers."

The written plans and maps were still scattered across a large table at the back of the room. Once the barrels exploded, they weren't going to be useful to anyone but it was still better to get rid of them just in case someone came sniffing around later.

He waited until Clara nodded again and headed out of the warehouse, carefully pulling a hood over his head. The streets weren't safe for Sebastian Redwood. At least for a couple of hours. Then it wasn't going to matter anymore.

Oscar couldn't just sit and wait, it was simply impossible. Hayden and Karina were attending the big ball, pretending as if nothing was happening, and he really didn't envy them that duty. Having to smile and lead polite conversations while the entire city was on the brink of destruction wasn't something Oscar could do right now, but spreading panic wouldn't help anyone. Gods, Hayden was probably going insane.

The plan was going well. The guards had attempted to arrest Redwood and Clara had helped him escape. One poor guy was shot in the leg but he was going to be paid handsomely for his suffering. The other arrows seemed to have narrowly missed. Oscar grinned at that thought. Clara never missed. But one wounded soldier was most likely enough to convince Sebastian she was on his side, the other shots were just for effect.

Despite the soldiers chasing them and several more people following them secretly, the trail had ended in the alleyways of the Lower City. Which meant Clara was somewhere out there, alone with her delusional brother, who was about to commit mass murder. How could Oscar stay safely in the palace while his wife was in danger?

He contacted his people across the city, ordering them to locate either her or her brother. Taking long strides to get to the meeting point as quickly as possible, he was too distracted to notice the shadows moving in behind him. Only after someone had tackled him to the ground and silenced his surprised yelp with a filthy rag stuffed into his mouth, Oscar realized how badly he'd fucked up.

Nobody knew where he'd gone. He'd rushed out of the palace without telling anyone, so worried about Clara he'd forgotten about his own safety. And it had backfired on him phenomenally.

"You wanted ropes and blindfolds?" a familiar voice growled into his ear as they twisted Oscar's arms behind his back, hastily wrapping a coarse rope around them. "You'll enjoy plenty of those tonight." A bag was pulled over his head. Then somebody kicked his stomach a couple of times for good measure before hurling him up and carrying him away, disoriented and utterly defenseless.

Chapter 68

C lara didn't have to pretend to be frightened anymore, especially after hearing Sebastian order his people to capture Oscar. Then he'd gone and left her alone with one of the men who had kidnapped her before. Seriously, what was he thinking? Did he have no regard for her emotions? Her life?

The man clearly didn't consider the 'don't touch my sister' order to be important, since he leered at her sleazily, reminding Clara of the two Ruthians that had ambushed her in the tower. This asshole was about to meet the same fate. Clara was done with arrogant men who thought a lone girl was nothing more than prey. Just a thing they could use for their entertainment. She needed to take this asshole out, and fast.

He didn't have much self-control, it only took him a minute to decide to move closer to her. The way his tongue kept sliding over his lips was beyond disgusting. Clara sniffled quietly and tried to back away, ending up against the wall. The man placed his hands either side of her shoulders, trapping her between himself and the wall.

"P-please don't," she whispered, moving her hands into position while playing the perfect victim.

"Don't worry," he grinned, "we are just going to have some fun."

That they were. But not the kind of fun he was expecting. He leaned forward toward her and Clara looked away, making a feeble attempt to push him away. She was hoping he would move in closer and try to kiss her now exposed neck, which he did. Men were so damned predictable, she smirked.

From this angle, he couldn't possibly see the blade she'd pulled out of the hidden pocket of her gown. He didn't notice it until Clara had plunged it deep into his back, right under the ribs at an angle where she hoped it would find his heart or lungs.

He groaned, his hand trying to reach the knife in his back as if he were trying to scratch a mosquito bite. Clara closed her eyes and had to bite on her lip not to start screaming as she pulled the dagger out and shoved it back in, again and again, until his lifeless body slid down to the ground.

She was trembling so hard she could barely hold the blade anymore and her cheeks were wet. But now was not the time for tears or mental breakdowns. She had to stop the explosions. Save the people. Save Oscar! The thought of Oscar in danger helped her bid her frozen body to move. She rushed toward the desk covered in parchments.

A map. Clara needed a map of the city. Preferably one with clearly marked locations of the powder barrels. It had to be here, right? That's why Sebastian had wanted the papers destroyed. It must have been. Her hands frantically flipped through the parchments, smearing blood all over them. Where was it?!

In her panicked state, she had completely overlooked a couple of larger parchments rolled up and stacked by the side of the table. When she finally realized her mistake and grabbed the biggest one, she sighed in relief. It was exactly what she was looking for.

A new wave of horror washed over her as she quickly scanned the list of locations. There were barrels in all the big squares where people were gathering for the festival, the barracks where soldiers who were off duty were celebrating, and... The wing of the palace where Karina and Hayden were hosting the grand ball for the most important nobles. Gods!

There was no time to ponder over it. Clara needed to reach the soldiers and hope Hayden had instructed them to listen to a crazy-looking girl covered in blood. She didn't spare a second glance at the body on the floor but she did pause to pick up the stolen bow along with the quiver of arrows, worried that before the night ended, she was going to need it again.

It didn't take long for her to run into a group of soldiers. "Hey! STOP!" they yelled at her after noticing her weapon and the blood on her clothes.

They were more than a little stunned when she didn't try to run away but rather, sprinted straight toward them. "Banana peel!" she screamed out as she got closer.

The men stared at her, clearly considering her insane, but their commander's face lost all color. "Where are we going?" he asked quickly, signaling his men to stand down.

The idea of using a secret passcode might have sounded completely stupid to an outsider, and Clara would never admit that it had actually come from a story she'd read a few months back, but it seemed to have worked.

"You are going to need more men. Gather everyone you can and spread around these locations," she paused to show the stolen map to the commander. "There will be barrels containing explosive dust in these locations that will kill everyone nearby if set on fire."

A few of the soldiers opened their mouths to protest or maybe laugh at her but the commander quickly silenced them, letting Clara continue. "There will probably be some men hanging around to set them off, they may be using fuses. The fuses look like long, sparkly ropes. I really don't know all the specifics. All I know is that if you don't stop them, hundreds of people will die. Including those in the palace."

"Yes, my lady." It didn't seem possible for the commander's face to grow any paler but somehow he'd managed it. Yet he was professional to the core, quickly regaining his composure to shout orders at his men. Several soldiers sprinted off toward the nearest patrols, one heading directly to the palace.

Clara stood resting against a wall, still trying to catch her breath after running across the docks. Now what?

Her part of the plan was done. The soldiers would take care of the rest. But what about Oscar? Was he still inside the palace? He should be attending the ball but somehow Clara doubted her husband would be at a party while the fate of the city hung on a thread and his wife was risking her life trying to prevent a massacre. Hayden and Karina no doubt hated attending the ball too, but their hands were tied. The royal couple simply had to appear on such an occasion unless they wanted to cause rumors that could quickly turn into a full-scale panic.

A small hand tapped her elbow and Clara flinched, pulling out her dagger again, stopping herself just in time to avoid stabbing the young boy that was standing next to her. Gods, is this what she'd become? Someone who mercilessly murdered people in cold blood? Drawing a blade at the slightest hint of trouble? She'd almost killed a child, for fuck's sake!

The boy looked at her with an eyebrow raised, his head cocked to the side in contemplation rather than fear. He certainly didn't seem like a sweet, innocent child. More like one of the pickpockets that roamed the city streets. Not that it eased Clara's conscience, but he probably wouldn't have let her stab him even if she'd tried. "What?" she snapped at him.

"Are you Lord Oscar's wife?"

Of course, Oscar had mentioned he was using the local kids to spy for him, this must have been one of them. "Yes," she nodded frantically, "do you know where he is? You need to warn him, they-"

"Too late," the boy shrugged, "they already took him. But...I might know where to, for the right price."

Clara had to fight off the urge to start strangling the stupid kid. Oscar's life was in danger and this ragged lowlife wanted to blackmail her? "You'll get your money. Now, show me!"

It would be better if she could take some of the soldiers with her but they needed every single man available to find the barrels and stop the explosions. Clara had to manage on her own. After all, this was a family matter.

Oscar was in some pretty deep shit this time. He had gotten himself entangled with the criminal underworld before but it had never gotten to the point where someone had actually abducted him with the intent of killing him, until now. Yet, all he could think about was whether this meant that Clara had failed.

He was frightened, yes, but not for his own life. Would Sebastian kill her? He didn't seem to care that he'd nearly caused the death of his own brother, but that was indirect. He'd argue that he'd just provided the papers to reignite the hostilities with the Ruthians and Nicolas was simply a casualty of war. Would Sebastian go so far as to directly order his goons to murder Clara?

They dragged Oscar inside an abandoned old building, at least he guessed it was by the shadows deepening outside of the blindfold and the smell of rotting wood filling his nostrils. Oscar prayed to every single god in existence, that when they finally removed his blindfold, Clara wouldn't be here tied up next to him. Or worse. He could very well imagine what a bunch of criminals might do with a pretty young girl.

No matter how much he struggled, there was no chance of breaking free, especially not with his hands tied behind his back. Strong arms held him up while someone slid a rope over his head. A noose, as Oscar discovered when it tightened around his neck.

When the hands let go of him, Oscar stumbled, nearly suffocating before he managed to regain his footing. He had to balance on his tiptoes in order to keep the noose loose enough to allow him to breathe, at least a little.

Only then did someone remove the bag from his head and Oscar found himself staring right into the face of Sebastian Redwood. Searching the room as best he could manage, Oscar didn't see Clara anywhere, which was either very good or very bad. What he did see didn't exactly comfort him, though.

The goons that had brought him here were leaving. It was in Oscar's favor, but still, it wasn't like Oscar could fight Redwood off from his current position. A barrel standing just a few feet away from Oscar made him shudder in fear. There was a sparkling rope coming out of it, stretching across the floor all the way to the exit. Oscar didn't have to guess twice to know its purpose.

Sebastian followed his gaze with a vicious smirk. "Aren't you a smart one? You have it all figured out, don't you?"

Still gagged by a filthy piece of cloth, Oscar couldn't exactly answer even if he wanted to.

Clenching his fists, Redwood stepped closer. "You know all my plans," he snarled, punching Oscar's stomach so all of the air rushed out of his lungs. "You're fucking my sister," another punch almost made Oscar stumble, only the tight pinching of the noose keeping him upright. "You walk around the palace like you own the damn place!"

Oscar braced himself for another hit but Sebastian kicked his knee instead, chuckling as Oscar struggled to stay up on his feet in order not to strangle himself.

It was a shitty position. Oscar couldn't breathe, couldn't think, the only thing he could focus on was keeping himself upright to allow for bits of precious air to pass through his constricted throat. His only two weapons, a brilliant mind and a quick tongue, were both useless at the moment.

It was a lost battle. There was no way he could escape this. The only reason he was still alive was that Redwood apparently wanted to beat Oscar to death himself. Or maybe just use him as a human punching bag before lighting up that devilish powder, tearing Oscar's helpless body to shreds.

At least, it seemed like Clara was safe. Sebastian would have no doubt gloated over discovering her betrayal. Perhaps she'd even managed to find out enough about Redwood's plans to thwart them.

If Oscar hadn't been so reckless and had just trusted her, he wouldn't be in this mess. The blame was all on him and nobody was rushing to his rescue this time. Perhaps he didn't deserve to be rescued.

Chapter 69

C lara paused to catch her breath, the stinging pain in her side forcing her to double over. Not to be outdone by the intense throbbing in her injured thigh, letting her know that the leg was going to give up on her soon unless she rested for a moment.

Damn, she really was in bad shape. But, to be honest, she hadn't expected to be running around the city in order to save her husband and stop her brother from massacring innocent citizens. Plus, she had just spent the past month mostly on bedrest.

The boy didn't seem winded at all. How unfair. "It's just around the corner," he urged, signaling her to keep going. Clara half ran, half limped to the corner of a building to cautiously peek into the next street.

There were nothing but warehouses around so Clara assumed they were back at the docks. A filthy, young girl, no older than six, appeared out of nowhere. She exchanged a couple of words with Clara's guide before melting back into the shadows.

"Most of the men have left," the boy announced, "it's only Lord Oscar and one other inside." Sebastian. Gods, Clara hoped Oscar was still alive.

"I hope you save him, lady," the boy grinned and pointed her to the right door. "He pays well."

Street honor apparently didn't command him to help a lady in distress, nor to try and rescue a well-paying customer. Clara couldn't blame him. It was obvious from the start that this was going to be her battle.

Sneaking around the city alleyways was not unlike sneaking around the forest, letting Clara put Rimea's lessons to use.

The building didn't appear to have any windows and the large gate used for loading and unloading goods was locked, making the small door at the side of the building the only way in or out that Clara could see.

Clara grabbed the bow and nocked an arrow before entering the building, knowing that she might have to react fast once inside. The door creaked but the sounds coming from the room behind them continued uninterrupted. The soft thuds interlaced by desperate gagging and gasping for air were sending shivers down Clara's spine.

Just as she'd expected, it was Sebastian beating a defenseless Oscar. Clara's knuckles turned white as she gripped her bow handle tighter upon seeing Oscar's desperate position.

Hands tied behind his back, Oscar was forced to balance on his tiptoes, while slowly being choked by a rope around his neck. Not only could he not fight back or evade the hits, but he had to take them while standing upright otherwise the noose would suffocate him. What kind of barbaric torture was this? Had Sebastian gone completely mad?!

One step forward was all Clara needed to get a clean shot, fully intending to aim for Sebastian's shoulder. Killing her own brother was a little too much to add to her conscience but she was determined to stop him from killing Oscar. Unfortunately, as she moved her foot forward, a piece of broken glass cracked beneath her foot. Her brother turned around, responding almost instantly.

Clara expected him to try and hide behind Oscar, perhaps even to pull out a blade and threaten to kill him unless she put her weapon down. That would be the reasonable thing to do. Also, it would be a very fortunate thing for Clara.

Being a few inches taller and more muscular than Oscar, Sebastian couldn't exactly use Clara's husband as a living shield since there would always be something sticking out. And Clara never missed.

Unfortunately, Sebastian must have realized this, because he jumped away from Oscar, grabbing one of the lanterns hanging on the wall. Clara's brows furrowed as she tried to guess the reason for his actions but she raised the bow, drawing the string and taking aim at her brother. Only Oscar's muffled cries stopped her from releasing the arrow. He was shaking his head vigorously, giving her a desperate look.

"You should listen to your husband, sister," Sebastian smirked, unfazed by the fact that she could kill him at any moment.

Clara hesitated. Something wasn't right.

Her eyes scanned the floor beneath her brother's feet, her heart sinking as she traced a sparkling rope running from the door to a barrel standing a few feet from Oscar. The powder. If Sebastian dropped the lantern, they were all going to die. Letting out a shaky breath, Clara slowly lowered the bow.

"Smart choice, you little bitch." The dim light reflecting in Sebastian's eyes gave him a ferocious look. "I have to say," he continued, shaking his head, "I had a failsafe for every possibility, even for this asshole messing with my plan. But you...I did not expect you to intervene. You were nothing but a useful pawn, an asset to be used and discarded. Do you really have to ruin everything you touch? Can you not, for once in your pointless existence, do something right?"

That hurt. Sebastian's words brought forth all of Clara's fears and insecurities that had been clouding her mind for years. Did she really fuck up everything? Sure, from Sebastian's point of view, it probably seemed that way, even though all Clara ever wanted was to live her life the way she wanted to, not the way someone else dictated.

"I did a lot of things right," she objected, fighting against a wave of doubts.

"One," her brother raised a finger, "you did one thing right in your entire fucking life. You gave the potion to the king."

Despite the horrible situation she was in, despite her exhaustion, the mortal danger, despite Oscar's constant suffering as he struggled to keep the noose from strangling him, Clara laughed. It was not something she could control, it just came out, reverberating through her entire being, shaking off all of her fears and doubts.

Sebastian stared at her dumbfounded, which made her laugh even harder. "You...," she tried to speak but her body refused to cooperate, her shoulders twitching as she tried to hold back the bursts of laughter, "you idiot... You...don't know? I never put that shit into the king's drink. Hayden is not crazy, he was just pretending to be so Oscar could get in on your little conspiracy!"

It probably wasn't a smart thing to reveal everything but Clara hoped it would throw Sebastian off enough for him to forget about the lantern and the fuse beneath his feet. But he was too smart for that. "Whatever. It doesn't matter anymore," he quickly shook off the surprise and straightened up, sounding calm again. "You let me go through with my plan and now it's too late to stop it."

"Are you so sure about that, big brother?" Clara asked and raised an eyebrow. "Because the map I gave the guards half an hour ago was very helpful. It was very considerate of you to leave it there for me, thank you."

Clara briefly considered lying to him about the warehouse being surrounded by soldiers but decided against it. Sebastian wasn't going to surrender. If he felt like there was no way out, he wouldn't hesitate to light the fuse and take Clara and Oscar down with him.

His expression twisted in rage, he snarled at her. "You fucking bitch!" He raised his foot to take a step toward her and Clara inhaled slowly, ready to shoot him the moment he moved the lantern away from the fuse.

But her brother didn't become the youngest diplomat in Orellian history by being stupid. Whether it was the flash of hope he saw in her face or he just realized his mistake, he quickly returned to his original position.

"Move away from the door, cunt," he hissed. "Or I'll blow us all up to pieces, that Levantian scum you love so much included. You never left him, did you? Gods, you are such a traitor! Seriously, how could you have stooped so low?"

Did he drink the insanity potion himself? Or had he always been such an asshole?

Clara slowly moved, leaving the door open and unguarded. The fuse on the ground stretched all the way out of the warehouse and Sebastian carefully followed it, holding the lantern right above it.

"How is loving a Levantian worse than planning to murder innocent people? Orellians, if you want to play the stupid nationality card?" Clara asked in vain hope to engage him in conversation, guessing that once he reached the door, she and Oscar were done for.

"It all serves the grand plan," Sebastian replied before smashing the lantern on the ground. It shattered with a loud noise, spilling burning oil all around. The fuse caught fire and the sparkling flames quickly started to advance toward the barrel.

No doubt Sebastian expected Clara to rush forward to try and douse the flames or free Oscar. To waste precious seconds, perhaps the last seconds of her entire life. But Clara was an archer.

The whole fucking point of being an archer was that you didn't have to rush anywhere. You stood in one place and solved problems from afar. And Clara had already figured out a solution to this particular problem.

She shot two arrows at the fuse, separating the rope at two different places, just to be sure. The sparks quickly reached the new end she'd'd created and, while she watched on with her breath held, the fuse died out.

The next two arrows grazed the rope holding Oscar up. They cut through enough of it so that Oscar's weight would tear the rest.

As much as Clara hated it, she couldn't rush in to untie or comfort him.

Another arrow nocked, she bolted for the door. She jumped over the pool of burning oil, wincing as the low flames licked her legs. Hopefully, the whole building wouldn't burn down with Oscar inside while she chased Sebastian. But Clara couldn't let him get away. Oscar would understand that. Gods, she hoped he was going to understand.

Sebastian didn't get far.

As smart as he was, he didn't realize that running in a straight line was not the best way to get away from an archer. Or perhaps he simply didn't think Clara would go after him, underestimating her once again. Clara was going to make sure that it was the last time.

An arrow went through his thigh, sending him tumbling to the ground. Groaning in pain, he grabbed his leg. Clara rushed over, ready to shoot him again in case he tried to get away.

His eyes narrowed, nothing but pure hatred in them now. "I'm your brother and the head of our family! I command you to stop with this nonsense!"

Clara snorted, fighting real hard to hold back another burst of laughter. He didn't even have authority over the people he'd hired, that man in the warehouse wouldn't have tried to rape her otherwise. Why the fuck did he expect her to suddenly obey his orders? Did he really think she was that gullible?

"Hey, kid!" she called out, looking around the empty street, completely ignoring her brother squirming on the ground just a few feet away from her. "Do you want to get rewarded by the king?!" She was sure the boy was still lurking around, waiting to see how the situation played out.

A short figure popped up from one of the side alleys and hesitantly moved closer. "I don't know. The king isn't exactly the safest person to deal with."

"But he is the richest one around," Clara appealed to the motivation that seemed to work best with the boy before. "And he would really appreciate it if you made sure this man didn't escape."

"The emperor is much richer!" Sebastian sensed an opportunity. "And he is going to pay you handsomely if you get rid of this woman and help me get out of here!"

Wow. It's not like Clara had expected chivalry but it still didn't feel very nice to hear her own brother trying to bribe a petty criminal to murder her. "He might be richer," she smiled sweetly at the boy, "but he is all the way beyond the western sea. And King Hayden is probably already on his way here. You look like a clever kid, you pick the smarter option."

The boy grinned and whistled sharply. A couple more kids crawled out of the shadows and approached Sebastian, one holding a big coil of rope.

"You stupid bitch!" Sebastian struggled against their small hands as they tied him up, but there were too many of them. "You were always a stain on our family honor, you fucki-OH!" The boy's ragged boot in Sebastian's stomach disrupted his tirade.

"Don't talk to Lord Oscar's wife like that, asshole," the little leader waggled a finger in Sebastian's direction.

Well, look at that, there was such a thing as street honor after all. "Thanks, kid," Clara nodded in appreciation. "Now go get the soldiers."

The muscles of her injured leg cramped as she was sprinting back to the warehouse, sending her tumbling to the ground. Her knee painfully banged against the cobblestones. Great, more bruises were exactly what Clara needed, not.

Not letting the pain stop her, Clara scrambled back to her feet and hobbled toward the door, frightened of what she was going to find inside. Was Oscar even still alive?

The oil on the floor was still burning when she barged in but, fortunately, it didn't reach the severed fuse or any of the walls. A tiny blessing from the gods? It would be only fair, given the amount of shit they'd already dumped on her head.

Oscar's body was collapsed on the ground, the skin on his face almost purple, and Clara let out a tortured scream as she leaped forward toward him. No, he couldn't be dead!

Her vision was blurred by tears as she quickly loosened the noose around his neck and cut the rope tying his wrists. He didn't move.

"Please, no," she sobbed, cradling his head on her lap, her fingers removing the rope before sliding along his neck trying to find a pulse.

This was all her fault. She should have stayed to help him, not chased after her stupid, treacherous brother. Or, better yet, she never should have married him, never should have told him she loved him. She was the cause of all of his problems.

If he had never met her, he would have been safe, not dying on the dirty floor of this warehouse, tortured to death by her own brother.

Over the sound of her sobbing and sniffling, she almost missed a wheezing gasp for air coming from Oscar's mouth. "Oscar?" she whimpered, desperately trying to calm down.

He probably couldn't breathe very well with his head lifted to her lap, so Clara gently put him back down, making sure his throat was straight to allow as much air through as possible. It proved a good idea since the moment she did it, his breathing became deeper.

Clara waited, holding her husband's hand, for what felt like the longest minutes of her life. The color of Oscar's face slowly changed back to its normal shade, except for his neck, which was still red and was no doubt going to be badly bruised. His fingers twitched and grabbed hers, desperately holding her while his eyes fluttered open. Only a hoarse groan came from his mouth when it finally opened but it didn't stop him from trying again and again.

"C...Clara?" he winced in pain. Talking must have been very hard for him. Clara could only hope that nothing in his throat was damaged permanently.

"I'm here," she sniffled quietly, "I'm sorry it took me so long. I had to settle some family issues first."

A corner of his mouth curled slightly to form a grin. "That family...of yours... Truly...something..."

"Yes, that's true," she laughed through the tears. "I'm really sorry, I've brought nothing but trouble into your life." She remembered saying the same thing to him once before and how he'd waved it off. Now it was even more true.

His fingers pressed into her hand harder. "No...you brought...love... All...worth it." He tried to raise his head to look around, quickly changing his mind while letting out a pained groan. "The...barrels?"

"I gave Sebastian's map to Hayden's soldiers, they seemed to be handling it before I ran off to find you. I'm really so-" A distant thundering sound interrupted her and her eyes widened in horror. There wasn't a cloud in the sky tonight.

Oscar closed his eyes. "Shit," he let out a strained breath.

One. Just one. Out of how many, twelve?

Trembling in despair, Clara waited for more sounds of explosions, tears rolling freely down her cheeks. This was all her fault. She wasn't fast enough, smart enough. Good enough. How could she have been? She was just a good-for-nothing seventeen year old girl, a fucking teenager. How the hell was she supposed to handle saving the entire city?

"Not your...fault." Oscar pulled on her hand, making her look at him through the tears. "You are...amazing. This was all...Sebastian. Did he...?"

Clara shook her head. "No. I shot his leg and your little friends are taking care of him until the soldiers arrive."

"You came...alone?" He raised his eyebrows. "I didn't think...you would come...at all. That anyone...would. I don't...deserve saving."

What the hell was he talking about? Who else would deserve to be saved more than him? "Did you suffer brain damage from lack of air? Because you sound stupid," Clara scowled at him, hurt that he would even think she wouldn't come to rescue him. "I will always come to save you. Alone or not."

"I love you." There was so much love in his expression, fresh tears fell from Clara's eyes. "I would give...my life for yours. I was...so scared."

Of course he was, being beaten to death while suffocating must have been a horrible experience. Before she could say something to comfort him, he slowly turned his head from side to side. "Not for myself. For you. I didn't know...if he..."

Clara leaned down and carefully kissed him, just a brief touch of her lips on his. "Remember what Kadri said? I'm indestructible." Oscar grinned, which was exactly Clara's intention. "I love you too. When he ordered those men to take you... I was hoping you would stay safe in the palace. You were supposed to be the smart one around here."

"I'm never smart...when it comes to you." He pulled on her hand to make her lean back down to his face.

Sure. The city was on a brink of destruction, Clara's brother was tied up in the middle of the street, guarded by underage criminals, Oscar had nearly died and still couldn't speak or even breathe properly. And what did he want to do? Make out on the filthy floor of this abandoned warehouse, next to a barrel full of explosives.

And, after all, why not? "I guess love makes us all stupid."

He smiled, his fingers gently caressing her hair. "Worth it."

Chapter 70

The heavy door in front of Clara was closed. She was standing here all alone, nervously shifting weight from one foot to the other, straightening her ceremonial gown for the hundredth time.

Karina's idea to carry the bow and quiver full of arrows on her back suddenly didn't seem so smart or attractive anymore. Clara's hair was carefully brushed and braided intricately to fall over her shoulder, the tip of her weapon and the feathered ends of the arrows sticking out from behind the other one. Combined with the beautiful emerald gown, it must have looked ridiculous.

But it was too late to do anything about it now, since the door was already opening soundlessly, revealing the large hall beyond. It was the throne room, the biggest hall in the palace, where the king usually greeted important foreign delegations. Today, there were no delegations coming. Just Clara, feeling tiny and lost as she walked down the aisle between rows of benches toward the dais at the far end of the room. Where Hayden and Karina now sat on their thrones.

Despite being filled with people, the room was surprisingly quiet. The loudest sounds were Clara's footsteps and the bottom hem of her gown swishing over the tiled floor. Clara tried to keep her head up and look only at the king, as etiquette commanded, but she couldn't help but notice several familiar faces in the gathered crowd.

Friska and Mina were in the back, proud smiles on their faces.

Larkin, Enzio, and the few men who remained from the group Clara had spent so much time with during her travels north, were saluting her. Not just mockingly touching their foreheads but real, proper military salutes.

Nicolas looked somewhat troubled, but his smile for Clara was sincere. Their mother was supposed to stand beside him but her spot was empty. Clara wasn't really surprised, even though it did hurt a little.

Sophia Redwood didn't believe that Sebastian was a traitor. She even went as far as accusing Clara of framing him to try and get her hands on the family riches. After her ridiculous outburst, not even Nicolas wanted to spend time around the woman who'd birthed them. He packed up his things and moved to the barracks for good. Sophia still had her money and the mansion but she was all alone in it now.

Lords and generals from Hayden's council were standing to either side of the thrones, Oscar among them. He gave Clara the brightest smile, nodding his encouragement while rearranging the cravat around his neck. His bruises had turned all shades of purple and yellow, a truly horrifying sight not fit for such an official occasion. At least he could speak without any issues, albeit still sounding hoarse.

Clara breathed in deeply as she stopped in front of the royal couple, lowering her head in a sign of respect, slowly bending down on one knee.

Hayden stood up, looking every bit the powerful and dangerous king. He was a far cry from the man who'd sat on the dirty ground of the kitchen tent, peeling potatoes and sticking his tongue out at his wife.

Karina followed him, staying a step behind. Just like Hayden, she was the picture of a mighty queen now, not the lowly wench scrubbing pots or the trembling woman bathing naked in a freezing cold lake.

Clothes really do make a big difference, Clara thought. Or perhaps it wasn't the clothes, but the air of authority that radiated from them in this moment, making every single person in the room wait reverently to hear them speak. Eager to follow their commands and fulfill their wishes. It was probably a good thing those orders didn't involve arresting Clara or dragging her into the dungeons as the sister of a traitor.

Clara forbade herself from thinking about Sebastian. He was alive, that much she knew. Oscar's little helpers kept their end of the deal and delivered him to the guards. Right now, Sebastian was most likely locked up in chains somewhere deep beneath her feet.

Clara didn't want to know what the king's people were doing to him or what his fate would be. Hayden didn't tell her and she didn't ask. That man wasn't her brother anymore. Not when the blood of dozens of innocent people and several soldiers who'd died in one of the squares was on his hands.

Only one of the barrel piles had exploded, the one hidden in a ceremonial bonfire in a square in the Lower City. The soldiers had searched the place high and low but didn't realize their mistake until the fire was lit and it was too late. All other threats were successfully eliminated, the men responsible killed or arrested. The whole city mourned the victims of the terrible tragedy. Thankfully, not many people knew how much worse it could have been.

Her head still bowed, Clara dared to peek up at Hayden. His expression was serious but when he noticed her peeking at him, the corners of his mouth fought to suppress a grin. Yes, that was the king she knew.

"Lady Clara Huxley," he spoke loud enough for everyone to hear, his voice echoing through the large hall.

Clara straightened her back and looked at him, her knee still touching the cold floor. "Your Majesty."

"Lady Huxley," Hayden repeated, "you have repeatedly proven your loyalty to the Kingdom of Orellia, to the queen, and to myself." Despite his serious tone, there was warmth in his eyes. "On several occasions you have risked your life to protect my wife and to protect the people of Orellia.

You have fought bravely and relentlessly. I would be proud if even half of my men were like you. Honestly, most of my men should consider you an example to follow." He raised an eyebrow and scanned the crowd, his gaze landing on each soldier present before moving on to the next.

The royal Master of Ceremonies standing at the back of the room must have been groaning at the king's impromptu additions to his speech. Poor man, Clara almost felt sorry for the headache this ceremony would be giving him. Almost. Women weren't normally featured in ceremonies such as these, especially not as main protagonists. As if forcing Hayden to stick to protocol wasn't difficult enough.

Hayden cleared his throat, looking down at Clara again. "If you were a squire, I'd knight you, but, well..." he shrugged, his hands pointing at her very non-squire-y appearance, his usual grin taking over his expression.

Clara's shoulders twitched as she suppressed a chuckle and she definitely wasn't the only one in the room. The Master of Ceremonies let out a quiet moan and hid his face in his palm. His job was certainly not one to be envied.

"Rise, please." Hayden offered his hand to help Clara up, which was probably a good thing since standing from a kneeling position while wearing a long gown brought a great risk of stumbling and falling.

Once she was safely standing straight again, the king let go of her hand. "Lady Clara Huxley, for your bravery, selflessness, unwavering loyalty, and for your invaluable service to the crown, you are being awarded the Red Lion Medal. Wear it with pride, just as your country is proud of you."

A wave of surprised whispers echoed throughout the room. They knew she was getting a medal but the Red Lion was something special. Only a handful of people were ever given this award, all of them national heroes. And until now, none of them wore a gown. A woman receiving the highest praise from the king himself was unheard of.

Karina smiled at her as she handed Hayden a small black velvet box. Clara fought not to giggle when the tip of the king's tongue poked out of the side of his mouth as he concentrated on attaching the pin to Clara's chest without actually touching her breasts. Keeping a straight face was almost impossible but Clara somehow managed to do it, not wanting to disrupt the ceremony, despite deeply disagreeing with it.

She had done nothing to deserve a medal.

If anyone should be given a medal, it was Oscar. He was the one who'd figured it all out. The one who'd nearly died protecting this country and its citizens. Not her. But Clara was outvoted, her opinion ignored.

Karina claimed that getting beaten was hardly a reason to receive a medal. Hayden didn't want his new Master of Whispers to be getting so much attention, it was a shady job after all. And Oscar had just grinned and reminded her that since he and Clara were married, half of the medal was going to be his anyway.

When the medal was finally secured to her chest, the red and black lion figure clearly visible against her green gown, Hayden took a step back and bowed his head. Everyone in the room followed suit, including the queen and the royal council. It felt surreal.

Fortunately, the moment passed quickly and Hayden straightened up again, pulling Clara into a hug while the rest of the room applauded. Clara caught a glimpse of the Master of Ceremonies rolling his eyes and leaving through the back door, shaking his head and muttering quiet curses.

"Hey, stop groping my wife." Oscar was the first to approach them, grinning at Clara and pretending to scowl at Hayden.

The king reluctantly let go, turning to her husband. "And here I thought that since I'm the supreme ruler of the country, everything and everyone in it belongs to me," he sighed.

"Yeah, sorry. The wrong type of country for that. I'm not sure people would be thrilled if you turned Orellia into a slavery empire." As usual, Oscar was being cheeky, pushing boundaries.

"Weren't you the one who wanted to start a harem?" Hayden chuckled and reached for Oscar's arm, hugging the surprised man. "I think I'm glad I didn't have you executed," he added after letting go of him, smirking at the sight of Oscar's dumbstruck face. "You two enjoy your vacation and don't get lost anywhere. Sadly, this war isn't over yet. I'm going to need all of my

heroes to bring down Odi. And the scoundrels will be handy as well."
The corner of his mouth curled up even further as he looked at Oscar.

They were headed off vacation. Oscar grumbled but Clara was glad to be in the saddle again, away from all the side glances and whispering that followed her throughout the palace. And while she was nervous about their destination, spending her time with Oscar, riding and talking, staying at inns along the road, (Oscar straight out refused to sleep in a tent ever again), was more than enjoyable.

Hayden insisted that, given his new position, Lord Huxley needed an escort. Oscar wasn't exactly happy about it but he managed to come up with a compromise – they brought Larkin along, plus a couple of other Levantian soldiers who wanted to visit their homes. The lieutenant's presence was also a great motivator for Mina to join them, even though she wasn't exactly thrilled by the prospect of being on horseback for so long. Clara felt embarrassed by the way they traveled in the end, like a true highborn lord and lady, accompanied by personal guards and even a maid.

With every mile bringing them closer to their home, Larkin and the soldiers seemed more relaxed and happier. Even Oscar smiled more often. Not just at Clara, he joked around with the men as well. Once they had gotten over their original aversion to him, caused by the abysmal reputation he'd had in Levanta, they'd readily accepted Oscar as a part of their group. That was Oscar. So damned irresistible.

It was late afternoon when they finally arrived at a big ornate gate, already opened so they could pass right through. Clara nervously clutched the reins. Oscar moved his horse closer to hers and leaned over to take her hand. "Don't worry," he soothed. "It's going to be alright."

Was it? Clara wasn't so sure anymore.

Oscar's parents loved Karina, no doubt they were hoping their son would one day marry her and become the king of Levanta. Then the war had happened and now Karina was unavailable and Oscar had been forced to settle for Clara. Surely they must have been disappointed over such a development, just like Sophia Redwood was when it became obvious her daughter wasn't going to marry the king.

Clara had half a mind to just turn her horse around and go back to the inn she'd spotted a mile back. She could come back here in the morning, looking at least a little more presentable. Not now, when she was exhausted after a whole day's journey, her hair loose from the braid and flying haphazardly around her head. She was dressed in her riding clothes, and probably smelled more like the dirt roses grew in, rather than the flower itself.

But Oscar didn't give her a choice. "Come on. They are going to love you." He sounded eager as if he couldn't wait to present her to his family.

Sophia was definitely on point when asking Oscar about his family wealth. The estate was huge and visibly luxurious, even just from the outside.

They headed first for the stables, a couple of stablehands rushing forward to help them dismount and take care of their horses. Clara dismounted from Betsie's back, taking her time to stretch her limbs, stalling so she wouldn't have to face Oscar's parents right away. Mina gave her an encouraging smile as she went to unpack Clara's things from the saddlebags.

"Well, well, well," a voice sounded from the stable entrance, making Clara quickly turn in that direction, "if it isn't my little brother. Finally crawling back home, Ossie?" The man wore a smirk on his face but the warmth in his eyes suggested he was just joking. He was more muscular than Oscar, clearly a warrior, but other than that, their features were surprisingly similar.

Oscar rolled his eyes as he turned to face his brother. "Dustin. I wish I could say it's good to see you again." Despite their brash words, the men embraced each other in a tight hug, patting each other's backs. "Is your wife visiting as well?" Oscar sounded strictly polite but Clara could tell he was hoping Dustin would say no. She remembered Oscar not being very fond of his sister-in-law. Were his brothers going to hate Clara as well?

"No," Dustin shook his head, "she's home on bed rest. We're expecting a baby."

Clara thought Oscar would reply with some snappy sarcastic remark but he surprised her, giving his brother a sincere, warm smile and embracing him again. "Congratulations, big brother. Come, meet my wife."

Clara tried to straighten her jacket and tuck a couple of loose curls behind her ear, but it was pointless. Fortunately, Dustin didn't comment on her appearance, bowing his head in front of her and kissing the back of her hand. "My lady." His smile was so similar to Oscar's Clara found herself smiling back at him. "It's an honor to meet you."

"The honor is mine. And please, just call me Clara."

Dustin's grin grew even wider. "It would be my pleasure." Oscar stepped next to Clara, glaring at his brother, warning him to back off. "Relax, Ossie," Dustin chuckled. "I'm just being friendly. Clara? I heard that you are an excellent marksman." His eyes found her bow tucked away in a scabbard attached to Clara's saddle, and he smirked in amusement. "You know, I'm something of an archer myself. Would you like to join me tomorrow so we could...compare our skills?"

Clara glanced at Oscar and nodded upon noticing his excitement. "Sure, why not?"

"Careful, brother," Oscar grinned, "your pride might suffer a fatal injury."

Dustin raised an eyebrow, clearly not believing that a woman could be good enough to beat him. "We shall see."

Great. Clara hadn't even been here five minutes and she was already competing with Oscar's brother.

"I'll take care of your people, Ossie," Dustin offered. "You should go greet Mom and Dad. They can't wait to meet your beautiful bride."

"Thanks." Oscar took Clara's hand and led her out of the stables to the courtyard, pausing for a moment upon noticing how tightly she had been clutching him. "Don't worry, Clara, please. My folks love you already and they haven't even met you yet," he whispered, leaning down to kiss her.

Hand in hand, they walked toward the mansion, Clara's heart skipping a beat when two figures walked outside to greet them. She calmed down slightly after seeing their kind smiles.

"Lord Huxley, Lady Huxley." Clara made a perfect curtsy, bowing her head deeply in front of Oscar's parents. Of course, her wearing riding pants sort of spoiled the effect, and she suddenly felt even more ashamed of her appearance, especially after seeing Oscar's mother who was wearing a beautiful ornate gown.

"Welcome." Oscar's father had a deep and strangely soothing voice. "It's a pleasure to finally meet you, Lady Clara." It looked and sounded like he really meant it. "I'm Alistair." He extended his hand toward her and when Clara reached for it, he grabbed hers and shook it. No kisses, no fake pleasantries or compliments. Clara really liked him. "And this lovely creature next to me is my wife, Eleonore."

Oscar's mother blushed when her husband pecked her cheek. "We are truly happy to welcome you to our home, Lady Clara."

"I... Thank you, I'm glad to be here." Clara was so taken aback by their natural and straightforward behavior she didn't know what to say. It was so different from all the pretentious pricks that often paraded around the Redwood mansion. But she should have known. Oscar was so kind and patient, he must have picked it up from somewhere. "Please, just call me Clara," she repeated the same thing she'd told Dustin.

Eleonore grinned at her. "It would be our pleasure." Her eyes found Oscar and she looked like she was barely holding back tears. "Come here, my dear boy!"

"Mom!" Oscar reluctantly let her pull him into a tight hug, rolling his eyes and sounding so much like a moody teenager it made Clara giggle.

Before she realized how incredibly inappropriate it was to laugh at their antics, Alistair had moved to her side. "Sorry about Ellie," he murmured, giving his wife a loving smile, "she always fusses over Oscar, especially after not seeing him for a while. I guess he's always going to be her little baby."

The way they rolled their eyes definitely ran in the family, since Alistair did it the same way as Oscar had just moments ago. "Be prepared that once she's sure she won't scare you away, she'll throw her arms around you as well."

Clara watched Eleonore whispering something into Oscar's ear. He nodded in response and they both looked at Clara. There were smiles on their faces, so it probably wasn't anything bad, but she still wanted to know what they were talking about. Oscar managed to squirm out of his mother's hold and went back to Clara, putting his arm around her shoulders.

"Come on, guys," Oscar said impatiently, "what kind of hosts are you? We're exhausted and starving and you are making us wait in the hallway like uninvited guests. I mean, I haven't eaten since Clara shot that squirrel for lunch and-"

"It was a rabbit!" she growled at him.

As he looked at her, he tilted his head to the side and raised an eyebrow. "Are you sure? It was very small." He didn't even bother masking the amusement in his voice, clearly mocking her in front of his parents to make her feel less nervous. And, to Clara's surprise, it was working. Especially since they didn't look at all offended and were smiling happily while listening to their exchange.

"It was a small rabbit. They aren't exactly born big," Clara defended herself. "And you'd know if it was a squirrel, they are much stringier."

"That's true," Alistair noted, his grin threatening to split his face in half. "Better than rats, though."

Clara chuckled, covering her mouth with her hand to preserve at least a semblance of respect toward Lord Huxley.

Oscar glanced between the two of them and shook his head. "Right, right. I forgot. Come on, Mom, let's leave the heavily decorated war heroes to share stories about eating rats and bathing in freezing cold lakes. I would very much prefer to have a proper dinner and a hot bath."

Oscar's parents were truly amazing. Clara had never imagined a family dinner could be so pleasant or funny, something to look forward to. Oscar and his brother kept bickering in a friendly manner throughout the evening, often joined by Alistair. Clara found herself laughing so often she had completely forgotten to be nervous. This was what she wanted her family to be like one day. Her and Oscar's, of course.

He kept smiling at her the whole evening, holding her hand, briefly kissing her cheek from time to time, making her blush. It was clear he was proud to show her off to his family, and even clearer they were happy for him.

"What was your mother asking you when we arrived?" Clara inquired when they were finally both in bed in Oscar's room, ready to go to sleep.

Oscar rolled to his side to look into her face, his fingers slowly sliding over her cheek. "She was saying that I finally look happy. I guess I do. Because I am finally happy, with you. Damn, now I will forever have to be grateful to Hayden for bringing us together."

Clara's heart suddenly felt so big it couldn't fit into her chest. "I'm happy too." Happy seemed like a lame word for how she was feeling.

"I love you," he whispered, leaning down to kiss her. "And I will love you even more if you kick my brother's ass with the bow tomorrow."

Shoulders twitching by suppressed chuckles, Clara nodded seriously. "I love you too, Oscar. And I don't think kicking your brother's ass is going to be a problem."

Interlude

T he low fire crackled quietly, casting dancing shadows over the small clearing. A horse was tied to a low bush with space enough to graze, his head lowered to the ground, scouring it for the best clump of grass, the saddle removed from its back and laid under a big tree, next to an unrolled sleeping mat.

The man wore casual clothes. A white shirt, leather breeches, sturdy jacket, and a thick cloak thrown loosely over his shoulders to protect him from the chilled night air. Despite the clothes being almost new, a perfect fit, clearly comfortable and made from high-quality materials, the man kept wriggling and pulling at the fabric as if he didn't like the way it felt against his skin.

It was no surprise. He hadn't worn civilian clothes in over thirteen years, not since he had joined the military training.

T he young boy was nervously clutching a small satchel filled with clothes, some food, and a few coins. Everything his poor family could afford to give one of their three sons who was leaving home to become a soldier.

Not that he particularly craved to be a soldier. But he didn't want to be a useless hungry mouth at a table where food was in short supply. Soldiers were given food and clothes, even paid once they graduated training. It seemed like a smart choice of occupation for a boy with no special talents.

"Just remember where your heart is, Lamar," his mother had told him before he left. "Soldiers often forget who they are and commit atrocious acts. You are a good man, never let that happen to you."

He was settled on an empty bunk in a large room, not sure what to do next. It was evening and although the sergeant had said that the cadets should be getting ready for lights-out, there was nobody else present. He overheard some noises coming from outside and curiously followed them, hoping he wouldn't get into trouble.

There was a small crowd of boys about his age, some of them a bit older. Lamar carefully weaved his way through the commotion, wanting to see what they were all looking at. It didn't turn out to be anything interesting though, just a dark-haired boy sitting on the ground, ferociously scrubbing a pot in a bucket of dirty water, just one pot from a huge pile next to him, while doing his best to ignore the boys staring at him.

Lamar looked around in confusion, unsure of what was happening. One of the older boys smirked, sizing him up and nodding, clearly pleased by Lamar's well-built body. "It's the prince," he whispered, jerking his head toward the dark-haired boy.

The prince? Lamar couldn't help himself but stare. The boy didn't look like a prince, he was all dirty and clearly tired, with dark circles under his black eyes.

The doubt must have shown on Lamar's face because the cadet next to him added, "I'm not kidding, ask anyone. That spoiled rich brat over there really is Prince Hayden, the son of King Rodric. Here," the boy stepped forward, grabbing one of the pots the prince had already cleaned, smearing mud and dirt all over it before handing it over to Lamar. "Make sure he's occupied until morning."

Lamar didn't exactly feel thrilled about it, knowing that as a new kid around here, it could have easily been him in that position, but he wasn't going to go against a whole crowd of boys just to protect a prince. What the hell had the precious royalty ever done for him?

His parents barely managed to put enough food on the table to feed their children. Hayden had no doubt been fed from a silver spoon, eating several-course meals every day, while Lamar often had to go to bed hungry when the only thing left for dinner was a piece of stale bread. Which he'd given to his little sister.

"Won't we get in trouble?" he asked, weighing the pot in his hand. "The king-"

The cadet's laugh interrupted him. "That's the best part. He's one of us now, the same piece of shit as you or me. The sergeants were given clear orders not to give him any special treatment."

It still seemed a little short-sighted. Wasn't the prince going to become the king eventually? Even if it took ten or twenty years, wouldn't he remember who'd bullied him during training? But Lamar wasn't really given a choice as the boy next to him nudged him forward. "Go on. Unless you want to join him?"

No, Lamar certainly didn't want that. The prince gave him a furious glare when Lamar carefully added the dirty pot to the pile but didn't say anything. Lips pressed into a tight line, Hayden finished cleaning the pot he was holding, dipping it into a bucket to wash it off, setting it on the ground in front of Lamar, snarling at the boy as if daring him to take that one too.

Lamar shivered and quickly retreated to the safety of the crowd. Prince or not, that kid was scary.

For the next few days, Lamar was so exhausted he barely paid attention to his surroundings. The drills were tough. Worse than he could have ever imagined. He considered giving up more than once. Always tired, always hungry. Especially since the rations were meager as the older boys took most of the food before the new cadets had even reached the table.

The prince was still here, suffering alongside the rest of them. Even worse since the boys continued to pick on him. He barely ate or slept but never complained. Lamar found himself reluctantly admiring Hayden. The poor kids were used to being hungry and beaten. But there was no doubt that until now, Hayden could have had any food he desired at any given time. Not just the few spoons of plain oatmeal and a scrap of moldy bread which were their rations on a good day.

Lamar felt awful whenever he joined the other boys in tormenting the prince but he was too afraid to stand against them. Still, it bugged him, like an itch that just wouldn't go away. Was this what shame felt like? His mother had called him a good man, but he was far from it at that moment.

Seeing the other cadets punch Hayden's face and shove him to the ground, kicking him in the stomach because he'd dared to refuse them his food rations, was the last straw for Lamar. It was one thing when they forced the prince to do their laundry or polish their boots. Not very nice or honorable, but tolerable. But brutally beating someone like this, four against one, that was just too much.

"Hey! What the fuck are you doing?!" Lamar yelled at them, moving closer.

The boys stopped and turned to him, arms crossed in front of their chests, their narrowed eyes giving him a clear warning. "We're just settling some scores with His Highness. It's none of your business. Move along." Or join him. He didn't have to add that part out loud.

"Leave him alone." Lamar was done with being ashamed of himself. It was about time he started being the good guy again.

One of the cadets stepped toward him. "Listen, you lit-"

The prince used the distraction to jump up from the ground and throw himself at the boy, taking him by surprise. They rolled in the dirt, exchanging several punches, but the other three quickly reacted, grabbing Hayden's arms and pulling him away from their friend. He struggled against them but they held him tight, waiting for their leader to pick himself up and approach them, raising his fist to punch the now helpless prince.

The hit never landed. Lamar made sure of it, grabbing the boy's wrist and hitting him square on the chin, sending him stumbling away. Lamar didn't pay any more attention to him, turning to the boys holding Hayden, ready to attack them as well. A sharp whistle made him freeze on the spot.

"What the FUCK is going on here?!" a strong voice hollered from behind them. All the boys quickly dusted off their clothes and stood up straight. "Were you little shits fighting?"

One of the bullies immediately pointed at Hayden. "It was his fault! His fucking Highness and his little asskisser attacked us! We were just defending ourselves!"

"Is that so?" The sergeant scoffed, leaping forward to grab the boy's collar. "Are you telling me that the two of them decided to attack the four of you?" he hissed straight into his face. "Or is it possible that they were just defending themselves? After you bullied the shit out of them for days? Despite me SPECIFICALLY telling you last time that I will not tolerate any of that shit around here?!"

The boy gulped but didn't answer, glancing at his friends, silently begging them for help.

Lamar was surprised. He'd assumed that bullying was something to be expected, even tolerated by the drill sergeants. That it was simply part of training. Now he felt even worse for having joined in on it.

Receiving no answer, the sergeant smirked, pushing the cadet away from him in disgust. "You are out. All four of you. I gave you my one warning last time and apparently, you were all too stupid to learn from it. And King Rodric certainly doesn't need soldiers this stupid. Pack your shit and get out of here."

The boys' faces lost all color and Lamar felt sorry for them. A lot of kids here had nowhere to return to. Even Lamar couldn't just go back home, he'd have to find a job somewhere and work his ass off to make a few meager coins so his family wouldn't starve.

"They're telling the truth." All faces quickly turned toward the prince. With surprise, Lamar realized that it was probably the first time he had ever heard him speak. "It was my fault. I attacked them." Hayden crossed his arms in front of his chest, looking up at the sergeant defiantly.

"Is that so?" The man clearly wasn't buying his story. The boys around the prince nodded, while Lamar frowned at him. What was he doing? "Well then," the sergeant shrugged, "you know what the punishment is." Hayden nodded sharply, spitting out some blood without saying a word. "You four assholes report to the kitchen. Now! And you two," the sergeant pointed at the prince and Lamar, "with me."

For the first time, Hayden hesitated. "It was just me. He had nothing to do with it!"

"Oh really? Because I clearly saw him punch one of those idiots. So, what is the real story, cadets?"

While Lamar had to admire the prince for trying to take all the blame on himself, even to the point of protecting those who had been tormenting him for days, he just couldn't allow it. "I did punch him to protect the prince," he admitted.

"Wow, are you going to lick his boots as well?" the sergeant scoffed contemptuously, turning around and walking away. "MOVE IT!" he yelled at them.

"I didn't need your help," Hayden hissed quietly as they walked side by side.

Lamar rolled his eyes. "Sure, you were winning all on your own. You're such an ungrateful prick."

Lamar's resolve faltered when he realized the sergeant was leading them toward a group of poles at the edge of the training grounds. Then, taking a deep breath to calm his rising nerves, he continued on. Getting whipped was not something he desired but that didn't mean he was going to back down.

He tried to put on a brave face as he hugged one of the poles and let the sergeant tie his hands on the other side, watching with horror as Hayden stepped to the next one. But...he was the prince? The king's son, the heir to the fucking throne, surely they wouldn't...?

It turned out, they would. The sharp pain caused by the whip biting into the skin on his back quickly drove all thoughts from his mind, forcing Lamar to focus all his energy on not screaming. Both of them suffered the whipping in silence, save for the heavy panting and an occasional groan, their blood coating the whip evenly as the sergeant alternated between hitting the prince and Lamar.

The pain lingered long after the punishment was over and the sergeant had left. Nobody came to untie them. Apparently, they were supposed to stay there until morning.

"Thank you," Hayden mumbled so quietly that Lamar barely even heard him. "I was not being ungrateful. I just didn't want anyone else to get in trouble because of me."

Lamar carefully glanced to the side, not wanting to break the scabs forming on his back by moving, surprised to see that the prince looked calm now. Just like Lamar, Hayden was kneeling on the ground, his forehead resting against the pole, his usual furious expression gone. He seemed almost normal.

Shrugging was an exceptionally bad idea, sending waves of pain throughout Lamar's body. "I deserved it." It felt like the whip washed away at least part of his shame and guilt. "I'm sorry for joining them, I'm normally not such an asshole. And I'm definitely not saying that just so you won't have me executed when you become king."

Hayden chuckled, groaning in pain as the movement irritated the skin on his back. "Don't worry. No hard feelings. It takes guts to go against the crowd."

"I should have done something earlier. By the way, since I'm already on my knees in front of my future king, I'm Lamar. Just so you know what to write on the execution order," he grinned, trying to mask his nerves with humor.

Cursing as his shoulders twitched in suppressed laughter, Hayden slowly turned his head from side to side. "You are an idiot. I like that. I'd shake your hand but..." he moved his tied hands up and down a few inches, "I guess it can wait until morning. It's going to be a long night. It always is. Oh, and I'm Hayden, but you probably knew that already."

"I think I've heard someone mention your name, yes," Lamar smirked. Realizing what the prince's words meant, he raised an eyebrow. "Not your first time?" What kind of a sick country were they to have their crown prince flogged repeatedly?

Hayden snorted in amusement. "No, definitely not my first time. And most certainly not the last time either."

And it wasn't. For either of them.

Lamar grinned over the distant memories, stoking the fire with a long stick, sending a pillar of flares up to the night sky. They'd become fast friends during that long night they'd spent together tied to the poles, their teeth rattling in the cold night air, with blood drying on their backs. They'd been inseparable ever since.

A lot of people believed Lamar had befriended Hayden just to get on the good side of the future king, but that was never his motivation. He liked the prince and was often surprised by how selfless and humble a kid from the royal family could be. Despite his obvious anger issues, Hayden was a good and loyal friend.

When King Rodrick suddenly died and the young prince was forced to take the crown, he'd remembered Lamar, choosing him as his personal bodyguard, raising Lamar up to a position greater than the poor boy could have ever hoped to achieve.

Lamar still had his doubts whether Hayden should have hired someone with better skills and more experience to lead his personal guards. A fifteen-year-old boy was hardly the wisest pick for such a position. But Hayden trusted Lamar indiscriminately and Lamar had strived to improve his skills every day so that hopefully one day, he would be good enough to actually deserve his position.

He'd devoted his life to protecting his king at all costs, against threats coming from the outside but also, at times, from Hayden himself. Lamar's fingers touched the healing gash on his lip. It wasn't the first time the king had punched him while yelling at him, but it usually only happened when he was drunk. And Lamar quickly learned to ignore whatever Hayden said while he was drinking. This time it was different.

It was a set up, sure. They had talked it through beforehand. Lamar had known what the king was going to say. That he was going to kick him out of the palace guard like a lowly criminal. Like a traitor. The captain had agreed to it, the stakes were too high and he had a secret mission from the king to fulfill. But it still hurt. He blinked a couple of times, trying to chase the stupid tears out of his eyes, poking the fire angrily again.

His stallion raised his head, neighing quietly, and Lamar immediately jumped up, grabbing his sword. The animal sensed another horse nearby which, at this time of evening, most likely meant trouble.

A lone mare trotted along the path toward his fire, a small figure wrapped in a cloak slouched on her back. "Are you going to stab me or help me off this devious animal?" a familiar voice snapped at him as the horse came closer.

"Laina, what the fuck are you doing here?" Lamar raised both his eyebrows but put his weapon down and reached for the maid's hips, helping her down to the ground.

"What does it look like I'm doing?" Her legs were a little wobbly and she glared at the poor mare. It was no secret that Laina was not a fan of horseback riding or of horses in general. "I'm going with you."

"Going where?" As far as Lamar knew, the maid was not part of the plan.

She rolled her eyes and passed by him, extending her hands toward the fire. "To Cchen-Lian. Where else?"

"How do you even know about that? You know what, it doesn't matter," Lamar waved his hand. "You're going back in the morning. This is my mission, I don't need you to help me."

Her eyes narrowed as she swiftly turned and hissed at him. "What the fuck makes you think I'm doing this for you?!" Lamar took a step back, surprised by the fury in her eyes. "I don't give a shit about you! But this plan is too important to be fucked up by a stupid sword-swinging brute like you. What exactly were you and the king thinking?! You don't know anything about that country, you don't even speak the damn language!"

Lamar had to admit that last part was painfully true but it didn't mean he was going to give up. "I have contacts-"

"From Shuen? On people who might not even be alive anymore? Or are loyal to the emperor?" Laina scoffed and shook her head. "Admit it, Lamar, you are hopeless. I'm coming along. It's not like you have the authority to make me go back anyway, you know, not being the captain of the guards anymore."

What an infuriating woman! Lamar closed his eyes and slowly counted to ten to stop himself from slapping her. The smug, victorious smirk that greeted him when he opened his eyes again had him balling his fists and starting the count again.

"Great, so it's decided," she declared, sitting herself down by his fire. "Now, I really hope you have something to eat. I stole some of Karina's jewelry so we can sell it in the next town and buy some proper food, but right now, I'd settle even for those disgusting rations you soldier people seem to love so much."

"What?" Lamar ran his hand through his short hair, staring at Laina, having absolutely no idea what to say or do. This was his mission, a very dangerous one at that. He had to make her leave. But how, when she shut down every argument he could think of and acted like her coming with him was a sure thing. "Wait, you stole the queen's jewelry?"

Laina shrugged dismissively. "Well, she did specifically forbid me from going. This way she can't send the guards to bring me back. Unless she wants to see me punished for stealing from the queen. Which she doesn't. At least, I hope not. Anyway, I can't go back, so you are stuck with me now."

"I-You... What?"

"Right, I forgot that stupid people have small brains," she rolled her eyes again and pointed at her chest. "Laina. Stay. With Lamar," she pointed at him. "Food?" Her finger moved toward her open mouth.

Flabbergasted, he went to his saddlebags and pulled out an apple, battling the strong desire to throw it at her head. This mission had just turned into a nightmare.

Afterword

W hew. This was a long one, wasn't it? Certainly the longest book I've ever written (and probably going to write). If you have made it all the way here, give yourself a pat on the shoulder. Good job! You have traveled the continent with Clara and watched her grow into a confident, strong woman. Clara is probably my favorite character from the series and you will be meeting her a lot. She invaded Whatever It Takes 3 and stole part of the narrative for herself. She features as a side character in The Pirate Queen and in another standalone spin-off I'm currently working on. She just can't stay away!

I'm grateful you have decided to read my books and that you liked the first one so much that you gave this one a chance, even though it's a really big book. And don't worry, the story doesn't end here! As hinted in the Interlude, the next book will feature Lamar and Laina as the main characters. It was supposed to be a fun book full of witty banter that would make you laugh. It turned out...well, much darker than anticipated. You will meet Hayden and Karina as well as Oscar and Clara in book 3. It is scheduled for publishing in October 2023 and you can already pre-order it on Amazon.

If you enjoyed this book, I'd like to hear from you and hope that you could take some time to post a review on Amazon. Your review doesn't have to be long or elaborate, even one or two sentences will be greatly appreciated. I'd also be grateful for a short review/rating on Goodreads.

If you want to know more about my other projects, follow my Facebook page: Author Anna Svoboda

Acknowledgements

Writing a book is hard. Finishing a book is even harder. This story never would have been created without the support of my family, my husband, and the fact that my toddler liked to sleep a lot.

I'd like to thank all my loyal readers for their support and the encouraging comments. You guys kept asking for paperbacks for so long that I finally relented and forced myself to publish the book properly! I never would have had the courage to do this without your support. As much as I would like to list every single member of my FB group Anna's Fiction Addiction, I can't, because the book would be insanely long and expensive.

Thank you, Mojgan, for your proofreading and valuable feedback.

Special thanks to the absolutely amazing Che Dunlop for editing the books. You are a treasure and I have learned a lot from you. Every time I write "a bit" these days, I immediately pause, thinking, "Oh, no! Che would hate this!". Then I have to delete the words and replace them with something else. You truly raised my books to another level.

Also By
Anna Svoboda

The Girl From the Other Side

Have you ever wondered how The Amityville Horror would play out if the ghosts actually tried to protect the people from an ancient evil? Wonder no longer, I have a book that answers all your questions!

Being a ghost can get really boring. 17 year old Jessica Robinson could tell you all about it. Sure, every once in a while, she has a bit of fun scaring the poor folks who bought the suspiciously cheap manor house by the lake. But after they run away screaming in the middle of the night, she's stuck in an empty building again with no escape and only her fellow ghosts as company. She doesn't even know who killed her. With no way of solving her own murder, is it a surprise she feels a little down in the dumps? There isn't even a flickering lightbulb at the end of this dark ghostly tunnel that is her gruesome afterlife.

Even though he is very much alive, Aiden sometimes feels like a ghost himself. His moms never ask his opinion about anything, least of all whether he wants to move into a haunted house. It's not all bad though, since the ghost who appears by his bed each night turns out to be a beautiful young woman. However, when magic comes to play and it turns out that Aiden's sister might become the next target of a mysterious serial killer, his life gets a little too interesting.

Available on Amazon and Kindle Unlimited.

C ome, Butterfly

On her 45th birthday, Diana's world crumbles as she loses her job and confronts her husband's infidelity. Seeking refuge in a hotel bar, she encounters a mysterious stranger who introduces her into the intoxicating world of BDSM.

Diana decides to leave her old life behind and explore the depths of pleasure and submission with the hot stranger. Their time spent together raises more questions. Why does it seem like he can read her mind? And why does he keep calling her his "little human"?

Come, Butterfly is a tantalizing BDSM erotica that explores the intricacies of desire and personal growth. While the plot takes a backseat, the story focuses on character development and the exploration of intense passions. Expect a "happily ever after" ending, albeit one that may not unfold as expected.

Please note that Come, Butterfly contains various kinks and potential triggers, including dominance, submission, bondage, spanking, edging, forced orgasms, anal play, wax play, double penetration, monster sex, threesomes, and more. Enter this world of sensual discovery with an open mind and a readiness to indulge in your deepest desires.

Available on Amazon and Kindle Unlimited.

Made in United States
North Haven, CT
13 May 2024

52471725R00332